ZERO DAYS

ALSO BY RUTH WARE

In a Dark, Dark Wood

The Woman in Cabin 10

The Lying Game

The Death of Mrs. Westaway

The Turn of the Key

One by One

The It Girl

ZERO DAYS

RUTH WARE

SCOUT PRESS

New York London Toronto Sydney New Delhi

Scout Press
An Imprint of Simon & Schuster, Inc.
1230 Avenue of the Americas
New York, NY 10020

First Scout Press hardcover edition June 2023

SCOUT PRESS and colophon are registered trademarks of Simon & Schuster, Inc.

For information about special discounts for bulk purchases, please contact Simon & Schuster Special Sales at 1-866-506-1949 or business@simonandschuster.com.

The Simon & Schuster Speakers Bureau can bring authors to your live event. For more information or to book an event, contact the Simon & Schuster Speakers Bureau at 1-866-248-3049 or visit our website at www.simonspeakers.com.

Interior design by Jaime Putorti

Manufactured in the United States of America

10 9 8 7 6 5 4 3 2 1

Library of Congress Cataloging-in-Publication Data is available.

ISBN 978-1-9821-5529-2
ISBN 978-1-9821-5531-5 (ebook)

For my dad, who was paranoid about online security
before *it was fashionable*

SATURDAY, FEBRUARY 4

MINUS EIGHT DAYS

T he wall around the perimeter was child's play. Six feet, but no spikes or barbed wire on the top. Barbed wire is my nemesis. There's a reason they use it in war zones.

At five foot two I couldn't quite reach to pull myself up, so I scaled a nearby tree with a sturdy branch overhanging the car park, lowered myself until my feet made contact with the top of the wall, and then ran softly along it to a place where I could drop down out of sight of the CCTV cameras that circled the building at intervals.

On the other side of the car park was the fire door Gabe had described, and it looked promising. A standard half-glazed door with a horizontal release bar on the inside. I saw with satisfaction that it was poorly fitted, with a gap at the bottom that you could practically get your hand through. It was the work of about thirty seconds to slip my long metal slider underneath, swing it up so the hook caught on the bar, and pull firmly down. The door opened and I held my breath, waiting for the alarm—fire doors are always risky like that—but none came.

Inside, the lights flicked on automatically—big fluorescent squares in a tiled ceiling that stretched away into the darkness like a chessboard. The far end of the corridor was still pitch-black, the sensors there not yet picking up my movement, but the section I was in was bright as day, and I stood, letting my eyes adjust to the glare.

Lights are a bit of a double-edged sword. On the one hand, they're a huge red flag to anyone monitoring the security cameras. There's nothing like a screen lighting up like Christmas to catch a security guard's eye and make them glance up from their phone. But you can sometimes style it out if you're caught walking confidently around a building at night when the lights are on. It's much harder to explain your presence if you're creeping along an unlit corridor with a torch. You might as well be wearing a striped T-shirt and carrying a bag marked *Loot*.

Right now it was 10:20 p.m. and I was wearing my "office" clothes—black trousers which looked like they could be the bottom half of a suit but were actually stretchier and more breathable than any regular office wear, a dark blue blouse, and a black blazer that was standard, off-the-rack from Gap. On my feet were black Converse, and I had a gray Fjällräven backpack slung over my shoulder.

Only my hair was out of place. This month it was dyed a fluorescent scarlet that wasn't close to any natural shade and didn't really fit in with the slightly stuffy atmosphere of this company—an insurance group called Arden Alliance. Gabe had suggested a wig, but wigs were always a risk, and besides, I was getting into character. Jen—I had decided my imaginary office worker was called Jen—worked in customer services but had fond memories of her gap year after university and still thought she was a little bit cool. Jen might have buckled down to achieve promotion, but her hair was the last flicker of a personality she hadn't quite abandoned to the nine-to-five. That, and perhaps a touch too much liquid eyeliner, plus a tattoo on her shoulder blade that said *stick 'em with the pointy end*.

The eyeliner was real—I didn't feel properly dressed without a smooth flick of Nyx Epic Ink. The university degree was imaginary. So was the tattoo. I wasn't sufficiently into *Game of Thrones* to ink it, though admittedly if I had been, Arya was the best character.

Jen had been working late, lost track of time, and was heading hurriedly home for the weekend. Hence the comfortable shoes. The backpack was for her office heels—although that was where my role play broke down. Jen might keep heels in her backpack. Mine was full of housebreaking tools and computer equipment loaded with some deeply shady software Gabe had downloaded from the dark web.

I walked softly down the corridor, my rubber soles silent on the carpet, trying to look as though I belonged here. On either side were the doors of empty offices, just the occasional LED glowing in the darkness where people had failed to turn their computers off properly for the weekend.

A photocopier in an alcove blinked hypnotically and I stopped, glancing up and down the hallway. It was illuminated behind me but dark around the corner up ahead, the motion sensors not yet detecting my presence. So much the better—the lights might alert security, but that worked both ways. The guards were unlikely to be coming from behind me; that corridor was a dead end out to the car park. If they came from up ahead, the lights flickering on would give me enough warning to double back or duck into one of the offices. Gabe would probably tell me to get on with finding the server room—but the chance was too good to miss.

Behind the copier were, as I'd hoped, a tangle of wires and two LAN ports for hooking up devices to the main company network. One was in use, connected to the copier. The other was empty. Heart beating, I glanced up and down the corridor and took one of the little Raspberry Pi computers out of my backpack.

The Pi was smaller than a paperback book, and I slid it down behind the copier, nesting it snugly into the mass of abandoned pages that had fallen off the back of the document feeder. I plugged it into a power socket and snaked the LAN cable into the empty port. Seconds later my Bluetooth earpiece crackled and my husband's deep voice came into my ear, strangely intimate in the hush of the deserted building.

"Hey, babe . . . your Pi just came online. How's it going?"

"Okay." I spoke quietly, not quite a whisper but not much more. "I'm just trying to get my bearings." I tugged a stray photocopy over the Pi, hiding it from view, then shouldered my bag and continued up the corridor, rounding the corner. "How are you doing?"

"Oh, you know." Gabe's tone was dry. "Just a little *Dark Souls* on the PS. Not much I can do until you get me into the server room."

I laughed, but he was only half joking. The part about *Dark Souls* might not be true—I knew full well there was no way he'd be gaming; on the contrary, he was undoubtedly hunched at his monitor anxiously tracing my progress on the blueprints we'd obtained from the planning department—but the bit about the server room was. This was always the hardest part of any job for Gabe—where he had to just sit back and listen, powerless to help if I ran into any trouble.

"Where are you?" he asked now.

"In a corridor running east-west from that fire door you found. This building is— Oh, shoot."

I stopped dead.

"What?" Gabe's voice was alert but not overly alarmed. *Oh, shoot* wasn't what I would have said if I'd just stumbled into a guard. That would have been something a lot stronger.

"There's a security door up ahead. Was that on the plans?"

"No," Gabe said a little grimly. "They must have updated." I could hear his fingers racing across the keyboard. "Hold up, I'm trying to get into the security system via your Pi. What can you see?"

"There's a PIR sensor." I looked up at the blinking infrared oval mounted above the door. I was just out of range.

"Okay, then wait, the sensor might trigger an alarm."

"Well, duh," I said. I knew that, of course. I wasn't worried about the door itself—between us, Gabe and I could get through most things. But a PIR sensor usually meant a motion detector—and activating it after hours risked some kind of alert to the guards. Still, the fire door hadn't been alarmed, which was a good sign. I began walking closer.

"Jack?" Gabe said. His fingers stopped clicking. "Jack, honey, talk to me, what are you doing? We don't want another Zanatech."

Zanatech. Ugh. One word: *dogs.* I've got nothing against them as pets, but I hate security dogs. Those things can really do damage. And they can run. Fast.

I ignored Gabe and took another step, holding my breath.

The sensor lit, registering my presence, and I shut my eyes, bracing myself for the sound of alarms, running feet . . . but the only thing that happened was the door swinging smoothly open.

"*Jack?*" Gabe's voice came into my ear more urgently as he heard my exhalation. "What just happened?"

"It's fine. The door's open. Don't think it's set anything off."

I could literally hear Gabe clenching his teeth on the other end of the line, trying not to snap the retort he wanted to make, but I knew the words he was holding back. He'd wanted me to wait while he tried to access the security system via the Pi and figure out if the door was alarmed. But that could take hours, and in this job, doing nothing was a risk in itself. Sometimes you just had to go on your gut—act on impulse.

Besides, it wasn't *really* impulse, and Gabe knew it. It was instinct, honed by years of doing exactly this kind of thing.

"You *hope* it hasn't set anything off," he said at last, and I grinned. I could afford to be magnanimous. If there had been an alarm screaming out, or worse, the sound of barking, while Gabe yelled *I told you so*, I would have been laughing on the other side of my face. But one of Gabe's many good qualities was that he wasn't a sore loser. I could tell he'd already moved on to the next challenge when he asked, "Where are you now? Lift lobby?"

"Yes." I looked around me. The lobby was furnished with a tall yucca and a futuristic metal chair. "There's three corridors coming off and . . ." I looked up at the dial above the lift doors. "Blimey, fourteen floors. Do we know where the server room's supposed to be?"

"Hang on," Gabe said. I heard the click of computer keys. "Looks like IT's on the fifth floor, so start there. What floor are you on? Ground?"

"I'm not sure." I looked around me. "The car park's on two different levels."

A long sign opposite the lift listed the different floors. Apparently I was on the first. And *5—IT and HR* was helpfully listed four lines above. So much for Gabe's computer wizardry.

I sent him a quick snap of the sign on my phone, captioned *no shit sherlock*, and I heard his rumbling laugh come over the earpiece as the message landed.

"Look, what can I say—we tech heads are used to being asked to solve problems people should be able to figure out themselves."

"Go screw yourself, Medway," I said amiably, and he laughed again, this time a low, meaning chuckle that made my stomach flutter.

"Oh, I would, but I've got someone much hotter in mind. And she's going to be home in an hour or two. *If* she gets off her arse."

I felt a smile tug irresistibly at my lips, but I made my voice stern.

"I won't be home at all if you don't get me into the server room, so keep your mind on the job and leave my arse out of it." I looked at the lift panel. It was the high-tech kind where you had to beep your card and select a floor. "The lift's got a card reader on it, so I'm assuming the upper floors are pass-card protected."

"Well, I probably can't override that until you've got me access to the server room, so time to get your steps in, babe."

I sighed theatrically and looked around for the fire escape route—aka the stairs. A labeled door in the corner of the lobby showed me the way, but before I took it, I dropped a bugged USB stick outside the lift doors. Gabe had handed me half a dozen before I left, innocent-looking little things loaded with a Trojan horse program of his own devising. With any luck, someone coming in on Monday would pick it up and plug it into their computer in an effort to locate the owner. When they did, they would find a bunch of bland Word documents and a sneaky little bit of code that would embed itself in their hard drive, make contact with its mothership, and allow read/write access to their computer as long as it was connected to the internet.

Coming out onto the fifth floor I dropped another USB and then touched my headset.

"You are in a small lobby," I said to Gabe in a robotic voice. "Corridors lead to the north, east, and west. To the south of you is a lift. In the distance is a tall, gleaming white tower. No, wait, that last part's from *Colossal Cave Adventure.*"

"Drop USB device," Gabe said, and I laughed.

"*A,* that's three words. And *B,* I've already done that. As you'd know *if* you'd managed to hack the CCTV system. So—which corridor?"

I glanced up and down the three equally featureless hallways, listening to the click of Gabe's mouse as he tried to make sense of the layout.

"You came in the fire door we talked about and lift C is at your back, is that right?" he asked.

"Yes. At least, I assume it's lift C. There's a door marked HR to the left, if that helps."

"Yeah, it does. You need the corridor straight ahead, I think."

I gave a thumbs-up, remembered Gabe couldn't see me yet, and then walked across to the glass door straight in front of me. This time it didn't slide open automatically.

"Okay, we're at another security door—and I'm on the wrong side. There's a card reader. What next, Inspector Gadget?"

"Anywhere to enter a code?"

"Yes, a key panel. Numerical."

"That's something. Give me a second. I don't know if I can override it yet, but I might be able to get the code off their system via your Pi."

I nodded and stood, arms crossed, listening to the frantic click of Gabe's fingers racing across the keyboard and his voice as he muttered the occasional swear word under his breath. I felt that smile tug at my lips again, and for a fleeting moment I wished I were with him, in our living room at home, so that I could snake my arms around his broad torso and press a kiss to the back of his warm neck where the black hair was shaven short in an undercut. I loved Gabe, loved everything about him, but this was the time I loved him most, when he was head-down and completely absorbed in his work. It wasn't just the sexiness of watching someone doing something they were very, *very* good at. It was the camaraderie, the sense that it was him and me against the world.

And, well, sometimes against each other. We might be husband and wife, but that didn't mean we weren't competitive. I was good at what I did too. Very good, as it happens.

While I waited, I strolled across to the keypad and entered *1234*. Nothing happened, just a brief red light on the sensor. I shrugged. I hadn't really expected more, but it was always worth a try. Then I typed in *4321*. Nothing again. I didn't risk a third attempt in case there was some kind of lockout, but something else occurred to me and I fished in my bag for the can of compressed air at the bottom.

"How's it going, honey?" I asked Gabe while I unscrewed the cap. I got a muttered grunt in response.

"Not great. I'm in their system, but I can't seem to access the admin side. Trying to get into someone's emails to see if they've mailed the code to anyone."

"Well, tick tock, Medway. *If* you want me home anytime soon. Time to get off *your* shapely arse, maybe?"

The only answer I got was a low growl, half frustration, half laughter.

I fitted the can of condensed air to the crack in the door and pressed the trigger. There was a long, loud hiss of air being forced through the narrow gap—and then the door slid open. I let out a delighted crow. Gabe's fingers stopped clicking.

"Uh . . . what just happened?"

"Just me, solving problems tech heads should be able to figure out themselves."

"Wait, you got the door open? How?"

"You know it, baby. Condensed air through the gap. The temp change confuses the PIR sensor. Hack *that*."

"Oh, fuck you."

"I thought we already established that was your job, Mr. Medway?" I teased, and heard Gabe's annoyance at being beaten a second time dissolve into laughter.

"Yeah, we did. And talking of shapely arses, hop to it, babe. Tick tock."

"Tick tock," I agreed, and began walking down the corridor, the lights coming on one after the other as I did.

It was a long hallway, lined with offices like the ones four floors below, none of them server rooms. I peered inside an unmarked door—but it was a closet, filled with janitorial supplies and a mop and bucket. Another light flicked on. I could see right down to the end now, where the corridor turned. That was all of them; if someone was coming from ahead of me, I would get no warning. There was a crackle from my headset.

"Still nothing?"

"Not yet," I said shortly, and then halted, listening.

"Did you—" Gabe began.

"Shh!" I hissed. He didn't need to be told twice. There was a soft click as he muted his mic, so that even his breathing wouldn't distract me.

There was a noise coming from up ahead. Not footsteps, thank God, but the low hum of computer fans and of air-conditioning working overtime. You hear server rooms before you see them.

"I've got it," I whispered back to Gabe. "At least, if I haven't, they've got a Cessna behind that door up ahead."

As I drew closer, I could make out a vented door with a sign reading NO ENTRY EXCEPT TO AUTHORISED PERSONNEL.

Ignoring that, I tried the handle. It was locked, of course, but the fact that there was no keyhole was a bummer. A physical lock I could probably have picked, but this door had only a swipe card reader to the left of the handle. No panel to enter a code. And the door was well fitted, with absolutely zero gap underneath. There was almost certainly some kind of internal release button, but I doubted I could press it with so little room to maneuver. The vent was installed so that the louvres angled downwards, not up, and the aperture was too small to be useful. Even if I jimmied off the grille, I couldn't fit through, and besides, I wasn't really supposed to damage anything.

"Babe?" I heard in my ear.

"There's a swipe reader. No way of entering a code."

"Balls." I knew Gabe would be pulling thoughtfully at his beard, trying to figure out our options. Encoding a swipe card wasn't hard if you had the equipment and knew the code, but we didn't know the code. And even if he managed to dig it out of the intranet files, I was here and the encoder was back at home. We had to finish this tonight.

"Up and over?" Gabe asked, his question chiming with my own thoughts, and I nodded.

"You read my mind."

Glancing up and down the corridor, I took stock of the rooms to either side of the server room. To the left was an ordinary office with a glazed wall fronting the hallway and two desks. The door probably wasn't locked, given it was a shared space, but the glass wall wasn't ideal—anyone walking down the corridor would see me in there. To the right . . . and now I felt a jolt of satisfaction. To the right was a restroom. Men's—but that didn't make any difference for my purpose. The point was that the corridor wall was solid plasterboard.

"Houston, we have a toilet," I muttered to Gabe.

"Easy as *A, B, WC.*"

"Easy for you; you're the one sitting on your arse at home," I shot back, and heard his answering laugh as I swung open the door.

Inside I stood for a moment, peeling off my jacket and waiting for my eyes to adjust as the lights flickered on. Behind me, against the corridor wall, was a bank of sinks. To my right were two urinals, and directly ahead were the stalls. I pushed open the door of the leftmost cubicle and saw to my immense satisfaction that it was a standard design—a bowl resting against a cistern sturdily boxed in to chest height. The new fad for concealing cisterns inside the wall is sleek but rubbish for what I needed.

I put the toilet lid down, climbed onto it, and then jumped on top of the cistern, where I stood, crouched below the paneled ceiling. I waited a beat to take stock, making sure my balance was centered and my equipment secure, then pressed gently upwards on the ceiling panel.

It shifted immediately, a cloud of dust and dead flies fluttering to the bathroom floor, and I pulled myself up, praying as I did so that the wall between the two rooms would be solid enough to hold my weight. It creaked gently as my biceps flexed, and again as I folded one leg up and inside the narrow aperture. But nothing gave, and in less than twenty seconds I was lying flat on my belly in the shallow void between the drop ceiling and the real one. It was very, *very* hot. The heat was coming from the snaking silver ducts of the air conditioners working hard to cool the racks of servers in the room below. When I pulled out my torch and swung it around, I could see the crawl space stretching away into the darkness ahead of me.

Carefully, very carefully, I put the torch between my teeth and edged my way across the ceiling, keeping as close to the supporting wall as I could. Then I dug my nails into a ceiling tile right above what I judged to be the corner of the server room. It pulled up as easily as a trapdoor, but the drop beneath was daunting. Banks of blinking servers, too tightly packed to be climbable, and an eight-foot fall to the floor. I could lower myself down—my upper-body strength was pretty good—but there was a high chance I would not be able to reach to pull myself back up. Which left one fairly urgent question: Did the server room door open from the inside without a swipe card?

Lying flat across the dividing wall, I leaned down between the struts and flashed the torch through the gap in the ceiling. By craning my head I could see there *was* some kind of panel beside the door handle, but I couldn't make it out—the shadow from one of the server banks made it impossible to see any detail. It might be a door release . . . or a fire alarm. Or simply a light switch. I would have to get closer to check.

With great caution, I laid aside the panel I had just lifted and commando-crawled further across the ceiling, closer to the center of the room. The supporting struts creaked a little but didn't move, and I held my breath as I began to pry up a second panel. This one was stiffer for some reason, maybe held in place by the air-conditioning duct taped over the adjacent panel, and I found myself straining at the edge, pulling at it with all my strength. One corner gave and I pulled harder. One whole side had come loose . . .

And then, with a sound like a crack of thunder, the entire panel snapped in half and I sprawled backwards.

For a long moment I lay there, frozen, the broken panel in my hand. The bang had been so loud that my ears were ringing, and I could imagine it echoing through the narrow ceiling space all along the hallway, reverberating through the ducts, making the whole ceiling vibrate like a drum. I could feel the gritty dust settling around me, the carapaces of tiny insects floating down to land in my hair and on my face, and I could hear Gabe's panicked voice in my ear.

"Jack. Jack! Are you okay? Babe, are you all right? What just happened?"

"I'm okay," I whispered. I put my hand up to the earpiece, checking that it was still secure. My fingers were shaking with shock. "I—I just snapped a ceiling tile."

"It sounded like a gunshot!" I could hear the relief in his tone, and suddenly, piercingly, I wished he were here with me, and I knew he was feeling the same. This was the hardest part—when something went wrong, or almost did, and the other person could do nothing to help. "Christ, sweetheart, don't *do* that to me. I thought you'd been shot."

I nodded soberly.

"I'm fine, but fuck, Gabe, that was *really* loud. If anyone's still working on this floor, they'll definitely have heard."

"Well, I can't get into the CCTV system to check until you've plugged in that drive," Gabe said. The teasing had gone from his voice and he sounded like he was worried but trying not to show it—both because he didn't want to pass on his nerves to me, and because he knew I didn't always take protectiveness well. "For real, love, are you okay?"

"I'm *fine.*" I laid the broken tile aside and propped myself back onto my elbows, cautiously patting myself down. My heart rate was slowing and nothing seemed to be missing from my pack or pockets. Then I realized—the torch had fallen through the hole in the ceiling and was lying on the floor of the server room, pointing away from the door. I still had no idea whether there was a release button.

Well, fuck it, there was only one way we were getting into that server room—and if I couldn't get out, so be it. If I had to sleep there, I could cope. I'd done worse.

I made my voice firm.

"I'm going down."

Gabe's laugh was a little tremulous.

"You know I love it when you talk dirty, babe, but now's not the time."

"Fuck you," I grunted, hauling myself into position, and this time his laugh sounded reassured.

"That's my girl. How big is the drop?"

"Eight feet? Maybe nine? Not more."

"Good luck. Break a leg. I mean, don't."

"I won't," I said tersely. I braced myself on the struts surrounding the ceiling panel, assessing the drop, dipped my fingertips into the climber's chalk tied onto my backpack, and began to lower myself slowly into the apartment, my muscles tense with the effort of controlling my descent. *This* was why I spent five boring mornings a week in the gym. Not so I could fit into my skinny jeans, and certainly not for Gabe, who didn't give a rat's arse what my dress size was. But for this. This moment when everything depended on the strength of my biceps and the tenacity of my grip.

Well, this and running from security guards, but I hoped it wasn't going to come to that tonight.

A few moments later I was hanging by my fingertips, arms at full stretch. I glanced down. I was maybe three feet from the floor. The drop was further than I would have liked, and I wished I'd worn something more shock-absorbent than Converse, but my fingers were already protesting. I counted to three.

And let go.

I landed on all fours, silently, like a cat.

"I'm in," I said to Gabe.

"You're bloody brilliant. Do I tell you that often enough? Now, have you got the thumb drives and that second Pi?"

"Yeah." I straightened up and dug in my pack for the padded envelope Gabe had handed me just a few hours ago, filled with his carefully prepared devices. "Where do I put them?"

"Okay," Gabe said, and now there was no teasing left, and his voice was pure concentration. "Listen carefully: here's what I need you to do . . . "

IT WAS MAYBE FIVE MINUTES later that I plugged in the final drive, then wiped down my sweating palms, straightened up, and looked around for my torch. For a minute I couldn't see it—but then I noticed a glow coming from underneath the furthest bank of servers. I must have kicked it there by accident when I dropped down.

It was right at the back, but I was able to hook it out with my metal slider and now I swung it around the room, aiming it at the panel beside the door.

A green knob. Unmarked, but it *had* to be a quick release, didn't it? Fire regulations surely meant that locking employees into rooms filled with masses of electronic equipment was a big no-no.

Before I pressed it, I glanced at the ceiling. There were two panels missing: one dislodged, the other snapped in half. Damaging fixtures and furnishings hadn't been part of the plan, but accidents couldn't be helped—everyone knew that. Perhaps I should climb up again via the men's loos to replace the panel I'd moved across, though.

I was considering this when Gabe's voice crackled over my earpiece, a new note in his tone.

"Babe? You still there?"

"I'm just leaving. What is it?"

"They're onto you. I've just got access to their cameras. There's a guard coming up the back stairs and another by the main lift. They're leaving the third floor now."

"How much time have I got?"

"Two minutes, tops. Maybe less."

"Should I stay put?"

"No, they're searching rooms. Someone must have heard the noise."

"Okay. I'm going for it."

With a frisson of trepidation and excitement, I pressed the green button. For a moment nothing happened and my stomach lurched. Had the guards somehow disabled the override? I pulled the handle— and the door swung inwards.

"Where are they?" I whispered as I ducked into the corridor. The lights flickered on as I retripped the motion sensors. As soon as they came into the lobby, the guards would know that someone was on this floor.

"Think it's the fourth." Gabe's voice was terse. He must be hunched over the monitors, trying to match the layout of the building to the camera views he was seeing. This was the stuff I sucked at—blueprints and tech gobbledegook—and that he lived for. "Hey, I can see you."

I glanced up, and sure enough there was the unblinking black eye of a security camera. I blew Gabe a kiss and pictured him grinning back, then wondered whether some puzzled guard in the back office was watching this same camera.

Gabe's voice broke into my thoughts with a new urgency.

"Nope, scrap that. You've got a guard directly ahead, about to go into the fifth-floor lobby. Turn around, head for the back stairs; you may be able to get down before the guy below finishes on the fourth. Don't run—he's right underneath you, he'll hear the noise."

Silently, obediently, I began speed walking in the other direction, thankful for the rubber soles of my shoes. I was almost at the stairs when Gabe spoke, sharp and peremptory.

"Abort! He's on the stairs."

Fuck. I couldn't say anything, and Gabe knew it. He could see his wife on the monitors, caught like a mouse between two cats. There was no way out. I would have to hide.

"Duck in an office," he ordered, but I was way ahead of him, already trying door after door. One locked. Two locked. Who *were* these people? Didn't they trust their colleagues? A *third* one locked. Frantically I dug in my backpack for my lockpicks and stuck them in the keyhole, digging around with a force that was as likely to break the picks as trip the lock. But luck was on my side, and with a heart-quickening *click*, the lock gave. I slid inside, wrenched the locking mechanism shut, and stood with my back to the wooden door, trying to quell my thumping heart.

"I can see you," Gabe said urgently in my ear. Craning my head to one side, I realized he was right. Even flat against the door, I was visible through the office window, and the guards were getting closer. Gabe had muted his mic so that I could listen better, and now I could hear their footsteps in the corridor, their voices getting louder.

I had only seconds to decide what to do.

They're searching rooms, Gabe's warning came into my head. If they opened the door, I was sunk.

I flung myself onto the floor, rolled sideways under a sofa, and lay there, my face pressed to the carpet, my heart thudding in my ears. For a moment I had a sudden, surreal image of my imaginary office worker, Jen, and what she would make of this, and I had to suppress a hysterical urge to laugh.

Instead I lay, holding my breath, twisting the ring on my left hand round and round with my thumb. It was my usual tic in moments of stress—a habit somewhere between biting my nails and crossing my fingers, only one that involved Gabe. It made sense; at least half the time, my fate was in my husband's hands.

Outside the door I heard the footsteps stop and the rattle of a handle.

"This one's locked as well."

"They're all locked on this floor," said another voice. "Here, I've got the master."

I heard the jangle of keys being thrown and stifled a laugh as the catcher missed and they fell to the floor.

"Do me a favor and just hand it to me next time?" I heard, and then the scratch of a key in the lock and the door opening. A torch swung around the space and I held my breath, praying they wouldn't direct the beam under the sofa. There was the sound of a roller chair being moved . . . then the *shhhhhh* of a door closing.

I let out a trembling breath as quietly as I could.

"Nothing in there," I heard from outside. "What about the bogs?"

"Empty." The second speaker's voice had an echoing quality, as though he was speaking from inside the bathroom itself. There was a pause and then, "Wait, hang on a sec . . ."

From my position under the sofa I could see nothing, and very carefully I raised my hand and touched my headset.

"Talk to me," I mouthed, the words barely above a breath.

"They've discovered the ceiling panel," Gabe whispered back.

Shit.

"Have a look at this," the second guard said.

I listened to the sound of footsteps as the first guard, the one who had searched the office I was in, made his way up the corridor.

There was a creak as the bathroom door swung open . . . then a gentle thump as it soft-closed behind him.

I was slithering out from under the sofa when Gabe's voice crackled to life in my ear, a low scream of urgency.

"Go, go, go. Now!"

I didn't need to be told. I was already on my feet, wrenching open the door, looking up and down the corridor, unsure which way to go.

"Opposite way from the lifts!" Gabe said, and I took off, pounding down the corridor, careening round the corner, where I would have face-planted into another set of security doors had Gabe not already triggered them. They stood open, waiting for me as I skidded through into a little lobby.

"Fire door to your right," Gabe said, and I slammed through, finding myself in a vertiginous stairwell, spiraling down into darkness. The heavy fire door banged shut behind me, but I didn't care. I'd already blown my chances of a stealthy exit. Nothing mattered now except getting away.

Down one flight. Down two. My heart was hammering in my ears.

"You're nearly there." Gabe's voice in my ear. "You can do this— three more flights and then hang a sharp left and you're at another fire door."

"Wh-what if there's an a-alarm?" I panted. Another flight. One more to go after this.

"Fuck the alarm. The other door wasn't alarmed. But if there is I'll override it. You got this, you hear me? *You've got this.*"

"Kay." I was too out of breath to talk now. Last flight and I staggered left, ducking back under the stairs. Sure enough, there was the fire door—and outside lay freedom.

I banged on the bar, wincing preemptively for the sound of a siren—but again, none came. I made a mental note for the report, but that could wait. For the moment, I was outside, in the blessed fresh air.

"Fuck!" Gabe howled in my ear, laughing now, the shaky, half-hysterical laugh of someone watching a movie with their heart in their mouth. "Jesus. You were incredible. I didn't think you were going to make it."

"I didn't either." My heart was banging in my chest, but I forced myself to slow to a walk as I crossed the car park. If there were more guards out here, no point in making it obvious who they were looking for. "Oh fuck me, I did *not* enjoy that."

Gabe laughed, that chest-deep dirty rumble that I loved.

"*A*, I most definitely will, and *B*, we both know that's a lie. You loved every minute of it."

I felt a grin spread over my face.

"Okay . . . I did enjoy it a little bit."

"A little bit? You looked like you were having the time of your life."

"Are they still searching for me inside?"

"Yeah, they're still poking around on the fifth floor. One of them's opened up the server room, but they haven't noticed the drives. You did brilliantly, babe."

"I know," I said modestly, and heard Gabe's answering laugh.

"Have you got it from here? I need to get inside the network before they figure out what's going on."

"Yeah, I'm almost at the car. See you in . . ." I glanced at my phone. "Forty minutes? Traffic should be clear this time of night."

"You want me to order some food?"

I realized that I was starving. I never ate before a job—running around on a full stomach doesn't feel great—but now the idea of food made my mouth water.

"*Yes*," I said emphatically. "A large pizza with mushrooms, peppers . . . No, actually scrap that. What I really want is the porto-bello veggie burger from Danny's Diner with truffle mayo and extra onion. Think they'll still be open?"

"Should be."

"Great. Don't forget the slaw. And extra fries. No, make that sweet potato fries. And tell them *not* to put it in the same bag as yours. Last time I was left picking your gross bacon jam out of my veggie burger."

"Copy that. No fries. Extra bacon. See you soon, babe. I love you."

"Love you too," I said, and then, with a happy sigh, I hung up and disconnected the earpiece.

Scaling the wall was harder this time round, with aching muscles and a heart still pounding with spent adrenaline, but I scrambled up a recycling bin and dropped down from the top of the wall just around the corner from where I'd left the car, already rummaging in my bag for the key as I straightened up. I wasn't even looking, but if I had been, it wouldn't have made much difference. Because when I rounded the corner they were waiting.

I walked straight into the arms of the head of security.

SUNDAY, FEBRUARY 5

MINUS SEVEN DAYS

P lease try him again." I knew my voice was getting testy, and I tried to keep it calm. If you react, the person you're talking to reacts back. First rule of social engineering: stay pleasant and others are much more likely to do the same. But this was bloody annoying. What was the point of *having* a get-out-of-jail-free card if the guarantor didn't pick up? "I can assure you he knows all about this and can vouch for me."

"Let me get this straight," the police officer said wearily, rubbing his hand over his face. "You're a—what did you call it? A *pen* tester?"

"Look, it's a stupid name, I get that. It's short for penetration tester."

The officer snorted, the security guard holding my bag smirked, and I felt my irritation rise even further.

"It's a real thing, I assure you. I stress-test security systems for a living."

"And your husband's a hacker?"

"He's not a hacker"—well, that was a white lie, because Gabe absolutely was a hacker, just not in the sense that the police officer meant—"he's a pen tester too. We both are. He handles the digital side, I do the physical stuff. Companies hire us to try to break into their systems, then we report back and tell them what they could be doing better. Look, read this." I held out the letter Gabe had handed me this morning, and he shone the torch over it.

"'To whom it may concern: this is to confirm that I have authorized Jacintha Cross and Gabriel Medway of Crossways Security to conduct a physical and digital penetration test at the offices of Arden

Alliance,'" he read aloud, and then shrugged, looking across at the security guard. "I mean, what do you think? Is that company paper?"

"I've got no idea, mate," the guard said. He looked like he was thoroughly bored of the whole thing and just wanted to go back to his desk, rather than stand around in a windy car park. "They subcontract out night security. I'm employed by Baxter Bland. Looks okay to me, I mean it's the same logo on all the signs, but she could've printed that off the internet for all I know."

"And this Jim Cauldwell . . ." The police officer tapped the signature at the foot of the letter. "He's the—what did you say? The Cisco?"

"The CISO," I repeated patiently. "The chief information security officer. We're here at his request, and that's his personal mobile number. Look, could you call *your* boss?" I asked the security guard. "I appreciate you're not employed by Arden Alliance, but Jim said he'd cleared this with the on-site security firm, so someone on your end should be able to confirm I'm legit."

"You're joking, ain't you?" The security guard looked at me like I was insane. "It's gone midnight on the weekend. No way I'm calling my boss on his home number, even if I had it. He'd have my guts for garters."

I suppressed a groan. We'd picked a Saturday for the pen test deliberately because Arden ran only a skeleton staff that day, just customer service operatives and the bare minimum of security and IT. Sundays they were closed completely, which meant that with luck Gabe would have had all weekend to poke around in their systems before IT got back on Monday and discovered what we'd been up to. Now that choice seemed like a very, very bad idea. Evidently Jim Cauldwell had clocked off for the weekend along with the rest of his colleagues.

"I'll try this CISO guy again," the police officer said with barely disguised annoyance. The subtext of *I should be out catching real criminals* was very clear. "But if I can't get hold of him this time, you'll have to come down to the station with me."

I sighed. This was turning out to be a long night.

* * *

SOME TWO HOURS LATER WE were at the police station. Jim Cauldwell *still* hadn't picked up (I was going to have to talk to Gabe about putting some kind of penalty clause in the contract in case this happened again; it was the second time this year) and the officer was starting to talk about arrest. *Fuck.* I could take a night in the cells—I'd had worse—but if things really spiraled and we had to get lawyered up, this was going to get expensive.

"Can I please call my husband?" I was trying to keep the panic out of my voice, but it was there, a little tremulous edge that somehow had the effect of making me sound less than legitimate. "Honestly, this is all a huge misunderstanding. He may be able to get hold of someone else at the firm."

"Sure," the police officer said wearily, and he pushed a phone across the desk. My bag, complete with what the officer had dubiously described as "computer equipment, lockpicks, and tools for housebreaking," had somehow been left at the front desk, along with my phone. Even if I wasn't actually under arrest, it felt pretty close to it.

Fortunately I knew Gabe's number by heart, and I dialed it now, the telephone keypad sticky with overuse under my fingers. It rang . . . and rang. The knots in my stomach tightened, and I found I was twisting my ring round and round my finger, the chipped stone flashing in the light from above. This was . . . weird. Jim Cauldwell might have forgotten to change his do-not-disturb settings before going to bed; this wasn't exactly a normal nightly occurrence for him. But Gabe? He'd never have turned off his phone while I was still out on a job. On the other hand, I *had* told him I was already at my car, and it was . . . I looked up at the clock above the desk. Jesus, it was nearly two a.m. Maybe he'd fallen asleep?

"He's not picking up," I said now, not trying to keep the groan out of my voice. I put down the phone and the officer looked at me as if he knew exactly how I felt. "Look, I'm sorry—what did you say your name was?"

"PC Williams," the officer said.

"Look, PC Williams, I know this is a huge waste of your time, and I'm really sorry. I don't know what else to say. We were asked to break into the building, and the CISO can confirm that. We were told that number would be manned twenty-four hours when we set up the contract, but clearly the idiot who hired us forgot and turned his phone off."

"And there's no one else you can call?" PC Williams said. "No one who can confirm you are who you say you are?"

"You've got my ID, but if you mean is there anyone who can confirm I'm a real pen tester, not some nut job with a can of compressed air, then no. Not until office hours." I put my head in my hands. The adrenaline of the chase had worn off and I was so tired I felt close to tears. "At least . . ."

Oh God. No. The knots were back.

Not him. I'd rather spend the night in the custody suite.

"At least?" prompted Williams, and I bit my lip.

"Never mind."

No. There was no way I was calling *him*. Not even if it meant getting arrested.

"Just do it," I said now, resignedly. "I get it—you have to do your job. Arrest me."

The officer sighed and shook his head, but not as if he was denying what was going to happen—more like a world-weary acknowledgment of the inevitable. I knew he didn't want this any more than I did—the paperwork, the hassle, the very likely possibility that this would all be sorted out in just a few hours when the CISO got up and saw the reel of missed calls on his mobile.

On the other hand, I *had* been found breaking and entering, with a backpack full of fake paperwork and badges, alongside some pretty shady tools. I would have arrested me too.

"Let me go and speak to my colleague," he said now, pushing his chair back with a painful screech, and I nodded.

As the door closed behind him, I slumped down in the plastic seat, letting my head hang back as I stared at the ceiling tiles. They looked solid. More solid than the one I'd snapped, anyway. I thought about my life choices, about how much I hated Jim Cauldwell in that moment, and about Gabe, who was—inexplicably—apparently snoring his head off right now instead of doing what we'd been paid to do, which was get inside the mainframe of Arden Alliance and do as much poking around as we could before we were detected. It was incredibly unlike him to just shrug and go to bed. Normally it was me who came home, shoved a takeaway down my throat, and collapsed, worn out by climbing over walls, ducking under cameras, and picking locks with my adrenaline pulsing the whole time. Gabe was typically still going when I woke up the following day, hunched over his desk, testing and poking and probing the limits of the security systems the company had in place.

Getting caught was, in some senses, what we both wanted. Red-teaming, acting the attacker, was fun, but presenting the report to the security team afterwards never was—running them through everything they'd done wrong, all the mistakes they'd made and opportunities they'd missed to put a stop to the hack. What you wanted—what the client was hoping to hear—was "This part of your security held up—your guys did a good job."

Unfortunately, this time, even though I'd been picked up, I couldn't honestly say that—principally because I'd been caught as a result of my own mistakes rather than any particular professionalism on the part of the guards. I'd been an idiot to snap that ceiling tile and an even bigger idiot to leave my car parked out front of the very building I was burgling—if I hadn't done that I could probably have got in and out without being caught, even though they should have seen me on the monitors, or had some kind of alarm in place on the fire doors. You shouldn't be able to open multiple fire exits after hours, undetected. I was going to have to ream them a new one in my report *and* fess up to my own incompetence. A double whammy of unpleasantness, and very likely my stupidity in getting caught would distract from the very real holes in their security and provide plausible deniability for what was, after all, a pretty sloppy setup.

I just hoped Gabe had found something to make the night worthwhile, something they couldn't ignore with an *Oh well, they caught you in the end, didn't they?* shrug. Unencrypted passwords. Sensitive client data. Some kind of admin access which would give an actual hacker the opportunity to *really* wreak havoc.

I was thinking about that, and wondering again why Gabe wasn't picking up, when a familiar voice came from behind my shoulder.

"Well, well, well. Look who we've got here."

I sat bolt upright and swung around, fury pulsing through me.

Jeff Leadbetter. *Shit.*

"If it isn't Jack fucking Cross." He was grinning like a cat that's found a particularly juicy mouse in a corner it can't escape from. "What have you done this time, Cross?"

"You know I haven't done anything." I folded my arms across my chest, trying not to let him see how much his presence rattled me. "I just can't get hold of the guy who hired us."

"Sanjay said we had a girl with a weird story about testing pens"— he gave a laugh that shook his broad shoulders—"and I thought, you don't get too many of those around here. If you needed someone to vouch for you, why didn't you call me?"

You know why, I thought, but I didn't say it.

"I had no idea you'd be on duty," I said tightly.

Jeff grinned. "Well, you know what they say. No rest for the wicked. You're looking good, Cross. All that ducking and diving must keep you fit."

What could I say to that? *Fuck off* was what I wanted to say, and he knew it. But we also both knew that wasn't the kind of thing someone on the brink of arrest could say to a senior serving police officer. At least I could stare him out of countenance. *I* had nothing to be ashamed of, after all.

But Jeff was watching my hand, where I was nervously twisting the ring on my finger. I dropped my arms, cursing the stupid habit, but his eyebrow had already gone up, and now he looked at me, a shit-eating grin spreading across his face.

"Well, well, well. Engaged, Cross? Someone's finally gonna make an honest woman out of you?"

"Married, actually," I gritted out. *Not that it's any of your business*, I wanted to add, but forced myself to shut my mouth.

"Bit less Cross these days, eh?" Jeff said, and then cracked up at his own pun.

"I didn't change my name, if you must know."

Jeff smirked at that. "We both know I wouldn't have stood for that, Cross."

Yeah, well Gabe isn't an insecure dickhead with a patriarchy complex, I thought.

"Is she legit then, sir?" Williams's voice broke in from behind Jeff's shoulder, and Jeff turned and laughed.

"Yeah, she's legit. At least, she is what she says she is, if that's what you mean. We go back a long way, don't we, Jack?"

"Yes." I pressed my lips together.

"I could tell you some stories." Jeff looked me up and down, taking in my tight-fitting blazer and stretch trousers with an expression that was only just short of outright lascivious.

I could tell some stories too, I thought, but we both knew it was too late for that. I had tried to tell those stories once before, right around the time we broke up, and it hadn't ended well.

Of all the police stations to get hauled into, why, why, *why* did it have to be this one? It wasn't even the one where he normally worked; that was over on the other side of town. Either he'd been transferred, or he was covering someone.

There was silence, and I knew what he wanted. He wanted me to ask. He wanted me to *beg*. He wanted me to say, *Please, Jeff. Please help me.*

Well, I wouldn't say it. Not even if it meant a night in the lockup.

"So . . . should I release her, sir?" said the voice from behind Jeff, and I felt a surge of relief. I had almost forgotten PC Williams's presence. Jeff couldn't do anything while he was there. For a moment Jeff said nothing, just stood there grinning down at me, and I felt my nails dig into the desk in front of me. He couldn't . . . could he? He wouldn't make some excuse, send Williams away, make me spend the night alone in an interview room, listening to that slow, soft voice that even now sent shudders running down my spine?

But then he laughed and shrugged.

"Just messing with you. Go on." He was talking more to me than to Williams, even though it was Williams who had asked. "Scram. But don't forget you owe me one."

"Oh, I won't forget," I said tightly, with just enough venom in my voice to leave him in doubt as to what exactly I was referring to. I stood up, tugged my jacket straight. "I never forget. You can be sure of that."

"Don't I get a thanks?" Jeff said. He didn't move out of the doorway, his broad body filling the space.

I gritted my teeth.

"Thanks."

There was a short pause, and then Jeff gave another laugh and moved aside.

"Go on then, get out of here. And stay out of trouble."

It was only when I came out into the chilly night air of the street that I felt it—the cold, wet patches under my arms, the sweat of pure panic.

I was still afraid of Jeff Leadbetter. And maybe I always would be.

It was nearly four a.m. before I got back home to Salisbury Lane, and I was half-drunk with exhaustion, my eyes scratching with tiredness as I wove mechanically through the near-deserted residential streets of South London. I'd considered leaving the car at Arden Alliance, but it was parked in a restricted zone, and I knew that when I finally did get to bed I would probably sleep for twelve hours. The chances of me waking up in time to rescue it before it got clamped (or worse—towed) were slim.

Instead I'd taken an Uber back to where the security guard had picked me up, and driven slowly home, windows down, hoping that the bad instant coffee the police had offered me before I left would keep me awake for at least another hour. But as the streets unfurled hypnotically in front of me, I was forced to admit that this might have been the wrong decision—first I took a false turn, finding myself in residential streets I didn't recognize for a surprisingly long time before I managed to make my way back to a road I knew. My sleep-fuddled navigation was only an inconvenience, though. The real problem was that I was in very real danger of falling asleep at the wheel—the absolute last thing this night needed. Somehow, though, the combination of the chill night air in my face, the coffee, and the angry screeching of the Runaways on the car stereo kept my eyes open, and finally, *finally*, after one of the longest, shittest nights I could remember, I was pulling up outside our little two-up, two-down.

On the doorstep I fumbled in the backpack for my keys, stifling a yawn, and almost dropping them when I finally found them. I caught them just before they hit the tiled front path, and then spoiled my dexterity by knocking over a milk bottle. A far-off dog began barking hysterically. I cursed my own clumsiness and stood, half expecting to see the hallway light click on and Gabe's sleepy figure come down the stairs, but nothing happened. He must be deep asleep.

It took me two or three tries to get the key in the lock. I was so tired, I felt almost dizzy with it. But as soon as the door swung open, I knew something was wrong.

It was the smell that hit me first—and for a minute I couldn't understand what it meant. All I knew was that the normal, comforting scents of cooking and laundry and that particular ineffable smell of *home* weren't there. Or rather, they were, but they were drowned out by something else. Something completely unexpected, and so out of context that for a moment I couldn't place it. It was a strange, fetid, iron-rich, almost *sweet* smell that reminded me of . . . of . . . what was it?

And then I placed it. It was the smell of the butcher shops along the high street.

It was the smell of blood.

Even then I didn't understand. How could I?

I didn't understand when I saw the smears of red on the hallway floor.

I didn't understand when the living room door handle was slick and sticky under my hand.

I didn't understand when I walked inside and saw him—Gabe— slumped over his computer, in the largest pool of blood I had ever seen.

Because—because it couldn't be *his*, could it? There was no way one single human being could hold all that blood. There must be some explanation—some awful, twisted, crazy explanation.

"Gabe?" I whimpered. He didn't move. The computer screen in front of him was black, only the lights from the big PC tower flickering in the dark puddle that spilled from the desk, across his lap, and onto the floor.

I didn't want to step in it, but there was no other way.

"Gabe," I called, more desperately, but still he didn't move, and at last I put one foot into the sick, slickish slime, feeling its thickness clutch at my shoes as I moved across the carpet.

There was a sob stuck in my throat, and as I reached him and touched his shoulder, it escaped, a mewling howl of distress that sounded like an animal in pain.

"*Gabe*, Gabe, wake up, wake up!"

He didn't say anything, didn't lift his head or show any signs of having heard me, and now I put my shoulder to his, forcing him to sit up, sit back in his chair.

He was unbearably heavy—fourteen stone of bone and muscle—and I wasn't sure if I could move him, but then, all of a sudden, he shifted, his weight flopping back in his chair, and I saw what they had done to him.

It was his throat. It had been cut, horribly, brutally, in a way I couldn't make sense of—it wasn't the neat surgical slash I would have imagined, but a fleshy mess protruding from a ragged hole, as if someone, some*thing* had ripped his windpipe out through the front of his neck, leaving a wound like a great scarlet laughing mouth.

A huge wave of sickness came over me and I lurched back, stumbling through the lake of blood, my hand over my mouth, my breath coming fast and erratic and a nausea building inside that threatened to overwhelm me.

Gabe.

I couldn't take my eyes off him, off his head, lolling backwards at a sick, unnatural angle that looked so profoundly dead, there was no way I could try to deny the reality of what had happened.

And yet. And yet his face was *still Gabe*. That strong, curved nose, like a Roman senator. Those cheekbones. The shape of his lips. The roughness of his beard, and the softness of the skin at the base of his neck. All of that was still Gabe, still the man I loved. But it was his dead body that I was looking at.

My legs were about to give out, and I groped my way to the sofa and pulled myself onto it, holding my knees to my chest and rocking, rocking. I was making a strange sound, I realized. Something halfway between a wail and a whimper and formed of Gabe's name.

This couldn't be true. It couldn't be happening. It *couldn't*. Not to Gabe—sweet, funny, capable Gabe, whose large, strong hands could pry off a stuck lid or splint a blackbird's wing with equal dexterity. *My* Gabe, who could fix anything, mend anything, make even the most terrible day okay with one of his huge, all-encompassing hugs.

But there was no way even he could fix this.

I don't know how long I sat there, staring at Gabe's body, at the flickering computer lights reflecting back from the dark pool of blood. Ten minutes? Twenty? I was shaking uncontrollably, and horribly, unbearably cold.

But at last I got ahold of myself. I knew what I had to do—what I should have done the moment I walked in the door.

My hands were stiff and trembling as I felt in my backpack for my phone. I had it, I knew I did. I had booked the Uber on it, but it still took me a long time to find, and when I drew it out the screen was blank and dark.

I had to hold on to the wall as I made my way through to our little kitchen, where there was a phone charger. It took me three tries to get the USB lead into the socket, my hands were still shaking so much. Metal ground against metal, leaving reddish smears across the screen as I tried and failed and tried again. But at last it was in.

The start-up took a painfully long time, cycling through its various animations and logos, the brightness hurting my eyes.

And then my lock screen. I opened it up and pressed the phone icon.

I dialed 999.

And I waited.

When the operator came on the line, I wasn't sure at first if I would be able to speak, but my voice, when it came out, was surprisingly steady.

"Police," I said in answer to her questions. I swallowed. I had to keep it together. I *had* to keep it together. I had already left it too long. "And please hurry. My husband—he's been murdered."

T he next few hours had the surreal, bright cadence of a waking nightmare. First came the sound of the sirens, screaming closer and closer. Then the emergency lights, saturating everything with a strange pulsing blue glow. Then the hammering on the door and the officers storming in. They asked questions that hadn't even occurred to me. Was the house secure? Could anyone still be on the premises? Did Gabe have any enemies?

It seems strange to say it, but I hadn't even considered that. Now, at the thought of someone hiding upstairs while I keened over Gabe's body, I felt cold all over again. But whoever it was, they were long gone.

And as for the rest—of course Gabe didn't have any enemies. Of *course* he didn't. The idea was absurd. Everybody loved him—his friends, his clients, his *family*. Oh God, I had a sharp flashing image of trying to tell Gabe's parents the news, and the realization of what had just happened rose up again, threatening to overwhelm me.

They took me upstairs, where a kind female officer helped me step out of my stiffening, blood-stained clothes and into clean, dry sweatpants, and then finally that same officer led me downstairs, shivering helplessly to where a police car was waiting.

As we passed through the hall—*my* hall—I turned my head and caught a glimpse of white-overalled forensics officers through the living room doorway. They had laid down mats across the floor and were setting up bright lights that illuminated everything with a horrible white glare.

For a brief moment the room seemed to spin on its axis. I looked away. I tried to breathe. I concentrated on putting one foot in front of the other until I reached the door of the police car.

I don't know how long I sat there in the back seat. I was shaking, in spite of the blanket someone had wrapped around me and the hot, dry air from the car heaters. Eventually someone came out and beckoned to the officer sitting beside me. She got out, and they had a low conversation, and then she climbed back in, this time into the driver's seat, and twisted to speak to me.

"Jack, are you okay to come with us to the station? We won't keep you too long, we just want to get everything clear while it's fresh in your head."

I nodded mutely. In truth it wasn't okay. I couldn't imagine anything I wanted to do less than go down there and live through the hideousness again and again and again. I wanted to crawl away into the darkness and scream into the night. I wanted to push past the officers in the hallway and cradle Gabe's body in my arms and tell everyone to fuck off and leave us, leave us alone.

I wanted to drink until I passed out.

But I had to do this—for Gabe, if no one else. I knew the officer was right; there was a window of time for tracking down whoever had done this, and I'd already wasted precious minutes, maybe even hours, by going into shock in the living room.

Another officer, a much younger one, climbed into the seat beside her and turned around to introduce himself.

"Hi, Jack, I'm Detective Constable Miles. Thank you so much for coming down to the station. We're going to make this as quick as we can, but we do want to make sure we're not missing anything. Have you got everything you need?"

I nodded, though it wasn't true. I had lost Gabe. He was the only thing I needed. Nothing else mattered.

J ust run me through the timings once more," the woman sitting opposite me said. Her voice was kind, gentle even, but her words made me want to cry—or scream—or do *something*. I was so tired. I hadn't slept for over twenty-four hours, and I had spent the night dodging security officers and climbing through ceilings before coming home to the most traumatic experience I had ever witnessed. My vision was blurred with tiredness. Most of all I was numb and dazed with a grief I hadn't even started to accept, let alone process.

Now I was sitting in an interview room with DC Miles, the young officer from the car, and his partner, DS Malik. She was watching me across the table with a mixture of patience and sympathy.

"I can't," I whispered. "I can't do this anymore. I can't."

"I know. I know this is really hard. But you've been so helpful leading us through Gabe's associates and so on—we just want to make sure we have the sequence of events absolutely correct, and then we can let you go."

I wanted to put my head in my hands—shut everything out. But I could do this. I *had* to do this. For Gabe.

I took a deep breath and steeled myself for one last rendition.

"I left the police station at . . ." I began, and then stopped in confusion. What had I said before? I couldn't remember the timings anymore. The events of the night were starting to blur. "I'm sorry—I'm just so tired. I think it was about two a.m. Or no, later. I remember seeing it was two a.m. in the interview room." I rubbed my eyes, feeling my head swim with exhaustion. "I got an Uber back to Arden Alliance, where I'd left the car. You can probably check the pickup time on the app if you need to know exactly. Then I got into my own car and drove home."

"And your phone was switched off for all this?"

"Not switched off—the battery had gone. I don't know when. I called the Uber on it, so it was working when I left the station, but it must have gone down after that."

"And you weren't using satnav or anything?"

I shook my head.

"No, our car doesn't have it, it's too old. Look, I don't mean to be rude, but why does this *matter*? What does my satnav have to do with Gabe's death?"

"We're just trying to get as clear a picture as possible," DC Miles said. His voice should have been soothing—his tone was clearly meant to be sympathetic—but for some reason all of my hackles went up.

"But I've told you all this, I've already told you. This is like—it's Kafkaesque. My husband is dead and you're asking me about my phone battery?"

"And you got home when?" DS Malik asked, as if I hadn't spoken. Her voice was kind, but brisker, as if she sensed that sympathy wasn't what I wanted.

"I think it was sometime around four a.m.—I remember looking at the clock on the dashboard as I turned into our road. I parked, then opened the front door and I found—" I shut my eyes, remembering the horror. The image of Gabe's mutilated throat rose up in front of my eyes and I opened them again, feeling a jolt of that remembered terror and disbelief. "Well, you saw."

"No footwear marks, no sign of a struggle?"

"None." I shook my head. "Any footprints you saw—that was me. There was nothing, no sign of anyone leaving—just a smear of blood on the living room door handle. I remember that. Because I saw it first, and I knew something was wrong."

"And Gabe, how was he sitting when you found him?"

"He was kind of slumped over his computer," I said. The numbness was stealing back over me, and I felt myself beginning to shake again, not uncontrollably like before, more a strange, steady shivering in spite of the warmth of the interview room and the hot mug of coffee clasped between my hands. "If it hadn't been for the blood, I might have thought he was just asleep. He was—" I swallowed, almost unable to think about it. "He was still wearing his noise-canceling headphones. I think whoever killed him—whoever killed him, they must have come up from behind and—"

I stopped. I couldn't say it. Something in my throat seemed to close up and I just shook my head.

"And then you did what?" DC Miles asked.

"I tried to lift him up. I thought—I don't know. I think I thought maybe he'd passed out, hit his head or something. I'm not sure what I thought. I kind of pushed him back in his chair; he was really heavy and at first I wasn't sure if I could move him—and then all of a sudden his weight shifted and he kind of flopped and I saw—I saw his—" I stopped. "His neck, it was—" I stopped again, breathing deeply through my nose, trying to hold it together.

For a long moment Malik and Miles said nothing, just watched me trying to control myself, and then Malik pushed a box of tissues across the desk and said softly, "I'm sorry. I know how hard this is. What did you do after that? This was around four a.m., yes?"

"M-maybe." I swallowed, blinking away the blurriness in my vision. "Maybe later. I honestly don't know. I think I went into shock. I just curled up on the sofa and—I kind of lost it. I couldn't—I couldn't process what was happening."

My hands were shaking harder now. So hard that I was becoming afraid of dropping my coffee. I couldn't drink it anyway. Instead, I put the mug down and held on to my knees to try to stop the trembling. How could I explain what had happened—the way my system had simply refused to compute this sequence of events? I thought of Gabe, coding late into the night, swearing each time his program crashed. *Error: an unhandled exception has occurred.* That was how I had felt. I had blue-screened. If only I could show Malik and Miles the error message—make them understand.

"I just . . . I just shut down," I said. My voice was a whisper. "I can't explain it. I didn't pass out or anything but I just—I couldn't move. I couldn't do anything. I know it was stupid. I should have called right away. I know that. I just—I *couldn't.* I couldn't process it."

I swallowed again. It felt like the tears I should be shedding were stuck in my throat. I hadn't wept since I had found Gabe's body—perhaps because I knew that if I gave way, I might not be able to stop.

"I'm sorry." I looked up at them both, hearing the tremble in my voice. "I'm *so* sorry. If I could go back and call you right away, I would, but I can't change what happened, and I've told you everything I know. My husband is *dead.*" The last word came out as a wail. I don't even know why I said it—I knew they had to do their job; I wasn't pleading for special treatment on account of Gabe. I just needed to say it. To hear the words coming out of my own mouth, to try to make it real.

I wanted to cry. I wanted to let it out—the unbearable grief and exhaustion. Why? Why couldn't I cry? It felt like something inside me was broken.

Perhaps the officers saw the desperation in my face, because DC Miles exchanged a glance with DS Malik and she shrugged, and then nodded.

"We're terminating the interview with Jacintha Cross. The time is . . . eight oh two a.m. on Sunday, fifth February."

She clicked off the recorder and then leaned forward to me.

"Thank you, Jack. I know that can't have been easy, but you've been really helpful. We're going to hang on to your phone, okay? But if you need to call anyone, you're welcome to use the phone here."

"Can I go home, then?" I asked. My voice was croaky. Malik grimaced sympathetically and shook her head.

"I'm really sorry. It's still a crime scene. Have you got anyone you can stay with in the meantime?"

I shut my eyes, trying to think, running through the list of people I could call on. My brain felt like it was short-circuited, little fritzes of false connections flashing up and disrupting my attempts at figuring this out. Gabe—slumped over his computer. Gabe—his head flung back, his throat spewing out of his skin, like something out of *Alien*. Gabe. *Gabe*.

"My sister," I said at last. "I could go to my sister. She lives in North London. Could you call her?"

"Sure. What's her name?"

"Helena. Helena Wick. 07422 . . ." I ground to a halt. *Shit*. What was Hel's number? I'd learned it by heart years ago, back when I first started doing penetration testing and didn't have Gabe to call on if things went south. But I was so tired I could barely remember my own name, let alone anything more complicated. "07422 . . ." I tried again, and this time the remaining digits came with a rush, like a nursery rhyme, reeled off without pause. "I think that's right. It's a long time since I dialed it from memory."

"No probs," DC Miles said. "Leave it with me."

He disappeared and then came back a few minutes later and said, "She's expecting you. We'll give you a lift in a patrol car."

I nodded. A sense of immense weariness was washing over me. The police interview might be over—but somehow the idea of calling Helena had made me realize something I should have known all along: that this nightmare was only just beginning. I would have to tell Hel what had happened. And then her husband, Roland. And they would have to tell their twin girls—something two little four-year-olds should never have to understand. How could they comprehend something I could barely process myself—that Uncle Gabe would not be coming to see them ever again? That he was gone?

And after Hel, it would be Gabe's parents, and our friends, and the bank and the broadband company and—and—and—

I thought back to when our parents had died, the numbing stream of admin, the endless spreadsheets that Helena had compiled. Inform the mortgage company. Tell the insurers. Cancel the TV license. Write to the GP. It had gone on and on and on for months.

I couldn't do it all again. Gabe hadn't even made a will, that I knew of. Why would he, when he was barely thirty and as healthy as anyone we knew?

"Jack?" DS Malik said, and I looked up, and realized the police officer was speaking to me.

"I'm sorry," I said. My lips were dry and stuck together. "I—I wasn't listening. Can you say that again?"

"We're ready to go," she said gently. "If you want. Okay?"

"Okay," I said. But it wasn't true. I wasn't okay. I would never be okay again.

Hel was standing on the doorstep as the patrol car drew up outside their neat little white-painted London semi, her face twisted with worry, a worry that cleared, but only slightly, as we came around the corner.

"Jack." She hurried down the checkered front path and I fell into her arms, burying my face in the familiar scent of her hair. "Oh my God, Jack," she said again, and her voice cracked. "I can't believe it, I can't believe it's true."

"We'll leave Jack with you, Mrs. Wick," DS Malik said. Her tone was sympathetic. "Is there a number we can use to be in touch? We can't release her phone yet, unfortunately."

"Yes," Hel said. She sounded distracted. "Yes, of course. I mean, I guess . . . mine? Probably? You've got it, right?"

"Yes, we've got it. Is there a landline to the house?"

"Yes," Helena said. She made a frantic motion to someone inside, who I guessed was Roland. "Rols, Rols, can you give them a card?"

"Sure," Roland said, and I heard his footsteps retreat up the hallway and then come back.

"Thank you, Hel," I said. I pulled away from her, but she kept hold of my hand. "I'm so sorry—this must have been—"

"Fuck that," Helena said shortly. Her hand tightened around mine, her grip crushing my ring into my knuckle, so hard it was almost painful. "Don't be stupid, Jack, you don't have anything to apologize for."

She took the cards Roland held out to her and passed them to DS Malik.

"There you go. That's my office number at the bottom—I'm a journalist and I work from home. You'll always find me on either that or my mobile. And that one"—she pointed at the other business card, underneath—"that's my husband's. He's a solicitor."

"Great," DS Malik said. "Thanks. And Jack, thanks for being so patient. I know this has been a horrendous experience. We'll be in touch very soon, and you'll be assigned a family liaison officer who'll be able to help you through the process and hopefully answer any questions you have. She'll be in contact sometime on Monday, I imagine. Is there anything else I can do before we leave you?"

I shook my head. I wanted nothing more than to curl up in the small white bed in Hel's spare room and cry myself to sleep. But the tears still wouldn't come.

WHEN I WOKE, THE STREET lamps were lit in the road outside, the yellow rays slanting under the curtains Helena must have drawn before she left the room. They fell on my face, making me blink and struggle to sit up, squinting against the glow.

For a moment I knew where I was—Hel's attic room was as familiar to me as my own bed—but not why, and I sat there, feeling an ache in my head and a bone-deep tiredness in my limbs, and trying to remember what had happened and why I felt such a strange sense of dread. The clock by the bedside said 6:45 and I rubbed my eyes confusedly as I realized—the street lamps must have only just come on—it was dusk, not morning. The realization gave me an odd sliding sense of everything being upside down, out of kilter, off-balance.

Then it came to me. Or no, *came* is the wrong word. It didn't just come, it hit me—sucker-punched me with a blow to the gut that left me doubled up and gasping with grief.

Gabe was dead. Gabe was *dead.*

For a long time I simply sat there, curled over my knees, my head in my hands, trying to make sense of it, trying to cram the fact into my brain. Was this going to be what it was like, every morning from now on? Was every day going to be a process of waking up, reaching for his warmth, and losing him all over again?

I remembered how my grandfather had been after my parents died. The way he would look around vaguely, ask for our mother, and Hel would say gently, "Mum's dead, remember, Grandad? She and Dad died two years ago." And then three years ago. And then four.

And every time, he would react with the same grief, his face crumpling, his blue eyes filling with unexpected tears. The shock wore off a little as the years passed—as if the knowledge *had* lodged in there somewhere, in spite of his Alzheimer's—but the grief . . . the grief never lessened.

After a while, as his memory deteriorated even further and the dementia made its last ravages on his brain, we simply stopped telling him.

"They're on their way, Grandad," Hel would say. Or, "I don't know, Grandad. Do *you* know where Mum is?" and he'd say, comfortably, "Oh, she'll be making tea, I expect. Would you like a cup?"

Maybe that would be me. Hel coming in with a cup of coffee. *Gabe just rang. Said he'd call back later.* And the strange thing was, I *could* almost imagine it. If I shut my eyes, I could picture him— back at the house, hunched over his computer, typing away on some impenetrable bit of code, utterly absorbed. The thought gave me a kind of peace, the idea that he could be out there somewhere—just beyond my reach. But it was a dishonest peace, and I knew that as much as I could fool myself if I tried hard enough, all I was doing was pushing the pain further down the line until the moment I stopped pretending and let the agony wash back over me.

At last, I forced myself out from under the covers and stood up, swaying a little. I stank. Mostly of sweat. The smell was the combined exertions of a night spent running around Arden Alliance, evading security guards, and then a morning in a hot interview room being interrogated by two police officers, and then a day passed out in the same clothes under a winter duvet. I smelled of adrenaline and fear—a smell I knew well from my fairly frequent brushes with tricky situations, though I had never been so scared as I was last night.

Someone had *killed* Gabe. But why? What could sweet, funny, loving Gabe have possibly done to upset anyone to that extent? Had they got him mixed up with someone else? But how—how could a case of mistaken identity get taken as far as murder? It didn't seem credible. But then, neither did any of the alternatives.

As the room settled around me, I tried to push the questions away. I couldn't answer them—I had spent half the night and most of the morning going over variants of the same in my own head and with the police. And I realized now that I was extremely hungry—almost faint with hunger, in fact. I hadn't eaten or drunk anything apart from coffee for more than twenty-four hours.

The smell of something deeply savory—sausages, perhaps—was wafting up the stairs. And suddenly I had the strangest feeling of dis-association. Because how *could* I be hungry when Gabe was lying in a police morgue somewhere, dead and gone forever? How could anything as mundane as food possibly matter?

And yet it did, and I was. The smell of the sausages brought water to my mouth, leaving me almost dizzy with hunger. And I knew that Gabe would be the first to understand that. *You've got to eat*, he would always tell me before a job. *You can't think on an empty stomach.* And I needed to think. I needed to think very badly indeed.

Hel had left towels and a change of clothes—not mine; they must be hers—on the foot of the bed, and I took them into the shower with me, dumping them onto the toilet lid before stepping into the cubicle and turning on the water.

It was hot and fast—much better than the stuttering pressure at my house—and I turned my face into the blast and closed my eyes, hearing the deafening hiss of the water in my ears, and feeling the jets pummeling my face—and for a moment I wished that I could stay there, muffled away from the world, eyes closed, ears blocked with water, unable to feel anything except the stinging needles of hot water against my skin.

But I couldn't. And at last I soaped my hair, dried myself off, and got dressed, ready to go downstairs and face a world without Gabe.

"OH, JACK."

Roland looked up as I stepped into the kitchen, my wet hair combed behind my ears, my stomach growling. As I tried for a smile, he stood and held open his arms, and I felt my throat close up. I shook my head, even as I walked into his hug, no, no, *no. Please don't be nice to me, Roland.*

But he was—and something about his hug, the feel of his arms around me, made me choke up like nothing else had. He wasn't Gabe—he was about six inches shorter and a couple of stone lighter, and he didn't have Gabe's beard or his heat or his indefinably comforting smell. But he was a man, and he was kind, and he wanted to comfort me—and that was so painfully close to what I wanted right now, just not from him, that it was almost unbearable.

At last I pulled myself away. Roland let me go, but there was something sad in his expression as he did.

"Please, don't be too nice to me, Rols. I just—" I swallowed, trying to find the words. "I'm only just holding it together, and I can't—I can't lose it. If I do, I might not—"

"Got it," Roland said. His eyes were full of an anguished sympathy, but I saw the way he squared his shoulders, and the smile he tried to put on his lips. "Operation Stiff Upper Lip commences."

Hel was at the cooker, her back to me, but I knew that she'd seen the little exchange play out, and I knew that she knew that what I needed right now wasn't sympathy but just to get through the evening without breaking down—and the best way to do that was a semblance of normality.

"How many sausages?" she said to me over her shoulder, her tone determinedly brisk, and I felt a wave of gratitude wash over me. "They're veggie."

"How many are there?"

"Twelve. The girls are in bed, so they're all for us."

"I'll have my full share then—four," I said. My throat ached with the effort of trying to speak normally, but my voice was almost steady. "Thanks, Hel. I'm starving."

"Mash? Gravy?"

"Yes. And yes."

Hel ladled sausage, mash, and onion gravy into three dishes, while Roland cleared aside sippy cups and Playmobil figures and laid out knives, forks, and glasses. Within just a few minutes we were sitting around their little table, and I was inhaling a glass of red wine that felt so good it was a little frightening. For a moment I just sat, my eyes closed, feeling the warmth of the wine filter through my bloodstream, numbing everything, and I thought . . . *I could stay here. I could stay in this warm, wine-fogged world where Gabe's absence hurts just a little less.* I had never understood substance abuse until that moment; even in the worst moments of my life before—the jackknifing lorry that had crushed my parents' car when I was seventeen, the grueling breakdown of my relationship with Jeff just a few years later—even in the middle of complete despair, I had never experienced the urge to opt out of *feeling.* But now—now if I could have made the pain go away, I would. If I could have crawled back into Hel's spare room and never come out, I would have done it. Because there was nothing left, apart from the tearing pain of Gabe's absence.

"Jack?" I heard, as if from a long way off. And then, "Jack, are you okay?"

I forced open my eyes. Roland was looking at me with concern.

"Yes, sorry. I'm okay." I cut a piece of sausage and put it in my mouth, chewing dutifully to show him how okay I was. But it tasted . . . good. Even with Gabe dead and my whole world crumbling, it still tasted good. I chewed, and swallowed, forcing the mouthful past the painful lump of unshed tears that seemed to be lodged permanently in my throat.

"Top-up?" Roland said, holding out the bottle. He had already started pouring when I spoke, reluctantly.

"That's fine, thanks, Rols. I don't want to be—I might need to speak to the police tomorrow."

"You're right," Hel said. She put her hand out and squeezed mine. "You *definitely* don't want to be hungover. What time are you seeing them?"

"I'm not sure. They didn't specifically say they wanted to see me, but they didn't seem . . ." I stopped, trying to put into words the uneasiness I'd felt during the interview. "They didn't seem completely happy with the timeline. They made me go over it several times. They said they might have more questions."

"The timeline?" Hel frowned and put down her knife. "What do you mean? What timeline?"

"I'm not sure. They started off asking about the car journey— why it took me so long to get back from Arden Alliance, and why my phone was switched off. But the thing they really kept harping on was the length of time I left between finding Gabe and calling the police. They seemed to think it was suspicious."

"How long was it?" Roland asked. He exchanged a glance with Hel.

"I don't know," I said honestly. "Maybe thirty minutes. Maybe longer. I know—I know it was incredibly stupid, but I just—I think I went into shock. But the thing is, he was so completely and obviously dead. The blood was cold, and sticky. It wasn't like I could have done anything."

The memory of it—the butcher shop smell, the mess of tendons and flesh spewing from Gabe's throat—it rose up in front of my eyes again, and I shuddered and clenched my jaw, holding my knife and fork tightly in my hands so my fingers wouldn't shake.

"Have they offered you a solicitor?" Roland asked now. His words chased the pictures in my head a little further away, and I looked up, puzzled.

"No, I mean . . . Actually yes, I think they did ask me if I wanted one, but I said no. Why?"

"I'm just . . ." He exchanged another glance with Hel, and I saw that both their faces were worried. "Well, look, maybe this is the law-yer in me, but the whole thing . . . the timing, and what you said about your phone, it's a bit . . . concerning."

"What do you mean?" I was puzzled. "You're not saying—they can't possibly suspect *me*, could they? Why would I—" I felt my throat close again, swallowed hard. "Why the fuck would I—"

Hel took a sip of wine and then set the glass down carefully.

"Because from what you said, this . . . it sounds like a hit, Jack."

"A hit?" Her words had stopped me in my tracks. "I'm sorry, did you say a *hit*?" The idea was so unexpected as to be bewildering. Whatever I had imagined as the root of Hel's concerns, it wasn't this. "But what—*why*?"

"Why do I think it's a hit? Because the—well, the method." I could tell she was trying to pick her words, but the picture rose up in front of my eyes again, Gabe's throat spilling out, raw and bloody through his skin, as if someone had pushed a knife right through behind the jugular and ripped it out, forward, severing arteries, tendons, and everything else in between. "That's how the professionals do it. I've covered a few stories about contract killings and . . . it's pretty distinc-tive."

"I didn't mean that." I gritted the words out through clenched teeth, trying to keep away the images Hel had conjured. "I meant why on earth would anyone want to kill Gabe? A botched robbery or something—okay, I could see that. But a hit? It makes no sense!"

"Well, that's the issue, isn't it? Why would anyone kill someone like Gabe, some lovely guy with no shady past, no enemies, and no secrets? But, Jack, it doesn't *sound* like a robbery. It just doesn't. It sounds like someone got in there, slit his throat, and got out, without leaving much of a trace. That's not a botched burglary—that's something else."

I was silent for a moment, her words sinking in as I realized she was right. How had I not seen it before? I thought of the questions that had come up in the police interview, questions about associates, our finances, had Gabe ever gambled, had he been mixed up in anything criminal, did he have any enemies. No, no, and no. Except . . .

"Well, he . . . he does have a past." I said it reluctantly, forcing the words out, feeling disloyal to Gabe, although it wasn't like he kept it a secret. If it came up, he was honest about it. He even did some outreach work with schools and youth groups, talking about what happened. It wasn't a secret—but it also wasn't something he was proud of. And it wasn't something I had ever shared with Roland or Helena. "Kind of. But I can't see how it's relevant."

"What do you mean?" Roland was frowning. "What kind of past?"

"He was convicted of hacking, at seventeen. He got sent to . . . I'm not sure, actually. Some kind of juvenile prison, I think. Then he was banned from using computers for a few years. But it was years ago— like fifteen years or something. I truly can't see how it could have any kind of repercussions today."

Hel sat, silent, chewing her lip. Then she shook her head.

"No, I can't see it either. Which is why I'm worried."

"What do you mean?" Her concern was infecting me, giving me a strange, ominous feeling, which in turn translated into a prickle of anger. "I feel like you're talking in circles, Hel. Spit it out, whatever it is."

"Look." Hel put down her glass again with a thunk. "There are two kinds of people who hire contract killers. People mixed up in organized crime—and spouses. And since Gabe has no connection with organized crime . . ."

My jaw had dropped, and it took me a long moment to find my voice. When I did, it shook with fury.

"What the *fuck* are you saying, Hel?"

"Keep your voice down, you'll wake the girls," Hel said in a low whisper. "And don't be stupid. Of *course* I wasn't suggesting you took out a contract on Gabe, that's absurd. I would never even *think* such a thing. But look at the facts—you've got no alibi. Your phone was switched off. There's no sign of breaking and entering. It looks like Gabe either let a stranger into the house—which frankly seems unlikely—or someone gave them a key. And then you waited half an hour to call the cops."

"I *told* you—" I broke in, but Helena spoke over me, her voice hard, as if she was trying not to let her feelings get the better of her.

"I know, Jack. I *know.* And I understand completely—but I'm extremely worried the police aren't going to. If they ask to speak to you again, I think you should take a lawyer."

I was silent for a moment, considering what Hel had just said. Stacked up like that, it did sound bad. But surely, *surely* no one could believe I would kill Gabe? What motive could I possibly have?

"What do you think?" I said at last to Roland. "You're a solicitor. Is Hel right, should I take someone? I mean, surely it'll look worse if I turn up with a lawyer in tow? Like I have something to hide."

"I think she is right, I'm sorry," Roland said. "Crime's not my area, but I'm pretty sure that's what my colleagues would say. I can give you some names if you want."

"I don't need a fucking lawyer!" I exploded. The tears were back, prickling at the edges of my eyes, making me irrationally furious with Helena and Roland, who were only trying to help. This wasn't their fault—*none* of it was their fault. But I wanted very much to lash out at someone. I wanted to hurt someone—and if it couldn't be them, it would probably be myself. "This is ridiculous." The sobs were rising up now, threatening to choke me, and I stood, pushing my plate away, suddenly too tense and full of pent-up grief and rage to sit, pretending everything was fine.

"I know." Hel stood up too, facing me. "I know, Jack. It's ridiculous—and ridiculously unfair and it's just—it's just unbelievably *shit* that this has happened, to anyone, but to you and Gabe in particular." Her voice was choking up, but she forced herself on. "But I'm just—you're all I've got left, Jack. I don't want you to take *any* risks with this, do you understand? And I'm worried for you—I'm really, really worried. So please, if you get asked to come in again, call a lawyer. Yes?"

I felt my rage deflate inside me like a pricked balloon, leaving only an intense weariness, close to despair. I felt my shoulders droop.

"Okay," I said, the anger suddenly trickling away. Maybe it was the unintentional pathos of Hel's cry, *You're all I've got left, Jack.* Because the thing was, it wasn't true—for Hel at least. She had Roland, and the girls, and her work. Yes, we were the last members of the family we had grown up with—our parents and grandparents all gone, no aunts or uncles, only each other. But she had made her own family, a new one—with a future that was bright and beautiful and loving. And until yesterday, I had been in the process of doing the same thing.

But not anymore. Now Gabe was dead, and with him, that future had been ripped away.

"Okay. If they ask me in again, I'll call a lawyer. I promise."

"Thank you," Hel said. She put her arms around me. "Thank you, Jack. I'm sorry, I know I'm being a mama hen, but you'll always be my little sister. I love you."

I shut my eyes, pressing my forehead into her shoulder.

I love you too, I wanted to say, but I couldn't make my throat form the words. I could only stand there, holding Hel, trying not to think about everything I'd lost.

MONDAY, FEBRUARY 6

MINUS SIX DAYS

thought I wouldn't be able to sleep that night, having spent all of the previous day passed out in Hel's spare room, but when I finally went up the stairs at just gone midnight, I did. It wasn't good sleep, though—the room was hotter than I was used to at home, and I tossed and turned, running from someone or something who chased me, doggedly, relentlessly, never letting me escape.

One of the twins woke in the night with a bad dream and called out for Hel, and I woke too, blinking and dazed, listening to the wailing cries and trying to piece together who and where I was. It didn't hit me this time, the reality of Gabe's death. Instead it was already there, hanging over me like a weight that had never left. It was like the specter I had been running from all night but had never managed to outpace.

Sometime later I woke again, this time to the noise of a school day kicking off. Filtering up from the bedroom below, I could hear Kitty, the younger of the twins, complaining about putting on her school top. It was scratchy, she said. She didn't like the label. And downstairs Roland had the radio on, the faint sound of Radio 4 coming up the stairwell.

Dragging myself upright, I reached automatically for my phone—and then remembered it was with the police. Damn. For a long moment I sat there, pulling myself together mentally and physically, and then I grabbed the borrowed robe off the bottom of the bed and padded downstairs for breakfast.

"Jack!" Roland was at the counter, doling out sandwiches into Tupperware boxes while tapping at his phone. "Good morning! How did you sleep?"

"Okay," I said. It was a lie, but he didn't need to know the truth. "Thanks. Can I . . . should I help myself?"

"Yes! Please. Sorry, it'll calm down in a sec. This is peak pre-school madness, but we'll be out the door in a few minutes. You're coffee in the mornings, aren't you? You know where it is."

He nodded at the tall larder cupboard in the corner. Glancing up at the clock, I saw it was ten past eight. Later than I'd thought.

As I spooned out coffee into the pot, I heard the sound of pounding footsteps on the stairs and Millie, the older twin, burst into the kitchen sobbing.

"Daddy! Kitty got toothpaste on my top!"

"Okay, okay, calm down, it's not the end of the world." Her father lifted her up onto his knee, dabbing with a kitchen towel until the stain was just a pale shadow against the royal blue. "Good as new."

"But I can still see it!"

"You'll be fine, sweetie. Right, shoes on. Where's Kitty?"

"Here!" Kitty clattered into the kitchen, shoes already on, hair plaited, evidently determined to expunge the toothpaste accusation by being the perfect schoolchild. She looked at me without any surprise at seeing her aunt, gray faced and bleary eyed at the kitchen counter. "Hello, Auntie Jack! I did my shoes myself."

"They're on the wrong feet, pickle," Roland said patiently, kneeling down to help Kitty swap over her red buckled shoes. At the sight of the shoes, my heart contracted. They were so little—each one small enough to fit in Roland's palm. Kitty stood, staring down intently as Roland refastened her straps, as if to check that he was doing it correctly. Then he straightened.

"Right. All set? Book bags?"

"Yes," the twins chorused.

"Water bottles?"

Kitty didn't have hers, and there was a moment of panicked hunt, this time with Kitty on the verge of tears before Helena came running down the stairs with it in her hand.

"Got it! It had rolled under the bed. Right, go, go! You'll be late!"

There was a chorus of "Bye, Mummy; bye, Auntie Jack," and another brief threat of tears from Kitty, who had apparently thought Hel was walking them to school . . . and then the door closed behind them, and Hel let out a sigh of relief.

"Thank Christ. God, I love having kids, but if there's one thing I won't miss, it's the school run. How are you?"

"Okay," I said, though it wasn't really true, and Hel knew it. "Listen, do you have a spare phone knocking around anywhere? The police have mine, and I really need to . . ." I stopped. What I really needed to do was start telling people what had happened to Gabe. At the very least I needed to put an out-of-office on the Crossways Security email address. We had clients lined up, a job booked in for next week. Arden Alliance would be expecting their report. And that was without even thinking about Gabe's friends and family, who would be starting to wonder why he wasn't reading the family WhatsApp group messages or returning emails.

"Sure," Hel said quickly, seeing my chin start to quiver. "You can have my old phone, the one the girls play with. It's perfectly functional. I think Rols might even have a spare SIM somewhere. He got a free one when he got his phone."

"That would be amazing," I said gratefully. "Even if there's no SIM, if I can use your Wi-Fi . . . "

"Hang on," Hel said. "I'll be back."

She left, and I heard the sound of her feet heading upstairs to the living room, and the noise of doors opening and closing as she rummaged through the girls' toy box and then Roland's office, which was off the back of the living room. Then her feet on the stairs again.

"Sorry about the stickers." The Motorola she held out wasn't that old—it was the same model as my last one, in fact—but the case was plastered with My Little Pony unicorn stickers. "And I might . . . hang on, there's something a bit gross on the screen." She was scrubbing at it with a baby wipe. "I think it's jam. Here you go. The pin is 1234, but it's logged into my Gmail so feel free to do a hard reset. I assume you don't want to see my messages."

"Are you sure? Won't the girls be annoyed if I wipe all their games?"

"Probably, but it'll be good for the little square eyes. They've still got the iPad so I'm sure they'll cope. And I found this in Roland's desk." She was holding a small cardboard folder, and now she opened it up and pulled out a SIM card, snapping it out of its plastic surround. "God, why do they make these things so tiny? I preferred it when they were a size you could actually see with the naked eye."

I didn't answer, I was too busy googling *how to reset Motorola Play*. I was halfway through the steps when Hel's own phone rang, and she stepped over to the window to answer it.

"Hello? Yes, that's me. Oh . . . oh, sure. Hang on. She's right here." She put her hand over the receiver and said in a low voice, "It's for you. The police."

My stomach swooped. I took the phone from Hel's hand.

"Hi, Jack speaking."

"Jack, hi." It was DS Malik. "Sorry to disturb you so early, but are you free today? Could you come into the station?"

"Of course." I found my heart was beating fast. Had they found something important? "Have you got any leads?"

"We've got a number of lines of inquiry and we're hoping you might be able to help us with some of them, but I'd prefer to talk it through at the station."

"Of course, what time would suit?"

"Say . . ." There was a pause, and I heard Malik leafing through a notebook, or perhaps a diary. "Say eleven a.m.?"

"Sure. Thank you. See you then."

I hung up and handed the phone back to Helena.

"Have they found anything?"

"I don't know." I looked down at the unicorn phone in my other hand. It had finished the reset process and was asking me to log in as a new user and enter Hel's Wi-Fi password. "I think possibly . . . yes? They've asked if I can come in at eleven. But they clearly didn't want to talk about it over the phone."

"God, I hope they've got a lead."

"Me too." I felt my throat close up as I said the words. The idea that whoever had done this to Gabe was still out there . . . I still couldn't fully process that realization.

"Have you eaten anything?" Hel asked now.

I shook my head. "I'm not really hungry."

Hel gave me a look that was pure mother hen, and I sighed.

"I know, I know, I have to eat, blah, blah. The truth is I feel a bit sick. I've got to—" I looked down at the phone in my hand. It had connected to my Google account, and the notifications were pinging onto the home screen. Unread email. Unread email. Unread email. "I've got to start telling people. I can't leave clients hanging, and Gabe's parents . . ."

I broke off. I couldn't even say the words.

"I can do it," Hel said urgently. "Honestly, Jack, no one would expect you to be ringing round, not twenty-four hours after Gabe—" She stopped, not wanting to say the unspeakable, and waved her hand as if to indicate, *after all this.*

But I shook my head. She was probably right—and there were definitely people I could let her deal with. But not Gabe's parents, and not his best friend, Cole. They deserved to hear from me, and they deserved to hear before the police got in contact, which they might be doing right now, for all I knew. I couldn't let the first they learned of Gabe's death be a call from Scotland Yard.

"No, I have to do at least a handful of people myself. I *need* to, Hel. I promise I'll lean on you for the work stuff, but John and Verity, and probably Cole, I have to call them myself."

"Okay," Hel said resignedly. "If you really feel you have to. But first you're going to call your lawyer, yes?"

"Not now," I said, and then seeing her expression, I held up a hand. "Hel, I *will* call her, I promise, but please stop bugging me. I just—I have to get this out of the way first. I can't let Gabe's parents hear about this through the grapevine."

Even Hel could see the justice in that one, and she nodded, albeit a little reluctantly.

"Can I borrow a laptop?" I asked, as much to change the subject as anything. "For the work stuff, I mean."

Hel nodded again and picked up a battered MacBook from the sideboard.

"Knock yourself out. Password is powerpets, same as the Wi-Fi. All lowercase. Safari is logged into my Gmail, but you can open up an incognito tab or use Chrome. And the phone should be working now, I've activated the SIM. The number's on there if you need to give it to anyone." She pointed at the cardboard sleeve that had contained the SIM.

"Thanks," I said, and then, impulsively, I moved across the kitchen and hugged her. She smelled like home, our home, our childhood home, the smell I remembered from walking through my parents' front door after staying with friends and inhaling like it was oxygen. "I love you."

"I love you too." Her arms tightened around me, and I could feel everything she wanted to say. How unfair this was. How eagerly she would have taken this grief away from me if she could. But neither of us were the kind for big emotional speeches, and at last she let go, coughed, and moved towards the stairs.

"Okay, well, I'll be upstairs if you need me. Shout, okay?"

"Okay."

"And I'll drive you down to the station. If we leave at ten thirty, that should be fine."

"Ten thirty. Sure." I looked at the phone in my hand. It was just after nine. I had ninety minutes to destroy Gabe's parents' world.

       *   *   *

IT WAS ABOUT FORTY-FIVE MINUTES later that I shut down the laptop with a sigh, knowing that I had done the easy tasks, and that now only the impossible ones were left. I had emailed the clients we had in the diary, not giving much information apart from explaining that I'd had a *serious family bereavement* and that Crossways would be closed for at least a fortnight and would not be able to fulfill their job. I gave them the choice of waiting to be rescheduled or contacting one of the other security companies that I rated, and then I changed the out-of-office response to say something along the same lines. I didn't say that Gabe was dead—I couldn't bring myself to type the words—but I was fairly sure that I wouldn't need to. It would probably be in the papers very soon.

Now I had to contact Gabe's parents, John and Verity, and his best friend, Cole. The only question was what order to do it in.

I decided to call John and Verity first—if only because I thought the police would probably track them down fastest. Their home phone number was stored in my contacts as "Gabe's parents," whereas Cole was down simply as "Cole Garrick," with nothing to spell out his relationship to Gabe.

But when I rang, the call went to answerphone. "You've reached the Medways," Verity's pleasant voice came over the recording. "Sorry we can't come to the phone. We're either out or on the other line. Please leave a message and we'll return your call as soon as possible."

There was a beep and I sucked in my breath, wondering what to say. Fuck. *Fuck.* Why hadn't I thought of this? They were probably out walking the dog. Or maybe Detective Sergeant Malik had already rung them, and they were speeding down the motorway from Oxfordshire to London.

"Hi," I said at last, realizing that I had to say something. There was a crack in my voice. I tried to harden it, knowing that I couldn't break down, not like this. "John, Verity, it's Jack. Something . . . something has happened. It's, well, it's serious. Could you call me? I'm not on my usual number so you'll need to call me on . . ." Shit, what was the number of this phone? I grabbed for the paper folder that Hel had left on the side and read off the number. "Okay," I ended, lamely, but unsure what else I could say. "Oh, and it's pretty urgent." Then I remembered the appointment with the police. I couldn't very well take their call during a police interview. "I won't be around between eleven and . . . I don't know. Maybe one? So if you don't get this message until after eleven, then, yeah." Oh God, I was screwing this up. "Call me," I said again. And then, "Bye."

The answerphone beeped halfway through the *bye*, putting me out of my misery, and I hung up. My throat felt choked, but I had a sense of reprieve, in a way. I wasn't sure how I would have coped with John and Verity's grief and shock while my own was still so raw.

I gave it ten minutes in case they had just been in the garden or upstairs, but no one called back, and now it was almost ten o'clock. I had only half an hour to contact Cole. If the police hadn't already done so. But when I brought up his number on the phone, I couldn't quite bring myself to dial it. Because Cole *would* pick up. He was welded to his phone, twenty-four/seven. And I had no illusions what I was about to do to him.

Unlike me, Gabe was an only child. But he and Cole were closer than plenty of siblings I'd known, and had been in each other's lives almost as long. They'd met at primary school, and had formed a kind of chalk-and-cheese friendship that had apparently baffled the teachers. Gabe had always had a touch of anarchism about him—Verity had said once that even at age five, he'd been the kind of child for whom a button marked *do not press* was an irresistible temptation—not out of any malice, but just because he couldn't *not* find out what it did. He'd scraped through his exams, too busy exploring the chaotic online world he'd just discovered to study hard, and then at age seventeen, he'd pressed one button too many and found himself on the wrong side of the law—a mistake it had taken him a good decade to recover from.

Cole, on the other hand, had been the perfect student—grade As in all his exams, a first from Cambridge, an internship at Apple, and then headhunted by Cerberus, an up-and-coming IT firm in the UK that had risen, in the last few years, to become an establishment player in the tech industry. On the face of it, they had nothing in common, and no one on the street would have pegged them for friends—Cole in his crisp white T-shirts and pristine Adidas, Gabe in his ripped jeans and Doc Martens.

But in spite of their differences, Cole and Gabe's friendship had endured, bonded at first by their shared fascination with computer games, tech, and coding, and then later by something much deeper—a genuine, bone-deep love for each other that you had to be blind to miss. I had never seen two men hug goodbye like Cole and Gabe did—holding each other so hard it was like they didn't want to let go. Cole had told me once that Gabe's time in prison had been one of the loneliest periods of his life.

And now I had to tell him that Gabe was gone—for good.

When I dialed Cole's number he didn't pick up straightaway, it just rang and rang, and after the first few rings I began to get the same creeping sense of release that I had with John and Verity. It was stupid, because of course I wasn't off the hook; I would still have to have this conversation, but it felt like putting off homework—a kind of relief, even if it was a false one.

But just as I was about to hang up, there was a click and Cole's breathless voice came on the line.

"Hello? Who's this?"

"Cole? It—it's Jack."

"Jack?" His voice went faint, and in my mind's eye I could see him pulling the phone away from his ear to look at the display, making sure he hadn't imagined it. When he came back on, his voice was puzzled. "Are you all right? This isn't your number, is it?"

"No." I swallowed. "No, I'm—I'm not really all right. Cole, something's happened."

Oh God, this was hard. This was so hard. Harder than I had even imagined.

"What's happened?" His voice, puzzled, kindly, with an accent painfully similar to Gabe's, made my stomach curl with grief. I wanted to put the phone down and howl.

"Cole—" My voice cracked, a huge painful lump of unshed tears seeming to lodge in my throat. "Cole, it's Gabe—he—he's—"

I drew a long, shuddering breath, trying to force the word out.

"Jack?" Cole sounded a mix of confused and alarmed. "Gabe's what? What's happened?"

"Oh God, Cole, he's *dead*." The last word came out not as the factual piece of information I had been trying for, but as a long, almost incoherent moan of pain.

"*What?* What the— Jack, did you just say Gabe is *dead*? Wh— How? What happened? *How?*"

I nodded, forgetting he couldn't see me, and put my hand over my eyes, closing them as if that could shut out the memories that had begun to crowd in, unwanted. They weren't like ordinary memories, little pictures recalled at will. They were more like PTSD flashbacks, unbearably real. For a moment I could almost smell the blood. The thought made me gag.

"I came home from work." My voice was shaking, but I tried to keep it steady enough to get the words out. "And he—his throat had been—" I didn't want to say it, but the images in front of my mind's eye were too vivid to push away and the words came in spite of myself. "His throat had been cut."

"Wait, are you saying he was *murdered*?"

"Yes. But I just—I can't believe it. I can't believe it."

"I can't believe it," Cole said, echoing my words back to me unconsciously, his voice uncomprehending, bewildered. "It makes no sense. Gabe? Who would harm Gabe?"

"I don't *know*. I thought at first, maybe a burglary gone wrong, but—"

Hel's voice came back to me, reluctant but full of a horrible kind of certainty. *From what you said, this . . . it sounds like a hit, Jack.*

"Fuck," Cole was saying, almost whispering, as if to himself. "Fuck. *Fuck.* They—they cut his *throat*?"

"I'm so sorry," I choked out. "I didn't want to tell you like this but I thought the police might be in contact."

"Jesus, Jack, don't apologize!" It was Cole's turn, now, for his voice to crack. When he spoke again he sounded close to tears, and I shut my eyes, wishing I had been able to do this in person. What I wouldn't have given for a hug at that moment . . . "I'm just—God, *I'm* the one who should be sorry. What can I do? Can I do anything to help? Anything?"

"I mean—not really." I leaned on the kitchen counter, my head in my hands, supporting myself as though the weight of all this was too much for my body to bear. "There's not much any of us can do until the police have finished investigating. But you could tell people, if you can face that? I just— I know I should—but I can't."

"No, oh God, of course not. Of course I can do that. Who do you want me to tell? Everyone?"

"I mean, not a Facebook post or anything. But if you could just tell our friends, let them know what's going on. I don't want the people who knew him to hear about it from the evening news."

"What about John and Verity?" Cole asked. "Do they know?"

"No." I bit the inside of my lip, thinking. Gabe's parents knew Cole well—he'd spent enough time at their house as a kid that they regarded him as something close to a second son. They certainly had his phone number, and there was a strong chance Verity would ring him if she couldn't get hold of me. "I called them, but they weren't picking up, and I have to leave now for the police station. So they know something's wrong, but not what. I guess . . . I guess if they call you, then just come out with it—it's better they hear it from you than social media. Explain I was trying to contact them. I'll try them again as soon as I'm back."

"Of course," Cole said slowly. "God, Jack, I'm just—I'm so sorry. I can't take this in. Do the police have any leads? Do they know who did this?"

"I don't know," I said. I rested my forehead on my hand, pressing the knuckles into my eyes. "My sister, Hel, she thinks—" I stopped. It was somehow incredibly hard to say any of this; saying it made it real in a way that was almost unbearable, but I forced the words out. "She thinks that maybe it was a hit. Because of the method. Like, someone was targeting Gabe. Do you—did he seem worried at all when you last spoke?"

"Christ." Cole sounded like I'd punched him in the stomach all over again. "No, I spoke to him . . . Friday, I guess? We were talking about going for a beer—he sounded completely normal. Is that the police theory too?"

"I don't know. They seemed completely at sea yesterday, but they rang me this morning and asked me to come down to the station, and it sounded . . . well, I thought it sounded like they might have found something. Maybe. But I'm not sure—I don't know if I should be discussing this stuff." I had no idea what the rules were. Was I allowed to talk to people about what had happened? What if the police wanted to keep some pieces of information back? "Look, it's probably better not to repeat any of this," I said at last. "I might be totally wrong."

There was a long silence, as if Cole was trying to take in what I had just told him. I didn't blame him. When he spoke again, it sounded like he was trying to pull himself together.

"Jack, listen, if I contact people—I need to know what to say. How do you want me to put this? And they'll want to know if they can get in touch with you."

"I—" I hadn't thought about that one. Part of me couldn't face the calls, the curiosity, the *sympathy*. It was different with Cole and Hel; Hel was family, and Cole had loved Gabe as much as I did . . . but Gabe's other friends, especially the ones I didn't know so well . . . "I guess just say the truth—we don't know what happened. The police are investigating. As for me . . . the police have my phone. So people can't contact me on my usual number. This one is borrowed from my sister and I'm not sure how long I'll have it. Maybe you could tell them I'm only on email for the moment?"

"Sure. I mean of course. And I can pass on messages if anything comes up."

"Thank you." I looked up at the clock. "Cole, listen, I'm so sorry, I have to go. I'm due at the police station soon. Are you—"

I wanted to say, *Are you okay? Are you going to be all right?* But it sounded so transparently stupid. Of course he wasn't okay. Neither was I. Both of us had just had our lives ripped apart.

"Listen, Jack," Cole said, filling in the silence. "Anything you need, okay? *Anything*. I mean that. Gabe—he's—" He stopped. I heard him swallowing on the other end of the line, trying to control himself as he corrected the tense. "He was, well, he was pretty much like a brother to me—you know? Which makes you my sister. So you call me, okay? Day or night—literally."

"Thanks, Cole," I whispered. And then I put the phone down and sat staring into space until Helena came down the stairs.

B y the way, what did your solicitor say?" Hel asked as we pulled into the car park behind the police station. "Are they meeting you here?"

I said nothing, and she yanked on the handbrake and turned to face me, her expression stony.

"Jack. Please tell me you *did* call the solicitor?"

"I didn't get round to it."

"Jack—" Hel began, but I cut in.

"Look, you've made your views on this perfectly clear. But I just think—I don't know. I just think it looks really weird and antagonistic if I start getting lawyered up. I have nothing to hide. If some lawyer starts telling me not to answer questions—that's not what I want. I *want* them to find Gabe's killer."

"I know you do," Hel said. "And I know you have nothing to hide. I just hope the police realize that." She drummed her fingers on the wheel. "Look, I can't make you do this, but will you swear to me that at any hint, *any* hint at all that things are going sideways, you'll stop the interview? Don't agree to say or do anything until the lawyer gets there. Just say, 'I'm exercising my right to have a lawyer present, and I won't be answering any questions until he or she gets here.' Okay?"

"Okay," I said. "But honestly, I think you're being neurotic."

"I really don't think I am, Jack. I don't want to be brutal about this, but there's a reason they always suspect spouses. You've got means, and you've got opportunity. The only thing they're lacking to make a case is a motive. So please, please be really careful not to give them one."

But she'd gone too far with that last remark. I didn't say anything, just looked at her, and she grimaced.

"Sorry, that came out wrong. Look—I *know* you had no reason to kill Gabe, and I'm probably being paranoid. But have you got one?"

"A motive?" I felt my voice sliding up an octave. "Are you shitting me? Of course I don't have a fucking motive. What would that even look like?"

"I didn't mean that—I meant, have you got a lawyer."

"Oh." I paused, trying to remember. "Yes, we've got this woman . . . Melanie, her name is. She works for a firm called Westland Law. We've used her a couple of times when things went south during jobs."

My phone beeped with an email and I looked down at it automatically. It was a client, expressing sympathy and telling me not to hurry back on their account, but the clock at the top was showing eleven a.m. and I turned and unclipped my seat belt.

"Okay. Here's hoping they've found something."

"Hear, hear. Do you want me to wait?"

"Better not. I have no idea how long it'll take. I can get a cab back if need be."

"Sure. Okay, well . . . take care." Hel leaned across the car to kiss my cheek and I hugged her back. "Love you."

"Love you too."

"Have you got any money?"

I was about to roll my eyes and tell her to stop fussing when I realized I actually didn't. I didn't even have a credit card—I had left my wallet in Hel's spare room.

Hel saw my expression and pulled out her purse.

"See? Mother hens are good for some things. Here, it's all I've got in cash, but it'll have to do." She held out two notes, a ten and a twenty, and I made a face and took them, tucking them into my phone case. "And repeat after me: Hel is always right."

"Hel is always right," I said, forcing myself to smile at her. Then I climbed out of the car, feeling her eyes on me as I crossed the car park and opened the door to the police station.

Inside the station it was noisy and smelled of cleaning fluid and used coffee cups. As I waited in line to speak to the officer behind the front desk, I couldn't help scoping the place out as if I were on a job. Two exits—one to the street, unmanned; one to the interior of the station, no lock as far as I could see. There was probably an activation button under the desk. One fixed CCTV camera in the corner with a huge blind spot that covered most of the right-hand wall—not a very good design for a police station. The odd thing was that I had no memory of any of it from before. Shock had wiped half the night's events from my brain—which felt strange, but no stranger than mechanically assessing the building's risk profile in a world in which Gabe no longer existed.

When it was my turn, I gave my name and explained I was here to see DS Malik. The officer behind the desk smiled politely and told me to take a seat, but I had barely done so before Malik herself came out through the interior door. I tried to read her body language. She didn't look like someone who had solved her case, and I felt my anxiety spike a little as I stood up.

"Hi."

"Jack, hi, thanks so much for coming in. There are just a few points we wanted to clarify from our last interview. If you could follow me through here . . ."

"No problem." She led me through the door, her pace quickening as we passed a warren of rooms and back offices. "Have you got any leads?"

"Your family liaison officer is the best person to talk to about that. Has she been in touch?"

"Not yet."

"Okay, well, I'll chase that up," Malik said. She ushered me inside an interview room that was similar to the one we'd occupied the other night.

"Jack, hi." DC Miles was already there, and as I entered he stood up and shook my hand. I noticed again how young he was—barely out of uni, by the looks of it. There was a tape recorder on the desk and as we sat down, Miles clicked it on and looked at DS Malik, who nodded and spoke.

"Interview commenced at eleven twelve hours, Monday sixth February. DC Alex Miles and DS Habiba Malik interviewing witness Jacintha Cross, also known as Jack Cross, in connection with the death of her husband, Gabriel Medway. Jack, this is a voluntary interview under caution, which means that you're not under arrest and you can leave at any time. However, a decision to arrest may apply should that happen and you decide to leave without being interviewed." She stopped and took a breath, and I found myself frowning. They hadn't said that yesterday . . . had they? But before I had a chance to question what the change in wording meant, Malik was continuing. "You do not have to say anything, but anything you do say may be used against you in evidence, and it may harm your defense if you do not mention, when questioned, something you later rely on in your defense. You also have the right to free, independent legal advice, and you can ask for a solicitor at any point. You can also ask for a consultation away from the interview room if needed, for advice, before you return to the interview. Do you understand these rights?"

"Um . . . yes," I said slowly. I was still trying to figure out what had been different about the wording of the caution. Perhaps Hel's paranoia was affecting me, but I was certain they hadn't said the part about the decision to arrest when they interviewed me the last time. But what did the change in tone mean? Was Hel right?

"Jack, we've brought you back in because there's just a few things we need to clarify about the statement you gave us the other night," Malik said, and I nodded. She was leafing through a notebook, looking for something, and then stopped as she found it. "Right. So, you told us the other night that you thought you left the police station about two a.m., is that right?"

"Um . . . yes, maybe just after. I remember seeing it was about two a.m. while I was still inside the station."

"Sure. Okay, and then you took an Uber back to your car, and drove home, arriving about . . ." She checked something in her notebook. "About four a.m. Is that right?"

"I think so. Maybe a bit after."

"Right. It's just . . . look, maybe you can help us out here, Jack, but we're struggling to make these timings add up. It's about half an hour's drive from the station to where you say you left the car."

I frowned more deeply. I didn't like that *you say*. Surely they knew damn well where I had left the car? It was a police officer who'd picked me up.

"That sounds about right," I said, trying to keep my voice even.

"Then another half hour . . . let's be generous and say forty-five minutes from Arden Alliance to your house. So that takes us to three fifteen at the latest. But you didn't call 999 until almost five a.m. That's . . . well, look, it's a big chunk of time unaccounted for."

I felt a brief flash of anger flare inside me but pushed it back down. It was their job to tie up all the loose ends, I knew that. But it took everything I had not to snap, *Shouldn't you be catching Gabe's killer instead of grilling me?*

I took a deep breath.

"Well, first of all, I was incredibly tired driving back and I took a couple of wrong turns. I'm not sure how much it added to the journey, but I'd be really surprised if I made it back much before four."

"Okay."

"And then, as I said"—*like I told you already* was the subtext I was trying not to underline too heavily here—"I went into some kind of shock when I found Gabe's body. I know I should have dialed 999 the second I found him, but I just—I didn't. I couldn't. Don't you understand that? It isn't every day you stumble across—" I stopped, the memories rising up, threatening to choke me. "Across your hus—" My voice was wobbling, and I changed tack, trying to keep in control of the situation. "But look, it doesn't matter anyway—surely you can tell that Gabe was dead long before I got home? I told you—the blood was sticky and clotting, and it's not just that; I rang him from the station, and he didn't pick up. I think—"

I stopped again, trying to control my wavering voice, which was going high and plaintive as a child's. *Don't cry, don't cry, don't cry.*

DS Malik said nothing, just watched me trying to get ahold of myself and then silently pushed a box of tissues towards me. I snatched one, almost angrily, and balled it in my fist.

"I think he was dead then," I said. My voice was flat and hard with the effort of not giving way to my tears. "When I called. I thought at the time it was strange. He was planning to wait up—we'd talked about ordering food—but it isn't just that. Gabe would never, *never* have left me hanging like that. He never relaxed until I was home safe. By two a.m. he would have been beside himself with worry; there's no way he would have let his phone go to voicemail like that—not if he were alive. I think he was killed before two a.m. Which means all this"—I waved a hand at the recorder, encompassing their questions and their obsession with my timeline—"is complete bullshit. At two a.m. I was in the police station across town. You *know* that. This—this is just a huge waste of time."

I was breathing hard. I had come in here hoping, expecting even, to be given an update on Gabe's case, to be told they had a lead. Instead . . . the feeling was brittle with disbelief. Instead Hel was right. I was being treated like a *suspect.*

"Okay," Malik said smoothly, changing tack. "Thanks for clarifying the timeline a little, Jack, that's really helpful. Can you tell us what you did after you found your husband's body?"

"I *told* you." My voice was shaking in spite of my attempt to keep it level. "I tried to move him, I tried to wake him up—and then when I realized how—how h-hopeless it really was, I went and curled up on the sofa. I was there for . . . I don't know. Maybe twenty minutes? Maybe longer."

"You didn't touch his computer?"

"What?" That question was a surprise. "No. No, of course not! I didn't give a damn about his computer."

"You didn't remove anything? You didn't notice anything was missing?"

"I didn't remove anything?" I was totally confused now. "What are you talking about? It was a desktop, there was nothing to remove. Do you mean a drive or something?"

"A hard drive," Miles said with an encouraging smile, like he was trying to be good cop to Malik's . . . I don't know. Fucking ridiculous cop. "Did you take out Gabe's hard drive, Jack?"

"No! Absolutely not!" I stared at him, trying to read his expression. "I didn't touch his computer. Wait, are you saying the hard drive is missing?"

"And what about the kitchen knife?" Malik asked now, from the other side of the table. I turned to face her, feeling dizzy with the abrupt about turn.

"Kitchen knife?"

"Do you recognize this?" She pushed a photograph across the table and then spoke to the tape recorder.

"I'm showing Jacintha Cross a photograph of a large kitchen knife with a logo in Japanese script."

My heart seemed to skip a beat.

I did recognize it. It was—it was *our* knife. Gabe's knife, in fact, the big solid Japanese one that he used for slicing and jointing, and which had cost the best part of three hundred pounds. He had added it to our wedding list in spite of my protests that it was crazy to spend that much on a knife—and in return he'd given way on the ridiculous faux sheepskin rug I'd wanted for the bathroom, which had got instantly matted and stained with toothpaste and shower water. The rug had lasted until our second wedding anniversary, when I had given up and thrown it out. The knife was still sharp as ever, and in practically daily use.

So yes, that was our knife. But it was covered in rusty dark stains. Stains that looked a lot like . . .

I felt the blood draining from my cheeks.

"That—that's our knife. We got it as a wedding present. Is that—is that the knife that—"

I stopped.

I felt incredibly cold all of a sudden—and very afraid.

"For the benefit of the tape, Jacintha Cross has identified the—" Malik said, at the same time as I spoke, interrupting her.

"I've changed my mind. I want a lawyer."

Miles and Malik exchanged glances, and then Malik nodded.

"Okay. No problem, Jack. Interview suspended at . . ." She looked up at the clock. "Eleven nineteen a.m." The recorder clicked off and she stood up, stretching her back. "I'll go and sort that out. Are you happy to wait here?"

I nodded, but in truth I wasn't happy. I was anything but. I should have had a lawyer. I should have had a lawyer right from the very start. What had I done? Hel's voice came back to me: *Repeat after me: Hel is always right.*

"Do you have a lawyer you want us to call?" Malik was asking. "If not, we can appoint one for you."

"Yes," I said. I racked my brains for the name—I had told it to Hel only just outside the police station, but the shock seemed to have driven everything from my head. "Melanie . . . oh God, what's her surname. Melanie Blair from Westland Law. Do you know her?"

"Yeah, I think we've dealt with her before. Okay. Let me go and make a few calls. Hold tight."

She left the room, the door swinging slowly shut after her, and Miles and I sat in uneasy silence. Miles ventured what was probably meant for a sympathetic smile, but it came over more nervous than anything else, and I couldn't bring myself to return it. I didn't feel one bit like smiling. Our knife. *Our knife.* What did that mean? Where had they found it? I remembered them taking my prints the night Gabe died, and at the time I had assumed it was to eliminate them from the ones found at the scene. Now the simple action had suddenly taken on a much more sinister bent.

We had been sitting there for maybe ten minutes when Malik came back and stuck her head around the door. Her eyes were on her colleague, not me.

"Al, could I have a quick one?"

"Sure." He stood up, gave me another slightly awkward smile, and slid out of the room, and I was left alone, trying to figure out what this all meant. Was I seriously a suspect? But how? *Why?* Surely they could tell that Gabe had been killed long before I got home?

But could they? It dawned on me that I had no real idea how accurate time-of-death estimates were. I could just about have made it home by three. The fact that I hadn't, they had only my word for that. Could they really tell for certain, four or five hours after the fact, whether someone had died at two or three a.m.? Suddenly I wasn't sure, and I wished more than ever that I'd called the police the instant I walked through the front door and saw Gabe's blood on the floor.

In my pocket the borrowed phone vibrated and I pulled it out. It was another email, but not from a sender I recognized. Sunsmile Insurance Ltd. Subject line: *Important: paperwork attached.* Was this a pen test Gabe had set up and forgotten to put in the diary?

More to have something to distract me from the agonizingly silent wait than because I really thought it was important, I clicked to open it up.

Dear Ms Cross,

I'm delighted to confirm your joint life insurance policy with Mr Gabriel Medway is now active.

Please read the attached policy schedule carefully as it covers some important exclusions and conditions of cover, and keep it safe as you will need it in the event of a claim.

Your cover started from the date of your first payment, 1st February, and renews annually on the anniversary of your policy.

Congratulations on choosing the peace of mind only Sunsmile gives,

Sue

Sunsmile Insurance

What the . . . this made no sense. I certainly hadn't taken out a life insurance policy. Had Gabe? But surely he would have told me? We had never bothered before. We didn't need one for the house—we had paid for it outright with Gabe's savings and my share of the money Hel and I had inherited from our parents—and as freelancers we weren't covered by most income protection plans anyway, so cover for loss of jobs or sick pay wasn't really an option. As for the rest, the chances of either of us dying had seemed—until a couple of days ago at least—so remote as to be laughable. We'd always told ourselves that it would be different when we had kids. Then it would have seemed like the responsible thing to do, to protect them in the event of something happening, however unlikely. But until then, surely it was just a waste of premiums.

Was it spam? Some kind of strange phishing attempt? For a moment I considered replying to the email to try to find out more—but when I glanced up at the sender details, in spite of the personalized footer, the email address was a generic Do Not Reply. It was quite possible that Sue wasn't even a real person.

A PDF was attached at the bottom of the email, and in spite of my misgivings and Gabe's voice in my head lecturing me about trusting strange attachments, I clicked it.

The text was already small, and on the tiny phone screen it was almost impossible to read, but I could make out the first few lines.

Gabe and I had apparently taken out a life insurance policy, in each other's favor. And the payout was one million pounds.

I dropped the phone. It clattered to the tiled floor with a noise that made me jump convulsively, my nerves already stretched to the breaking point, and I scrabbled to pick it up, my breath loud in my ears.

This was impossible. It was *impossible*. Even if Gabe had set something up, which was unlikely, one million pounds? It was an absurd sum—almost twice the cost of our little house. Far, far more than we needed to live on, either of us.

No, if this was real—and it seemed like it might be—there was only one explanation. Someone else had set it up. And more than that. Someone was setting *me* up.

I was being framed.

The thought was almost unbelievable, and staring down at the phone in my hand, I still couldn't quite make the realization sink in, even though it seemed to be the only explanation. But how? *Why?*

I couldn't answer either question. Instead, what lurched over me with a shocking pulse of adrenaline was a realization: The police had my phone. Which meant they had access to my Gmail account. Which meant I had a matter of hours, maybe even minutes, before they noticed this email too.

I *had* to show Malik the email, get my side of the story in, before whoever had the phone put two and two together and made five.

I stood up, feeling little electric prickles of shock running over my skin, and went to the door. When I pulled it open there was no one outside, and I was about to stick my head out and call for Malik when Hel's voice came into my head again, her tone warning. *There's a reason they always suspect spouses. You've got means, and you've got opportunity. The only thing they're lacking to make a case is a motive. So please, please be really careful not to give them one.*

Fuck. *Fuck.* I had no idea what I should do. Sit tight and wait for the lawyer? But if they discovered the email in the meantime, it would look very, very bad that I hadn't mentioned it.

No. I should show it to Malik now, this minute. After all, I'd done nothing wrong. If I got in there fast, before her colleagues stumbled on the email, I could trust her to listen to my side of the story. *Yeah, because trusting the police went so well last time*, said a sarcastic voice inside my head, and this voice wasn't Hel's—it was my own.

I thought of the last time I'd called the police—this exact force, in fact—to report my boyfriend, a serving police officer, for domestic abuse. Not only had they not listened, hadn't even filed a report, as far as I knew, they'd done something worse: they'd retaliated. Parking tickets for places I'd never been had begun to appear through my letter box. I was the victim of "random" stop and searches at strange times, getting hauled down to the station when they found lockpicks in my bag and questioned for hours until I could prove I wasn't a burglar. I got dropped calls in the middle of the night; I was turned down for car insurance when my car was flagged as stolen. And all of it had started from the moment I dobbed Jeff Leadbetter in to his colleagues—and they went running straight to him.

And okay, Malik wasn't Jeff. She hadn't even been on the force at the time I'd reported him, as far as I knew. But this was far, far higher stakes than a bad breakup. If I got this wrong, I could end up in jail for the rest of my life, and Gabe's killer could end up walking free.

The only thing they're lacking is a motive. Don't give them one.

I was still trying to make up my mind when I heard Malik's voice approaching from up the corridor, and ducked swiftly back inside the interview room, my heart thumping.

" . . . know, but I just think we should nick her," I heard. The voice was faint but coming closer and accompanied by the click of heels.

"Okay, yeah, her prints are on the knife, but I still feel—" Miles began, but Malik broke in impatiently.

"The knife's the least of it, Al—it's everything else." The footsteps had come to a halt, as if Malik had stopped halfway up the corridor, the better to make her case. "The timings are fishy as hell, her phone was *conveniently* switched off so we can't check her movements, and then to top it all off she waits the best part of an hour to dial 999."

. "I just—" Miles tried again, but Malik was barreling on.

"Not to mention the SOCO's initial report says there's absolutely no sign of a break-in. Explain that."

"The perp could have rung the doorbell," Miles said, rather meekly, and Malik let out a snort.

"You think our vic would let some stranger into the house and then sit there quietly with his headphones on while they cut his throat? He was built like a tank. No, sorry, I don't buy it. I say we nick her now. End of."

"How's that meet the necessity test, though?" Miles said. "I mean, what's really changed since the other night? If the boss didn't think it cleared the bar then, I just don't see how anything's different today. Bottom line, she's not really changed her story, and she's not a flight risk, is she? She's cooperating. She's attending voluntarily."

"Call it my Spidey sense or whatever, but I just don't trust her. It's all far too convenient the way she's got an excuse for everything—the phone loses charge, then she gets 'lost' on the way home"—I could practically hear the air quotes—"and then this supposed 'blackout' or whatever she's claiming happened when she did finally get in. No, I'm sorry, Al, taken all together it's just too much. I'm not buying the grieving-little-widow act. I'm going to talk to Rick before her solicitor gets here."

"Well, you're the boss," Miles said, and I could hear the shrug in his voice. "Want a cuppa before we go back in?"

"No, I'm fine, thanks. I want to catch Rick before he goes for lunch, see if I can get the thumbs-up. Solicitor reckons she's going to be at least half an hour, so it's not like we're in any hurry."

"Kay. I'll just ask her if she wants anything, then see you back in the interview room?"

Malik made some kind of agreement, and then I heard the sound of footsteps starting up again, this time coming closer.

I slipped soundlessly back to my seat and sat down, my heart beating fast, trying to figure out what all this meant.

Someone was setting me up for Gabe's murder. They *had* to be. From what Malik had just said—no sign of forced entry, no evidence of an intruder—this wasn't a case of mistaken identity or a botched burglary. This was a hit, by someone good enough to break in and kill Gabe without leaving any kind of evidence, and now they were covering their tracks by framing me. And unless they'd made a mistake, which they hadn't so far, it would come down to whether Malik believed me when I said that I hadn't taken out that policy.

My hands were trembling. I remembered back when I first started going out on jobs, the way I would get the shakes beforehand. I remembered Gabe kneeling in front of me. *Breathe in through your nose, three, two, one . . . out through your mouth, three, two, one. In through the nose, three, two, one . . . out through the mouth. You've got this.*

I found I was breathing, slowly, shudderingly, my teeth clenched against the panic. *Think, Jack, think. You've got this.*

Okay. So I couldn't confide in Malik. She'd made it very plain that all she was waiting for was evidence of my guilt—and if I showed her that email, I would be handing that to her on a plate. Could I delete the email? That would remove it from the server, and might buy me some time, at least until the solicitor got here, but I was clearly on their radar. It was almost certain they had set up some kind of backup on my phone, to make sure I didn't wipe any incriminating data. It was what Gabe would have done, I was sure of that. And I knew enough from talking to him to know that nothing is ever *really* destroyed, not just by pressing delete and emptying the recycle bin. If they had me in their sights, they would comb that phone until they found something.

On the other hand, if they'd seen the email already, and clocked me deleting it off the server . . . well, that would just about finish me. It would look like I was attempting to destroy evidence. So no. I couldn't do that. It would be suicide.

But sitting here with the email lurking in my inbox, waiting for someone to read it, that felt equally impossible. It would be just a matter of counting down to my arrest. And if that happened, I had absolutely no confidence that Miles and Malik would find Gabe's killer. As far as Malik was concerned, I was already guilty—the email would be the final nail in my coffin. I could have coped—almost—with being arrested for something I hadn't done, even the idea of going to trial for it, but what I couldn't cope with was the idea of Gabe's killer walking around out there, free and laughing at us both. By the time my case got to court, no matter what the verdict, whoever had done this would probably have fled the country, covering up their tracks and making it impossible to ever get justice.

So that was it. Two choices—hand Malik the email now or wait for her to find it—both of which almost certainly ended up with Gabe's killer going free.

Or could I . . . The thought came to me, almost as an impossibility. Could I just . . . leave? I wasn't under arrest, after all. Not yet. I was, what had Miles called it? *Attending voluntarily.* But then I remembered Malik's words at the start of the interview. *You can leave at any time. However, a decision to arrest may apply should that happen and you decide to leave without being interviewed.*

That was what that had meant—that veiled threat. You are here voluntarily—but we'll arrest you if you try to leave.

Fuck. *Fuck.*

In through the nose, three, two, one . . . But I hadn't got this. I hadn't got this at all. I was flailing, and badly. If only, if *only* Gabe had been here, whispering in my ear via the headset, or better yet sitting beside me, real and warm and inexpressibly reassuring. But he wasn't. I was alone. And I had no idea what to do.

I was sitting, my head in my hands, trying to figure out my options, when the door handle turned and Miles's smiling face came through the gap.

"Hiya, Jack, sorry for the delay, we were just trying to get hold of your solicitor. She's on her way; she'll be about twenty minutes. Would you like a drink of anything? Tea? Coffee?"

"Um . . ." I swallowed, hoping that the maelstrom of emotions churning inside me didn't show on my face. *Think of it as a job—this is just another job. You're playing a role.* "Um, yes, thanks so much. Tea would be great." He nodded and was turning to leave when something occurred to me. "Decaf, if you have it. Or even peppermint? But don't worry if you haven't got any, normal's just fine."

Miles looked doubtful.

"Yeah, I'm not sure if we'll have any of that, but I'll have a look."

I let out a shuddering breath as he shut the door. I didn't want tea and I certainly didn't care whether it was decaf, but I had banked on kindly, well-meaning Miles trying to make it happen, and even a few minutes' delay as he asked around his colleagues for whether anyone had peppermint tea was a few minutes in my favor.

Because, somehow, a realization had settled over me—a cold, hard certainty.

I wasn't waiting here to get arrested for a crime I hadn't committed. I was getting out.

I forced myself to sit very still as I listened to Miles's footsteps disappearing down the corridor. When at last the sound faded I stood and walked to the door. My heart was hammering, but I made myself breathe in through the nose, out through the mouth. This was just another job. I'd done this a hundred times before, hadn't I?

In my head, I rehearsed the stories I would use if I was challenged. If Malik or Miles caught me, I would say I was on the way to the toilet. If someone else found me, I would give a false name. Kate was a good one. No surname unless they pressed me, but there were enough Kates around my age that there was always a strong chance of finding one in any organization. Beyond that, I would have to improvise. I wasn't dressed smartly enough to pass as a solicitor and I didn't have any of my usual kit. This would be down to whatever I could find in the station, and how far I could blag my way out of any given situation.

Miles had turned left, Malik presumably right, but by the sounds of it Malik had been going to find a colleague, which meant there was a strong chance she would be closeted in an office somewhere, whereas Miles might be returning with the tea any moment. Besides, right was the way I had come, and my best chance at finding the main exit.

I turned right. The corridor led past a row of interview rooms, offices, and closed doors. I walked quickly and purposefully, my coat slung over my arm, trying to look like someone who belonged, someone with places to go and people to see.

Left at the corner. Straight on past some kind of locker room. Then a T junction where I had to turn . . . damn, I couldn't remember. I hesitated, trying to recall the route I'd taken with Malik that day. Normally, on a real job, I paid close attention to the building's layout, but an hour ago it would never have occurred to me that I could end up in this situation, and I hadn't made any particular effort to remember our route. I shut my eyes, trying to visualize the turns we'd taken. Past the entrance desk. Through a door. Along a corridor past a photocopy room and then . . . left . . . surely? Yes, left. Which meant I had to turn right.

I turned, walking swiftly along the deserted corridor, and my spirits gave a little glad leap as I recognized the open door with the photocopier inside. I was on track. This whole thing was almost too easy. A few minutes, maybe less, and I would be outside in the fresh air.

And then I got to the door.

I remembered coming through it the other way, but now I remembered something else, Malik tapping something to the left of the doorway. At the time I hadn't even thought about it—I'd just assumed she'd pushed some kind of release button, but now I saw it: a beige plastic card reader. Presumably she had been holding some kind of fob or card, and it was that she'd tapped against the reader. Shit. *Shit.* There was a "break glass" fire alarm button next to the reader which *might* unlock the door for safety reasons, but it was a big gamble—too big for me to risk. If I set off an alarm it would bring every officer in the building running towards the exit—and me.

What could I do? With my tools I could possibly have forced the metal plate—it looked like a simple electromagnetic contact—but I had nothing but the clothes I was standing up in. Was there a way around, or a back exit? Arrests were an occupational hazard for pen testers, and from the rare occasion that I had got as far as the custody suite, I knew that they were extremely secure, but that the rest of the police station wasn't usually Fort Knox. When I was dating Jeff, for example, the station he worked at—but I pushed that thought away. I couldn't deal with thinking of Jeff right now. Encountering him would be the only way this situation could get worse.

Suddenly I heard footsteps, a woman's shoes, coming from around the corner of the corridor. Should I stand my ground? Try to tailgate through the door? But it might be Malik—in which case I'd be sunk.

I dithered for what felt like an eternity but was probably only a second or two, then at the last minute I lost my nerve and ducked into the photocopier room, bending over the copier as the person passed behind me. It wasn't Malik. I couldn't see exactly who it was, but I could tell from the shape that it was someone older and heavier. She paused at the door, and I heard the click of the reader activating, then she passed through.

Damn. *Damn.* I should have gone with my first instinct and tried to blag my way out behind her. I'd done it often enough on jobs—claimed my pass wasn't working, or simply rushed through like someone in a hurry. Nine times out of ten you got away with it. But the stakes were higher now, and that ten percent chance of getting challenged was the reason I'd lost my nerve.

Letting out a shaky breath, I looked around the little copier room, trying to see something, anything of use. An abandoned pass was too much to hope for—but a fire plan of the floor wasn't unreasonable, and it might show another exit.

There was no plan. But instead my eye lit on something almost as good: a marker—a thick, sturdy Sharpie.

Picking it up, I went back into the corridor, looked up and down to make sure no one was watching, and then stood the pen upright at the bottom of the door, its tip leaning against the corner between the door jamb and the door itself. Thank God I was on the inside of the door. Doing this trick from the outside was much harder to pull off.

Then I retreated back into the copier room, folded a piece of paper into the size and shape of a credit card, and waited. And waited.

It had been probably no more than three or four minutes since I'd left the interview room, but I was painfully conscious of the fact that Miles would be returning very soon, if he hadn't already done so. Say a couple of minutes to boil the kettle. Another sixty seconds to stir the tea, find the milk. If he'd bothered to hunt around for decaf tea I might have another couple of minutes, but I couldn't bank on that. And if he did return to find the room empty, then how long would it take him to raise the alarm? Sixty seconds? No, I'd dealt with people like Miles before, and they weren't that decisive. Malik now, if she found the suite empty, she would have everyone on red alert before you could say *knife*. But Miles . . . no. He wasn't that kind—he was the self-doubting, chain-of-command type. Which meant he'd probably try to locate Malik first, make sure that she hadn't taken me down to custody. And then? Well, if I was lucky he'd give me the benefit of the doubt and search the toilets, but there were no guarantees on that front, and once he found Malik, I was pretty sure the game would be up. Malik looked the kind to act fast and ask questions later.

I was still pondering when I heard footsteps again, a man's this time, coming purposefully down the corridor. Not Miles. Someone in heavier shoes, with a more assertive tread. An officer in uniform passed the door of the copier room, and I heard the tap of the card reader, and the door swinging open. But when it swung back, I didn't hear the *clunk* of the lock clicking back into place. The sound as the door swung shut was rather different—a plasticky crunch.

I waited for the police officer to notice the sound, stoop, examine the floor . . .

In through the nose, three, two, one . . .

Nothing. Just the noise of footsteps receding.

I let out my breath and walked as fast as I dared out of the copier room and up the corridor, and this time, sure enough, the door was open, just a crack. The Sharpie had toppled unnoticed into the gap and prevented it from closing.

Just in case anyone was watching I touched the folded piece of paper to the reader, miming someone tapping their pass, and then I pushed open the door, kicking the Sharpie aside as I went through. The door closed behind me, and I was out.

The next part would be the hardest. I was so close—but I had to pass the front desk. Would the officer on duty remember me? Would he wonder why I wasn't accompanied by either Malik or Miles?

I had been holding my jacket when I went in, and now I put it on, winding my scarf around my throat to hide as much of my distinctive red hair as I could. Why, oh *why* hadn't I listened to Gabe when he'd said, "Well, they'll certainly remember you on CCTV."

But it was too late for that. I just had to walk fast and hope that no one had registered me.

The door to the car park was coming up—and so was the front desk. The officer on duty was shielded from me by the foyer wall, but I could see someone talking to him, complaining about something, judging by the body language.

"Sir, please don't take that tone," I heard from the officer, his voice pitched somewhere between weary and threatening.

I quickened my pace, right to the edge of what could be considered normal, and almost without thinking about it moved to the right-hand side of the waiting area, into the CCTV blind spot that I'd noticed earlier. *Breathe in through the nose, three . . . two . . . one . . . Out through the mouth, three . . . two . . . one . . .*

I was almost at the door.

"Excuse me," I heard coming indignantly from behind me, and I had to fight every instinct in my body to stop myself from turning, checking whether it was me the officer was addressing. "Excuse me, but I'll have to ask you to leave if you—"

It wasn't me. He wasn't talking to me. My hand was actually on the main door, I pushed it open—and then I was out, into the car park, my knees trembling, my muscles weak with relief.

The urge to call Hel was overwhelming, but I knew I couldn't spare the time to do that; I needed to get away. I could call her from the cab if I had to. Half jogging now, I crossed the little car park towards the road, running through my options in my head. Not Uber. I hadn't set it up on the borrowed phone and besides, it was too traceable. A black cab, then. I could only pray that one stopped. Did I have any money? A memory came back, Hel shoving two notes into my hand, me slipping them into the phone case . . . *Hel is always right.* Bloody hell, she was. If I got out of this I would never ignore her advice again.

A cab was coming towards me, yellow light on. I waved my hand, trying not to look too much like someone about to go on the run. Somehow articulating the words in my head for the first time brought the reality of the situation home to me. Oh God, what had I done?

"Hi," I said, a little breathlessly, as the taxi pulled up next to me. "Hi, thanks, could I go to . . ." I stopped. Shit. Where? I had to get out of London, but before that I needed clothes, food, and most importantly, money. Hel's was the obvious answer—but the police would expect me to go there, and I had no idea how much time I had. What I really wanted was to get my go bag from my own house, but that would be suicide.

Or . . . would it?

"Come on, love," the driver said, a bit impatiently. "You coming or going?"

"To, um . . . Salisbury Lane," I said, making up my mind and getting in the taxi. Was I mad? "SE10. Do you know it?"

"Yeah, I know it," the driver said, and swung into the traffic. I found myself looking back, towards the station, as he pulled away, holding my breath as if at any moment blue-light cars might start pouring out of the compound, but nothing happened.

I sat back in the seat and tried to decide whether I could really risk what I wanted to do.

But the more I considered it, the more I convinced myself that it wasn't a crazy idea. Yes, it was a risk—but it wasn't as big a risk as all that. There would probably be an officer on the door, but for that very reason it was the last place the police would expect me to go. Their first port of call would almost certainly be Hel—who would tell them, truthfully, that she'd dropped me at the station. Then . . . well, then, I guessed they would start to look other places. Maybe even track my borrowed phone. But hopefully by that point I would have been in and out.

Reaching into my pocket I turned off the phone, and then leaned forward and spoke to the driver.

"Actually, I said Salisbury Lane, but where I really want to go is Salisbury Gardens, do you know it?"

"Uh . . ." The driver scratched his head, thinking. "Is that that little kinda cul de sac round the corner from Salisbury Lane? The one with the pub at the end?"

"That's the one. Could you drop me there?"

"Yeah, sure. Same difference to me."

"And if you don't mind not going past—" I stopped. I had been going to say *not going past the top end of Salisbury Lane*, where my house was, but suddenly it struck me that that was stupid. I was in a cab. The police weren't going to notice someone driving past in a cab, and I might be able to check out the lay of the land, see if the CSIs were still processing the house.

"Yeah?" said the driver, and I shook my head.

"Never mind. Sorry, just having a brain fart. You carry on."

"Home, James, and don't spare the horses, eh?" said the driver with a laugh, and I nodded. But I didn't laugh back. Home, yes. But I wasn't sure who might be waiting for me.

IT WAS MAYBE TEN OR fifteen minutes later that the taxi turned into Salisbury Lane, and for a moment I had a sharp, almost unbearably vivid flashback to the last time I had made that turn—weary after a long night talking to police, happy to be almost home, completely unsuspecting of what I was about to find.

As the car made its slow way down the road, bumping carefully over speed humps, I peered out of the window at my own house, trying to make out any movement inside. There was none—or none that I could detect. The curtains were closed, the front door was shut, and

I could see no signs of police presence at all, save a single patrol car parked directly in front of the property, a shadowy form behind the wheel. Either they had finished processing the scene, or they were waiting for a specialist team to come in.

There were no lights on in the house, in spite of the fact that the day was dreary and gray, and the other cars parked in the road were all ones I recognized as belonging to our neighbors. I let out a breath. *Out, three, two, one . . .*

"Here all right?" The driver's voice broke into my thoughts as he turned the wheel, swinging into Salisbury Gardens, and I felt something in my stomach writhe with nerves.

"Yes, great. Thanks so much. How much do I owe you?"

"Twenty-two pounds forty-five. Call it twenty-two."

I handed over Hel's notes.

"Could I have five pounds change?"

The driver nodded and counted out the change, and I pocketed the coins and slid from the car, my heart beating hard as I walked down Salisbury Gardens to the rather disreputable garages at the far end.

To the right of the garages was a little overgrown lane, once used by the bin men, before the days of wheelie bins in front gardens. Now it was full of nettles and brambles, but it was just passable, enough people forcing bikes and children's play sets down it at intervals to keep it relatively clear.

At the near end was a locked gate, with a combination I was supposed to know but couldn't remember, but it was easy just to swing myself up and over. No one was likely to notice, or to say anything if they did. We didn't live in that kind of neighborhood.

The houses looked very different from the back, and it took longer than I had expected to find ours, almost to the point where I thought I might have missed it, although I couldn't think how. But suddenly there it was—white-painted wall; little square of scrappy grass; the thorny rambling roses I had planted, more for security than because I particularly liked the flowers. They had grown since then, and now they covered the whole of the garden wall, an effective deterrent to anyone trying to scale it. Cursing my security-conscious past self, I shrugged off my coat, shivering as the bitter February wind chose that moment to gust up the alley, and flung it over the top of the wall, effectively blanketing the carpet of roses. It wasn't much, but it helped a little, though I could still feel the thorns digging deep into my palms as I pulled myself up to crouch atop the wall.

I let myself quietly down into the garden, retrieved my coat, then ducked immediately behind the patio table, my heart beating fast in case anyone had seen me. No police officers stuck their heads out of the back door, though, and after a few minutes I straightened and looked ruefully down at my bloodied hands. There was nothing to be done apart from pull out a couple of the biggest thorns, wipe the blood on the back of my jeans, and then turn to face my next challenge: getting inside the house. Without my tools, without even my keys, which were still in my bag at the police station, it wasn't a simple task—but the fact was that Malik was right: Gabe would never have let a stranger into the house and then sat down with his noise-canceling headphones on while they slit his throat. No, someone had broken in, and without a trace, which meant I could too.

I had two things immediately in my favor: First, I didn't have to worry about forensics. My fingerprints and DNA were already all over the house, so I had no need to wear gloves or cover my clothes. And second, I knew the layout, and the weak spots.

The problem was, *what* weak spots? Working in the industry, with a ton of expensive computer equipment in the house, meant that both Gabe and I were pretty security conscious, and the downstairs was clearly a write-off. The back door had a mortise lock and sturdy bolts from the inside, and the ground-floor windows were double locked, with burglar alarm sensors to detect breaking glass. I knew the code, of course, but I also knew that while opening the front door gave you thirty seconds to override the alarm, smashing any of the windows would trigger it immediately, and I needed enough time to get inside and up to the spare bedroom before the cop in front of the house came blundering in.

The upstairs, though . . . that was more hopeful. Glancing up and down the row of backyards, I dragged a patio chair over to the little single-story kitchen extension and pulled myself up onto the flat roof.

It was, if anything, even colder up there, the wind making me stagger momentarily as I got to my feet. The puddles on the roof were iced over and I picked my way past them carefully. If I slipped now, I was done for.

Immediately in front of me was the bathroom window. It was closed and locked, like always, but I noticed something puzzling. The ventilation fan in the top half of the sash wasn't turning.

Normally we left it open—the bathroom had three outside walls and was cold and prone to damp; keeping the vent turning was the only thing that kept mildew at bay. On a windy day like today it should have been spinning round at a rattling pace. But now the spokes were silent and static. Had the police shut it off? Why would they?

I examined the fan. It was made of clear plastic. I could see there was a crack running through the outer part of the fitting, a crack I didn't remember being there before—and I had stared at that fan every morning and every night since we moved into Salisbury Lane, every time I brushed my teeth or washed my hands. Now, as I looked at the fan with fresh eyes, I realized something—something that made my stomach drop with a mixture of hope and dread.

The fan was loose.

Whether it had always been that way or whether someone had jimmied it out with tools, the fan itself was only wedged into the circular cutout, and now, as I inserted my nails beneath the plastic surround, it came out easily.

From there, it was the work of seconds to stick my arm through the hole, down to the bathroom window latch, turn it, and lower the top sash with a squeak of damp wood.

I was in. And unless I was sorely mistaken about that crack, this was likely the way Gabe's killer had entered the house, breaking the fan as they did.

The thought made me feel a momentary wash of sickness—whoever had slit Gabe's throat, I was almost certainly standing in their footsteps, my feet resting where theirs had, less than forty-eight hours ago. The last person to touch that fan, this window latch, the last person to drop the sash and slide their way quietly through the narrow opening just as I was now doing—that was the person who had killed Gabe.

For a second, as I lowered myself to the bathroom floor, I thought I might throw up. It wasn't just the realization that I was following the same route as my husband's killer, it was everything—the nauseating mix of the familiarity of home, and the terrible alienness of what was happening. The bathroom was still full of my clutter, makeup spilling out of containers, nail varnish leaking onto the shelf of the mirrored cabinet. Gabe's beard wax was sitting by the sink, and the sight of it brought a lump to my throat. But there was fingerprint dust on the door handle, and when I stepped out into the hallway, plastic duck boards had been laid across the floor to preserve the blood spatter and footprints. In the air was an alien tang of chemicals—presumably from the wipes and sprays they'd used to process the scene. Most of all, most sickeningly of all, I could still smell Gabe's blood, that metallic butcher shop reek that had assaulted me the moment I opened the front door just a couple of nights ago.

Suddenly, I was not sure if I could do this. I stood for a long moment, holding on to the banister, fighting the panic that was threatening to overwhelm me. Gabe's absence had never felt so huge and so *real* as it did now. He was *gone*. I had spent every waking moment since his death trying to understand that simple fact, trying to *believe* it, but now, here, surrounded by our shared belongings, the knowledge crashed over me like a wave, one too big to fight. I found I had sunk to my knees, still holding the banister, and a moan was coming from my mouth. It was Gabe's name.

I wanted him so much. In that moment I would have given anything—*anything*—to hear his key in the lock, his voice calling up the hallway, *Babe, I'm home.*

I shut my eyes. *Babe, you got this.*

I didn't have this. I didn't have this at all. I couldn't do it.

Except I had to. Because no one else was going to.

Dragging myself upright, I took a long, shuddering breath and forced myself down the hallway, to the room that functioned as our spare room and my office, trying to focus on what I needed to do and get out.

In here it was easier to ignore the police presence. They had clearly been through the room in a cursory fashion: my laptop was missing, and so were some of our files, but otherwise it was largely undisturbed. I mentally crossed my fingers as I made my way over to the built-in wardrobe in the corner. If what I wanted was gone, then this whole trip was for nothing, and I had just wasted an hour of precious time.

I knew exactly where it should be—at the bottom of the wardrobe, half-hidden behind a pile of suitcases, a box of Christmas decorations, and a collapsible laundry rack. The junk was still there when I opened the door, and I lifted it out, stacking it piece by piece behind the door, and breathed a sigh of relief. There it was: an unassuming little forty-liter rucksack, one half of an identical pair. My go bag.

Gabe had had one for years, ever since he started working in online security. It wasn't uncommon for him to get a panicked "we've got an urgent situation" call from a client, and to have to jump in the car to spend an unspecified number of days and nights combing through server logs. His was full of computer equipment, diagnostic tools, spare leads, and cables—plus a spare pair of underpants and a vacuum-packed tub of his favorite coffee.

Short-notice calls for physical pen testers were less common, and before I met Gabe it had never occurred to me to have a go bag myself. But he had nagged me into it on the basis that "you never know," and now I was more thankful than I could say.

I unclipped the top and took a quick look inside, checking that everything was still there, but it seemed to be completely untouched. I guessed that the police had focused all their efforts so far on the actual crime scene and hadn't given the rest of the house more than a cursory once-over for anything obvious. After all, there would be more than enough time to comb through looking for weapons and drugs once the scene downstairs was processed.

I made a quick, rough inventory of what I knew was in there: spare laptop and charger, mobile phone charger, and a couple of changes of clothing—mostly the kind of comfortable dark stuff I typically wore on jobs. I also had a bunch of tools and equipment that the police would certainly have confiscated if they had found them, including lockpicks; various shims; a sheaf of fake credentials and badges for companies like Intel, Hewlett Packard, and various office-cleaning firms; and a device for cloning security passes. There were also some more practical bits and pieces reflecting the long days and late nights that jobs often entailed—snacks and energy bars, painkillers, water, and a wash bag containing the basics for a bathroom refresh.

Finally, there was a credit card which was probably useless to me now, and at one point there *had* been £100 in cash. Unfortunately, at some point Gabe or I had clearly raided it for taxi money, since the notes were no longer there.

There wasn't much I could do about the cash, aside from cursing my former self; the only question was what else, if anything, I needed. I tried to think. I didn't want to add too much weight or bulk—as it was, the bag was just about small enough to pass as a commuter's backpack, which meant I could blend in on the Tube or in an office. Strapping on a tent would make me stand out, as well as making the whole thing more tiring to carry. But there was enough space at the top to add some essentials. I had a pair of fake glasses in there already—along with an arm brace and sling that had got me out of a number of sticky situations in the past. It was amazing how helpful people were to a woman with her arm in a sling—holding open security doors, entering pins on keypads, that kind of thing. But I probably needed warmer clothing. The kit had been put together on the basis of passing unnoticed in an office, not going on the run.

There was a basket of clean washing on the landing, waiting to be put away, and I grabbed a few pairs of socks, some warm tops, and extra underwear, as well as a fleece hoodie that could double as a pillow or—in an emergency—a fake baby bump.

What else—my passport? But no, that was pointless. By the time I got to a port, my name would be on a watch list, and besides—I needed to be here. My single aim was to figure out what had really happened to Gabe, and I couldn't do that from the Cayman Islands, even if I were able to get there.

I was about to pack up and leave when an idea occurred to me: Gabe's private key—the code that gave access to his Bitcoin wallet. He had told me once where it was, and now I couldn't remember. It was written down in the back of a book, I knew that, I just couldn't recall which one. Shit. *Shit.* Why hadn't I made more of an effort to commit it to memory? I shut my eyes, trying to remember. He had said it like it was funny, that much I recalled. Like a joke. Where would you hide a key?

Most of our books were downstairs, in the living room, and I couldn't face going down there, not yet at least. I told myself it was because I was worried the police officer stationed outside might notice someone moving about behind the thin curtains, but in truth, it wasn't that—or not completely. The truth was that I wasn't ready to go back down to where Gabe had died.

There were a couple of bookcases in our bedroom, and I decided to try there first. If I didn't turn anything up, then I could decide whether to risk the living room.

Our bedroom was somehow harder to enter than the spare room. It just looked so *normal.* There were my clothes, strewn carelessly over the little antique sofa at the foot of our bed. Gabe's jeans, neatly folded over the radiator. His book was still splayed on the bedside table, along with a handful of change. Even the duvet was still rumpled the way we had left it the morning before the Arden Alliance pen test. How long ago was that? I counted back. One . . . two . . . that would be three nights ago, the last time I had slept in my own bed, with Gabe's body pressed against mine. It felt like another lifetime—like a different person had lain there with him, one who wasn't rubbed raw with grief and ambushed by unwanted memories every few minutes. If only. If only I had stayed there with him, his warm body wrapped around mine. If only I had told him I didn't feel well. If only I'd *known*. But I didn't. I couldn't have. And if I had—if I'd stayed home, curled up on the couch, watching TV instead of sneaking around in Arden Alliance's server room, then maybe none of this would have happened. Or perhaps I would be dead too. Would that really be so bad?

I knew that I should get what I needed and get out, but I couldn't stop myself from walking slowly across the room to Gabe's side of the bed and crawling into the space his body had left. I lay down and pressed my face into his side of the pillow, and it smelled of *him*. It smelled of Gabe.

I felt the tears threatening at the back of my throat, and I knew in my heart that what I was doing was dangerous. I was going to lose it, and the police were going to find me there, hours later, still hugging Gabe's pillow, having sobbed myself into catatonia. But God, I didn't want to leave. If I could just stay curled up a few minutes longer, my eyes closed, pretending that everything was okay, that Gabe was just downstairs making coffee, that any minute he would be coming up, cups balanced in his hands as he tried to open the bedroom door with his elbow . . .

I felt an animal howl of grief rise up inside me, but I pushed it back down and forced myself to sit up, swing my legs over the side of the bed, and take a deep, shuddering breath.

You got this.

I don't, I thought desperately. *I do not, in any possible sense, have this. And if I do have it, I don't want it—I don't want all of this on my shoulders, being left up to me.*

But I had no choice. And I knew that if it had been me lying there, my blood all over the living room floor, there was no way Gabe would have curled up in the dent I had left in our bed and given up. No way at all. He would not have rested for a single moment until he had tracked down whoever did this and destroyed them.

Gabe would never have given up. So neither could I.

I stood up.

His bookshelf was beside his bed, the water glass from three nights ago still sitting on it, the mark of his lips on the rim, but I toughened my heart, pushed the glass aside, and began looking through the books, my head to one side as I read the titles on the spines. *A Confederacy of Dunces*, nope. *Fermat's Last Theorem*, nope. *The Cement Garden. Empire of Pain. The Music of the Primes.* Nope, nope, and nope.

I scanned the shelves, growing frustrated now, looking at the familiar, Gabe-ish mix of literary novels and sciencey nonfiction. Our tastes had never converged that much—I leaned more towards Neil Gaiman, Ursula K. Le Guin, Robin Hobb—your basic sci-fi/fantasy nerd. Which made it all the harder to recall the title that Gabe had mentioned. Still, it was none of the ones here, I was ready to swear to that.

And then I saw it. Not upright on the shelf but lying crossways, wedged into the gap between the books and the shelf above. Old and battered, the schlocky 1960s jacket peeling and a little torn.

The Glass Key, by Dashiell Hammett.

I heard Gabe's deep, amused voice rumble in my ears. *A key for a key, get it?*

I pulled it out, carefully, because the paper was old and brittle and I could feel the glue on the spine was ready to crack, and opened it up.

Inside the front cover were three long codes, carefully written out in pencil, each over twenty characters long, and a mix of numerals and letters.

One of those entries—and I had no idea which one—represented somewhere north of twenty thousand pounds, although the amount fluctuated so much that it was impossible to know on any given day how much was in there. And all I needed to access it were these numbers.

There was no time to write out the full strings, and I certainly couldn't memorize them, so I picked up the book and stuffed it in the top of the rucksack. As I did so, a noise from outside made my pulse jump.

It was a noise I knew well, one I'd made myself just a few nights ago, in fact. It was someone kicking over the milk bottles on the front step.

"Balls," I heard from the front garden. "Sorry, just tripped over the milk bottles."

There was the crackle of a radio, inaudible words blaring out under a blast of static, and when I peered cautiously through the bedroom curtains, I saw a police officer standing in front of my door, holding a mobile phone.

I hadn't thought it would be possible for my heart to beat any faster, but now it sped up.

"Yeah," I heard. "Yeah, gotcha. Heading in now, but I'm pretty sure she won't be here. I've not seen anyone except the postman. Hang on. Key's a bit stiff."

Shit. *Shit.* I had to get out of here.

Shouldering the bag, I ran as swiftly and quietly as I could down the corridor, but I had barely made it halfway to the top of the stairs when I heard the second key turn in the front door. For a moment I froze, looking longingly at the bathroom door—but it was in sight of the front door, which was about to open at any second. Instead I turned around and bolted back into our bedroom, pulling the door closed behind me.

Inside I stood with my eyes shut and my ear pressed to the door, the better to hear what was going on downstairs. There was a metallic bang as the front door flung open and the latch banged against the hallway wall (my paintwork!) and then the heavy tread of a police officer stepping inside my house.

I held my breath, listening, wondering what I should do.

"I'm inside," I heard, faintly, from downstairs. "Can't see anything amiss. Let me just have a recce."

There was an answering crackle from the radio, and I heard the officer's feet on the hallway floor, and the screech of the squeaky board as he stepped into the living room.

Thanking God for old Victorian houses, I carefully turned the handle of the bedroom door and put one foot out onto the landing—only to bolt back inside as I heard the crackle of the radio and the officer's footsteps in the hall again.

"Nothing down here. I'll just take a look upstairs."

Shit. Now I was really trapped. There was no way I could leave with him coming up the stairs, and no way he wouldn't come into the bedroom. Would he search the wardrobes? Under the bed?

For a moment I stood frozen in indecision, and then, at the sound of a creaking tread on the bottom-most stair, I shook myself out of it. What I had told myself back at Arden Alliance was just as true now as it had been then: In this job, doing nothing was a risk in itself. Sometimes you just had to go on your gut.

I ran across the bedroom, avoiding the loose floorboard under the window, wrenched open the wardrobe door, and leapt inside, yanking the door shut behind me.

Just in time.

The clothes were still swinging on their hangers when I heard the bedroom door creak open and the sound of the officer's boots on the rug. My heart was thumping in my ears and I clasped the bag hard to my chest as though it could muffle the sound. Through the crack of the wardrobe door I could see his shape, dark against the window, and I watched, breath bated as he bent and looked under the bed, then straightened. Even through the door, I could hear the heavy sound of his breathing. He sounded like he had a cold, or perhaps was asthmatic. Could police officers have asthma? If he wasn't very fit then I *might* be able to outrun him. I just hoped it wouldn't come to that.

I closed my eyes, willing myself not to make a single sound, even though the wardrobe was painfully cramped, and the faux fur stole I had bought for Hel's wedding was tickling my nose. *Please, please,* I begged him telepathically. *Please get the fuck out of here . . .*

And then, almost as if I'd willed him into it, he turned and I saw him walk back towards the door.

I let out a silent, shuddering breath of relief.

And then I sneezed.

For a second, stupidly, I almost thought I'd got away with it—that the officer had put it down to a noise from outside.

And then he turned on his heel and came back into the room and I knew I was sunk. There was only one thing in my favor now, and that was the element of surprise.

With a wild yell, I crashed out of the wardrobe, sending the doors flying open and the officer tripping backwards in shock. He recovered and came for me, round the end of the big bed, and I dodged right, not left, as he had apparently been expecting, leaping over the mattress and using its spring to catapult myself towards the bedroom door.

"Stop!" I heard him yell from behind me. "Stop! Police!"

But I didn't. I wasn't stupid enough for that. Instead I pounded down the corridor and then paused with a split second of indecision at the landing. Downstairs and onto the street, or out the back the way I had come?

Both had risks; in front of the house was the police car and the very real possibility of another officer inside it, warned by the commotion inside the house.

But going out the back meant if they closed off the alleyway, I would be trapped.

There was no time to weigh up the options. Barely pausing, I slammed into the bathroom, yanked open the sash window, and threw myself out onto the icy roof, rolling across the graveled surface with the puddle ice crackling at my back.

There was no time for the careful, controlled descent I had planned. Instead I almost launched myself off the other side of the roof, into my neighbor's garden—his fence would make one more obstacle for the police if they were coming out of my back door.

"Stop!" I could hear from behind me, and the sound of heavy, panting breaths. "I am ordering you—"

I landed with a thump, the shock radiating up through my knees, caught sight of my elderly neighbor's startled face, gazing out of his kitchen window, then straightened painfully and made for the gate into the alleyway. I *had* to get out before the officer called for backup and the alley became a dead-end trap.

The gate was padlocked, and there was no time for picks, even assuming the rusted mechanism worked. Instead I threw the go bag over into the passage, backed up, and took a short run up to the wall. I dug my fingers into the crumbling mortar at the top, ignoring the screeching protest of my nails as they cracked and splintered, scrabbled until my foot found a convenient loose brick, and then pulled myself up to flop chest-down on top of the wall.

I felt it as soon as I landed, a stabbing pain in my side, just below my ribs. Glass? A knotty bit of clematis? There was no time to pause and check. From up here, I could see the police officer levering himself painfully out of the bathroom window, his radio to his mouth, and I could hear his wheezing breaths and the crackle of response codes.

Ignoring the tearing noise from my coat, I swung one leg over, then the other, and landed on all fours in the back alleyway.

From here, I ducked down below the shelter of the garden wall, so the officer on the roof couldn't see me, and ran in the wrong direction—not towards the open end of the alley, but the other way, towards the blind end. At last, when the sound of the police radio had faded into the distance and I had reached a promising-looking gate on the opposite side of the alley, one with a bright shiny padlock. These gardens belonged to the houses on Lancaster Lane—a terrace that backed onto Salisbury Lane, and shared our back alley. If I could just get access to one of those houses . . .

I pulled out my picks and, with trembling fingers, set to work as fast as I could, praying that I could get it open before Officer Wheezy made it over the garden wall. Luckily it wasn't anything fancy, just a regular off-the-peg lock from Halfords, and it was only a few moments until it opened with a reassuring click, and I slipped through into the neat little garden inside.

There, I stood up, smoothed my hair, and tried to calm my trembling breathing. This bit was going to be the hardest in some ways. I just had to hope my cheerful girl-next-door demeanor would see me through.

With my best confident smile, I rapped on the door, and stood back and waited.

For what felt like a long time, no one came, and I looked over my shoulder, feeling my anxiety rising. But just as I was considering trying another garden—or getting out my picks again—I saw a shadow behind the glass, heard the sound of a key in the lock, and saw a woman's astonished face peering out at me.

"What the hell are you doing in my garden?" She had a baby on her hip. I made my smile a little wider, and a lot more rueful.

"I'm so sorry. The gate was open." A lie, of course, but I just had to hope she'd blame her partner. "I'm your neighbor from number . . ." I paused infinitesimally, not wanting to give my own house number in case the police came knocking. "Forty-five. My name's Ella. This is so stupid, but I locked myself out. I thought I could get out of the gate at the end, but I couldn't remember the code. Do you know it?"

"I've got no idea." She looked me up and down, apparently reassessing her initial hostility. I smiled at the baby and it smiled back. From far up the alley I heard a crash and the faint sound of swearing. It sounded like the police officer was over the wall. I willed the woman to make up her mind—but I couldn't ask. She had to offer. And then, thank God, she did. "You want to come through the house?"

"Would you mind? I'm *so* sorry." She stood back and I followed her, into a tiny kitchen that was a messier, more kid-friendly version of ours, cupboards fastened with child locks and a fridge spattered with magnetized letters. "Thank you—you're a lifesaver." I was chattering now as the back door closed behind us, almost giddy with relief. "I feel like such a plonker—turns out the key doesn't work in the back door."

"Ours is like that." She was thawing a bit as she led me through the narrow hallway to the front door. "Only locks from the inside. No worries. What number did you say you were?"

"Forty-five." I had to pray she didn't know her neighbors too well, but this was London, and we were far enough down the road I thought the odds were good. "Really nice to meet you."

"Nice to meet you too." We were at the front door now, and I opened it and stepped through, barely trying to disguise my relief at the empty, patrol-car-free road outside.

"Thanks again," I said. "Take care."

"Take care," she echoed, and then the door closed behind me.

As I turned out of Lancaster Lane onto the main road, I shoved my hands into the pockets of my coat to stop them shaking. The relief I had felt at getting away from Officer Wheezy was fading, and I could feel a growing pain in my side where I had landed on top of the wall. There was no time to stop and investigate. The most important thing was to put some distance between myself and Salisbury Lane, where the police cars were probably already amassing. After that . . . God. What should I do? I needed money. And a plan.

Hel. I needed to contact Hel and explain what had happened. But I couldn't go to her house—that would be the first place Miles and Malik would go. I tried to still my racing brain enough to think through the next few steps. Could I call? They probably hadn't tapped Hel's phone yet—I was hazy on the logistics surrounding this, but I was pretty sure that monitoring phones needed a warrant, and that took time. So Hel's end was probably fairly safe right now.

But they *would* seize her phone records eventually—so whatever I did now, they would discover it when they came to comb through her texts and call logs. Did that matter? I tried to think it through. This phone, the pink unicorn-stickered phone Hel had handed me that morning, was a goner as far as traceability went. I had used it to call too many people connected to me and Gabe, and besides, the SIM card was almost certainly registered to Roland's account. It was useless to me from today. Which meant that I might as well burn it one last time.

I turned it back on and dialed Hel's number.

"Jack!" Her voice when she answered was pleasant, cheerful, no hint of concern beyond what she was already feeling about having her baby sister interviewed by the police. "Are you done? Shall I come and collect you?"

"Listen," I said abruptly. "Hel, I've done something really stupid. No"—as she broke in, trying to ask questions—"I don't have time to explain now, but I'm in deep shit. You were right, I *am* a suspect."

"Okay," Hel said. There was a slight tremor in her voice, but I could tell she was trying to keep calm. "Okay. But . . . they haven't arrested you?"

"I didn't give them the chance. I walked out of the interview."

"And they let you go?"

"They didn't exactly . . . know. But they do now. And I'm pretty sure there'll be a warrant out for me."

There was a silence at the other end of the phone. I could hear Hel's breathing, and I could tell she was trying very hard to keep hold of herself, not to shout *What have you done?* down the phone at me, much as she probably wanted to.

"I need cash," I said into the charged silence. "As much as you can spare. But don't go to the bank, just whatever you can get out of an ATM." If she was being followed, a trip to the bank would be a huge red flag. "And . . . warm clothes. A sleeping bag." Shit. What else? A *plan* was what I really needed, but right now I didn't have one, beyond getting out of London before I was arrested. "Oh, and one more thing. Bleach. For my hair, I mean. I need to get rid of the red."

"Okay," Hel said tightly. "What time and where?"

"I don't know." I tried to think. "How long do you reckon you'll need to get everything together? We probably shouldn't leave it too late. The more time we give the police to get warrants and put you under surveillance, the harder this is going to be."

"It's . . ." I could hear her voice go faint as she took the phone away from her ear to look at the time. "It's just gone half one now. Say an hour to get everything ready, then half an hour to make sure I'm not being followed. But I'll have to pick the girls up at three. Fuck. That doesn't leave much time."

"What time does Rols finish work? Or could you slip out after supper?" The thought of finding somewhere inconspicuous to hang out, shivering, until after dark wasn't very enticing, but it didn't sound like I had much choice.

"No, wait," Hel said slowly. "The girls . . . that could work."

"What do you mean? I meet you at the school? I really don't think—"

"Not the school, but . . . maybe the shopping center? The one on the main road, where the cinema is. We quite often stop in there to go to the loo on the way home or get a snack, and there are loads of entrances and exits."

"I don't know, Hel." I tried to keep the worry out of my voice, but it crept in anyway. "I don't like the idea of the girls being mixed up in this. What if something goes wrong? How are you going to make sure you're not being followed if you've got two four-year-olds in tow?"

"None of us have a playbook for this, Jack." Hel sounded testy, but below it I could hear her concern. "This is the first time I've done this too. But I feel like sticking to my routine is probably the safest, don't you? If I *am* under surveillance, then the police will be on red alert for anything out of character. Whereas picking up the girls, walking them home, going to the toilet . . . all of that is what I do every day."

"Okay," I said slowly. "So . . . what's the plan, then?"

"There's a public toilet on the ground floor, next to Urban Outfitters. It's got two entrances, one into the cinema and one into the main shopping center."

"Okay. We'll meet in there. What time?"

"Say . . . three thirty? It might be a few minutes after if the girls are tired, but I'll do my best."

"Okay," I said again. I glanced up and down the street. "Hel, I'm going to have to dump this phone, do you mind?"

"I expect the girls will be crushed at losing their progress on *Pretty Pawz*," Hel said, with a kind of grim humor. "But they'll live. Now, go. And don't get caught."

It was almost two hours later that I arrived at the shopping center Hel had described, hot and extremely footsore. I had walked from Lancaster Lane rather than take a taxi or a bus—painfully conscious that I had used the best part of Hel's thirty pounds already, and that if she didn't manage to make contact with me this afternoon, that might be all my resources for the foreseeable future. I had Gabe's Bitcoin, of course, but I was fairly sure that no reputable exchange would start handing out cash—not without showing ID, anyway. A bus would have been cheaper, but London buses no longer took cash as payment, only contactless, and I didn't want to risk that. I had no idea whether the police were already monitoring my cards.

Along the way I had stopped at one of the omnipresent little stands selling tourist tat and *I ❤ London* T-shirts and bought a plain black baseball cap with the Tube logo on the front. With my collar pulled up and the baseball cap pulled down, my face was effectively hidden from cameras and prying eyes, but I still felt painfully conscious of my pillar box red hair. Why, why, *why* had I gone for such a ridiculous color?

A memory came to me, sharp and painful: Gabe burying his face in it, his lips against my temple, his voice in my ear, *It's the exact color of Virginia creeper on the turn . . . I love it so much . . .*

I had laughed. *Okay, Wordsworth.*

Now his words, the memory of them whispered in his deep, soft voice, made my heart hurt.

But I couldn't think about him now or I would lose it, here in the street in front of the shoppers and tourists. I had to keep putting one foot in front of the other, keep trying to figure out what to do about this unholy mess I'd got myself into.

For I'd had plenty of time to think about my decision on the long walk from Lancaster Lane and to wonder whether I had done something unutterably, unforgivably stupid in bolting out of the police station. I had no illusions about what I'd accomplished—in that one split second, I'd changed myself from a person of key interest to the police into suspect number one, a fugitive with a giant red target painted on their back. Because why would someone run unless they were guilty? That would be the police logic—and I couldn't fault it. There was only one problem with it. I *wasn't* guilty.

I could have stayed. I could have shown the police that email and said, *Look, I didn't set this up, something is wrong, someone is framing me for Gabe's death.* Because surely there would have been some way of tracing that email back to the source? *Someone* had filled out that form, had sent it off, had processed the payment. And that someone *had* to be the person who had killed Gabe—didn't they?

Why had I done it? Why had I taken such an insane risk?

I knew the answer. Because with Gabe dead, I didn't really care what happened to me—but the thought of sitting in a cell, unable to so much as make a phone call, while the police pursued false lead after false lead in the hope of convicting me, was unendurable. Not because of what it meant for me, but because every moment they spent pursuing me, the real killer would be disappearing into the shadows—and I wouldn't be able to do a thing to stop them.

If the police weren't going to find Gabe's killer, I would. And if I had to put a target on my back to do it, so be it.

It had felt like impulse, that decision to run, even to me. But I had spent years acquiring the bone-deep knowledge that had informed my choice to trip the security door back at Arden Alliance instead of waiting for Gabe to fix the problem for me. It was like I'd always said: sometimes, often, to do nothing was to run a risk in itself. Yes, this decision had stakes a million times higher than Arden Alliance. And yes, I could have waited. Hel would probably have said I *should* have waited. I could have shown Malik the email and waited to see what she made of it.

But waiting would have been a risk. And a big one—because that was the thing, the stakes *were* a million times higher than some routine pen test. There were two giant what-ifs hanging on a decision to wait, questions that my freedom depended on.

First—what if the person who'd set up that insurance hadn't made any mistakes? What if they'd used a secure browser and a VPN—something Gabe used fairly routinely himself, enough that it wouldn't necessarily come over as suspicious—and spoofed the payment back to Gabe's own account? It wasn't impossible they'd ticked every single logistical box, swept up every single bread crumb. In that scenario, there might be nothing but my word for it that this wasn't a fresh, steaming motive right there on a plate—and Malik had already shown me that my word wasn't worth very much to her. The police had failed me once; there was no reason they wouldn't fail me again. The thought of what that failure might look like—me locked in a cell, unable to escape, while Jeff Leadbetter poured poison into Malik's ear about what a psycho I was and Gabe's killer laughed up his sleeve—that image made me feel like throwing up. It was that what-if, processed in a split second in the interview room, that had made me run.

But the second what-if had occurred to me only on the walk back from Lancaster Lane. And in some ways it was more frightening. It was this: What if the person who'd set up that insurance was . . . Gabe?

I had no evidence that he had. We'd never even discussed it. But something, some*one* had caused Gabe's death. I had no idea what or who, but now, looking back over the last few weeks and months, I had begun to wonder whether maybe Gabe had seen this coming on some level.

I don't mean that he had known he was going to die—that was absurd. Gabe wouldn't have sat there and waited for a hit man to come and get him. He would have warned me, called the police, done *something* to protect the both of us. But there were a handful of things that, looking back, made me wonder. A certain jumpiness that wasn't completely in character. A few times I'd spoken to him and he'd been zoned out, staring at his device long enough that I'd had to physically tap him on the shoulder to get his attention. He'd shaken his head and said, *Sorry, babe, work stress*, but none of that was normal. Gabe loved his work. Of course, he didn't like grappling with taxes or dealing with invoicing headaches, no one did, but the furrow lines between his brows and his deliberate vagueness . . . those had been new.

The more I thought about it, the more I was sure that something *had* been bothering him in the week or so before his death. Something minor enough that it hadn't rung any alarm bells for me at the time, but there had been *something*—something more serious than I had realized, and maybe something more serious than even Gabe himself had realized. And if he *had* been mixed up in some kind of trouble, some encounter that had made him feel just paranoid enough to want to make sure I was protected if anything happened to him, then . . . yes. In that case I *could* just about see him doing this. And maybe even doing it without saying anything to me—telling himself that this was totally ridiculous, of course it was, no point in worrying me with his paranoia, but you know, no harm in setting up some kind of nest egg, just in case he fell under a bus.

And if that was the case, if Gabe really *had* set up that insurance himself, I had absolutely no way of proving that I hadn't known about it. And far from protecting me after his death, Gabe might just have condemned me to rot in prison for his murder.

The thought made me want to cry—the idea of Gabe carefully looking out for my interests, and in the process being the one to inadvertently snare me in a trap of his own good intentions.

Don't think about it, I told myself as I walked. I wouldn't—*couldn't*—cry. Nothing draws attention like a weeping woman weaving her way along a busy high street, even one with her head down under a baseball cap. I had to stay inconspicuous.

I was getting close to the shopping center's main entrance when something caught my eye, and I stopped. It was a phone box, but the phone inside had been vandalized, and a laminated notice was taped to the glass. *Out of order*, it read.

Glancing up and down the road, I slipped inside the box, recoiling momentarily from the stench of piss, and then, carefully, I peeled off the sign.

The tape crumpled, sticking to itself, but the notice itself was fine, and I slipped it inside my jacket and then let myself out of the phone box, mentally apologizing to the next person who tried to make a call.

INSIDE THE SHOPPING CENTER IT was hot, stifling, even, compared to the February chill outside, and I instantly began sweating in my jacket and cap. But I couldn't afford to take either off, so wiping the perspiration off my nose, I pushed through the crowd of people, trying not to glance too obviously behind me.

It was highly unlikely I'd been followed. The police had no way of knowing where I was, or that I was heading here. Hel was the surveillance risk, and she wasn't due here for another . . . I felt automatically for my phone before remembering that I had dumped it in a bin a couple of miles from Salisbury Lane. Instead, I glanced up at the big clock that dominated the atrium. Another fifteen minutes. I had plenty of time.

Even so, I weaved my way deliberately through the thickest part of the crowd, up an escalator, and then through the cinema foyer before going into the upper floor of Urban Outfitters, and down the steps inside the shop.

I had exited the shop and was looking around for the toilets Hel had mentioned when I realized something. The pain in my ribs, the pain where I'd bruised myself landing on the chunk of clematis, it had dulled to an ache as I walked, but now it was hurting in a different way. It was . . . stinging. And there was an ominous tickling sensation that wasn't just the sweat prickling on my skin.

Pausing in an inconspicuous corner by a rack of plastic plants, I slipped my hand up under my jacket. When I brought it out, my fingertips were red. And not just tinged with blood, but slick with it. Somehow when I'd thumped down on that wall I had cut myself badly.

I swore quietly, wiped my fingers on my jeans, praying the blood wouldn't show up against the dark denim, and tried to think what to do. I had to stop the bleeding before it soaked through my clothes and made me even more conspicuous than I was already. It was too late to phone Hel; she would be on her way, probably with the girls in tow. I would have to buy first aid supplies. There was a big pharmacy across the way, a Boots, that would probably have everything I needed and more. The problem was that the cap covering my hair had taken almost every last penny I had.

I stood for a moment, sizing up the shop opposite, considering my options.

I had shoplifted before. I wasn't proud of it—but Hel and I had dealt with our parents' deaths in very different ways. She had put her head down, gone to journalism school and made top grades. I had . . . not. I had spiraled, acted out, dropped out of school. And, somewhere along the line, I had started shoplifting. Not because I needed to; our parents hadn't been rich, but they'd had a modest life insurance policy that meant Hel and I had enough money to live on, if we were careful. But because it made me feel . . . alive. In control. Predator, not prey.

I had turned out to be good at it. Very good. And for someone flailing in school and bombing her exams, there was something exhilarating in finding an area I could excel in. Even then, without any training, I had understood how security systems worked—how to figure out the camera blind spots, how to exploit the changes in shifts, how to disable the various types of security tags the different shops used. I had never told anyone—not Hel, not my friends. I had never even used the stuff I'd stolen—I couldn't, not without Hel asking where I'd got the money for a designer handbag or how I'd afforded those jeans. Half the time I went back the next day and dropped whatever I'd taken discreetly in the changing room, ready for the assistant to hang it back on the rack. The rest of the time I donated my haul to a charity shop.

I'd been caught eventually, of course. I'd gone back to the same shop too many times, and there was one security guard who was better at his job than the rest, better than me. But it was that kindly security guard who had told me I was wasting my talents, that there were legitimate jobs for people like me, people who liked figuring out how security systems worked and finding the weaknesses. The idea that I could get paid for this . . . *paid* for running rings around systems and breaking into buildings . . . that was a revelation.

I hadn't stolen since. I had promised the guard I wouldn't, if he let me go. Now, looking at the brightly lit store opposite, I realized that I was about to break that promise.

THERE WERE NO TAGS ON the dressings. That was something. But a box of ten cost nearly ten pounds, which was nine pounds more than I had, and although I hadn't had a chance to look at the puncture wound under my clothes, the amount of blood on my fingers suggested that a 50p pack of economy plasters wasn't going to cut it. Looking up and down the racks of first aid supplies, I considered my options. I was still wearing the rucksack and cap—which wasn't ideal. I couldn't afford to take the cap off in case someone recognized my hair. But with it on, with the bulky bag on my back and my coat buttoned up to hide the bloodstains, I looked like a shoplifter—the worst, most amateur kind. Back in my heyday I could have lifted half the contents of this store and walked out with my head held high. But right now I looked shady, and if I was pulled over for a bag search with a rucksack full of housebreaking tools, there was no way I would be able to talk my way out of the situation. Which meant I had to be careful. A security guard strolled along the end of the aisle, glancing at me without comment, and I made up my mind: *One item only. And don't leave without paying.*

Picking up the dressings and holding them out in front of me, well in sight, I headed purposefully to the self-service checkouts, not breaking my stride as I passed the display of chewing gums and breath mints and palmed a cheap pack of Wrigley's Extra.

At the till I shifted the box of dressings into the hand holding the gum, ensuring in the process that the gum was underneath, and then swiped. The barcode reader beeped, and *Chewing Gum, £0.70* flashed up on-screen.

I put the gum down in the weighted bagging area, hovering the box above it with my free hand, and quickly tapped *Payment* on the screen in case anyone was reading over my shoulder. I needn't have bothered. The staff member manning the tills wasn't a security guard, just a regular checkout person. She was examining her nails over by the far side of the queue and wasn't even looking in my direction. I dropped the pound coin in the change slot, praying it wouldn't get spat out—and when *Payment Accepted* showed on the screen I closed my eyes, not trying to hide my relief.

The receipt came out along with the change and I grabbed both, then walked purposefully towards the entrance, keeping my head high and my back to the security camera. As I exited the store, I let out a shuddering breath. I had done it. For the first time in almost ten years, I had stolen something—and I had got away with it. It was a weird, not entirely good feeling.

THE BATHROOM WAS EMPTY, ALL five stalls gaping wide, and I wasted no time in washing my hands and getting the *Out of Order* sign out from under my jacket. I stuck it to the door of the middle stall. The tape was reluctant to unpeel from itself, but at last I got it fixed, slightly lopsidedly, and slipped into the cubicle. I locked the door behind me, put down the toilet seat, and then sat, lifting up my feet to sit cross-legged so that my presence was invisible from the outside.

Then I shrugged off the jacket, pulled up my top, and examined what on earth I'd done to myself in my neighbor's garden.

The first thing I thought was that there was a *lot* of blood. More than I had expected, and enough to make my stomach churn unsettlingly with memories of Gabe. It had trickled down my stomach and soaked into my jeans, and my stomach and ribs were smeared so thick it was hard to see what was actually wrong. My T-shirt was black, thank God, but when I touched it the fabric was stiff and wet.

By the time I'd cleaned the cut with spit and toilet paper, the wound itself didn't look quite so bad—but it didn't look great. As I stared down at the small, ragged puncture oozing dark blood, I wished I knew more about first aid. This was no scrape from a clematis. There must have been something sticking out of the top of the wall—a metal spike, or a shard of glass maybe. Whatever it was, I had flung myself down on it with enough force that it had gone clean through my jacket and my top and into my stomach, just below my right lower rib.

It hurt, but not as much as I would have expected, more a kind of low throb. Mostly I was just furious at my own stupidity for not running a hand along the top of the wall before I threw myself onto it.

What I really wanted—what I should have stolen—was some kind of antiseptic. But I couldn't face shoplifting a second time, and besides, the possibility of missing Hel was unthinkable. Instead, I unpeeled a dressing from its plastic backing, pressed it over the wound, and fished a clean top out of my rucksack. Then I waited.

The next few minutes ticked past very slowly indeed. Without even a borrowed phone, I had no way of knowing what time it was, but even so, from counting the seconds in my head and listening to people come and go, I was sure that I had been here for more than ten minutes. A lot more.

"Always out of bloody order!" I heard one girl say, apparently looking at my sign. "Fucking ridiculous."

"It's people putting baby wipes down the loo, innit," her friend said. It sounded like they were applying makeup in the mirror; her voice had that slightly distorted sound of someone making a lipstick mouth. "Pipes aren't meant for it."

"Are you done? The film started at half past."

"Oh, relax, there's always loads of ads. It's only—" There was a pause. "Only twenty to."

"Yeah, but I like the trailers. And besides, I want to get a Coke."

"Keep your knickers on," the other girl grumbled, but I heard the click as she capped her lipstick. "There. Happy? Come on, then."

I heard the sound of music as the cinema door swung open, muffled again as it closed behind them, and I suppressed a groan. Twenty to. What had happened? Had Hel realized she'd been followed? How long should I give it before I gave up and left? Another ten minutes? Another twenty?

The minutes continued to tick past, and I was just making up my mind to cut my losses and give up before the cleaners came and investigated the *Out of Order* sign when the shopping center door swung open, and I heard a familiar little piping voice.

"But Mummy, *why* can't we have a Krispy Kreme?"

"Because I said so," Hel snapped. She sounded worried, and close to the end of her tether. "And because they're full of sugar, and you already had an after-school snack. Now, into the toilet, the pair of you."

I cracked open the cubicle door and said, cautiously, "Hel?"

Hel swung round and her face flickered through a gamut of different emotions in the space of a few seconds—from fear, to shock, to utter relief.

"Jack! Oh for Christ's sake." She flung her arms around me, her voice muffled in my hair. "I thought I'd missed you. I'm sorry we took so long."

"Oh God, Hel, no, don't apologize. I'm the one who should be apologizing. Are you okay? Was everything all right, you know, getting here?"

Were you followed was what I wanted to ask, but I didn't want to say it in front of the kids. No point in making this situation sound scarier than it already was.

"So-so," Hel said, making a rocking motion with her hand. "I'm pretty sure there was a plainclothes guy outside the house, but they peeled off when I went inside the school gates. We came via the playground, just to make sure. Quite hard for single blokes to hang around there unnoticed. But that's what held us up; once we were there I couldn't exactly get away without ten minutes on the swings. Thank God Kitty needed the loo."

"Mummy," I heard from inside the cubicle, "I've done a poo. Can you wipe my bum?"

Hel gave a sigh.

"Yes, okay, I'm coming. But you manage at school, Kitty, so I don't know why you need my help at home. You're a big girl now."

"I can wipe my own bum," Millie said virtuously from the stall next door. "I did it at break."

"Jesus wept," Hel muttered.

"Look, I should get out of here," I said. "Did you bring everything?"

"Yes. It's all in here." Hel pulled a Tesco carrier bag out of her capacious Cath Kidston mum tote—the tote that usually held spare T-shirts for the girls, snacks, and school reading logs. "I'm sorry I couldn't bring more; I thought carrying a suitcase to school would raise alarm bells. But there's clothes, a sleeping bag, hair bleach, a pay-as-you-go phone I got from Tesco, and two hundred and fifty pounds. I'm sorry I couldn't get more money—I hit the daily withdrawal limit for my card."

"Seriously, do *not* apologize." I was rummaging through the bag, relief pulsing through me as I saw what Hel had managed to cram in. Underneath the sleeping bag was a navy sweatshirt and a gray beanie, and I pulled off my jacket and baseball cap and swapped them for the jumper and knitted hat. Carefully, I tucked the stray strands of red underneath the edges of the beanie, hoping I didn't look too obviously like someone hiding their hair, and then stuffed everything else into the go bag.

With my face uncovered but my hair hidden, I looked sufficiently unlike the figure who had walked into the shopping center side of the loos that I thought I would pass muster on CCTV as a different person.

"Did you pay cash for the phone?" I asked as I slung my arms into the straps of the rucksack, wincing a little at the pain the action provoked.

"Yes, I paid cash. And for the SIM too; I got it from one of those dodgy shops on the high street and it's prepaid up to a hundred pounds of credit. Listen, Jack—" She had taken hold of my hands, and now she looked down at the blood still grimed under my nails. "Wait, is that blood? Are you okay?"

"It's nothing, honestly. Just a cut. You're an absolute fucking legend, Hel."

"Mummy, my bum is *still* pooey," came from inside the cubicle, in the chidingly imperious tones that only a four-year-old could manage. "Are you *ever* going to stop talking?"

"I said I'm *coming*," Hel growled.

"Go." I put my arms around her again, hugging her more fiercely now, conscious of the fact that this might be the last time we saw each other for . . . well, I didn't want to think about that, about what might happen if I didn't manage to fix this. "Sort out Kitty. I love you, Hel."

"I love you too." Hel's voice cracked.

"Mummy, I'm going to count to three," I heard as I swung the door open, "and if you're not wiping my bum by the time I finish, then I'm going to be very, very angry. One, two—"

I stepped out into the bustling shopping center.

I was surrounded by a hundred people—shoppers, staff security guards. And yet I had never felt more alone.

I left the shopping center through a different entrance from the one I had come in by, and then stood outside in the street, trying to work out what to do.

What *could* I do? The gravity of my situation, the enormity of what I'd done when I stood up and walked out of the police station, was only just starting to strike home, and if I thought about it too much, the weight of the realization threatened to crush me. I was a fugitive. I was on the *run*. It was almost impossible to believe.

I was, I suddenly realized, extremely tired. And I also had probably only limited time to get out of London. The police would likely still be searching my neighborhood, then fanning out towards Hel's, hoping for me to pop up on their radar, making contact with a friend or going to familiar ground. But sooner or later they would figure out that I had made a break for it. And at that point the net would widen, and they might start contacting other forces.

I had to get out of London and go somewhere . . . unexpected. And then I could take some time to figure out my next move.

The problem was, where to go? Cities were expensive, and full of surveillance equipment and police. But remote communities were small and noticed strangers, particularly lone women popping up in the middle of winter.

Somewhere in between then.

But first, I had to change my hair.

Without it, I was just an ordinary woman, anywhere from twenty-five to thirty-five, height and build on the slight side, dressed in nondescript clothing and with nothing unusual about her. With it, I was instantly recognizable. CCTV would pick me out in a moment, and there was a limit to where I could plausibly wear a hat or a hood.

I thought, briefly, of finding another public toilet—but the bleach would take a while to work. No, a cheap hotel would be better. Or, even better still, a backpackers' hostel. There I would melt in among the other young people with their rucksacks and transient stays.

Pulling Hel's burner phone out of my pocket, I opened it up and typed in *backpacking hostel, London*. There was one around the corner, and it took cash. Hoisting my bag over my shoulder, I began walking.

"HOUSE RULES ARE NO MUSIC in the dorms after ten p.m.," said the bored girl on reception. She had a strong Australian accent. "Headphones are fine. No food or alcohol in the bedrooms—use the dining room for that. No smoking in the building—cigarettes *or* weed. It *will* set the fire alarms off and you *will* be chucked out, so just don't do it, kay?"

"Okay," I said. "I don't smoke."

"Sure," the girl said with a wave of her hand. "Of course you don't. Top or bottom?"

"Sorry?"

"Top or bottom bunk?"

"Oh . . . I guess . . . top?"

The girl nodded and plonked a plastic card and a small locker key down on the counter.

"Key for the hostel," she said, pointing to the card. "Also the key for your room. You're in bed five."

"And this?" I held up the locker key.

"Key to the luggage cage." She glanced at my rucksack. "Maybe you won't be needing that. One night, you said?"

"Yeah."

"Twenty-four pounds."

I rummaged in my pocket and pulled out two of the notes Hel had given me. The girl shook her head and pushed a card reader over the counter, tapping it with her fingernail.

"Sorry, we don't take cash."

"What? But you have to. It said you did on your website."

The girl shrugged.

"Website must be out of date. Card or contactless."

"I can't do card," I said evenly. I was trying to keep my voice level and pleasant, but I felt like crying. It seemed like a hundred years since I'd slept, a hundred more since I'd been happy, or able to relax. I was in the middle of a waking nightmare, and this stupid chick wouldn't take cash? "My bank is overdrawn. I have cash."

"Card or contactless," the girl repeated. I stared at her. I didn't know what to do. "Sorry," she added, but she didn't sound it. "There's a place in Maida Vale that might take cash."

She held out her hand for the keys.

I stared down at them, thinking of the long walk to Maida Vale, the taxi I couldn't afford, the police who might even now be following Hel home from the shopping center. What the fuck was I going to do?

"Here," said a deep American voice from behind me, and some- one leaned over my shoulder and tapped their phone on the card reader. It beeped chirpily. *Payment accepted* read the screen.

I turned and looked up, unable to believe my eyes. A tall Black guy with neatly styled locs stood behind me, hands in pockets. As our eyes met, he gave a little deprecating shrug and a grin.

"I—oh my God, I mean—thank you!" I was stammering, but I hardly knew what to say. "Honestly, you've saved my life. *Thank* you. Oh, and here." I held out the notes, but he shook his head.

"Nah, we're good."

"But I can't—" I tried to think how to phrase it. He wasn't much younger than me. If he was doing this in the hopes of a date or something . . . well, that was so far off the cards it was laughable and I should probably let him know. But what if he was just a Good

Samaritan? How could I tell him without sounding hopelessly up my own arse? "I'm only here for one night," I managed. "If I don't pay you back now—"

"We're good," he repeated, and smiled. He had a kind smile. I felt something inside me begin to crack. "I don't need paying back; people been good to me along the road. I'm just happy to help a damsel in distress."

In spite of myself, I smiled back. The old-fashioned phrase sounded so funny in his drawling American accent.

"Listen, do me a favor, Red, pay it forward next time you see someone in need, yeah?"

"I will," I said. I bit my lip. I wished I could tell him what his kindness meant to me, but there was no way of saying anything without making myself even more conspicuous than I already was. "Thank you, seriously. Wh-what's your name?"

"Lucius." He held out his hand and shook mine. His was large and warm, and for a piercing, painful second, the feel of his fingers against mine reminded me of Gabe. "Lucius Doyle. What's yours?"

The question caught me off guard.

"Sorry?"

"Your name." He smiled, amused, his wide grin curling at the corner with a tug of laughter. "I take it you *do* know it?"

Fuck. Why hadn't I thought of this?

"K-Kate," I said, remembering, belatedly, the name I'd cooked up at the police station. "Kate . . . Hudson." The surname came out of nowhere. I didn't know any Hudsons—but it felt like a suitably anonymous, unmemorable name, without being too obviously pseudonymous.

"Like the actress?" Lucius asked, and I mentally slapped my hand across my forehead. Of *course* like the bloody actress. That was why the surname had tripped off my tongue.

"Yes," I said with an attempt at a laugh. "But no relation, sadly. As you can probably tell."

"You'll need to sign in," the front desk girl said, with a very plain *hate to break in* yawn. "Name, address, email, phone number."

"Of course," I said, breathing a sigh of relief that she was giving me an out with Lucius. I owed him—but that didn't mean I could afford to let my guard down with him, and I'd come perilously close to doing so. I filled in the form she slid across the counter, making up a fictional address in Cornwall and praying she wouldn't notice the postcode was complete BS, because I didn't know the real one for Padstow. I was pretty sure it wasn't EX24.

I took my time over it, making my writing intentionally hard to read when it came to the email address and phone number. I didn't think they would check them, but if they did, a plausible smear of ink would give me an out.

When I looked up, Lucius was gone.

said I'm almost done!" I shouted. That was the third time someone had banged on the shower room door, and I couldn't completely blame them. I had been in here for almost an hour, first cleaning and re-dressing the puncture below my ribs as well as I could, and then applying the hair bleach. It was only supposed to take thirty minutes, but the red dye had proved stubborn and I'd had to have another go, thanking God that Hel had thought to give me two packs. Second time around it smelled even worse, and now not only were my eyes watering, but my nose was tingling and the skin on my scalp was beginning to hurt. *Do not leave on for more than 30 minutes* said the packet. I'd done twenty the first time, but it hadn't been enough, so this time I'd left it for the full thirty. Maybe all my hair would fall out. Would a bald woman be less conspicuous than one with bright red hair? I doubted it.

At last the timer on the burner phone pinged and I stepped back into the shower, leaning over to keep the stream of water away from the fresh dressing on my ribs and watching the creamy white foam swirl into the plug hole. At least not too much of my hair seemed to be disappearing with it. When I stepped out of the shower, shivering now, I looked into the mirror, unsure what I was going to see. My hair was still there, thankfully, and at last the red was gone. A girl with draggled white-blond hair stared back, looking strangely startled; like me, but with all the color drained out.

As I raised my hands to run them through the fragile wet strands, I saw that my fingers were shaking. I hadn't eaten for . . . I tried to think back. Not since breakfast, and then only a snatched piece of toast. I'd been subsisting on shock and fear. Now as the banging came again and I jumped convulsively, every nerve jangling, I realized that I had to get some food inside me or I was going to faint.

"I said," I tried to keep the sob out of my voice as I dragged my jeans up over wet, trembling legs, "I am fucking *coming*. Give me a break."

"This isn't a fucking spa, you know," the girl standing outside snapped as I opened the door. She was pretty and very tanned. "There's three showers for the whole bloody place. Jesus. The nerve of some people."

She pushed past me through the narrow doorway, deliberately shoving me with her shoulder as she did.

"Fuck you very much," I said bitterly, swallowing back the lump rising in my throat. I wanted—God, I didn't even know what I wanted. I wanted to curl up in the rented bunk and pull the curtains around my mattress and hide from all of this until it had gone away. I wanted to wake up tomorrow and find this whole thing had been the worst nightmare I'd ever had. I wanted to find whoever had done this to Gabe and rip off small parts of their body, one by one, until they bled to death, slowly, agonizingly. I wanted to go home, sink my face into Gabe's chest, and wrap my arms around his warm, solid body. I wanted to listen to his heart. I wanted to *cry*. Why couldn't I cry?

Instead I got my laptop out of the luggage cage and made my way down to the communal dining room, where I bought a Pot Noodle from the commissary, topped it up with boiling water from the electric kettle in the corner, and curled up in the window seat to eat it.

As I forked the scalding noodles into my mouth, I tried to ignore the griping pain in my side and concentrate on figuring out my next move. Tomorrow I should get out of London, that was a given. But where? And in the meantime, I needed to make contact with Hel, to let her know I was okay, at least for tonight. I just wasn't sure how. I knew her number off by heart, but if I texted her from the burner phone there was a strong chance the police would join up the dots, and once they had this phone number, I would be instantly traceable.

I could email her—Gabe had installed VPNs on all our laptops, so in theory there was no way to track my location from an email, not if I crossed all the T's properly. But I had to assume that the police might eventually read anything I sent—and Hel's reply along with it.

I opened up the laptop. The first thing I did was disable all the location services. Then I fired up the VPN and connected to the internet. My heart was thumping as I hovered the mouse over the web browser icon. I knew logically that the VPN ought to shield me—it protected my web identity from anyone on the hostel's Wi-Fi network, and meant that anyone trying to trace the email from Hel's end would be able to follow the threads back to the offices of the VPN operator but no further. But, unlike Gabe, I didn't fully understand the technology behind it. I knew how VPNs worked—roughly, at least. But was I safe opening Gmail in the normal way? Or should I use Tor, the anonymized dark-web browser that Gabe employed for checking out the shadier hacking forums? Did Gmail even *work* in Tor?

I sat there for a good five minutes, my finger on the trackpad but not quite clicking, and then I gave up and pressed. The police were highly unlikely to be monitoring Hel's email right this second, and if they did eventually manage to trace me back to the hostel, I would hopefully be long gone.

Inside Gmail, I scanned down the list of work emails and routine updates, checking for anything important. Nothing jumped out until my eye came to the email I had received from Sunsmile Insurance— the email that had started all this. My stomach turned over at the sight of it, as I relived that moment when I'd realized the truth of what was happening to me. Was it really only this morning? I felt like I had aged fifty years since reading it.

The email sat there, read but otherwise seemingly untouched, but I had no way of knowing if the police had been all over it, if perhaps they were already in touch with the insurer. If they were, there was nothing I could do about that now. I just had to keep going, putting one foot in front of the other.

I was still staring at the unread messages, trying to think of what I could truthfully say to Hel to reassure her, when my computer pinged and a new email notification flashed up in the corner of my screen.

My eyes flicked automatically to the sender.

It was from Jeff Leadbetter.

For a minute I didn't do anything. I didn't open it. A part of me wanted to—Jeff worked with Miles and Malik, for God's sake. He might have information I could use, or let something slip about how close the police were. But at the same time, this was Jeff we were talking about. He *was* police. And he was also the man I'd spent five years trying to avoid and forget.

The email squatted, unread, at the top of my inbox, an unexploded bomb of possibilities. What if there was a virus attached? There were no attachments, or none that I could see, but Gabe had told me once about an exploit that used embedded images to hijack the computer, worming their way in as soon as the email was opened. I swallowed, hard. Then I navigated to my settings and ticked the box labeled *Ask before downloading external images.*

Finally, with the feeling that I was taking a giant, possibly insanely stupid leap of trust, I opened Jeff's email.

Well well well, it began.
   Who's been a naughty girl then.

I nearly shut it back down. A kind of enraged nausea welled up inside me. How had I ever dated this man, let alone slept with him? The thought made me feel sick.

But I forced myself to keep reading.

Had a call from Habiba Malik today. Said her colleague Alex had been having a very interesting chat with a friend of mine—right up until the point when the aforementioned friend slid out of the interview. Without telling anyone. And then the boys over in tech turned up some veerrry dodgy stuff on your phone apparently.

Serious talk though, Jack—you're in trouble. Big trouble. And you know there's no way you can keep this up? I don't know what you're trying to achieve but I don't think civilians realise how hard it is to stay under the radar. You'll run out of money, you can't use your cards, you can't use your phone, there's no way you can leave the country, and if you're reading this the tech boys have probably already traced your IP address. You're fucked basically, excuse my french. But you know that, right?

Listen, take my advice. Turn yourself in. This is only going to get worse the longer you delay getting caught. Because you WILL get caught. Everyone does in the end. No, turn yourself in, get a good lawyer, cop a plea.

Why did you do it anyway? Was he hitting you? Screwing around? You should have come to me. I'd have sorted him out for you. In a purely professional manner appropriate for a serving officer of course ;)

J

By the time I finished reading the last line, the fear and nausea were gone—burned away by the only emotion that remained: a searing fury. Without giving myself time to think better of it, I stabbed the reply button, then began to type, hitting the keys so hard the computer rocked against my lap.

Jeff. Fuck you. No seriously FUCK YOU. How absolutely dare you—the idea that Gabe would ever, EVER physically abuse me, that is RICH coming from you of all people.

Are your superiors reading this? Did they authorise you to send that pathetic screed in the hopes that I would con-

*fide all my secrets to you, maybe beg to be rescued, or give
away something about my location? Well I hope they ARE
reading this, because I have something to say—something
I tried to say five years ago, only no one wanted to hear it.*

*To whom it may concern: I dated Jeff Leadbetter from
the age of 20 to 22. He treated me like shit for at least 80%
of that period, and when I finally pulled myself together and
left him, he hit me, threatened me, and then stalked me for
six months. And when I reported it to the police, his colleagues swept it under the rug.*

*So fuck you, Jeff, and fuck you whoever is reading this.
And no, it goes without saying, I didn't kill my husband. But
someone did, and whoever it was broke into our house via
the vent on the bathroom window, and then cut his throat.
It took me about five minutes to find that out—five minutes
it could have taken you too, if you weren't so busy trying
to convict me. So do your jobs, get out there, and fucking
CATCH THEM.*

Furiously, my fingers physically trembling with rage, I hit send
and watched the email swirl away. Then I put my head in my hands
and tried to figure out what I had just done, and whether I'd made a
huge mistake.

A large part of me knew that I'd probably done exactly what the
police had been hoping I would do with that email—assuming they'd
known about it. They must have known it would make me angry—
even someone who knew nothing about my past with Jeff couldn't
have read those mocking, patronizing sentences as anything other
than a goad. And so I'd responded, falling into the trap like any forum
poster taking the bait of an internet troll and firing back.

But perhaps the police hadn't banked on Gabe's VPN—a superse-
cure one which bounced through several countries that were known
for their lack of cooperation with UK and US law enforcement.

Well, whatever I had just done, I was committed now. There was no unsending the email, and if I *had* given away my location, I might as well accomplish something useful at the same time.

Deliberately pushing Jeff Leadbetter to the back of my mind, I opened up a new email and filled in Hel's address at the top. That was the easy part, but when I tried to think what to say, I struck a brick wall. *I'm okay?* Except I wasn't. *Don't worry?* She absolutely should.

Dear Hel, I managed at last.

I'm safe. I can access emails but you should assume the police are reading anything you write here. So far, so pointless. How could I get her a message that actually mattered?

The thought came to me with a bitterness that stuck in my throat, that this would have been so much easier if I actually *had* killed Gabe. If I'd had some warning, I could have prepared—I could have had cash and burner phones up to the eyeballs, and a properly researched protocol with Hel for secure message exchange. Instead I was making it up as I went along, drowning in grief, and trying not to screw things up more than I already had done.

I was still trying to think what to say when my email notification pinged again, giving me a little jolt of adrenaline. Was it Jeff replying already?

But when I flicked back to my inbox, the top email wasn't from Jeff. It was from a name I only just recognized—Julian Archer, an old friend of Gabe's. And the subject line was *My heartfelt sympathy.*

Dearest Jack, read the preview pane,

I just heard the terrible news from Cole Garrick . . .

I closed my eyes. I couldn't face it—the shock, the sympathy, the questions.

I shut down the browser.

But something stuck with me from Julian's email—Cole's name. And with it, Cole's voice in my ear, from our call that morning on Hel's unicorn phone. *Anything you need, okay?* Anything. *I mean that.*

Cole knew as much about computers as Gabe did, and probably more about mobile phone security, which was his professional area. He, of all people, would be able to tell me what I needed to know— how to communicate safely with Hel. The police would have all my friends and family on their list already, but Cole—I couldn't remember the last time I had rung him before this morning, and even then I'd used Hel's old phone, not mine. Before today, our communication had always been through Gabe. The police would work their way around to Cole eventually, I had no doubt about that, but they would have no reason to put him top of the list.

Most importantly, Cole was Gabe's best friend. If something *had* been going on in Gabe's head the last couple of weeks, something that he hadn't felt able to tell me, for whatever reason, Cole was the only other person he might have confided in. I *had* to find out if Gabe had set up that life insurance policy or not, and there was a chance— not a very high one, but a definite chance—that Cole might know, one way or the other.

But how could I get in touch with him without putting us both on the police's radar?

I was still trying to figure it out when a deep voice came from in front of me.

"Hey, what happened to your hair, Red?"

The words jolted me back to reality and I looked up, slightly alarmed at the idea that someone was keeping track of my appearance. Then I realized—it was Lucius, the guy from reception. Of course—he had seen me with red hair that afternoon.

I gave a shaky laugh.

"I don't know . . . just fancied a change, I guess. You know what they say—blondes have more fun."

"I hear ya. Though you were looking pretty serious there. Everything all right?"

The question was kindly phrased, but the absurdity of it made a near-hysterical laugh bubble up inside me, threatening to escape. Instead I stared at him, wondering what to say.

Well, I was just wondering how to get in touch with my dead husband's best friend without being fingered by the police. Any ideas?

"I—I've got a tricky email to write," I said at last. "To a friend. I was just trying to think of how to phrase it."

"Ah," Lucius said. He smiled, a kind one that made his eyes crinkle. He was older than he had looked at first, I realized. Probably my age or more. "You know what? My rule of thumb is, if you can't write it, say it. I always find face-to-face is better for the big stuff."

Face-to-face. I chewed my lip, wondering if this was the stupidest idea I'd ever heard, or if the man was a genius. Face-to-face. I knew where Cole lived. I knew where he worked. It was highly, *highly* unlikely he'd be under surveillance—not yet at least. Could I just . . . find him?

"You know . . ." I said slowly, "I think you might just be right."

"I'm always right," Lucius said with a wink. "G'night . . . Blondie."

"Good night," I echoed. As he disappeared up the stairs to the dorms, I shut down the laptop, threw my Pot Noodle cup in the bin, and stood, with a new sense of . . . not hope exactly, but at least a kind of purpose. I had a plan—albeit a pretty cursory one.

I was going to get some sleep. Then I would find Cole.

TUESDAY, FEBRUARY 7

MINUS FIVE DAYS

When I woke, it was with a sense of complete disorientation. I was lying in an unfamiliar bed, surrounded by purple curtains, and there was a low, throbbing pain below my right ribs. The room was extremely warm, my hair smelled of bleach and cheap shampoo, and I could hear other people's breathing.

Then it came to me—I was in the hostel, lying on a thin mattress in a curtained bunk, and my roommates were asleep, which meant it was likely still early.

I pulled myself up against the pillows. My head was aching, my side hurt, and I had the sensation of not having slept at all, although I knew I had. But my dreams had been filled with horrible nightmares—images of Gabe, soaked with blood, lurching upright with a ghastly grin and begging, *Please, help me*, as his cut throat whistled with every word; sweaty chases through hot shopping centers with a policeman on my tail who looked a lot like Jeff Leadbetter but wore Hel's coat and pushed the twins in a buggy in front of him—an image that should have been funny, but in the dream had been anything but.

For a long moment I sat, waiting for everything to stabilize, for the sickish feeling of dread to subside and the pieces of the day to sink into place. At last, realizing that this wasn't going to get any better, I parted the curtains, swung my legs over the side of the bed, and climbed down the bunk ladder to the floor.

Down on the ground, I got dressed as quietly as I could in the semidarkness. The burner phone said that it was 6:34 a.m. Cole was an early riser—he went to the gym before work most days and was usually at his desk at his office in Limehouse by nine at the latest. Which meant I had just enough time to walk across London to intercept him before he got there. The only question was what to do about my bag. It was heavy—heavier than I really wanted to drag with me, and it would be safe in the luggage cage under the bed. But I didn't know whether I would be coming back—it was all too possible that answering Jeff's email last night would turn out to have been a huge mistake. In the end I unlocked the cage and dragged the rucksack out, swinging it onto my back with a grimace.

In the lobby, I left the keys on the counter and then let myself out into the early-morning chill of a London February.

THE WALK TO LIMEHOUSE WAS longer than I had thought, and by the time I began to weave my way through the narrow streets of Wapping, down to the river and Cole's office, the traffic was humming, and I was getting more and more anxious.

It wasn't only the ticking clock of Cole's arrival that was making me concerned. I had never felt so conscious of the hundreds and thousands of CCTV cameras London possessed, had rarely even noticed them before today unless I was on a job. Now, as I ducked down alleyways and walked swiftly past the entrances of Tube stations, I felt painfully aware of them—the little plastic lenses following me as I passed, capturing my image, storing it on disk or passing it remotely to some control room back in Scotland Yard. The only saving grace—and a fact I tried to keep reminding myself of as my paranoia mounted—was the fact that there *were* so many of them. Looking for one person in the thousands of images churned out by London's vast surveillance web would be not so much like looking for a needle in a haystack as like looking for one particular grain of sand on a beach. I just had to hope that facial recognition wasn't yet at a stage where computers could cut out the humans and scan for a particular set of biometric features. They couldn't do that yet . . . could they? It felt like only yesterday that I'd been reading sarcastic blogs about iPhones failing to distinguish between Chinese faces.

Well, if they could, there was nothing I could do about it for the moment. All I could do was get to Cole's office and intercept him before he disappeared inside for the day.

Cerberus Security was a tech company that specialized in privacy and security apps for mobile phones. It had started out small, with an ad-blocking app that had proven unexpectedly successful. Later it had expanded into password managers, antivirus apps, and software aimed at worried parents trying to keep tabs on their kids.

The company was housed in Kynes Wharf, a massive black-painted wooden building right down by the Thames. In its day it had been a cotton warehouse, receiving bales from all over the world off ships that made their way up the river at high tide. Now it had been converted into hipster offices. Once upon a time, Cerberus had occupied just the top floor, back when Cole had joined the firm barely out of university. In the years since, it had expanded to take over the entire building, slowly pushing out the other tenants, and Cole had risen with it.

Now, as I swung around the corner, I saw an intermittent stream of young people coming from the opposite direction. They didn't look like the office workers at Arden Alliance—most of them were too young, and they were for the most part not dressed in suits and ties. I would have fit in fine here with my blond hair and Converse. But I wasn't intending to go inside—not yet, anyway. Instead I waited, scanning the approaching workers for Cole's face and trying not to meet the eye of the boxy CCTV camera mounted on top of a high wall, nestled amid the barbed wire like a strange bird. Jesus. They were everywhere. I moved away, turning to face the Thames and its expanse of stinking low-tide mud, though I knew it was stupid—if the police requisitioned footage from that camera, my image was already captured. Turning my back now wasn't going to help.

I looked at my phone, anxiety coiling in my stomach. Ten past nine. Had I missed him? The thought of braving the reception desk with their *Do you have an appointment?* and their *Can I see some ID?* was not a pleasant one.

And then I saw him. My stomach did a flip.

He was striding along, head down, looking at his phone, with his hood up, shading his face. His dark blond hair, or what I could see of it, was wet and uncombed, as if he'd come straight from the gym showers, and he looked gaunt and unshaven, and a lot like he hadn't slept. Cole had always borne a strong resemblance to the lead in an American high school drama—handsome, clean cut, a total contrast to Gabe's dirty, bearded sexiness. I had once heard two teenage girls in an airport gigglingly debate whether he was Zac Efron. Now he looked—well, he looked like a man whose best friend had been brutally murdered, I supposed.

"Cole," I called, keeping my voice low. He looked up, then around, puzzled, apparently not sure where the call had come from. I took a breath. "*Cole*, it's me."

He stopped at that, this time looking directly at me, puzzled. Then recognition clicked, and his expression changed to shock.

"*Jack?*" His voice gave me the same little gut-wrenching jolt I had experienced on the call yesterday. "Are you—wait, have you done something to your hair? I barely recognized you."

"I need to talk to you." My face felt stiff with the effort of holding everything in check.

Cole nodded, plainly concerned but trying not to show it too obviously. "Of course." He waved an arm at the door of Cerberus Security. "Come on in."

For a moment I hesitated. It felt like a truly terrible idea, walking into his office under the eyes of his colleagues and receptionists and security staff. But what was the alternative? Having this conversation out in the street? Both seemed impossible.

"Could we—" I swallowed and glanced up and down the street, clocking once again the security cameras, the guard just inside the office foyer. "Is there a coffee shop, or somewhere we could go and talk privately? I don't want—" I stopped, not sure how to say what I meant. What I was trying to say was that I didn't want to get him in trouble if the police came asking questions after our meeting, but how could I blurt that straight out?

Cole stood looking down at me for a moment, worried puzzlement etched between his dark brows.

"Depends how private you want. We could go back to the flat?"

Cole's flat was only ten minutes' walk from Cerberus, a gorgeous penthouse in a converted warehouse overlooking the Thames that'd had Gabe groaning that he was in the wrong job the first time Cole had shown it to us. It would be quiet . . . and private. But somehow the suggestion made me uneasy. A building that fancy was sure to have CCTV, and it wasn't impossible the police might have staked it out already. There was also the question of Cole's girlfriend, a beautiful model-turned-artist called Noemie. I didn't want to drag her into it if I could possibly help it.

"Is Noemie there?" I asked at last, and Cole shook his head.

"She's in San Francisco for work."

"I just think your flat—" I stopped, glancing at his colleagues streaming past. There was no way I could say what I wanted to—that the police were after me, and his flat felt too dangerous. Even standing here left me itchy with a sense of exposure I couldn't articulate. But Cole seemed to understand.

"Okay, look, I have an idea. An old church, round the corner. It's never locked this time of year; the vicar leaves it open in case rough sleepers need a place to warm up."

I nodded, and he led the way back in the direction he had come, through a couple of narrow alleys, and out into a deserted graveyard, with a small, soot-stained church dominated by a pair of enormous yews. In the corner were a couple of tents and a homeless man rolled up in a sleeping bag. His eyes were closed. I shivered in sympathy and put a handful of coins—all the change I had—in the empty paper cup beside his carry mat. He didn't stir, and I only hoped he would wake up before someone else helped themselves to the money. Then I hurried after Cole.

I couldn't help looking over my shoulder, checking for cameras as we made our way up the path between the fallen gravestones, but there were none, or none that I could see. The tall wooden door looked closed—but when Cole pushed it gently, it swung inwards, and together we slipped through the entrance and into the church.

Inside it was chilly and quiet, with a sense of being almost but not quite abandoned. As I followed Cole down the aisle we passed straight-backed pews silently facing a rather dusty altar. Little silvery motes floated in the thin pale light filtering through the stained-glass windows.

"How did you know about this place?" I whispered.

"I walk through the graveyard at lunch sometimes," Cole said. His voice was not quite as low as mine, and it echoed in the rafters. "Just, you know, to get away from the desk. And one day this old lady, she was throwing out the flowers, and she asked me if I'd like to come inside, see around. But Jack, listen—what's going on? Is everything okay? I mean—" He stopped, swallowed. "Sorry, that's an incredibly stupid thing to ask—what I meant—I just—"

He stopped again, and I shook my head, unable to express how very, very not okay everything was.

"No," I said at last. "Nothing's okay. I—"

Cole held out his arms, and I walked into them, still shaking my head, feeling his grip tighten around me. I stood, pressing my face to his warm chest, feeling the rise and fall of his breath, overcome for the first time in what felt like days by the crushing agony of what we had both lost.

We stayed like that for a long time, simply standing in the silent chancel, my forehead pressed against the softness of his hoodie, feeling his shoulders and rib cage shaking with unspent emotion. He was crying, I realized, and the thought gave me a stab of guilt. He was crying— why couldn't *I* cry? Gabe was my husband—why couldn't I cry?

"It's so fucking unfair," he managed at last, his voice hoarse with tears and anger. "Oh fuck, Jack, how do we go on?"

"I don't know," I said, feeling my own throat ache with the effort of forcing out the words. Cole straightened and then swiped at his eyes with his free wrist, the tears soaking into the sleeve of his gray marl hoodie.

"Look, I know asking you if you're okay is a stupid question in the circumstances, but Jack, you look—"

He trailed off, but I knew what he meant. I had seen myself in the blurred, toothpaste-spattered mirror of the hostel bathroom as I brushed my teeth that morning, and even I had been shocked by what I'd seen. It was impossible that I had lost weight in the three days since Gabe's death, but it looked as if I had—my pointy face had turned from gamine to gaunt, my features strangely small and undefined without my usual cat's-eye flick of eyeliner.

With my white hair and un-made-up face I looked like a ghost— which, in a way, I was: the ghost of the woman who had left Salisbury Lane just a few nights ago for Arden Alliance. That woman had been happy, safe, a loving wife with a loving husband. I was none of those things. I was—the word hung strangely in the silence, unspoken. I was a *widow*. And I was a wanted person.

"Cole, I'm sorry to do this to you, but I didn't know where else to turn."

"Sorry to do what?"

I took a deep breath.

"Look, I have to tell you this up front so you can decide if you want to help me. Because if you do—"

"Jack, *what*? Seriously, whatever it is, I'll do it. Don't even think about it. Just tell me—whatever it is, tell me."

"I'm wanted." I said the words baldly, unsure how else to phrase it. I had spoken more loudly than I meant, and the two words echoed around the nave, overlapping, chasing each other. Somewhere high above the altar a bird rose up, flapping its wings in alarm, and then settled again.

Cole blinked.

"I'm sorry, I didn't catch that. What did you want . . . ?"

"No, Cole." I lowered my voice. "*I'm* wanted. I'm wanted by the police. If you help me—there's a chance you could get prosecuted. And for God's sake, don't tell Noemie. I don't want to drag her into this."

"*What?*" His face, already alarmed, had turned suddenly pale, and for a moment I thought he was going to faint, ridiculous as it sounds. I had never seen anyone look so unutterably shocked. "You're wanted by the *police*? Are they mad? What happened?"

"They think I killed Gabe." As the words came out of my mouth, I heard a bitter, hysterical little laugh bubble up with them. It just sounded so crazy when I said it. How was I even speaking it aloud?

"No," Cole said, almost reflexively. "*No.* That's just—it's insane. No!"

"They think the timings of my movements that night don't add up. But there's something else. I found an email, in my inbox. It's a huge insurance policy that Gabe—*someone*—took out just before he died. They'll think it was me—or that I knew about it, at least. They think *I* killed him, and I did it for the money."

"An insurance policy?" Cole was blinking like someone punch-drunk, barely able to register what was going on. "I don't—but—"

He groped his way to a pew and sat, hands lifeless between his knees, as if trying to come to terms with what I had just said. I moved across and sat beside him.

"I know. I know, I was as shocked as you. But the police have my phone, and they know about the insurance. I don't know if I'm being set up, or if Gabe—" I swallowed. It was extraordinarily hard to spit out what I wanted to say. "If Gabe—if Gabe took the policy out himself, because he was afraid of something. That's what I came here to ask. Did he say anything to you? Before he died?"

"Jesus—no. He didn't say anything. Why—what—"

He stopped. His expression was utterly bewildered.

"If he didn't take it out," I spelled it out for him, "then someone is framing me. Do you understand? Someone killed Gabe, and they're framing me. It's not a burglary gone wrong, or a case of mistaken identity. Someone arranged a hit on Gabe, and they're trying to set me up to take the fall. And if he *did* take out the policy, then there's every chance he did so because he saw them coming."

For a long moment Cole simply stared at me as if he had no idea what to do or say. Then something seemed to snap into place inside him, and I saw him visibly click into a different gear—adrenaline-fueled problem solver, so similar to Gabe that it made my heart hurt.

"Okay," he said. He stood, walked down the gap between the pews to the side aisle, and then came back. "Okay. So. Damage control—the police are after you. What do they know?"

"They have my phone—unlocked," I added in answer to the question I knew was coming.

Cole winced. "Not ideal, but okay."

"They have most of Gabe's devices—phone, laptop, and so on. I gave them the passwords that I knew, but I don't know all his log-ins. Oh, wait—" The memory came back to me from the police interrogation. "They don't have his hard drive. Someone took it."

"Someone *took* his hard drive?" Cole sounded as puzzled as I had been.

"Yes, at least, it was gone. They asked me about it."

"The hard drive from his main computer?"

"Yes."

"Anything else missing?"

"I have no idea. I didn't look before I called the police—I didn't see any of his equipment when I went back to the house, but I assume the police would have seized it all."

"Okay . . ." Cole said slowly. "And what do you need?"

"Well, I have some cash. And I have clothes and a burner phone that Hel—my sister—bought me. But I need a way to talk to Hel. And longer term, I need somewhere to sleep."

"You can stay at m—" Cole began, and then shook his head. "No, sorry. Stupid idea, I can see that. They'll get to me eventually. Okay, no, first things first. Communication. Let me think . . ." He turned away, staring at the patterns cast by the tall stained-glass windows across the austere gray flags. Then he turned back. "I think Signal is your best bet. It's end-to-end encrypted, and there's a setting where you can make messages expire after reading."

"But you have to give your phone number to sign up to Signal, don't you? And that part's not encrypted. So if the police are monitoring Hel's phone, they'll be able to find this number, and then I'll be toast."

But Cole was shaking his head.

"No. You have to give *a* phone number, but it doesn't have to be *your* phone number."

"What do you mean? You have to verify it—I'm sure you do."

"You just need a number where you can receive a text message," Cole said. "Look." He sat back on the pew beside me, opened his laptop bag, and pulled out a MacBook. "There's a bunch of sites that can do this—we use them for development tools. They generate a throwaway number, and some of them you can use temporarily to receive texts. So . . . okay, let's pick this one."

He chose one site from a bunch of bookmarks, seemingly at random, and clicked through. Instantly a list of UK mobile numbers popped up on-screen, and he selected one and tapped *Open*.

"Right. Install Signal on your phone and enter that number."

I did as he said, typing in the unfamiliar number laboriously and going through the sign-up process until the only step left was to verify the number. I clicked, and a few seconds later a message popped up on Cole's computer screen.

"Click to verify . . ." Cole said, and tapped. There was a pause. He picked up his own phone, typing something, and as he did, my phone vibrated and the screen lit up. I unlocked it. A Signal message notification hovered at the top of my screen: *Do you read me Red Sparrow*, it said.

I stared down at the phone in my hand. For the first time in what felt like days, I found I was smiling.

"Cole, you are a fucking genius. *Thank* you."

"You can message Hel from that number now, and there's no way for the police to trace it. Is she on Signal?"

"I don't think so. She's more of a WhatsApp kind of woman."

"Well, don't worry, I'll get a message to her somehow, tell her to get in touch. You should probably assume the police can read the messages if they're monitoring her phone, but they shouldn't be able to trace your location from them."

"Okay. And *thank you*. Thank God you know this stuff."

"Part of the job," Cole said, a little grimly. "Look, I've been thinking about tonight. I wish you could stay at my flat—"

I was shaking my head even before he'd finished the sentence.

"—but it's not going to take the police long to come sniffing around. Noemie has a cottage, though. She bought it to work in, years ago. It's down near Rye, and we spend the weekend there sometimes. It's nothing fancy, I don't think it's even got central heating in fact, but it's quiet and isolated, and it's in Noemie's name so it's one step further down the chain from you. You could stay there while you figure out your next move."

His words gave me an uncomfortable knot in my stomach— perhaps because they echoed the questions that had been whispering at the edge of my subconscious all night: What the hell had I been thinking? And what was I going to *do*? I couldn't keep running forever.

"That's part of the problem," I said. "I—I honestly have no idea what my next move is. I didn't plan any of this, and now—now I'm stuck. My only way out is through."

"Through? What do you mean, through?"

"I mean, I have to find out who killed Gabe." There was an edge in my voice that sounded, even to my own ears, on the verge of desperation. "I *have* to. Nothing else matters."

"But, Jack . . ." Cole's face was alarmed. "If you're right—if this was a hit rather than just some punk after Gabe's computer equipment, or a burglary gone wrong—these people are dangerous. You could end up being killed yourself. I really don't think you should go poking tigers."

"I . . . don't care." It was the first time I had said the words aloud, though they had hovered at the edge of my conversation with Helena, unspoken, unadmitted even, but only just. "If it's that or rot in prison for the murder of the man I love—"

Suddenly I could barely speak. The unshed tears were back, thick and clotting at the back of my throat, making it hard to get the words out. The bitterness of it crashed over me again like a wave. Gabe dead. Our life in ruins. The police hunting me for a crime I hadn't committed and Gabe's killer—Gabe's *killer* . . . If I didn't think about it, if I just kept putting one foot in front of the other, concentrating on one step at a time, then I could keep going, just. But Cole's words had made me look up, had made me think about my situation and what I was doing, for the first time since I had left the police station. And the unfairness of it all made me gasp.

"Jack, no." Cole's voice was quiet, but there was something horrified there too. "Please, *please* don't say that. I can't send you out there wondering if you're going to do something stupid to yourself—"

"I've already *done* something stupid," I said flatly. "When I walked out of that police station. I marked myself as suspect number one. The only important thing is tracking down who did this, because if I don't find out who killed Gabe, my life is over anyway. I have nothing to live for, don't you get that?"

"Jack, *no*," Cole said again, and this time his voice cracked. "Please don't say that, Gabe wouldn't want—"

He stopped. I squeezed my eyes shut, feeling the threat of the ever-hovering tears that never seemed to actually come. Because that was the worst thing—he was right. Gabe wouldn't have wanted any of this. He wouldn't want me to be doing this, to be throwing myself into some twisted fantasy of revenge. But guess what—Gabe wasn't fucking *here*. He had gone and got himself killed, and left me here alone. So there was nobody but me to sort this out—nobody but me to decide what to do.

For the moment, I had the briefest, strangest hallucination—of the rubbery warmth of a Bluetooth headpiece in my ear, of Gabe's voice, low, intimate, keeping me company as he always did on a job.

You got this, babe.

I squeezed my fists tight, until my nails dug into the soft skin of my palms, hating him for the liar he was.

And then Cole's arms were around me again, and I was grinding my face into his shoulder, wishing, wishing more than ever that I could cry, that the tears would come, that I could lose myself in the release of sobbing.

"How could he leave me?" I was saying, my voice breaking on the last syllable. "How could he, Cole? Why didn't he fight them? Why did he let this happen?"

Cole didn't answer, he just stroked my back, but I knew the truth. Gabe left me because he didn't have a choice. Just like I hadn't had a choice when I'd run from that police station. I had seen no other option.

And I had no other options now—but to keep going, and to try to find out who had done this to Gabe. And after that? But I couldn't think that far ahead.

Solve the next problem. And then the next one after that.

Keep putting one foot in front of the other.

Until you can't walk any further.

B raving Charing Cross train station felt . . . well, it felt insane, if I was being honest. Walking across the concourse, in front of the very eyes of the British Transport Police officer standing lazily with his back to a pillar, it felt like I was walking into a giant public-transport-shaped trap.

But I looked, I knew it, very different from the woman who had bolted from the police station yesterday morning. My red hair was gone, and with Cole's help and a pair of scissors from his desk, I had cut the rest short, into a pretty good approximation of a white-blonde crop. I had also borrowed a pair of Cole's sunglasses and a coat that Noemie had left in his office—a beautiful, long, camel-colored trench that must have cost an unthinkable amount of money, I could tell from the softness of the wool as I pulled it on. But Cole was adamant: I had to take it. I could leave it at the cottage if I really wanted to, he said, but Noemie wouldn't care either way—she hadn't even noticed that it had been hanging behind his office door for six months. Beneath my jumper, I had rolled up the fleece and taped it around my belly in the semblance of a baby bump—a pretty good one, as long as you didn't touch it. The only thing slightly out of place was the bag on my back—it hinted at gap-year traveler more than yummy mummy, but I hoped I could style it out.

As I passed a darkened shop window at the entrance to the station, I glanced at my reflection. The police were looking for a red-headed fugitive in a cheap rain jacket. The woman gazing back at me was a well-dressed pregnant blonde in D&G shades and a coat that probably cost north of two grand. The effect was . . . well, it was pretty impressive, I had to hand it to Cole. I looked nothing like the frightened girl who had ambushed him outside his office just a few hours ago. Even so, walking directly past the police officer in the entrance was a bad moment.

At the ticket machine I paid cash, my fingers shaking as I tried to navigate the fiddly touch screen and feed the crumpled notes into the slot. As the tickets printed with agonizing slowness, I glanced up at the board to make sure I had the time and platform right. I didn't want to board too early and risk being trapped on the train if something happened. But I couldn't leave it too late either. I had five minutes to spare, which was about perfect.

The final receipt spat out into the tray, and I scooped everything up and swiped my way through the ticket barrier. The temptation to lower my head as I walked below the CCTV camera facing the barrier was almost irresistible, but I knew it was only one of many. Besides, hiding my face would attract all the wrong kind of attention. Instead, I reached into the pocket of the trench coat and drew out my phone, pretending to study the screen. A woman shading her face as she passes below a camera—massive red flag. A woman engrossed in Twitter as she crosses the platform—two a penny.

Still, I was sweating beneath the wool coat by the time I picked a carriage and tried to figure out the best seat to take. One by the door, for easy getaway if the police boarded the train? Or one further down the carriage, where they would take longer to find me? On the whole I preferred the entrance—the chances of them getting on at my exact carriage seemed low—but the seats there were all full.

I was still dithering when a young man in one of the priority seats stood up.

"Here you go, love."

For a moment I blinked, unable to work out what he was saying. Then I looked down and realized. My bump. The priority seats were for the elderly, disabled, and . . . pregnant.

I felt a flush of shame wash up my chest and reach my cheeks—even though part of me was laughing at myself. I was a fugitive, on the run from the police, wanted for *murder*, and it was the fake bump I had chosen to feel guilty about?

"I'm fine," I said, hoping that the blush wasn't too painfully obvious. "Honestly. I'll walk down."

"Nah, you're all good, love," the boy said. He had that weird mix of swagger and self-consciousness that seemed unique to males in their late teens. He ducked his head, picked up his bag, and began heading down the aisle, leaving the empty seat to me. "I don't like sitting near the bogs anyhow," he said as the carriage door slid shut behind him, which made me laugh.

It was two minutes until the train left, and as I slid into the vacant seat, my bag on my lap, I couldn't help peering out of the window, back up the platform. I was listening for pounding feet, shouts of *Police! Stop the train!*

But none came. The minutes ticked down until at last we reached 12:40—the time the train was supposed to leave. Nothing happened. I swallowed, aware that my neck and jaw were aching with tension. Why? Why weren't we going?

Then the train speaker crackled, and I felt a lurch in my stomach, a rush of nerves so strong I thought I might vomit. Was the train canceled? Were they holding us here for a "routine inspection"?

But then, after what felt like a pause of a thousand years, the conductor's voice came on.

"This is the twelve forty train for Ashford International, calling at Waterloo East, London Bridge . . ."

The familiar litany of stations droned on, and beneath the conductor's voice I could hear the *beep beep beep* warning as the train doors slid closed, and the engines began to fire.

" . . . Headcorn, and Pluckley, arriving Ashford International at fourteen hundred hours. We apologize for the late departure of this train, which was due to staff shortages, and we hope to make up time on the journey. Our next stop is—"

The train was picking up speed. We were moving away from the platform. And then we were out, into the bright crisp air of a sunny winter afternoon.

I let my head fall back against the seat, feeling myself exhale as if someone had pressed a release button.

I had done it. I was out of London.

"YOU CAN STOP HERE," I said to the taxi driver. He pulled in where I'd indicated and looked around the deserted car park doubtfully. In summer it was probably a sweet place, with a kiosk selling ice creams and plastic buckets and spades. On a cold February afternoon it was little short of desolate.

"You sure?"

I nodded. Taking a taxi had been a gamble—it was exactly these kinds of questions that I had wanted to avoid—but the alternative, walking five miles from Rye station along country lanes in the gathering dark, hadn't exactly appealed either.

"Yes, I'm sure. I'm meeting a friend."

The driver shrugged. "Eight pounds twenty pence."

I leaned over, counting out the change from the train ticket pound coin by pound coin and adding a tip so small I felt instantly guilty—but my supply of cash was dwindling painfully fast, and I didn't know when I would be able to get more. The driver didn't seem to bear any resentment, though, and got out cheerfully, in spite of the wind whipping across the tarmac, to unlatch the boot and remove my rucksack.

"There you go, love. Good luck with it."

He nodded at my bump, and I felt instantly even more guilty.

I waited until he got back in the car and completed a gear-grinding three-point turn to rejoin the main road, and then I turned and began to walk along the beach to where I very much hoped Noemie's cottage must be.

It was very cold. The wind had picked up the sand and was blowing it at knee height along the flat beach, so hard that even through my jeans I could feel the stinging particles hitting my skin like tiny needles.

My feet were sinking into the soft dunes, and my eyes were watering with a mixture of wind, sand, and sea spray—and for a moment I deeply regretted not getting the taxi to drop me at the cottage itself. But the risk was too great.

The burner phone had said it was only half a mile from the car park to the cottage, but as the dunes wore on, it began to feel much, much further, and I started to wonder whether I had made a mistake. My legs felt jelly-like with the effort of striding through the shifting sand; the rucksack on my back felt like it contained bricks, not clothes, tools, and a sleeping bag; and the wound in my side throbbed like a motherfucker.

I shook my head, blinking salt spray out of my eyes. What was the matter with me? This wasn't me. I was strong, capable, physically fit. Gabe might be the one in our relationship who got the lids off jars and heaved the washing machine out of its cupboard when the hose blocked, but I was the one who had the stamina and the endurance. Last month I had done a hill-running half marathon in aid of Cancer Research. And now I couldn't walk along a beach?

But the truth was, of course, Gabe *wasn't* that person anymore. Because he was dead. Any stuck lids in my future, any problems at all, in fact, I would be dealing with alone.

The unfairness of it hit me again, like a punch in the gut, and I found myself sinking down in the dunes and putting my face in my hands. Maybe I should simply give up, give in, lie down here on this beach and let the waves come in and take me out to sea. Because what did it matter? Who was I kidding to think I could do this alone, any of it? Least of all track down whoever had done this to Gabe. I might be able to scale walls and pick locks, but figuring out who had killed my husband? That was a job for the police. And they already had their suspect: me.

But I couldn't give up, and I knew it. I couldn't just sit there in a puddle of exhausted self-pity. Something steely inside me was already gathering my muscles, preparing me to pull myself up and continue walking. It wasn't even a conscious part of me—because the conscious part of my mind was the part that was telling me I was an idiot who should give up there and then. This was something else, something very deep, close to the core of me. It was the hard, indomitable part of me that refused to give in to the grief of Gabe's death—at least for now. It was the part of me that had stood there in the bathroom with the bleach fumes stinging my eyes, scrubbing over and over at my raw scalp until every trace of red was gone. It was the part of me that urged myself on during jobs— not to hand myself in to the security guards but to go that extra mile, get that extra file, even when Gabe was telling me in my earpiece that we had enough, that I could come home.

Well, there was no home left now. And no point in crying about it. I just had to keep going.

Slowly, I pushed myself upright, pressing my hand to my ribs to ease the throb as I got to my feet, and began following the path inland in the gathering darkness.

As I walked, the wind dropped, but in its place a mist began to gather in the hollows of the dunes, a curling sea mist that seemed to be creeping in from the channel behind me. At first it was just wisps, but then the wisps joined into a blanket, and the blanket thickened, until at last I could barely see my hand in front of my face. Putting on my phone's torch didn't help much either—it transformed the shifting darkness into a featureless white wall that reflected the torch's beam back at me with blinding intensity—and after a few minutes' stumbling, I turned it off and waited for my eyes to adjust.

I had no idea what time it was when I realized that the shapes in the darkness had coalesced into something that wasn't just a hillock or a tree, but something more concrete, and definitely building-shaped. It was just a few feet later that I crashed my shin painfully into a structure that was most definitely *very* concrete. At first I thought it was a fence, but then, feeling round with my hands, I realized. It was a railway sleeper, more than one in fact, stacked on top of each other. I had walked into some kind of bench, or maybe a raised flower bed, judging by the earth inside.

Carefully, feeling ahead of myself with outstretched hands, I walked towards the dark shape looming out of the mist. I prayed it was Noemie's cottage—but if it wasn't, I was starting to seriously consider just breaking in and bedding down. My phone was no help; the Google Maps marker was jumping about indecisively over about a square kilometer of map, and none of its guesses were particularly close to the marker Cole had shown me on his own phone back in London. *Location accuracy: low* it informed me helpfully. I remembered my text to Gabe: *no shit, sherlock.*

But as I got closer to the little building, I could see it fit the description Cole had given me—the corrugated roof, black walls, mustard front door. And then I spotted something that clinched it: a piece of driftwood nailed beside the door with the word *Spindrift* carved into it in faint, wind-worn writing. Hurriedly, almost shaky with relief, I dug in the front pocket of my rucksack and drew out the key Cole had pressed into my hand that morning.

It turned in the latch—and I was inside. Cold, hungry, and almost faint with exhaustion—but I was inside, and that was enough.

t was well over an hour later that I noticed that my phone had a message. I wasn't sure how long it had been sitting there. It had taken me that long to get the lamps lit, the fire in the grate going, and a kettle of hot water boiled. Cole had told me that the cottage had no heating. What he hadn't mentioned was that it also had no electricity. Well, it clearly *had* had power at some point; I'd found at least two sockets, and there was an electric reading lamp by the little couch. But either there had been a power cut, or it was switched off at the mains. Regardless, no amount of fiddling with the picturesquely ancient fuse box made anything happen, and in the end I had to make do with lighting the oil lamps and candles dotted around the place.

In the low warmth of the candlelight, the cottage turned out to be beautiful, but barely large enough to merit the word. It was a single high-raftered room, with a hand-crafted kitchen that had reclaimed wooden cupboards running along one wall, a china sink with a single cold tap, and a vintage 1950s stove that turned out to run off bottled gas. Opposite was a comfortable couch that folded out into a bed, and between the two were Noemie's easel, a small round table with bentwood chairs, and a little fireplace. On the walls were Noemie's paintings—broad, abstract landscapes in marine colors. The whole thing was small but utterly stunning, with a kind of Shaker-like simplicity, and I could see why Noemie had fallen for it. It must be the perfect place for an artist—somewhere totally quiet, off the beaten track. Somewhere she could really create.

There was nothing in the fridge, which was turned off, with the door propped open by a small Japanese urn filled with sea holly, but the cupboard by the back door held pasta and a couple of jars of pesto, and I was just sitting wearily down at the little table with a steaming bowl of fusilli when I saw the notification on my phone. I had a Signal message, from an unknown number. Hastily, I clicked through.

"Jack, it's me, Hel," it read. "Are you okay?"

My heart seemed to leap into my chest and I typed out quickly, "Yes! OMG yes, I'm fine. But this isn't your number?"

There was a pause, then the message flashed up.

"No. C advised me to get a burner phone too, in case the police seized mine. I've set the messages to delete but he said it was safer this way. Where are you?"

There was a moment's pause, then the phone pinged again.

"Or do you think you shouldn't say?"

I sat, chewing my lip, wondering what I could or should put in writing. If Cole was sure Signal messages were secure, then I trusted him. He was the expert on phone security, after all. And I didn't for a second think Hel would give me away—but I also didn't want to put her in the position of having to lie to the police.

"I'm safe," I typed at last. "And I have somewhere warm and dry to stay. That's probably all I should tell you."

"Good. I've been worried. But Jack, what are you going to do? Long term I mean?"

It was exactly what Cole had asked, and getting the same question from Hel made me feel even worse.

"I don't know," I typed, and then followed up, "I need to find out who did this, but I have no idea where to begin. All I have to go on is a broken fan. It's not much."

"A broken fan?" Hel's reply was puzzled, and I realized that I hadn't told her about breaking into the house and finding the crack in the bathroom window vent.

"Never mind," I wrote. "Long story. But I'm going to need something more substantial to figure out what's going on."

And then, even as I pressed send, it occurred to me. There *was* something—possibly, at least. If I was right, if Gabe hadn't set up that insurance policy, then someone else had. And maybe that someone had left a trail. The problem was, that kind of work—hacking into databases and looking for information trails—was very much more Gabe's area than mine. *Had been*, I reminded myself painfully. Had been Gabe's area.

"Actually . . . there is one lead," I typed out to Hel, just as a message came through from her.

"I've been wondering . . ."

"Crossed, sorry," I wrote.

"You go first :)" she typed back, with an uncharacteristic smiley—Hel wasn't usually much of a one for emojis, but this wasn't exactly a normal situation. "What's your one lead?"

"Okay. Well. I was just thinking—there IS one clue. The insurance."

There was a long pause. I could almost hear Hel's brain ticking. Then her reply came through.

"How do you mean?"

"Someone took that policy out. And I really don't think it was Gabe. It's just not his style."

Wasn't, I reminded myself bitterly. It *wasn't* his style. Would I ever get used to thinking of him in the past tense? It seemed impossible that he was gone, even though I'd cradled his dead body in my arms.

Hel's reply had already pinged through onto the mobile.

"Okay. But how do you prove that?"

"I'm not sure," I typed. "I could ask Cole. Maybe he could do something fancy with their system—figure out the IP address of whoever applied?"

There was another long pause. Then the message popped up. Just one word.

"Maybe." I could almost hear the doubt coming off the screen. For some reason I felt nettled.

"Okay then—what were you wondering?"

"Well . . . I don't know if you're going to like this . . ."

She paused again and I almost rolled my eyes. There was literally *nothing* to like about the situation I was in. Hel could hardly make that any worse.

The phone pinged again.

"But I was thinking . . . have you heard anything from Jeff Leadbetter lately?"

"Jeff?" For a second I was puzzled, wondering how on earth she knew about Jeff's email. She didn't—*couldn't*—surely? "What do you mean? Has he emailed you too?"

"He's emailed you?"

"Yes, isn't that why you asked?"

"No, what do you mean he's emailed you?"

I sighed, the sound surprisingly loud in the little cottage, audible even over the cracks and hissing of the fire.

"Oh God, he sent me this stupid goading thing about Gabe's death. I assume his bosses told him to do it. Probably hoping I'd email back and give up my location."

Hel's response came back quickly this time.

"Did you? Reply?"

"Yes, but I made sure to switch on the VPN. I don't think they could get anything off it."

There was another long pause. Presumably Hel was trying to figure out whether I had just done something incredibly stupid.

"That's a virtual private network," I added, in case Hel didn't know what I was talking about. "It hides your location."

There was still no response.

"Why did you want to know about Jeff anyway?" I tapped out, more to get her to tell me what she was thinking. The long pauses were making me nervous. I had an image of the police battering down Hel's door, seizing the phone, although it was far more likely she was just typing one-handed while trying to get the twins to bed.

"Hel?" I was just typing when her message came through.

"Look. I might be completely wrong, but let's say someone did kill Gabe. And let's say you're right, and they're framing you. We've both been assuming that was something to do with Gabe, but what if it wasn't? What if it was something to do with you?"

"What?" I was confused now, my tiredness getting the better of me to the extent that I couldn't quite understand what she was trying to say. "Hel, sorry, you're going to have to spell this out. What do you mean?"

"I'm saying, what if someone killed Gabe not to punish him, but to punish YOU? And now they're set on ruining your life. And the only person I can think of who's sick enough to do that . . ."

The message trailed off, but I had gone completely cold, because I knew what she wasn't saying now.

The only person she could imagine deliberately ruining my life, the only person *I* could think of who would want to do that, was Jeff Leadbetter.

For a long moment I didn't reply. I just sat there, trying to process Hel's suggestion. It couldn't be true. It *couldn't*. And yet . . . could it? For six months after we broke up, Jeff had made my life a nightmare. Speeding tickets that mysteriously appeared from nowhere. Dropped calls in the night. A two a.m. drug bust at my old flat, in Hackney, with six armed officers battering the door down and storming in while I slept. *Anonymous tip-off, love* was all the explanation I'd ever got, but I'd known the truth. Jeff. And if I'd been a different kind of person, a more reactive one, or even—God forbid—someone who still enjoyed the occasional joint or bit of coke, the way I had when I was younger, I could have ended up in jail or even dead, if things had gone really wrong.

The middle-of-the-night drug bust was the worst, and it had tailed off after that, going back to silent phone calls and the occasional "random" vehicle search. Finally, when I'd met Gabe and moved in with him, it had stopped completely. Naively, I had assumed that Jeff was frightened of Gabe, or had moved on.

But what if he hadn't? What if he had simply been biding his time, waiting to punish both of us?

It was fantastical. But then so was every other theory I had come up with.

My phone pinged again.

"Jack? Are you there?"

"Yes, I'm here," I typed. "Thinking."

"Thinking what?"

Thinking her theory made no sense, was the honest answer. Jeff? A cop? Staging my husband's murder just to punish me for some long-ago breakup? It seemed ridiculous—not least because I had seen him at the station right around the time Gabe must have died. But he *was* the only person I could think of with a grudge against us, and somehow, even as my logical brain came up with a hundred reasons why it couldn't be true, a question kept whispering treacherously at the edge of my subconscious. Was it *my* fault? Had Gabe died because of me?

I was sitting there, staring at the screen, trying to think what to say to Hel, when a warning flashed up. *15% battery.*

Shit. I had completely forgotten that with no electricity, I wouldn't be able to charge my phone.

"Listen, my battery's running low," I typed out to Hel. "I'd better go. But I love you."

"Love you too," she messaged back. "Stay safe, okay?"

"I will xx"

There was a brief pause while I waited to see if she would message back, but she didn't, and in the end I shut down the phone and simply lay there, staring into the firelit darkness, trying to process what she had said. The more I thought about it, the more unlikely it seemed—Jeff was a dickhead, sure, but he wasn't a killer. And more to the point, he was a dickhead with an alibi—one I could attest to myself.

But when I closed my eyes, trying to fall asleep, it wasn't with Hel's words echoing in my ears, it was Jeff's own, the words he had hissed at me as I packed my bag that final day, the day I had left him for good. *I'll make you regret this, you stupid cunt. If I can't have you, no one can.*

Back then, I was sure he hadn't really meant it. I'd put it down to hot air, empty words spoken by a man with an outsize ego and an inability to accept rejection. But now . . . well, now Gabe was dead. And I wasn't sure of anything anymore.

WEDNESDAY, FEBRUARY 8

MINUS FOUR DAYS

It was very, very cold when I awoke, and for a while I just lay there, huddled on the sofa, trying to work out what time it was. The fire had died down in the night and was now white ash and black cinders in the grate. I could see my breath every time I exhaled.

I had fallen asleep fully clothed, with a crocheted woolen blanket wrapped around me, which now seemed like a good decision. I might be cold and stiff, but at least I didn't have to get dressed.

What I did need, however, was to pee—and in spite of my ignoring it for as long as I could, the pain in my pelvis at last forced me upright. It wasn't just my bladder that hurt. Everything ached. My side where the puncture wound throbbed every time I tried to roll over on the couch. My thigh muscles from slogging through the dunes the day before. My feet from walking six miles on London pavements to Cole's office, and then three miles back in the opposite direction to Charing Cross. Even my fingers were stiff and sore—probably from clenching my fists to try to stop my hands shaking whenever I passed a police officer or a CCTV camera.

I felt like an old lady, every joint complaining as I pulled myself painfully to my feet, the blanket wrapped around my shoulders against the chilly morning air.

The bathroom was a little lean-to with a corrugated iron roof and was, if it was possible, even colder than the main room. I winced as my bare skin made contact with the freezing toilet seat, and then sat for a long time, my face in my hands, trying to work out what to do.

What I *wanted* to do was phone the insurance company, put on my pen testing hat, and try to inveigle some information out of them about that policy, even if it was just a time and date for when it was set up. But I couldn't do anything until my phone was charged. Every-thing hinged on that.

Which meant the first thing I had to sort out was the electricity.

The second . . . I had to try, somehow, to figure out if Jeff Lead-better was behind all this. I just had no idea how to go about that, let alone prove it.

Two coffees later, and with a small fire crackling in the grate, I felt a little less cold and a lot less hopeless—but I still hadn't been able to get the electricity to work, and without it, I wasn't sure if I could stay here.

I had switched the phone off overnight to conserve battery, but now I turned it back on and was surprised to see that it was almost eleven a.m. I had slept longer than I had imagined. More worryingly, the battery was down to eight percent.

I opened up Signal and messaged Cole.

"Cole, hi, it's me. I'm sorry to bother you, but I can't get the elec-tricity to work. Is there a central switch? I can't charge my phone and I'm almost out of battery."

I waited for a few minutes to see if he responded, but there was no reply. As I stared at the lighted screen, the battery bar ticked down to seven percent, and I felt a kind of panic rise up inside me. If I had no phone, I was well and truly fucked. I couldn't even use the laptop without it—I had been relying on the phone for a hot spot.

Another thirty seconds. Still no reply. Fuck. Fuck.

With a hollow feeling in my stomach, I turned off the phone.

I HAD TOLD MYSELF THAT I would check in for Cole's reply only every half hour, but I managed just two checks before the battery died completely, sometime between twelve thirty and one. After that I had no way of knowing the time, but it felt like it was three, maybe four hours later that I was seated in a rocker on the porch, well wrapped up in Noemie's camel coat, and reading one of the curling paperbacks I had found on the mantelpiece. The sun was dipping towards the horizon, the shadows lengthening, when I heard the purr of a car engine from far up the lane. I sat up, ears instantly pricked, listening and trying to figure out if the sound was getting closer or pulling further away.

With the crashing of the distant waves, it was hard to tell for sure at first, but at last I was certain, it *was* getting closer. Much closer.

A lurch of apprehension sent me stumbling to my feet, looking left and right with a sick feeling of panic. Shit. Why hadn't I prepared for this? My belongings were strewn all over the cottage. I couldn't afford to simply abandon the contents of my rucksack—that was everything I had in the world—but if I stopped to pack, it could be too late.

At last, heart banging in my chest, I made up my mind. I flung down the paperback, ran into the cottage, grabbed the phone and what I could of the rest of my stuff, and pelted back out, heading into the dunes.

Then I crouched between two stunted bushes and waited.

It felt like a hundred years. I was closer to the ocean now and could hear very little apart from the waves, the beating of my heart in my ears, and my own panting breath. I thought—though it could have been my imagination—that the engine sound had got louder and then stopped. But I wasn't sure. What I hadn't heard, I was fairly certain, was a car starting up again and pulling away.

Was it the police? A friendly neighbor come to check out the lights and smoke? Or just the postman?

The sun had dipped behind the headland now, and it was getting extremely cold, the wind picking up as it had last night around this time. I remained crouched, my arms wrapped around my rucksack, my head buried in its folds, trying not to think about what I was going to do. I couldn't stay out here all night—I'd freeze. But if the mist came in, perhaps I could make a run for it? I was still wearing the camel coat, and that felt like the one silver lining—not just for its warmth, but for the fact that its color blended almost perfectly with the rain-dappled dunes. If they really wanted to find me, they would do it, I had no doubt about that. My hiding place was no match for a proper search party, let alone police dogs, and I'd made no attempt to hide my tracks from the cottage. But if the visitor was just one casual person come for a cursory check, I might be able to slip away into the darkness when the sun finally went down . . .

I was still running back and forth over my increasingly desperate options when I heard it. The sound of a low whistle, not quite a tune, just a strange little up-and-down riff that sounded immediately familiar, and yet I couldn't place it. I stayed where I was, trying to work out what was going on. Was it just an evening dog walker, making their way to the sea, whistling as they went? Perhaps, but it was a strange tune to pick . . . not the kind of easy-listening foot-tapper that people usually hummed, and why was it so familiar to me? The melody gave me a strange pain around my heart—a kind of unhappy yearning out of all proportion to the brief snatch of notes.

There was a pause, and then the sound came again, a little closer but fading in and out with the wind, and then suddenly, with a lurch of shock, I knew. I knew where I'd heard it before, and why it had given me that strange, bittersweet feeling of loss: it was the opening riff to a Talking Heads song, "This Must Be the Place." And the reason I recognized it, the reason it had made my heart hurt, my body making the association even before my brain had slotted the pieces together, was that it was the song Gabe and I had danced to at our wedding, our first dance, swaying together on a Greek beach beneath strings of fairy lights as our friends and family stood around and smiled.

Only someone who knew us both intimately would have whistled those opening notes. Only they would have remembered, would have known what that song meant to me. Without second-guessing, without thinking about how potentially stupid I was being, I dropped my pack and stood—and there, two or three ridges away on the hummock of a dune, silhouetted against the sky and staring out to sea with a worried expression, was Cole.

"Cole!" I choked out, and he turned, his face lighting up as soon as he saw me.

"Jack!" He stumbled through the sand and threw his arms around me. "Why the hell are you hiding out here? Didn't you get my message?"

"The phone died," I explained, holding it out.

Cole swore. "I thought maybe I'd seen your message too late. I tried texting and then when I couldn't get hold of you I panicked, and thought I'd better drive down. When I got to the cottage and found half your stuff gone—" He trailed off, leaving me to imagine what he'd thought.

"I'm sorry," I said. "I heard your car and I didn't know what to do. I thought—well, look, never mind." I glanced up and down the darkening beach. It was deserted, but I suddenly felt very exposed. The thought of Cole driving down in his car, automatic number plate recognition clocking him every step of the way . . . "We should get inside."

Cole nodded, picked up my bag, and we headed up through the dunes, back to the cottage.

Inside Cole lit the lamps, and I rekindled the fire while he tried to figure out the fuse box in the little lean-to. At last he gave up and came back into the main room, shaking his head.

"I don't know what's wrong with it. Something's gone bang, and I think it's going to take someone with real qualifications to put it right, but look, I bought a battery pack, you can recharge your phone at least."

He pulled what looked like a chunky mobile phone out of his pocket and handed it to me, and I gratefully dug in my rucksack for the charging cable and plugged in my phone.

"How many charges will it do?" I asked as the battery icon began to tick reassuringly upwards.

Cole shrugged. "I don't know, but it does mine at least four times, minimum, and I can top it up in the car before I go."

"God." I sat down on the couch. "I have to say, Cole, I'm happy to see you, but . . . do you think it was a good idea to come down in the car? What if you were followed?"

Cole shrugged again, more ruefully this time.

"I know. I just—I panicked when I couldn't get hold of you. I kept thinking what would you do, stuck in the cottage with no electricity and no way of calling for help. And then I began thinking about the fact that we'd left it with barely any food and stuff. I think I just realized what a stupid plan it was."

"Are you kidding?" I walked over to him where he was seated at the table and put my hand on his shoulder. "It was a great plan. And I'm bloody grateful—you got me out of London. I just—I suppose I'm worried that if the police had you under surveillance . . ." I trailed off.

Cole rubbed his face unhappily. "I know. I know. But look—I don't think I was followed. I mean, I'm sure I wasn't. Those county lanes on the last bit—they're single-track roads where you meet one car an hour. There's no way to follow someone on those without them seeing you. And I got off the motorway at Maidstone, so that's it as far as automatic number-plate recognition goes. But, Jack, if they really start digging they're going to find this place. It's in Noemie's name, but I pay most of the bills, and I'm pretty sure I'm on the council tax. I come down here practically every weekend in the summer. It wouldn't take them long. This was only ever a stopgap. If you want to be untraceable, you need somewhere completely off the grid—not connected to either of us."

I nodded wearily. I knew what he meant. But I wasn't intending to be on the run for that long. I couldn't.

"You look tired," Cole said now. "Have you been eating?"

"Yes," I said, though it wasn't completely true. I'd had pasta and pesto last night, a cereal bar for breakfast, and then I'd tried to eat the rest of the cold pasta for lunch, but something about it had turned my stomach. Now I suddenly felt very hungry.

"Well, I bought food," Cole said, getting up. "And wine. I'm going to cook you a really bloody good dinner. I want you to sit there and do absolutely nothing, and for just a couple of hours we're going to pretend none of this is happening, okay?"

"Okay," I said. There was a lump in my throat—maybe at Cole's kindness, or maybe at the realization of how much, how *very* much I really did wish that were true.

For the next two hours we did just that. Cole cooked—some kind of amazing, savory dish of fried red peppers, noodles, and a shedload of miso, and I sat at the table and stoked the fire and drank the silky-soft red wine Cole had brought until my head was fuzzy and everything that had happened over the last few days took on a strange patina of unreality.

When Cole served the food, I wolfed down the whole plateful, and then half of the huge portion of seconds he immediately doled out, and then sat back, feeling so full I could barely think, and reached for the bottle.

"God, I just realized, I've probably drunk too much to drive," Cole said as I leaned over to refill first his glass, and then mine.

"Don't be silly," I said. "It's your house. You should stay."

"Are you sure?" He looked doubtful. "I mean, it's Noemie's house, technically." He looked at the hearth rug and I could see him calculating how cold it was going to be, wrapped in his coat, by two in the morning. "I guess I could sleep in the car."

"Cole, stay. It's a double couch. It won't be the first time I've top-and-tailed with a friend. Besides"—I found I was smiling for the first time in what felt like days—"I might actually wake up able to feel my fingers tomorrow if there's someone else to warm the place up."

"Okay," Cole said, although he sounded a little reluctant. "I'll have to leave early, though. I've got a meeting at ten in London."

"That's okay." I suppressed a yawn. "I'm shattered. I'll probably be asleep in about ten minutes."

"Is your phone charged?" Cole asked, getting up and beginning to clear the plates. I nodded and turned it on, half hoping that there might be a message from Hel, but there was nothing—only four increasingly anxious messages from Cole starting from just after my phone had died, asking me if I was okay and then announcing his intention to drive down.

But thinking of Hel had made me remember something—our conversation of the night before.

"Cole," I said now, "I'm really sorry, but I need to ask you another favor."

"Jack." He put the plates in the sink and came and sat next to me, his face serious. He took my hand in his, his fingers warm and gentle as they wrapped around mine. "Please, for God's sake, stop apologizing. I *want* you to ask me—don't you get that? I want to help. I'd have done anything, *anything* for Gabe. So please. Whatever it is—just say it. And if I can do it—it's yours."

"I don't know if you can, that's the thing," I said, and then I told him about Hel's theory about Jeff, and my own suspicions about the insurance policy. As I talked, Cole's face grew more and more grave, and when I finished he looked very worried indeed.

"I don't like this."

"But you do think it could be true?"

"Yes, I do. Shit. I mean—this is bad. When it was just a case of mistaken identity, some burglary gone wrong, that was bad enough. But if Hel's right, Jack, this guy is psycho. You could be in real danger."

"There's more," I said, a little reluctantly, and then I told him about the email from Jeff and my impetuous reply. "Do you think I did wrong? Answering it, I mean?"

Cole shook his head. "I don't know. God. I mean, replying probably wasn't the wisest thing if I'm being honest, but if anyone could set up a good VPN it's Gabe, and if it gets Jeff's colleagues poking into his background . . ."

"Do you think Hel *is* right, then?" I asked.

Cole looked taken aback. "I mean . . . I guess? Don't you?"

"I don't know," I said. My head felt thick and stupid, the food and wine making logical thought hard. "I just . . . I can see her point. It's like she said: it's nearly always spouses in this kind of case—spouses and exes. And Jeff is the only really significant ex I have, certainly the only one where we parted on bad terms. But it just . . . I don't know, Cole, it just doesn't *feel* like something he'd do. And he was there, at the police station, right around the same time I was."

"He could have hired someone," Cole said. "I mean, he's a cop. He must know the right people to talk to."

"It's not just that . . . it's the whole thing, the setting up of the insurance. It feels too elaborate. I just wish I knew the deal with that—who took it out, whether it's really connected to the killing. Is there a way of finding out?"

"Maybe . . ." Cole said. He rubbed his temple. He looked like he was thinking hard. "Shit, this stuff was Gabe's area, really. The easiest step might be to try to get hold of the policy documents, work out if there's any mistakes, something that might indicate someone other than Gabe took it out. If that's the case, it might be enough to get the police to take a look at the back end. If they could get the IP address of the person who set the policy up . . . Would Jeff have known enough to use a VPN, d'you think?"

"I don't know." My head was aching. "He's not very techy. I think they did send me the policy documents. Hang on."

I opened up my laptop, navigated to the email the insurers had sent me, and clicked to view the attachments. The one marked *A summary of your policy* looked the most hopeful, and I opened it.

A long PDF appeared on my screen, and I scrolled down it, scanning past the legalese for information about Gabe. There was his name, including middle name, all correct. Height. Weight. Occupation. Date of birth, correct. Moderate drinker. Nonsmoker—well, that last one wasn't strictly true. Gabe liked the occasional joint. But it was true that he didn't smoke cigarettes, and anyway, I wasn't sure that Gabe himself would have admitted to the odd toke on an insurance policy. It didn't seem that relevant. But there was a *lot* of information here, all of it correct, and I couldn't see how Jeff could have known half of it.

"This wasn't Jeff," I said aloud. "It can't be. There's stuff he couldn't possibly have known. I mean, how many people know Gabe's middle name is—" I stopped, corrected myself painfully, "—was Charles?"

"There's always phishing," Cole said, a little doubtfully, but I shook my head.

"Jeff's not savvy enough for that, I told you. It's not just that he's not techy enough; I don't think his brain would work like that. He's a 'use your connections to fuck them over' kind of guy."

"Wait." Cole put down his glass. "Hang on. Jeff's connections. What about the police database?"

"What do you mean?"

"This Jeff guy—he's a police officer, yes? And Gabe—"

"Was arrested when he was seventeen," I finished, suddenly seeing where Cole was headed. "Fuck. But he was a juvenile. Do you think it could still be on the system?"

Cole shrugged.

"Honestly? I have no idea. I know a conviction like that would be spent in terms of having to declare it, but I'd imagine it's still logged somewhere—and probably somewhere a guy like Jeff could take a look. I don't know what they keep on file, but I'd imagine date of birth, height, and so on are pretty much a given. Weight, well, Gabe's put on a few stone since he was seventeen, but nothing you couldn't size up from looking at him. And the rest . . ."

"As for the rest, you could probably make a pretty good guess. Fuck." The realization felt like cold water on the back of my neck. I ought to feel—not happy, exactly, but at least a kind of grim satisfaction that I might be getting closer to finding out what had happened to Gabe, and who had set this up. But I didn't—I felt instead a kind of unfolding horror. Because if it *was* Jeff, then the chance of the police solving this had just gone from slim to virtually nil.

It wasn't that I thought Malik and Jeff were in cahoots—not exactly. I couldn't see tough, driven Malik sitting down with a bent colleague and cooking up a plan to murder an innocent man and lock up his wife. That just didn't seem plausible to me. But the idea that they wouldn't push too hard to investigate one of their own, that they might treat a report from an unstable, hysterical girl with a history of "false" police reports against her ex with skepticism . . . yes. That seemed all too plausible indeed.

"If this is true," I said blankly to Cole, "how the fuck do I prove it?"

"Look." He put his arms around me, and I felt the same urge I'd felt the day before when he hugged me in the church—the urge to put my face on his chest and cry, as I would have done if he were Gabe. Only I still couldn't cry. I couldn't seem to let go enough to cry. "Jack," I heard his voice, close to my ear, the warmth of his body, his height, his presence somehow so like Gabe's, in spite of their differences, that it made a lump rise in my throat. "It's going to be okay."

We sat like that for a long time, Cole's arms around me, my cheek pressed against his chest, listening to his heart. For the first time in days I felt . . . safe. But I knew that was an illusion. Cole couldn't protect me from what might be coming any more than Gabe had been able to protect himself.

"I don't think it is," I whispered.

"Jack." Cole touched my chin, tilting my face to look at him. "Listen to me—it's going to be okay. I'm not going to let anything happen to you."

I wanted to believe him. I wanted to believe him *so* much.

The problem was, we both knew it was bullshit. That wasn't a promise Cole could make. And the worst had already happened. Gabe was dead. Me getting convicted of his murder . . . well, that would be just the cherry on a cake of shit.

I sat, silent, looking up at him, at his furrowed brows, his dark blond hair, his troubled blue eyes, turned deep navy in the candlelit dark. He put his hand to my cheek.

And then he leaned down and kissed me.

For a moment I thought—I don't know. I thought perhaps it was just his compassion for me, a gentle brotherly kiss meant for my cheek or forehead that happened to land on my mouth. But then his lips parted, his hands came up to cradle my face, and I realized he was *kissing* me. Properly kissing, his mouth open against mine, his tongue against my lips. And for a second, a strange, wine-muddled, longing-filled second, I let him. No, more than that, if I'm being completely honest—I did more than just let Cole kiss me; I kissed him back.

But then something inside me lurched, a sense of the deep, absolute wrongness of this, however much I wanted to feel someone's arms around me and their body pressing against mine. Yes, I wanted someone—their lips, their heat, the softness of their bare skin—but I didn't want just anybody, I wanted *Gabe*.

"No." I said the word indistinctly at first, my mouth muffled by Cole's. And then more forcefully, pushing at him with my hands flat against his hard chest. "*No!* Cole, I don't want this!"

Cole staggered back as though I'd slapped him, though in truth my shove hadn't been that hard.

"I'm sorry," he said, as if bewildered, though I wasn't sure if his bewilderment was at my actions or his own. "God, I'm so sorry—the wine—I just—"

"It's fine," I said tightly, though I wasn't sure if it really was. "We were both—look, I get it. We're drunk, we're both grieving—" My throat tightened. And the thing was, I could see how it might be true, for him as well as me. How that longing, that desperate longing for Gabe might turn into reaching for the person who had been closest to him. But Cole was with Noemie, and I—what even *was* I? His best friend's widow?

"I'm sorry," he said again. He reached out, but I took a step back, involuntarily, and his face crumpled as though he was hurt. "I'm so sorry. I'll sleep in the car."

"Don't be silly," I said. "You'll freeze."

"I'll put the heater on."

"You can't leave the heater on all night, the battery will run down. Come on, Cole. We're both adults, we"—*you*, I thought, though I didn't say it, but then it was true that at first, at least, I had kissed him back—"just made a mistake. We don't have to let it ruin our friendship. I've got a sleeping bag—I'll sleep on the floor."

"*No,*" Cole said at that, his voice emphatic. "No. If anyone's sleeping on the floor, it's me. I'm sorry—I was—I don't know what I was thinking, Jack. I was just confused. And I—"

He stopped.

"Yes?" I asked. I felt—I don't know. Confused, but also sorry for him. But he shook his head.

"Never mind." He pulled his phone out of his pocket, looked at it, and then sighed. "Look, it's nearly midnight. Let's get some sleep. And *I'm* going on the floor, okay? I don't want to hear anything more about it."

For a minute I thought about arguing—but then I gave in and nodded. Cole would be going home tomorrow, to a proper bed and a mattress. He could take one night on the floor.

"Okay."

For the next few minutes there was silence, while Cole unrolled my sleeping bag across the floor, and I pulled out the couch. I hadn't tried to unfold it the night before; I'd simply slept across the cushions, and now I struggled with the mechanism. It came with a bang, sliding out unexpectedly and hitting me in the ribs. The blow wasn't hard, but it fell exactly over the place where I'd sliced myself on top of the wall, and a hot wave of pain shot through me, making me cry out and drop the sofa bed, holding my hands over the dressing.

"Jack?" Cole said, straightening with a puzzled expression from where he was unzipping the sleeping bag. "What—are you okay?"

I couldn't speak. I could only stand there, my hand pressed to my side, making a movement that wasn't quite a nod or a shake and trying not to whimper with the pain.

"Jack, what the fuck?" Cole came across, alarmed now.

I could feel something hot trickling down my side from beneath the dressing. *Shit.*

"I'm . . . okay," I managed. The pain was receding, back to the low throbbing ache I was starting to get accustomed to. "I'm okay. I cut myself . . . climbing a wall. The couch just . . . it just caught me on the tender bit."

"Jack, no. You've gone gray. This isn't—let me see."

I shook my head. I wasn't taking my top off in front of Cole, not after what had nearly happened between us, but he must have read my thoughts, for his expression grew set and a little impatient.

"For God's sake, Jack, I'm not going to jump your bones, if that's what you're worried about. Yes, I was stupid for a moment, I'm not denying that. But you don't nearly faint from just getting scraped in the side by a couch; that's not normal. Show me what happened."

I closed my eyes. Then, reluctantly, I pulled up my T-shirt.

The first thing I saw was that the dressing—two days old now—was dark with old blood. More blood, fresh and red, was trickling out from beneath one corner. Cole gave me a look as if to say, *Can I?* And when I nodded, he began to peel back the wet corner of the dressing. I shut my eyes, feeling the pain intensify as the sticky edges pulled on the wound, but I could still hear Cole's shocked intake of breath as the dressing came clear.

"Oh Jesus, Jack . . . This . . . this doesn't look good."

I opened my eyes.

"What do you mean?"

I peered down at my side, trying to see past the bunch of rolled T-shirt Cole was holding in his free hand. In the other was the blackened, crusted dressing.

What I saw made acid nausea rise at the back of my throat.

The wound hadn't healed. It was still the same small, malignant puncture, just below my rib. But now the sides were puffy and swollen with the white, unhealthy look of flesh that's soaked too long in the bath. And the liquid that oozed gently out of the hole was a mix of blood and something more unsettling, a kind of sticky white fluid that didn't smell great.

"You need to get this treated."

"I can't go to hospital. They'll want ID and NHS numbers. Look, let's just try and—" I swallowed. "I don't know. Clean it up. I've got some more dressings in my rucksack, maybe I can get something from the pharmacy tomorrow."

"I don't think a pharmacy's going to cut it," Cole said. His expression was unhappy. "You need stitches, and probably antibiotics."

"Well, they're not going to just hand out a prescription for antibiotics without taking a name, are they? And I can't give them one. So unless you've got a better idea, maybe shut up and do something useful—like getting a cloth."

There was a silence. Then Cole nodded shortly, turned on his heel, and disappeared into the little outhouse bathroom.

I sighed.

I knew I was snapping at the wrong person—that Cole was one of the few people trying to help me here. But I also knew that although he was probably right, his suggestion was pointless. I needed stitches, and antibiotics, and a good night's sleep in a proper bed, and a way into the insurance company database—and a thousand other things I was never going to get. Antibiotics were the least of it—I needed *Gabe* and he was gone. So hearing from Cole about all the things I *ought* to be doing—it just wasn't helpful.

"I'm sorry," I said when he came back with a bar of soap and a clean washcloth and set them down on the table. "I know you were trying to help, and you're not wrong, but—right now, I have to concentrate on finding out who did this to Gabe."

"And how are you going to do that?" Cole said. He had moved over to the stove and had his back to me, heating up a pan of water, so I couldn't read his expression, but his voice was level, as if he was trying not to show his real feelings.

"I don't know. I need—I need to find out who took out that policy. *Fuck*, I wish Gabe was here."

There was a long silence. Cole, standing over the stove, seemed to droop, and I knew we were both thinking of the same thing—how much we missed Gabe, and what an awful, fucked-up situation this was. I wished, more than anything else, that this were just an exercise—with a clear objective, and Gabe muttering instructions into the Bluetooth headset in my ear.

So? a voice said inside my head, a voice that made my heart hurt with how much it sounded like Gabe. *Pretend this is an exercise. What's your objective?*

My objective was . . . well, it was what I'd just told Cole: to find out who'd done this to Gabe and expose them. That had always been my objective. It was why I'd run from the police station in the first place—because a target on my own back didn't matter, *if* it meant I was free to hunt Gabe's killer to ground.

No shit, Cross. What's your immediate objective?

That sounded like Gabe all right. Always asking the tricky questions. Because that one was undeniably tougher. My immediate objective was to figure out who had taken out that insurance policy. But I had no idea how to do it. I could call the company up—but I wasn't sure how much more information that would get me. Almost certainly, all they would be able to give out over the phone would be details that I already had from the policy documents, and if someone had told them about Gabe's death, possibly not even that. If *only* I

had access to the original files—there must be additional information on there, card details, for example, or call recordings. Someone
must have paid for that policy—who? If Gabe were here, I was certain
that together we could have hacked our way into the company files—
but hacking was his area. I really didn't have the first clue how to go
about getting remote access to a secure database. My speciality was
buildings—physically getting into places. But—

And then it came to me. If I could get into the offices of Sunsmile Insurance Ltd., then I wouldn't need to do any hacking. I could
just log into their database like a regular employee. And getting into
places I wasn't supposed to be—that *was* my job.

For the first time it felt like I had a plan, and I felt a little flicker of
something that might have been . . . was it hope?

"Cole," I said—and then I stopped. I wasn't sure why. Cole had
turned around from the stove, and now he looked at me.

"Yes?"

"Never mind," I said. I didn't know why I didn't want to tell him
my thoughts. I only knew that what I was about to do was dangerous,
and I didn't want anyone pouring cold water over the idea before it
was even half formed. If I was going to do this, I had to hold on to that
sliver of hope. It was the only one I had.

Cole picked up the hot pan and carried it carefully over to the
kitchen table.

"Hold your top up," he said. "This might hurt."

I nodded, and he dipped the washcloth into the pan, then dabbed
gently at the cut on my side.

It did hurt. It hurt a *lot*. A hell of a lot more, in fact, than it had
done just two days ago when I washed it out in the hostel bathroom.
When the skin was clean, Cole dabbed on some antiseptic cream he'd
found in the bathroom cabinet and then taped another dressing in
place, and I let out a shuddering breath.

"How does that feel?" Cole asked, looking at me with an expression halfway between worry and exasperation.

"Better," I said, though I wasn't honestly sure if it was true. I felt sick and wrung out, and the wound was stinging like a bastard. And the pan of water in Cole's hands was worryingly red. How much blood was I losing? But there was something comforting about having a clean dressing, and even the stinging sensation of the cream was sort of reassuring—in a *no pain, no gain* kind of way.

All of a sudden I felt immensely tired, and the sofa bed, with its soft mattress and knitted throw, was irresistibly tempting.

"We should get some sleep," I said, and Cole nodded.

"Good night, Jack." He blew out the candle on the table, and I tucked the spare dressings and cream into my rucksack and zipped my fleece back up.

"Good night, Cole."

Then I climbed onto the sofa bed, turned down the oil lamp, and lay down.

The fire had died down to glowing embers, and I listened more than watched as Cole pulled himself inside the sleeping bag, the synthetic fabric rustling.

There was the momentary glow of his phone screen as he checked the time, and then he turned in the darkness, his back towards me, and I heard him sigh.

THURSDAY, FEBRUARY 9

MINUS THREE DAYS

I opened my eyes. A thin gray moonlight was trickling through the curtains, and Cole was snoring on the hearth rug in front of the now-dead fire. The wound under my ribs hurt, and I was very cold, but I was also certain that neither of those things was what had woken me. Something else had prodded me from sleep.

Gabe had always said that what made me a great pen tester wasn't my physical skills. It wasn't that I was faster, stronger, quicker at picking locks, or more daring at scaling walls. There were plenty of guys more capable of forcing doors, or women with fancier kit. No. What had saved me, time and time again, what had made me a wickedly good shoplifter back in the day, was that I noticed stuff—stuff that other people didn't—and that I trusted my gut.

The blind spot in the cameras. The pause in a security guard's footsteps. The tag that could be deactivated with a ballpoint pen.

I had noticed something—before I was even fully awake. I just wasn't sure what.

For a few minutes I lay there, listening, trying to work out what it was that had made me startle awake, my heart already racing before I had opened my eyes.

It wasn't Cole getting up to use the toilet. It wasn't thunder—the weather outside was still, and through the crack between the curtains I could see nothing but calm whiteness—presumably the sea mist had rolled in again overnight.

And then I heard it—the sound that had propelled me into consciousness even before I'd fully recognized what it was.

A burst of static from a police radio, and a muttered call sign.

Heart pounding, I jolted upright and tiptoed across the bare boards to crouch below the window. Gently parting the curtains, I could see someone—I thought it could be Malik, though I wasn't sure—standing outside the house, speaking very low into a radio. Up the track, an unmarked black car was parked sideways across the road, deliberately blocking in Cole's Mazda, and further away I could see the glow of headlamps through the mist, twisting and turning with the narrow lane as another car closed in.

Whoever was outside must be waiting for reinforcements. I *had* to get out, before they surrounded the house.

A huge, sick wash of adrenaline coursed through me, but I pushed it down and instead concentrated on scooping my belongings into my rucksack with shaking hands. It was extremely cold—my breath was coming in white clouds—but I was too keyed up to feel it, shivering more with nerves than from the chill.

"Cole," I whispered. He was still asleep, snoring peacefully. "Cole, get up, I need the sleeping bag."

"Wha?" he mumbled, turning over, and I felt a rush of furious impatience.

"Get *up*. I need the—never mind." I yanked, trying to pull the sleeping bag off him. For a moment his body came with it—slithering across the rug—but then it jerked free, and I bundled it up as Cole sat upright, blinking and more than a little confused.

"What the f—" he said, his voice at normal volume, and I hissed at him in an agony of fear.

"Shut *up*, there's police, outside. I have to go."

"But—" Cole started, but I was already grabbing my rucksack and peering through the rear windows of the cottage. There was only one door, but at the back there were two large windows, one of which opened above a straight drop onto sand, the other onto what I strongly suspected was a gorse bush. The question was whether I risked the prickles, for the cover, and to break my fall. For a moment I hesitated, unsure. Then I went for the other window—the straight drop. The prospect of cover from the police was tempting, but the landing would probably make a noise, and if I got tangled in the bush I might never get out. The idea of flailing there painfully, twigs cracking, trying to stifle the sounds of pain as the thorns pricked me . . . it wasn't appealing.

The window gave a squeal as I pushed it up, and I winced, holding my breath. But there was no sign from the front of the property that anyone had heard, and I dropped my rucksack gently out of the window and then climbed after, lowering myself down the side of the shack with my feet braced against the wooden shingles, until I was hanging full length. The stretch made the area below my ribs screech with pain. I could feel the dressing pulling against the skin and the wound beneath opening up.

I let go, dropping soundlessly to the sand, on all fours as I always did, but this time, in spite of the soft landing, I had to close my eyes, biting my cheek against the pain in my side and waiting for the hot throbbing to recede.

I was just straightening up, one hand pressed to my ribs, when I heard the sound of an engine and the crackle of tires on tarmac coming from the front of the cottage. The reinforcements were here.

Drawing a deep breath, I shouldered my pack and began to run, into the mist.

I had no real idea where I was going, only that I was heading through the dunes, away from where the taxi driver had dropped me off. It was ridiculously hard, running through the shifting sand—the rise and fall of the dunes was almost impossible to see in the mist and darkness, and I was glancing over my shoulder for pursuers when I ran almost full pelt into something that stopped me short with a jolt.

Shit. *Shit.*

Barbed wire. My nemesis.

It looked to be the remnants of some long-forgotten fence, perhaps, coiling up out of the soft sand like a weed, and it had tangled itself in my shoes and jeans, hooking into the loose fabric and the skin beneath. I couldn't rip myself free without losing a chunk of flesh. Carefully, cursing my inattentiveness and the farmer for not picking up his fucking debris, I began to uncoil the strands.

From behind me I could hear sounds, someone pounding on the front door, raised voices, and when I glanced back, I could see the headlamps of a car piercing the mist, and something else—something smaller—the swing of a torch beam, perhaps. I unhooked another coil. I was almost free.

And then I heard it, a voice, maybe through a loudspeaker, though I wasn't sure.

"Jack!" It was a woman's voice. "Jack, it's DS Malik. We know you're out there, you've got nowhere to run. You need to turn yourself in."

I shut my eyes for a second. How. How the fuck had they found me? Had they tracked Cole's car?

I ripped the last coil off my shoe and began to run again, my feet silent in the damp sand but my heart and breath sounding painfully loud in the predawn hush. Even the waves seemed to have quietened.

"Turn yourself in, Jack!" Malik called. Was it my imagination, or was her voice closer? "You're innocent, we know that—this is all a big misunderstanding. We've spoken to your sister and she explained everything. We just want you to come home and clear it all up, clear your name and help us catch Gabe's killer."

A sob rose in my throat. I wanted—God, I wanted more than anything—to believe that was true, to believe that they really did think I was innocent. But you didn't send two squad cars after an innocent person in the middle of the night.

"You can't keep running, Jack," Malik's voice came again, and now I could see torch beams in the darkness, slicing through the mist like white light sabers. "We're tracking your phone. We know your location. I'm giving you the chance here to turn yourself in. Things are going to look much worse for you if you keep running!"

I thought I was innocent?

I almost wanted to shout it back to her, the bait-and-switch was so laughably transparent. But I didn't—I wasn't that stupid, and I couldn't spare the breath for shouting anyway—I needed every scrap of oxygen in my lungs to force myself forward through the dunes.

I ran on. And on. It felt like miles, though in reality it was probably not even one. But running in the dark through soft, shifting sand is no joke, particularly when you can't see the rise and fall of the ground and every step is jarringly unexpected.

After another few hundred meters the muscles in my legs were beginning to ache, the initial bolt of adrenaline wearing off, and the pain in my side was rising with every step. But I had to keep running—I had no other choice. *You can do this*, I thought. *Speed, stamina, strength; this is what you train for*. Except there were half a dozen of them, combing through the mist, and one of me—and my stamina was running out. I would have to stop running at some point. The only question was whether they caught me first.

And then I saw it, looming out of the darkness—a low concrete shack with a metal serving hatch at the front. In the summer it probably sold ice creams and slushies, but right now it looked like a World War II bunker. I glanced back over my shoulder and saw the beam of a torch slicing through the mist, not as far away as I would have liked. For a second I wavered. Keep running—or hide?

My breath was shuddering through my nose, and for an instant I put my hand up, feeling reflexively for the rubber earpiece, to ask Gabe for his advice—but I knew the truth before my hand even touched my bare cheek. I was alone. There was no Gabe here to tell me what to do.

The shutter covering the serving hatch at the front was padlocked from the inside and looked secure. I might have been able to pry it open with a crowbar; I had a small, slim jimmy in my rucksack which would probably have done the job, but it would be hard to force the shutter without making a noise, and impossible to do so without leaving a visible sign of what I'd done—a sign that would lead any pursuer straight to me. Picking the lock of the staff entrance at the back was a better bet, *if* I could do it fast enough. The torch beam was getting worryingly close—and now I could see another coming from the other direction, high up in the dunes ahead of me. They were closing in. Hiding had suddenly become not just the better option but the only option.

But when I rounded the corner of the shack, I saw that there was a door—but no keyhole, just an ancient numerical keypad made of painted metal, and beside it a rusting steel knob. A mechanical combination lock. Fuck. It made sense. The place was probably staffed by a multitude of casual workers, so giving all of them a key would be a headache. It also meant that if the code had four digits, there were exactly ten thousand possible combinations.

"Jack!" I heard from behind me, as if in answer to my misgivings, and my stomach lurched. Whatever I did, I had to do it fast. Doing anything was better than doing nothing. Quickly, I tapped in 1234, just as I had at Arden Alliance, and twisted the metal knob. It had been worth a try then, and it was worth a try now, but just like at Arden Alliance, nothing happened.

Unlike at Arden Alliance, though, the attempt wasn't entirely pointless. Touching the keys had shown me something—two of them felt different from the others. Smoother. Colder. The chipped paint had worn away, exposing the metal beneath. I longed to get out my torch, but I couldn't risk it, so instead I ran my fingers over the whole keypad, closing my eyes to better feel the change in texture. There were five that were perceptibly more worn than the others: 1, 4, 5, 9, and the * sign.

I let out a shaky breath. Four numbers, and an asterisk to finish the combination. That still left twenty-four possible combinations—perfectly doable, given mechanical locks rarely had a cutoff for failed attempts, but still more than I could manage with Malik and her guys combing the darkness behind me—even supposing I could keep track of the combinations in my head.

But I had broken enough combination codes to know two things. First, if asked to set a four-digit combination, a sizable chunk of people chose years. And second, because most people picked dates that were personal to them, that likelihood was doubled when the digits included 1 and 9. The chances were very high that the combination began with 19—which meant that it would be either 1945 or 1954. I had no idea which one was more likely, but it didn't matter. Without pausing to think, I typed in 1954* and twisted the knob so hard the metal gave a quiet shriek. This time, it turned.

The door swung open and I slipped inside, closed it silently, and sank down with my back to the cold metal, my heart thumping hard enough to make me feel sick.

Inside the shack was very quiet, the sound of the sea and the wind muffled by the thick concrete. It smelled of ice cream cones and sour dairy, overlaid with the slight fustiness of defrosted freezers. I was straining my ears for the sound of voices, but it was hard to make out anything above the rushing of my own blood in my ears and the pounding of my pulse.

And then I heard it. Closer than it had ever been before. Very, *very* close.

"Jack!" It was Malik. She sounded angry now, more than angry, furious. "Jacintha Cross, this is a police order. We have dogs on the way, and believe me, you do *not* want to be hunted down by the dogs."

I pressed my face into the pack. There was sand in the stitches where I had dropped it in the dunes. I fought the urge to cough.

And then I heard another voice, a male one. Not Miles but someone else, someone who made my pulse speed up to a sickening pace.

"She outfoxed you?"

It was Jeff.

"That little fucking bitch." It was a low growl of frustration from Malik. "I *saw* her, I'm telling you."

"If you say so." Jeff sounded more amused than annoyed. Then Malik's voice came again, sharper.

"Hang on a sec, what's this place?" There was the scrunch of boots on gravel as they came closer to the shack and stepped onto the concrete apron in front of the counter. I squeezed my eyes shut, as though that could make me somehow less visible. I wished, wished, wished more than anything that I had Gabe's voice in my ear, telling me I could do this. Because right now, I felt like I was about to lose it.

"Reckon she could be in here?"

There was a short silence, and then, shockingly loud, a sudden rattling bang as someone—maybe Malik—tried the shutter over the serving hatch, considerably less gently than I had.

"It's padlocked," I heard from Jeff. "Any signs of forced entry?"

"I don't think so." There was more rattling as someone, probably Malik, examined the edges of the shutter, but I knew they were solid. "Let's try round the back."

More scrunching. I felt bile rise in my throat and swallowed it down, hard. I had a sudden, sharp memory of hiding under the sofa at Arden Alliance while the security guards hunted outside, but I had never felt this scared on a job.

"Combination lock," I heard, more muffled this time; the door was evidently thicker than the shutter. Then a series of clicks as someone did the same as I'd done, jabbing random buttons. I pressed my face even harder into the rucksack, trying to still even my breathing. *Please,* please *don't notice the worn keys* . . .

"Fuck," I heard, in Malik's voice, her tone disgusted. "Well, I can't see how she could have got in here."

"I think she'll have doubled back, gone up to the road to try to hitch a lift. She's good with people. Persuasive. It's more her style," Jeff said a little condescendingly. There was an *I know what I'm talking about* edge to his tone. Malik gave an exasperated sigh.

"I'm telling you, she didn't double back. I *saw* something."

"Coulda been a rabbit," Jeff said with a shrug in his voice. Malik made a sound like she was trying not to tell him where to shove the rabbit.

"Well, either way, there's not much we can do until the mist lifts," she said tightly. "Let's fan out, check the road, and then when it gets a bit clearer we can try again."

Behind the metal door, I let out a shuddering breath.

I waited until the sound of their boots fell silent. Then I pulled myself to my feet, opened the door, and peered out the tiniest crack. I wouldn't have put it past Malik to have been waiting, silently, to see if I popped up, like Jeff's rabbit from a hole.

But she was gone. And so was Jeff. There was no one there, just the swirling mist.

I turned up the collar of the coat against the stinging sand, gently closed the door of the shack behind me, and then walked on, into the dark.

It was maybe two, three hours later that I stumbled wearily into the outskirts of Hastings. The sun was only just coming up, and I hadn't dared to hope for an open cafe, but to my amazement, there was one down by the port—not a fancy place, just a diner serving bacon sandwiches and tea to the fishermen and dockworkers. At the counter was a group of workmen who'd stopped off for a complicated order of hot drinks and breakfast baps.

As I stood behind the foreman in the queue, I felt my legs shaking with what might have been anything from hunger, to tiredness, to just plain shock.

What I was doing definitely wasn't sensible—I didn't know what Malik's next steps might be, but I'd been seen in a town only a few miles up the coast, and I was wanted for murder. It was surely only a matter of time before my picture was in the paper. The big question was whether the police knew about my hair. Had they found footage of me at the train station? Or were they still operating under the assumption that they were looking for a girl with red hair in an anorak?

Either way, I probably didn't have much time left. But that didn't matter. For the first time in two days, I had an idea of what to do next. It had been forming as I ran through the dunes, thinking over my realization of the night before, pondering how I could infiltrate Sunsmile without getting caught. Normally for a job like this, a big job, breaking into a company full of sensitive details, Gabe and I would have done weeks of phishing, cracking, and OSINT—gathering both covert and open-source information from all the places we could until we had a clear picture of who to target and how to get in.

I didn't have weeks. I might not even have days. I didn't have access to Gabe's library of hacking tools, password rippers, and Trojan horse programs. And if I got caught, I would have no get-out-of-jail-free card, no head of security to bail me out. But I *did* have a plan.

A prickle of excitement ran through me—and then I realized that I had reached the head of the line, and the server was standing with her arms crossed, waiting for my order. I bought a cup of tea and a toasted teacake and asked for the Wi-Fi password. Then I found an empty table and fired up my computer.

The first thing I did was what I almost always did when choosing a target. I went to Instagram and searched for any posts geotagged to Sunsmile Insurance Ltd. The head office was in Milton Keynes, and luckily the employees were an Instagram-savvy bunch who loved taking pictures. More importantly, Sunsmile was a big company. Small places, where the security guards knew every single member of every team, were something of a nightmare. But Sunsmile looked to have several hundred employees—and that was just the ones on social media.

I scrolled down the posts, page after page of them, taking down possible names, clicking through to profiles. I was looking for two things: women of about my age, ideally not too physically dissimilar from me, and holiday snaps. There was one more thing I was keeping an eye out for—a picture featuring a security pass—but that seemed like too much to hope for, so I wasn't holding my breath on that one. Firms had got much better about not letting employees post their passes, in part because of people like me telling them about the risks.

Somewhat to my astonishment, however, it was that which came up first: a man holding up his brand-new employee pass and grinning broadly. "First day nerves LOL!" read the caption.

I clicked through and enlarged the image. Oh, Brian from Finance. You lovely, lovely idiot.

He'd had the sense at least to obscure part of his real name, but that didn't matter for my purposes. I screenshotted the pass and saved it to my downloads, then went back to looking for likely targets.

Again and again I found people who seemed perfect—right age, right height as far as I could tell; some of them even looked like me—but when I clicked through, their feed showed them safely in the UK. And then I found her. Keeleybab2001, Sunsmile call center operator. Not holiday snaps—but something better: a photo of a baby covered in small red spots. The caption showed a horrified blue-faced scream emoji, and read "Poor lil bubs has chickenpops!!!"

I clicked through. Keeley Winston. Fortunately, she also had a Facebook profile with very slack privacy settings, and a quick scan of it gave me her date of birth, current whereabouts (Milton Keynes), and where she'd been to school (also Milton Keynes).

All I needed now was her phone number. Luckily, I was just getting started.

I took a long gulp of tea as I scrolled down Keeley's Facebook friends list, then picked a random contact called Katie who had commented on a fair number of Keeley's posts. It was the work of five minutes to set up a Twitter account using Katie's name and profile pic. Finding my next target was a little harder. I needed a mutual Facebook friend of both Katie and Keeley—whose Twitter DMs were open. Keeley's Facebook friends weren't much for Twitter, and I hit a blank wall again and again—until finally finding Gemma, PR manager for Wilkinstone's Travel. DMs open with the line "Hit me up for travel tips, tweeps!"

I clicked the little envelope and began composing my DM.

"Hey Gemma, organising a little cheer-up for Keeley—did you know poor little bubs has got the pox?!—but lost her number for the courier. Can you resend? Don't want to spoil the surprise Kx"

The message came back seconds later.

"Hi Katie, that is so nice!!! 0744 956 7652. Can I paypal you something for it?"

"No, all good," I wrote back. "Ur the best!"

Then I shut down Twitter and opened up Photoshop.

*   *   *

SOME TWO HOURS LATER I left the print shop in Hastings with Keeley Winston's brand-new Sunsmile employee pass in my pocket. It wasn't the best bit of forgery I'd ever done—printing the mockup directly on one of the card blanks in my rucksack would have been more convincing, but the print shop didn't have the facility to do that, so I'd had to make do with printing on shiny paper and then gluing the paper to the card. When I'd finished it looked okay—not good enough to withstand any kind of close scrutiny, but okay. But to be honest, if I got as far as being properly suspected, I was toast anyway. I was hoping to get away with just a casual glance—and at a casual glance it looked identical to Brian's, only with Keeley's name and my photo in place of his.

When I looked at my phone, I saw it was ten past ten. I had two options—and both had risks attached. I could try to phish Keeley's computer password now, or I could wait until I was actually inside Sunsmile Insurance.

If I tried now, I would be going to Milton Keynes safe in the knowledge that I had the information I needed to see the job through.

But I didn't have the equipment required to spoof a number, and a call from a random unknown mobile was much less convincing than one coming from her own company. If Keeley didn't rise to the bait, I would have to start again from scratch—find someone else away from the office today, get their number, fake their ID. And I was running out of time.

The problem was that the alternative was, in some ways, even riskier—to wait until I was actually inside Sunsmile, and try for the final piece of the puzzle then. If I failed at that point, if Keeley saw through my bluff, then I was sunk. More than sunk, in fact—if Keeley realized what I was trying to do, there was a good chance someone would be waiting for me at the Sunsmile reception with a team of security, as I tried to leave the building.

Yes, the second option was riskier—much riskier. But it also had a higher chance of succeeding. And so it was the one I was going to take.

I GOT OFF THE TRAIN at Milton Keynes at just past one p.m. I had left Noemie's camel coat balled up in the train toilets, and now I was wearing what I hoped was call center–appropriate clothing—dark blue jeans, a white T-shirt, and a dark jacket. I felt keyed up, sick with nerves, and the dressing beneath my rib was throbbing in time with my thudding heart, but aside from that I felt . . . well, I felt better than I had in days, to be honest. I felt like I was back in my comfort zone, on a job—a job that I couldn't afford to fail, to be sure, but how many times before had I felt like that? This was a pen test—just like any other. And I was very, very good at my job.

I was maybe five minutes away from the Sunsmile building when my phone beeped. It was a Signal message from Hel.

"Hey, are you okay? Didn't hear from you yesterday," she'd written. I felt a wash of serotonin, mixed with the strong feeling that this wasn't the time or place to have a heart-to-heart with Hel.

"I'm okay," I typed back. "Had a close shave last night—haven't really slept—but I'm on the track of something big. Might be the first bit of good news for days."

"WHAT?!" Her answer came through immediately, vibrating with excitement.

"I have a lead," I typed. "On the insurance policy. I can't talk now. I'll message as soon as I'm out."

"Wait, are you there right now??!!?!" Hel typed back, with an uncharacteristic number of exclamation marks.

"Yep," I replied.

Hel responded with a single shocked-face emoji. Then, "Be careful! Keep me posted. Over and out."

I shut down the app. Then I turned the corner—and the Sunsmile complex was sprawling in front of me.

THE BUILDING WAS EVEN BIGGER than it had looked from the photos on Instagram, and I felt a prickle of intimidation as I walked up to the glass door, but I pushed it open with what I hoped looked like confident familiarity. People were coming back from lunch, and I'd been crossing my fingers for the kind of glass security barriers that swung open or slid back like lift doors—they were fantastically easy to tailgate through. But unfortunately, Sunsmile had gone old school with metal turnstiles, the kind they'd had at the municipal swimming pool when I was a kid.

They were also annoyingly effective, and there was no way I could squeeze through with another employee without getting done for sexual harassment. I was going to have to blag it.

I walked up to the barrier with as much confidence as I could muster and didn't break stride as I swiped my plastic card on the reader. The jolt as the turnstile failed to unlock jarred my rib so hard I had to suppress a gasp, and the metallic clang was audible over at the reception desk. What I wanted to do was wince and press my hand to my throbbing side, but instead I looked down at the swipe card I was holding, keeping my expression mild and puzzled.

Then I tried again, this time pushing the barrier more cautiously with my hand. A small queue was building up behind me, people coming back from lunch, diverting past me with sighs to the other turnstiles as they realized what had happened.

"Mine went blank the other day," one of the girls said. "You'll have to get Derek to swipe you through."

Derek. If I'd had time to send up a silent prayer of thanks to a God I didn't believe in, I would have done.

"Derek!" I called across now, to the security guard standing behind the front desk. He looked up, his expression inquiring and helpful. "Derek, I'm so sorry—I don't know what's happened. My pass isn't working. Can you beep me through?"

I held it up, deliberately not moving from the turnstile. Don't let him get too close.

"It's . . . Keeley?" I said, putting just the smallest touch of chagrin that he hadn't recognized me into my voice. "Keeley Winston, from the call center?"

Derek peered closer, squinting at the ID from his position behind the desk, and then up at my face. I felt my heart quicken. Now was the moment. If he did actually know Keeley, I was utterly, utterly screwed.

And then he grinned.

"Sorry about that, Keeley," he said, and pressed something under the desk. "Don't keep it too close to your credit cards, yeah?"

"Oh, shoot. I didn't know that." I made a face, miming regret at my own stupidity. "Thanks, Derek."

And then the turnstile unlocked, and I was through.

I WALKED CONFIDENTLY FOR THE first few minutes, following the crowd of people, and then allowed myself to fall back from the cohort who had come through reception with me, waiting for a new group of lunchtime returnees to catch up. When I was satisfied that no one near me was part of the cohort I had come through the turnstiles with, I tapped a nice-looking girl on the arm.

"I'm so sorry, I'm an IT contractor and I'm supposed to be working on someone's machine in the call center, but I've got totally lost. Can you point me in the right direction? The person I'm looking for is Keeley Winston."

The girl laughed, but not unkindly.

"Oh God, yeah, it's a bit of a maze, isn't it? The call center is third floor, over in C wing. Take that lift over there. I'm afraid I'm not sure where her desk is, but someone up there will be able to point you in the right direction."

I nodded my thanks and hurried away up the corridor to the lift. But when I stepped inside and pressed the button for the third floor, nothing happened, and I realized to my dismay that it was swipe-card protected.

I stepped out of the lift and stood for a moment, considering my options. I had my rucksack with me, more for want of a place to leave it than because I'd particularly wanted to bring it—it was a little too big to look right as a commuter bag, but I'd had no choice. Now I was extremely glad.

Ducking behind a convenient potted plant, I dug in the pack and pulled out the sling I kept balled at the bottom for emergencies like these, then looped it over my head and put one arm, my right, into it. In my left, I held the rucksack, since I now couldn't wear it on both shoulders. Then I straightened up and pressed the lift button again, praying that it wouldn't arrive empty this time. My luck held. A kindly-looking guy in his late forties was already inside.

"Going up?" he asked as I stepped inside, and I smiled and nodded, and then began patting my pockets, miming hunting for my pass, almost dropping the rucksack as I did, and wincing as if the jolt had jarred a sprained wrist.

"Let me," the man said swiftly, and reached forward with his employee pass, touching it to the card reader. "Which floor?"

"Three. Thank you so much. I am *so* fed up of this wrist. I'm never ice skating again."

"I sprained my shoulder playing squash last year," the man said conversationally as the lift began to rise. "Absolute pain in the . . . well, I was going to say arse, but that's the wrong end, ha ha!"

I laughed, and the lift stopped at the second floor.

"Well, this is me," he said. "Hope the wrist is better soon." And he stepped out.

"Nice to meet you," I said with a grateful smile that was considerably more real than my sprained wrist. And then, as the lift door closed behind him, I shrugged hastily out of the sling, straightened my shoulders, and prepared for the final hurdle.

*   *   *

WHEN I STEPPED OUT OF the lift doors on the third floor, my first impression was that the Sunsmile call center was like every other office I'd ever pen tested, but louder and larger. A small labyrinth of desks and pods stretched away in a complex hierarchy that encompassed hot-deskers, people with little glassed-in booths, and the favored elite few with access to a door that shut and a window with real daylight.

The level of chatter was insane, and I fought the urge to put my hands over my ears as I wove my way among the booths, looking for someone kind to ask. At last I picked a girl who'd just put down her phone and was midway through the act of dialing someone else. Busy people were always the best—too distracted to ask the right questions.

"I'm so sorry," I said apologetically. "I can see you're tied up, but can you point me in the direction of Keeley Winston?"

"Keeley?" the girl said vaguely. "Think she's off sick, but her desk's over there." She pointed towards the corner of the floor. "Can't miss it, it's plastered with gonks."

For a minute I thought I'd misheard.

"Sorry, did you say . . . gonks?"

But the girl was talking into her headset again, and so I shook my head and moved away, towards the corner she'd indicated. Keeley must have been reasonably senior, because she had a half booth *and* a window—and when I drew closer, I saw what the girl had meant. The little booth was full of what I supposed must be the "gonks" she had referred to—little troll dolls with fluffy upswept hair and grinning faces. There were girl gonks and boy gonks, baby gonks and granny gonks. The effect was deeply unsettling and somehow also made me want to laugh—but I couldn't do that right now.

Instead, I sat down in Keeley's chair, fired up her computer, and looked around. What I'd been hoping for was the lottery win of pen testing—a password written on a Post-it and stuck to the monitor—but if Keeley did write down her passwords, she wasn't stupid enough to leave them in plain sight. Instead, I picked up the phone, took a deep breath, and dialed the number Gemma had given me. It rang. And rang. And rang . . .

I was on the point of giving up, sick with disappointment, when there was a click and the phone was picked up. Instantly I heard a baby wailing on the other end, and my heart lifted. The only thing better than someone busy was someone busy and distracted.

"Hello?" Keeley's voice was brusque and a little worried. "Who is this?"

I took a deep breath. *Do not fluff this.*

"Hi, Keeley," I said, making my voice as warm and professional as I could. "Sorry, you're probably wondering why it's your own number calling you! This is Kate from IT. There seems to be a problem with some of the computers—bit of malware's got into the system somehow—so we're having to do a manual scan on the affected machines. I've been trying to catch you all week and it's getting . . . well, it's pretty urgent, to be honest. I'm at your desk right now, is there any chance you could pop up and log me in?"

"Well, I don't know how it could have been me." She sounded a little defensive. "I've been off all week with Harry. He's got chicken-pops."

Pox, I thought but didn't say. Cardinal rule of phishing: Do not piss off your target.

"Oh, what a nightmare!" I said instead, filling my voice with sympathy. "I've got twin boys and they both had it a couple of months ago. I swear, I didn't sleep for a fortnight."

"Oh my God, tell me about it," Keeley said ruefully, and I could tell from the change in her tone that I'd succeeded in making a connection. "Bloody nightmare, isn't it." The wailing in the background intensified. "Look, Kate, sorry, this isn't a great—"

"Oh, totally, of course," I said. "Shit—I hate to drag you into the office for something that's not your fault, but I *have* to run this scan. It's a security issue."

"I can't come in!" Keeley sounded alarmed. "There's no one else who can take him. My mum's doing chemo; her doctor said she can't have him until the spots scab over."

"Look," I said confidentially, with the air of someone making up their mind. I lowered my voice. "This isn't completely . . . I mean, we're not supposed to do it this way, but I can see you're in a tricky situation. Do you want to give me your password and I'll do the scan without you coming in? Just—don't tell my boss. We're *really* not supposed to do this."

"Oh God, sure," Keeley said, the relief in her voice palpable. "They're all on my Rolodex under Harry Winston, but the main one is Harry24Sept. God, thank you *so* much, Kate. I really appreciate you doing this. I'm sorry, I would have come in if I possibly could, but—you know what it's like."

"Yeah, blokes don't get it, do they? My boss thinks I can just drop anything. I'm like, it doesn't work that way, dude!"

Keeley gave a shaky laugh and the wailing rose again in the background.

"Look, I'll let you go," I said warmly. "Take care, Keeley. Make sure you get some sleep too!"

"Thanks, yeah, I'd better go, Harry's kicking off World War Three. Take care, Kate. Bye."

"Bye!" I said brightly, and there was a click and the phone went dead.

I resisted punching the air in triumph, logged into the computer, and while it booted up, turned to the card marked *Harry Winston* on Keeley's Rolodex.

It was a treasure trove. Passwords to every single system neatly logged with not even the barest attempt at disguising them.

I closed my eyes, sending up a silent prayer of thanks to overly complex IT systems with unmanageable numbers of passwords and to distracted parents everywhere, and began trying to figure out the call-handling database.

The hard part was working out which icon on Keeley's very crowded desktop was the relevant one, and I had several false starts with a car insurance database and something that seemed to be some kind of employee intranet—but at last I fired up one that displayed a home screen with the Sunsmile logo and the legend *Sunsmile Life Insurance—a friend for life.* Pressing the search icon took me to a screen that said *Search by customer ID number, policy number, name, postcode.*

My heart was thumping as I typed in our postcode.

Three policies came up. Two were for people I'd never heard of—presumably neighbors who happened to have policies under Sunsmile. But the third—the third was the most recent, and it was Gabe's.

My fingers were shaking as I clicked through and scrolled down the customer record. There were copies of everything. The forms submitted, the payment receipts. I clicked onto the credit card they had stored on file, mentally crossing my fingers for a smoking gun. I'm not sure what I was expecting—a card registered to Jeff Leadbetter seemed like too much to hope for—but my heart sank when I saw the details. It was Gabe's name, Gabe's card, in fact; I recognized the number. It didn't make sense. Gabe was careful about his credit card details. It wasn't impossible he'd been phished, but that just didn't seem like Jeff. But then I clicked through to the ID section, and there, right in front of my eyes, was a scan of Gabe's driving license. And *that* stumped me. I could not imagine Gabe uploading his license anywhere apart from a real, kosher, secure site with a genuine need for his photo ID. Had I got this all wrong? Had Gabe *really* taken out this policy after all?

I scrolled down the page, looking for something, *anything* to give me a clue, but only one thing seemed out of place—the phone number attached to the record. It wasn't Gabe's number. But it wasn't Jeff's number either—or at least, not the one he'd had when we were together. I didn't recognize it at all. I wrote it down on a Post-it that

Keeley had thoughtfully left beside her monitor and put it in my pocket. A phone number wasn't much of a lead, but it was something. Maybe I could call it when I got out of here.

I was just about to X out of the database when I saw it, right down at the bottom of the screen—a small icon like a speaker. *Call Records* said the header. And there was one single date-stamped entry, from just over a week ago—three days before Gabe's death, in fact.

My heart started thumping again.

A phone call. An actual phone call. With whoever had set this policy up. And I had almost missed it.

There was a headset resting on the desk, and I picked it up and settled it over my ears, then clicked on the recording. I was fizzing with nerves, biting the inside of my lip so hard my teeth almost met in the soft skin. For a second nothing happened—just a whirling "loading" icon. And then a woman's voice came over the headphones.

"Hello, could I speak to Mr. Gabriel Medway?"

"Who is this?" said a man's deep voice.

I felt a rush of shock—swiftly followed by a sense of crushing defeat. Because it wasn't Jeff. It was nothing like him. It was far too deep—much more like . . . a feeling of dread was pooling in the pit of my stomach. It sounded much more like Gabe, in fact.

Oh God. Had I got this all wrong?

I had paused the call, my finger jerking reflexively on the mouse at the sound of a voice I hadn't been expecting, but now I rewound it to the beginning and started the recording again, this time steeling myself for the man's voice.

"Who is this?"

This time, even though I'd been expecting them, the words felt like a stab to the heart. Because it sounded like it *could* be him. I wasn't *absolutely* certain, though. The woman was coming through crystal clear, but the recording at the man's end wasn't brilliant. The line was crackly and his voice was distorted. I turned up the volume a notch and closed my eyes, trying to filter out all the call center distractions and focus on nothing but the sound of the voice in my ears.

"This is Jo from Sunsmile, Mr. Medway, you were in touch about setting up a policy with us? We just needed to clarify one point, it's regarding—"

"I'm sorry, could you email me about this?" said the other speaker, rather brusquely. He sounded rattled and annoyed at being called. "This isn't a good time."

And suddenly I was sure, absolutely sure, with a rush of relief that made my fingertips tingle: this *wasn't* Gabe. It was very like Gabe, very similar indeed—the same deep voice, even the same London accent. Almost anyone else might have been fooled. But I *knew* Gabe. His voice had accompanied me night after night, year after year, whispering in my ear for hours with encouragement, instruction, jokes, warnings. And although there was nothing I could put my finger on, nothing I could take to the police as a certainty, I was certain of one thing: The person on the other end of the line *wasn't* Gabe. Not in a million years.

"Of course, if you prefer," said the woman pleasantly, "but this really will only take a moment. It's just—"

There was a click, and the call ended.

I heard the woman sigh.

"And a nice day to you too, sir," she said, a little sarcastically to the dead air. And then the recording stopped.

My heart was thudding like a drum in my chest, so hard I could hear it in my ears.

I resettled the headphones, cupped one hand over my ear to shut out as much of the background noise as possible, and squeezed my eyes shut.

Then I turned up the volume as high as it would go and pressed play again.

I'm sorry, could you email me about this? This isn't a good time.

Again.

I'm sorry, could you email me about this.

I'm sorry, could you

I'm sorry

I'm sorry

I'm sorry

And then—I don't know how, but—I knew.

I heard the clatter as the mouse slid from the desk and fell to the floor.

I sensed the drag of the chair's castors against the carpet tiles as I pushed it back from the desk and stood on unsteady legs.

I felt the shake in my hands as I shut down Keeley's computer and flipped her Rolodex back to *A*.

But inside—inside I felt strangely numb. Inside I felt nothing at all.

"Are you okay?" a girl at the next desk said to me as I walked away. "Were you looking for Keeley? She's off sick with her kid."

"Yes, I know," I said. My face felt strangely hot and cold. I gripped the strap of my rucksack to stop my hands from trembling. "I'm from IT, I was just updating some patches on her machine while she was off. All done now."

It was an effort to form the words, but the girl didn't seem to notice. She simply nodded and went back to her next call.

I felt like screaming, but I couldn't. I had to get out of here, I had to figure out what to do. I had to figure out *why*.

Because the voice on the end of the recording, the voice I had listened to again and again and again . . . that voice was Cole's.

And I couldn't even begin to process what that meant.

My legs felt weak as jelly as I retraced my steps back through the maze of Sunsmile offices and meeting rooms, towards the main entrance. My heart was thudding, and I could think of only one thing. I had to get out of here and call Hel, tell her what I had discovered. Because it made no sense. Cole? *Cole?*

I was almost at reception, fishing in my pocket for my phone, when I rounded the final corner and saw them—a group of security men huddled around a screen behind the front desk. There were three of them, plus a guy in a suit who looked more like some kind of manager, and they looked worried. One of them was pointing to something on what I was horribly sure was a security monitor. Another was talking to Derek, the guard who had buzzed me in earlier. Derek had his hands raised defensively, as if making a counterargument to some kind of claim.

All the feeling seemed to drain out of me. Something was wrong. Something was very, very wrong. But how? I hadn't slipped up, had I? No one had challenged me. I hadn't noticed any suspicious looks from anyone in the call center, and I could *swear* that Keeley hadn't clocked anything during our phone call.

I had two choices now: barrel through reception at speed hoping nobody registered me, or back away. I was hesitating—after all, the altercation might be nothing to do with me—when a sound from outside caught my ear and sent my pulse racing even faster. It was the short *whoop-whoop* of a police siren, as a patrol car pulled up in the hatched "no waiting" box outside the office and turned on its blue lights.

Maybe they weren't here for me. But it was starting to look very much like they were, and I wasn't waiting around to find out.

I turned and hurried away, back into the building. I was looking for fire exit signs, but naturally all the ones in this area pointed back to reception, so I ignored them and began half walking, half jogging deeper into the Sunsmile complex. I had a strange feeling in my chest— panic, yes, but mixed with a kind of exhilaration, the pulse of adrena- line that always accompanied me on a job when things got tough. My hand went automatically to my ear again, feeling for the Bluetooth ear- piece, but of course, just as before, there was nothing there. It was like a physical reminder of Gabe's absence—I was on my own.

I was trying to put some hasty distance between myself and reception, while still keeping to a pace that looked plausibly like that of an office worker who'd forgotten she needed to pick up little Fred- die from nursery. Not sprinting. No one sprints in an office. But a kind of stressed half-run. The stressed part was easy at least. What was harder was keeping myself from breaking into a full-speed dash. I could almost hear Gabe in my ear: *Don't make yourself conspicuous, babe. Try to blend in.*

I am fucking trying, I thought. But I would have growled it with more conviction if Gabe had really been there. When I reached a deserted stretch of corridor, I shrugged off the dark jacket and fished in my bag for the pair of fake glasses I'd packed earlier—thick black frames that were hard to miss. As far as disguises went, it wasn't much, but the two changes together might confuse someone work- ing from a blurry CCTV picture.

At last I was deep enough into Sunsmile that the fire exit signs began pointing a different way—ahead of me into the complex—and now I followed them, glancing over my shoulder as I did to make sure no one was following me. From far behind me I could hear some kind of commotion—but I wasn't sure if it was the security guards or something unrelated. The latter seemed like wishful thinking, but whichever it was, they didn't seem to be on my trail.

I was just starting to feel optimistic when I rounded a corner and saw a guard up ahead, staring down at his phone.

Shit.

He hadn't seen me, he was too busy reading whatever was on his screen, but my imagination was already filling in the blanks. A text with my description. Maybe even worse—a screenshot from CCTV.

Shit. *Shit.*

At last I made up my mind and ducked into an office. It was empty and I sat at the desk facing the window and kicked my bag hastily into the footwell, then tried to slow my racing heart. The computer wasn't on, but I didn't have time to start it up. Instead, I pulled over some files and picked up the phone.

Above the hum of the dial tone, I could hear footsteps coming up the corridor. *Keep going*, I begged, internally. *Keep going!*

But they didn't. They stopped outside the open door, and I heard a slightly awkward cough.

"Well that's simply not good enough," I snapped into the phone. "We needed those numbers yesterday."

A trickle of sweat ran down between my shoulder blades, and I pressed back into the chair to soak it up.

"I don't know how to put this, Diane, but tomorrow is not Thursday." Unless of course it was. I had totally lost track. I shut my eyes, trying not to let the hand holding the receiver shake too visibly. There was another cough, this time accompanied by a very timid tap on the door. I sighed, put the receiver to my shoulder, and swung the chair around.

"Hello, yes? Can I help you?"

The security guard was standing outside the door, shifting his weight from one foot to the other.

"Sorry to disturb, but can I ask, have you seen any intruders?"

"Any intruders?" I tried to put every ounce of irritation possible into my voice. "I'm sorry, isn't that *your* job? I didn't realize we were delegating company security to account operatives now."

"I'm investigating a disturb—" the guard began diffidently, and I cut in, sharply.

"To answer your question, no, I certainly haven't. The only person who's disturbed me is *you*. Now if you don't mind, I'm in the middle of a very important call." I turned back to the phone, which was now beeping loudly to signal that it was off the hook. "I'm sorry," I said loudly into the receiver, fervently hoping the guard couldn't hear the noise above my one-sided conversation. "Where were we? Oh, yes, the"—*Shit, think of a plausible insurance term. Think, Jack!*— "ROI numbers I asked for. Now the question is, when are you going to stop messing me around and get me the figures? The meeting is *tomorrow*, in case I didn't make that clear enough. Or do you want me to walk in there and explain that the reason I haven't got up-to-date projections is because you couldn't be bothered to comply with a very simple request?"

I shut my eyes, pretending I was screening out the other speaker's excuses, but really trying as hard as I possibly could to listen for the sound of the security guard retreating. I couldn't hear a thing above the noise of the phone beeping in my ear. Was he still there? Did I dare look?

In the end I slammed down the phone as if disgusted, and swung round in my chair, ready to give the security guard a blast that would send him scuttling away—but he was gone.

I slumped back in the chair, feeling all the bravado seep out of me. That had been unbelievably close. A more decisive guard would have called my bluff—or smelled a rat. And if the next visitor was Derek, or one of the guys who had been reviewing the security footage in reception, I was absolutely sunk.

I had to get out of here. *Now.*

I picked up my bag and swung it over my shoulder, ignoring the stab of pain in my side. Then I ran, this time in earnest—in the opposite direction from the one I hoped the guard had taken. I was no longer trying to look plausible. The illusion that this was just any other job had faded. It wasn't. The stakes were much, much higher—and I had never felt fear or fatigue like this on any pen test.

My legs were shaking, but I forced myself on and took a left, following a fire exit sign. As I did, I almost barged into a woman carrying a cup of tea but managed to dodge with a muttered "Sorry!" and then took a right at random, more to get away from the woman's startled gaze than out of any sense of where I was heading.

And then, just as I had begun to think I must have taken a wrong turn and was going to have to double back, I rounded a corner and ran straight into a dead end. Only it *wasn't* a dead end. It was a huge fire door—just not the kind I had been hoping for. No friendly steel bar or informal back exit. This one had a green button behind glass, and a large sign above it reading *This door is alarmed. Do not use except in an emergency.*

I felt sick. Actually, properly sick. It was exactly what I would have told Arden Alliance, if I'd ever actually written that report—you shouldn't be able to sneak around opening up fire doors without setting off some kind of alarm. Now, just when I didn't want to, just when the stakes were highest, I had found a company that was doing the right thing. There was a slim possibility that the sign was a fake, to stop people nipping out for a sneaky cigarette—but somehow I doubted it. That button looked like it meant business.

Either way, there was nothing else for it. From behind me, further up the corridor, I could hear the growing sounds of voices, walkie-talkie call signs, and heavy footsteps. Whether the diffident guard *had* smelled a rat, or whether the woman with the tea had raised an alarm, it was clear security had figured out my route and were closing in.

I *had* to get out of here, even if it meant triggering mayhem. And actually . . . maybe a bit of mayhem wouldn't be the worst thing?

The thought gave me a blast of courage, and lifting my foot, I kicked with my heel at the glass covering the button. My first kick missed, but on my second try the glass shattered. I took a deep breath, pressed the button—and nothing happened.

The adrenaline drained out of me. I simply stood there, staring in stunned disbelief, listening to the sound of voices from up the corridor. There was no alarm—but the door itself remained resolutely closed.

This *had* to be a mistake. Surely? An unalarmed fire exit was inadvisable. A nonworking one was flat-out illegal.

The footsteps were very close indeed.

I raised my hand, ready to press the button again. But before I could, the door swung outwards with a slow, stately heaviness, leaving me blinking in the bright afternoon sun, and what sounded like a thousand fire alarms began screeching out across the complex.

For a moment I had no idea what to do. People started pouring out of offices to my left and right, shrugging on coats, swinging handbags over their arms in spite of strict instructions to leave everything, and grumbling to their colleagues about the interruption. And then, I realized—these people were my camouflage, my ticket to freedom.

Hauling my rucksack higher up on my shoulder, I lifted my chin, and trying my best to look as pissed off as possible, I walked out into the sunshine with the rest of them. As soon as I was around the corner, I began to run.

Twenty minutes later I skidded, panting, into Milton Keynes station, my hand pressed to my aching side, not even trying to hide my scarlet face and heaving chest. Partly because there was no way I could—I was too exhausted to even attempt to look fine—and partly because a train station is about the only place you *can* look like you're fleeing police without raising suspicion.

At the ticket barrier I stood, wheezing, one hand braced against the machine as I searched with the other in my pockets for the return half of my ticket. Thank God it was still there. I was trembling so much that it took three tries to feed it into the narrow slot, and then the barrier opened and I passed through, and sank down onto a bench at the side of platform 1, trying to look like someone who had just missed their train. In reality I had no idea what I was going to do next.

Every part of my body was shaking with adrenaline, and my side was throbbing with a hot white pain so intense that it was all I could do not to lean over the side of the bench and throw up—if I'd had anything in my stomach since the toasted teacake, I probably would have done. But it wasn't just the pain in my side making me feel sick—I was in even deeper shit than I could possibly have known, and not only that, but *somehow* the police were keeping tabs on me. They had traced me first to Cole's, and now to Sunsmile, and I had no idea how.

I had returned to the station more on instinct than anything else—the urge to get out of Milton Keynes stronger than almost any other. But now I had no idea where I was going or what I was going to do. I couldn't go back to Cole's. I definitely couldn't go to Helena's. What I really wanted was to go home. To have a hot shower, to lie in a soft bed, and to *sleep*. I wasn't sure how much sleep I'd had last night, but it couldn't have been more than a few hours, and since then I'd not had more than snatched moments to rest. Now, as the pain in my side ebbed back to a more manageable but still fairly worrying throb, I felt weak and shivery with exhaustion—my own bed the most seductive thing I could imagine. There was no use longing for it, though. Going home was impossible—even more impossible than going back to Hel's. I might as well sit here longing for Gabe—both he and my normal, everyday existence were gone, far beyond reach.

I was still sitting there, trying to control my breathing, when I heard a commotion behind me in the ticket hall. Glancing over my shoulder, I saw two uniformed officers at the barrier, flashing their warrant cards at the guard on duty.

My heart sped up to an almost sickening pace, and I looked around the platform, trying to figure out my options. Far up ahead I could see a train coming—but to which platform?

Moving casually, trying not to attract attention, I walked quickly down the platform to the overpass, my head down as if checking my phone. In reality every ounce of my attention was focused on the main station entrance behind me. The police officers had passed through now and were spreading out, one moving up the platform towards me, the other talking to some students near the entrance.

My heart racing, I slipped into the shadow of the overpass and began climbing the stairs. As soon as I was out of sight on the covered bridge above the platform, I yanked off the glasses, fumbled in my rucksack for the fleece hoodie, and dragged it over my head. With the hood up I looked, I hoped, completely different from the smart office worker who had blagged her way into the Sunsmile offices—more like a teenage boy than a grown woman.

The train was nearer now, close enough for me to see which line, and glancing up at the board I saw that it was headed for Birmingham, eight minutes behind schedule, and coming in at platform 6. It didn't match my ticket—but that was the least of my worries right now, because unfortunately the train wasn't the only thing getting closer. Peering back over my shoulder down the stairs, I could see that the officer who had followed me had stopped to talk to a woman in a white top and dark jacket and was now heading for the overpass.

I gulped, pulled the hood closer around my face, and jogged across the bridge towards the sign pointing down to platform 6.

"Hey!" I heard behind me, but I didn't stop. I had no idea if the officer was talking to me or someone else, but I wasn't going to wait around to find out. "Hey, son!"

His footsteps were speeding up. Below me the train drew into the station.

Oh God, oh God. Not now—please not now.

My side was throbbing, and I felt like I was going to throw up—but I made my legs work just a little harder as I ran down the steps towards the platform.

"Police!" I heard from behind me. But platform 6 was blessedly crowded, and as I flung myself around the corner at the bottom of the stairs, I found myself face-to-face with a gaggle of teens, all similar heights to me, two also wearing black fleeces with the hood up. I sent up a silent prayer of thanks to the god of teenage boys as the train doors opened, and I shoved my way through, with scant regard for good manners.

Close the doors, close the doors.

Inside, I pushed my way down the crowded aisle and into the next carriage.

As I did, the announcement came over the speaker.

"This is the delayed fifteen thirty-one service to Birmingham New Street, this train is now departing, please stand clear of the doors."

I held my breath, ducking my head to peer out through the window, at the platform. The police officer was standing there, looking irritated, speaking into his walkie-talkie.

And then there was a jolt that made me stagger and press my hand to my side, and we were moving. We were away. But that had been entirely too close for comfort.

As the train drew out of Milton Keynes, I felt the tension go out of my body with a rush that left me weak and trembling, and desperate to sit down. When I had picked up the go bag back in Salisbury Lane I'd congratulated myself on how light it was. Now, even though I'd eaten most of my provisions, it felt like a lead weight on my shoulder. I let it slide to the floor and looked around for a seat. I was trying to decide whether I was better off moving down another carriage or asking the woman opposite to remove her shopping bags from the seat next to her when I felt a trickle of something hot down the side of my stomach. When I slipped my hand up underneath the fleece, my fingertips came out red. The dressing must have come loose with all the running. I was bleeding again.

Shit. The fleece was black, so the bloodstains wouldn't show, but I couldn't afford to bleed onto the train seats or anywhere people might see. If there was one thing that would attract attention, it would be that.

There was a toilet sign over the doorway to the next carriage, so with an effort I pulled the rucksack back onto my shoulder and began squeezing along the aisle, desperately hoping as I pushed past a woman with her baby that I wasn't leaving smears of blood on her pram.

The toilet was the old type with a slam door and a lime-scaled loo which I wouldn't have been surprised to find emptied onto the track. But as I closed the door behind me and slid the bolt across, I wouldn't have cared if it was the toilet out of *Trainspotting*, I was just so thankful that it had a lock that worked, and a tap.

Hooking the rucksack over the back of the door, I pulled off first the hoodie and then my ruined white top, now adorned with a dark red poppy of blood that bloomed across one side.

My first thought, when I examined the dressing, was that it didn't look too bad—the running had just pulled the cut open again, and the blood had soaked through the gauze. Probably all I needed to do was stick on a new one.

But when I peeled off the corner of the soggy square, what I saw underneath made me blench.

The underside of the dressing looked even worse than the one Cole had helped me remove yesterday, soaked with a mixture of blood and what looked worryingly like pus. The wound itself was angry and swollen in a way that even I, someone with zero medical training, could tell wasn't good.

An infection would explain why I was feeling so strange—my legs so weak and jelly-like, my skin running hot and cold—and reluctant as I was to admit that Cole was right, I was starting to think he might be correct; I did need antibiotics. But that was a risk I couldn't take.

In the end I splashed warm water over the skin, flushing away as much of the gunk as I could and trying to ignore the queasy smell that came up from the sink along with the steam. The water stung, but not as much as I would have thought, and the sharp sensation was almost a relief from the constant low-level throbbing which had been gnawing at my side all day.

When the cut was clean, I patted it dry with toilet paper and then stuck on another of the dressings I had stolen from the shopping center. I held it against my ribs, shutting my eyes against the pain as I pressed down, and even through the layers of gauze and paper, I could feel the heat coming off the wound. There was nothing to be done apart from crossing my fingers and trusting to my immune system. Shivering now, I pulled the blood-stained top back over my head, dragged on the fleece, and tried to think what to do.

My ticket wouldn't work on this line—which meant I would somehow have to blag my way out at the other end. That might be easier at a small country station, maybe even one small enough not to have ticket barriers. The only question was where.

I dug in my pocket for my phone, to check the train's stopping points, but before I could open it I saw a Signal notification on the lock screen. It was a message. From Hel.

"Jack?" it read. "Are you there? How did it go?!"

A rush of relief spiked through me. *Hel.* God, I wanted nothing more than to talk to her—I wanted to blurt out this whole tangled mess and get her cool, analytical appraisal of what the fuck was going on and what all this meant.

Was it really possible that *Cole* was responsible for Gabe's death? He hadn't killed him—I was sure of that, or at least, as sure as it was possible to get without having witnessed the murder myself. The shock in his voice when I had told him, the anguish as he had stammered out "They—they cut his *throat*?" That hadn't been fake, I was sure of it. But the insurance—why else would he have taken out the insurance? That wasn't a spur-of-the-moment thing. He must have spent days getting hold of Gabe's ID, his credit card details, filling out forms. That was coldly premeditated in a way that made my head spin, and I couldn't begin to parse what it all meant.

Hel was the one person whose opinion I trusted more than anyone else's in the world—more than Gabe's, in a way, because Gabe was an optimist, and his perspective was always colored by wanting the best for people and believing the best of them. Hel was . . . well, she wasn't a pessimist exactly. But more of a realist. We had been through the same things, survived the loss of our parents when we were barely adults. We had both lost our trust in things turning out okay that night, in a way that Gabe never had. And besides, Gabe was gone.

Because of that, she was the only person who might, just *might*, be able to help me get to the bottom of this. But it wasn't just my own confusion stopping me from replying. There was something else, a feeling which I realized now, looking down at the lock screen, had been dogging me for some time, ever since I messaged Hel before I went into Sunsmile. I hadn't had time to think about it then, but there was something *wrong*. Something . . .

And then it came to me.

In fact, it was staring me in the face with its little round eyes.

Hel's shocked emoji, the one she had sent me two messages ago. And before that, the now-deleted "You go first" message with its uncharacteristic smiley face. Two emojis that she had never used in her texts before.

And something else came to me too—something that made me go first hot and then cold with realization, and then grope my way to the closed toilet lid to sit down before my jelly legs gave way to the rocking motion of the train.

Cole had been the one to tell Hel about Signal.

Cole had given Hel my throwaway number, had told her to message me on a burner phone. Except . . . what if he hadn't? What if this whole thing was a setup? What if the person I had been texting the whole time was . . . Cole?

The thought made me feel almost violated. And yet . . . it explained something that had been preying on me ever since I saw the police at Sunsmile, and which I had not been able to figure out since: how they had known I was there at *that very moment*. That was information I had only given to Hel.

Someone had betrayed me. And I was as certain as I could be that it wasn't Hel.

A nauseous wave of cold dread threatened to swamp me. But I had to be sure.

"Hel," I typed back, "this is going to sound really stupid, but I need to ask you something. What was the name of your childhood teddy? The big blue one?"

There was a long, long pause.

Then, "Jack, is everything okay?"

"It's fine, but I need you to tell me this, Hel. What was his name?"

Another pause.

"Fuck," the reply came back, swiftly this time. "It's bloody years ago. I can't remember. Bluey?"

I felt like I had just touched an electric fence—a jolt of panic so strong I bit the inside of my cheek. If I could have, I would have thrown the phone out of the train window. But it didn't open, and anyway, I couldn't afford to lose it.

There was a knock at the door, but I ignored it. Instead, I stared down at the phone screen in front of me, a mixture of disgust and fear coiling inside me.

"Why?" the message came back. But it was too late. I *knew.*

That teddy bear had been Hel's pride and joy. She had taken him to bed every night for sixteen years—and even then, he wasn't thrown away, just retired, with honors, to a shelf above the wardrobe. He was one of the few things she had taken with her when we cleared our parents' house, and now he sat on top of Kitty and Millie's wardrobe in their room. There was no way, absolutely no way short of a coma, that Hel could have forgotten Bluebell's name. It was engraved in *my* memory, let alone hers—the endless wails of "I've dropped Bluebell!" every night as he fell from the top bunk to the floor; the arguments every holiday over whether she could take him, and if so, whether he had to travel in the suitcase or could be carried in her arms; the terrifying twenty-four-hour scare when he got lost on the underground. The idea that Hel could have forgotten what he was called—well, it was laughable. She would as soon have forgotten Roland's name.

I wanted to cry. But I couldn't.

"I know," I typed back instead. "You can stop pretending."

Another pause.

"I'm sorry?"

"I know," I typed again, and pressed send. Then, "I know, Cole. I know everything."

There was another long, long pause, and then my phone began to ring.

As it did, there came another knock at the door, this one more urgent.

"I've got a desperate toddler out here!" I heard from the other side.

I stood, unhooked the rucksack from the back of the toilet door, and then opened it with an apologetic smile at the scowling woman standing with her little boy in the corridor.

The phone was still ringing as I moved to the far side of the little vestibule. The train lobby was the old-fashioned kind with a window that opened, and in spite of the cold wind blasting through I made no move to shut it. Hopefully the sound would cover our conversation.

I waited until I heard the lock of the toilet door slide shut, and as it clicked, the phone in my hand stopped ringing.

I was about to call back when something occurred to me, and I stopped and dug in my pocket. The Post-it with the number I had taken off the Sunsmile database was still there.

I took a deep breath—and typed it into Signal. Then I pressed call.

"You don't understand." It was Cole's voice, shaking, and for the first time since Gabe's death I didn't feel a rush of pain at how similar they sounded—just disgust, and disbelief at my own stupidity. How could I have thought Cole sounded like Gabe? They were *nothing* alike. *Nothing.*

"Oh, I understand," I said. My own voice was level, almost unnaturally so, with the effort of keeping it low. "I understand everything. Why did you do it, Cole?"

"You don't *understand*, I didn't want this—I didn't want any of this. I was trying to protect you!"

For a second, I couldn't find the words to reply. Then I did, spitting them into the receiver with a force that took even me by surprise.

"Fuck. You."

"You don't know who you're dealing with."

"A fucking lying, traitorous, murdering—" I stopped, searching for a word bad enough for what I wanted to call him. "*Cunt*," I finished, and now my voice wasn't steady, it was trembling almost as much as Cole's. "That's who I'm dealing with. How could you? How could you do it to him? He was your *best friend*."

"He was a fucking fool," Cole said, and there was real agony in his voice. "I tried to warn him off, but he wouldn't let it go. And you think all this is me? It isn't me. I never wanted this. I was doing the only thing I could, which was to try and protect *you*. There was nothing I could do to save Gabe. All I could do was make sure you walked out of this."

"You didn't protect me, you fucking *framed* me, you imbecile," I almost shouted down the phone, and then forced myself to lower my voice to a venomous whisper. "Are you seriously going to stand there and say that taking out that insurance was an act of protection? As if any amount of money could make up for Gabe's death! You didn't protect me, you gave the police a cast-iron case *against* me. Are you trying to tell me you didn't think of that?"

"Of course I thought of that," Cole snarled, "but if you're in prison, they can't murder you too, you stupid bitch."

"Who?" I demanded. "Who? Who are you talking about? Who would want to kill Gabe, who would want to kill *me*?"

"I can't tell you," Cole said, and now the anger and anguish were gone from his voice, and he sounded scared—genuinely scared.

"Cole, I swear to God, I'm recording this conversation, and unless you want me to release it on Twitter, right now, you need to tell me what's going on."

"No!" he yelped, as terrified as if I had brandished a live wire at his face. "Christ, Jack, do you want to get us both killed?"

"Then tell me!"

"They. Will. Kill. Us," Cole said, enunciating each word very slowly and distinctly, as if speaking to a small child. But I had the impression that he was doing so not to patronize me—though that might have been part of it—but to try to keep his own voice from shaking. "Do you understand that, Jack? They will kill me for telling you, and you for finding out."

"I. Don't. Give. A. Fuck," I spat back, matching my tone to his, with angry mockery. "Do you understand *that*, Cole? I'm facing life in prison. I've lost the only man I ever loved. I cannot tell you how little of a shit I give about the idea of someone cutting my throat too. In fact, you know what? At this point it would be something of a relief. The only thing, the *only* thing I care about is finding out who killed Gabe. If that gets me killed too, I honestly don't give a damn."

There was a long silence. A very long silence. I could hear Cole's trembling breaths at the other end of the line. It was clear that, perhaps for the first time, he really understood how far I was prepared to go with this.

"I can't tell you who," he said at last. His voice was very low. "I don't know who—but I can tell you why."

"Okay." It had started to rain now, the drops sliding sideways across the half-open window and spattering my face. I closed my eyes, feeling the coldness drip down my nose. It felt like crying, but it didn't soothe the ache in my heart. "Okay. Why?"

"Fuck," Cole whispered. "Fuck. *Fuck.* Look, can we do this face-to-face?"

"You must be kidding me." I laughed at that, a harsh rasp that jolted my ribs and made me wince. I pressed a hand to the dressing. "So you can hand me over to the police again? That was you who told them I was at Sunsmile, wasn't it? You must have been laughing up your sleeve when I spilled the beans to Hel. And when the police turned up at your cottage—they didn't follow you, did they? It was you, you called it in."

"I was *trying* to protect you," Cole said desperately, and the strange thing was that I could almost, *almost* believe him. "Please, Jack. *Please.*"

But I was done with this.

Cole had betrayed Gabe, and then he had betrayed me too—over and over and over.

"Cole," I said with finality, "I swear, if you don't tell me what you know right this second, I'm going to livestream this conversation to Gabe's Twitter account. I'm going to send it to every Discord group he ever joined, I will post it on Reddit and stream it on Twitch. And I will name *you*, on every single platform. I have no idea how many people that is—but Gabe's Twitter account alone has almost 100,000 followers. I'm pretty sure a bunch of them are *your* followers too. You want them to hear your voice, admitting your complicity in the murder of your best friend?"

"Fuck!" Cole shouted, so loud I had to hold the phone away from my ear. There was a noise at the other end that I couldn't quite decipher. It sounded like he might be sobbing. Then his voice came back, trembling and angry. "Listen to me, Jack. If you pursue this, if you tell *anyone* what I'm about to tell you—"

"You are done threatening me," I said coldly. "And I have no interest in hearing anything from you other than why my husband had to die. So spit it out, or get ready to go very, very viral."

"Do you know what a zero-day exploit is?" Cole demanded.

I frowned. "Is this some kind of test?"

"No, I'm answering your question. Do you know?"

"Of course I know. It's a way to hack into a device that hasn't been fixed. One that the software developer doesn't know about—hence the zero days. That's how long the developer has had to fix it."

"Correct. And you know that the serious ones—the ones that affect, say, every single person with an iPhone—they're valuable, yes? Like, hundreds of thousands of dollars valuable, on the black market?"

"Yes." I was properly puzzled now. Where was this leading?

"Well, Gabe found one. A big one. He came to me to ask for my advice about what to do. I told him his best bet was to go to the software developer and claim the responsible reporting bounty. But instead, he"—Cole paused, swallowed audibly at the other end of the line—"he decided to sell it on the dark web. I don't know who he went to, but he must have messed with the wrong people because they decided . . . well, they decided they didn't want to pay whatever he was asking. They decided they'd rather just take it. So that's what they did."

W hen I hung up on Cole, for a long minute I didn't do anything. I just stood there, trying to absorb what he had told me, barely even noticing the way the raindrops from the open window were blowing into the carriage and speckling the screen of the mobile.

Then I pulled myself together, turned around, and almost dropped the phone. The woman from the toilet was standing behind me, holding the hand of her toddler.

For a brief instant her eyes met mine, a direct and unblinking stare like a challenge. Then she turned and moved up the carriage, in the opposite direction from where I had been sitting.

I felt all the breath go out of me. How long had she been standing there? Not long, surely. Her toddler was too small to wait patiently silent while his mother eavesdropped on a stranger's phone call. Which meant that she had likely only caught the last part of our conversation.

Racking my brains, I tried to replay what I had said and figure out whether it would have sounded suspicious. Cole had done most of the talking, I remembered that. My input had been limited mostly to stuff about coding, hacks, and exploits—at least for the last few moments. But before that . . . I had mentioned Gabe's name, I was pretty sure of it. And I had talked about his murder. Or at least referred to Gabe being killed, I couldn't remember the exact words I'd used. However I'd phrased it, though, I was pretty sure I'd said enough to get someone curious searching for the case on their phone. *Fuck.*

Opening up the phone again, I pulled up Google and typed in *Gabe coder murder*, then waited as the screen filled with results.

The first one made me go first hot, and then very, very cold, so fast that it was almost sickening.

It was an article on the BBC, and the headline was "Wife of Murdered Coder Sought for Questioning." The preview image was a picture of me.

My hands shook as I clicked through to the story. It was dated and time-stamped earlier today, and at the top, immediately below the headline, was a large photo of me, taken from the Crossways Security website, captioned *Jacintha Cross is wanted for questioning in relation to the murder of her husband. Police have asked the public to report any sightings by dialling 999.*

Beneath the photo, the article continued.

> Police investigating the murder of digital security expert and "hacktivist" Gabriel Medway, who operated under the username Gakked in the online hacking community, have today released a statement confirming they are urgently seeking the programmer's wife, Jacintha Cross, who is wanted for questioning in relation to her husband's death.
>
> Ms Cross, who was initially interviewed voluntarily by the Metropolitan Police, has not been seen since Tuesday 7th February. Police are urgently seeking her in connection with their enquiry and have appealed to members of the public for their help.
>
> Jacintha Cross, 27, a security consultant who also goes by the name Jack, was last seen near the town of Rye in East Sussex but is thought to have left the area, possibly travelling by bus or train. She is described as white, 5'2", of slight build, with hazel eyes and mid-length, distinctively dyed red hair, but a police spokesperson cautioned that she may have changed her appearance.
>
> Detective Inspector Branagh of the Metropolitan Police said, "We are urgently appealing to members of the public for their help in tracking down Ms Cross, who may be travelling under a false name or with forged doc-

umentation. **We would ask the public not to approach Ms Cross directly, but to report any suspicious sightings to the police by dialling 999."**

Halfway down the article was a grainy blown-up shot of me walking through Charing Cross station, my head down over my phone. It was black-and-white, but you could tell that my hair was probably no longer red. Below were links to three pieces about Gabe's death, each illustrated with a photo of him taken from our company website. I knew I should click through, find out what information the police had already put out there, but his warm, friendly face, smiling out of the screen, felt like a punch in the stomach, and I couldn't bring myself to do it. Instead, I shut down the phone, but closing the screen did nothing to lessen the sick feeling of dread that had been building in the pit of my stomach the whole time I was reading. In one way, the article wasn't a surprise—it was, after all, only confirmation of what I already knew: that the police were looking for me and considered me a suspect in Gabe's death. But somehow, seeing the facts set out so brutally was still a shock, and the way the police had phrased their quotes . . . *who also goes by the name Jack.* How had they managed to make a simple abbreviation sound so shady? And as for *We would ask the public not to approach Ms Cross directly*—like I was armed and dangerous, for God's sake! The photo was good, as well. No mercifully blurred black-and-white mug shot. They had taken my professional head shot from the Crossways company website, along with Gabe's. It was high-res, well lit, and even with my hair bleached straw white and bags of exhaustion under my eyes, I was very recognizably the same person. Was the woman with the toddler already calling 999?

I glanced out the window, and then pulled up the train timetable on my phone. We were about fifteen minutes away from Northampton, but that was a big station which would almost certainly have ticket barriers and probably British Transport Police on standby. I absolutely could not afford any kind of altercation at a place like that. I'd be arrested within seconds.

The next stop was ten minutes further down the line, at a place I had never heard of—Long Buckby. Google showed it to be a small village with a station that didn't seem to have even a ticket office, let alone fixed barriers. It was exactly the kind of place I'd been hoping for. The only problem was that it was twenty-five minutes and two stops away. If—*if*—the woman with the toddler was calling the police right now, they would almost certainly board the train at Northampton. In ten minutes they could sweep the entire train.

I stood at the window, chewing my nail and considering my options. Option one was to get off at Northampton and try to tailgate through the barriers behind another passenger—but I didn't like my chances. In a rush hour crush with commuters pushing and shoving I might be able to pull it off, but it was only just gone four p.m. and doing the same thing in a sparsely filled station was much harder. Option two was to stay on the train and try to hide until Long Buckby. If I made it that far, I was probably home free. The problem was, if the woman with the toddler *had* called the police, then staying on the train past Northampton was pretty much a one-way ticket to jail.

Option three . . . but there I ran into a brick wall. The only remaining option was what my last resort had always been—to stop running and give myself up to the police. Obviously, I wasn't going to do that. It would make the whole thing pointless. Except . . . would it?

I took my hand out of my mouth. I hadn't seriously considered giving myself up before. But my trip to Sunsmile had changed—well, not *everything*. But it had changed a lot. I now had evidence backing up my story.

My statement to Cole had been a lie—I hadn't been recording our conversation; there wasn't any setting on my phone to allow me to do so, though I was pretty sure I could have found an app somewhere, if it had occurred to me in advance. But I hadn't thought of it—and so when I'd told him I would stream the conversation, it was nothing but bluff. Still, I *did* have a recording I could take to DS Malik: the one of Cole's voice sitting on the Sunsmile database. I just had to hope that when Malik and Miles listened to it, they were as certain as I was that the speaker wasn't Gabe. Because the problem was, Gabe and Cole did sound a lot alike. Same deep voice, same North London accent. It had been close enough to twist my heart with grief every time Cole spoke to me these past few days.

The problem was that even if Malik and Miles agreed that it was Cole on the recording, that might not let me off the hook. What if they thought we'd been in it together? Cole setting up the insurance in Gabe's name, me collecting on the policy. We wouldn't be the first couple to commit a murder for financial security and a new future. The fact that I'd been found hiding out at Cole's cottage would likely seal their suspicions.

No. I couldn't trust this to Malik and Miles—not again. They had proven already that they were willing to go for the easy solution rather than dig for a complicated truth. I couldn't afford to give them a second chance—not until I had got to the bottom of what was really going on. Because as much as I wanted Cole on the hook for his part in this, I wanted to find Gabe's killer more—and I was pretty sure that wasn't Cole.

That left me with two options: Northampton or Long Buckby. The only question was which.

I was still trying to make up my mind when the train began to slow, and eventually came to a halt with a screech of brakes. The silence after the roar of wind through the half-open window was like a strange vacuum. I could hear the patter of rain outside and the hiss and tick of the train's air brakes. From far up the carriage came a child's slow exhausted wail, and I knew how it felt.

Then a crackle came over the speakers.

"Sorry for the delay, ladies and gentlemen, we're being held for a few minutes at a red signal. There's a train ahead of us at Northampton and we're waiting for the platform. We should be on the move in just a few minutes."

I felt my heart begin to thump. Was there really a train ahead of us? Or was this some kind of ruse, to let the police get their officers in place, ready and waiting on the platform to board the train?

Shit. *Shit.*

But what could I do?

My eyes fell on the door, with its half-open window. If only it had been one of the old-fashioned trains, where you could lean out and unlock the door from the outside. But I was fairly sure those had been phased out. This one still looked pretty old, but it seemed to have some kind of central override—an illuminated display stated firmly *Door Locked*, and below it a poster read *To open door, wait for train to stop. Check door is adjacent to platform. Wait for unlocked light above. Open door window and unlock door.*

Which meant there was no chance of opening the door until we had reached the platform. Except . . . *Open door window.*

My thumping heart sped up. Could I?

The window was already halfway down, but it seemed to have stuck, and it was with a great effort that I managed to get it just a few inches further. Then I stood on tiptoes and put my head out through the narrow gap. There was nothing underneath apart from railway sleepers and gravel.

I put a hand to my side, thinking about the oozing cut beneath the dressing. This window was barely wide enough for me to wriggle through, and the ground was a good fifteen feet below the opening. I had dropped fifteen feet before. It is *not* a joke, even in tip-top condition. You feel it everywhere—in every bone and joint. I felt more than a little sick. But there were no other options.

I pushed the bag out first. The side pockets stuck against the sill, but I ground it through, and then listened with a wince as it ricocheted off the outside step and from there thudded to the ground. Then I grabbed hold of the top of the window surround and tried to hook one foot up and over the edge.

It was very high, and for a minute I wasn't sure if I could even get my foot up, let alone the rest of my body. It *should* be possible. I had vaulted a much higher wall when I broke into my own backyard in Salisbury Lane, but now my arms were shaking with fatigue, the pain in my side was screaming, and my muscles didn't seem to want to obey me.

For a moment I thought about giving up. But my bag was already on the ground outside. If I stayed on this train, even if the woman with the baby hadn't spotted me, even if I made it safely to Long Buckby, I would be completely and utterly screwed. I would have no money, no phone, no clean clothes, nothing.

I *had* to get out of that window.

The realization gave me a burst of adrenaline and I got first one, then the other foot up and over the sill. Then I swiveled, ignoring the scream of pain from my side, and slithered through the narrow gap on my stomach, lowering myself until I felt my feet touch the step outside.

I stood, my muscles trembling with exertion, holding on to the edge of the window above me, and risked a glance down, past my legs. The drop was terrifyingly high. It looked worse than it had from inside the train.

Carefully, I got down on my hands and knees and twisted shakily around until I was sitting on the bottom-most step. Below me was a daunting drop, onto what looked like painfully chunky gravel.

I swallowed. And then I heard the train's engines start up.

"Good news, ladies and gents," I heard from inside the open window. "We've received clearance to proceed to Northampton."

There was a jolt and the train began to move.

My heart was thumping so hard in my chest I thought I might be sick. What I wanted was to lower myself down slowly and carefully to the ground—but there was no time. We were picking up speed. I was going to get smacked in the face by a bush at seventy miles an hour if I didn't act fast—very fast. But it turns out it's very, very hard to make yourself jump off a moving train.

I was leaning forward, trying to psych myself up to do it—when I heard a noise from up ahead and looked right to see a tree looming over the track, its branches rattling against the roof of the train. It was too late to jump. If I did, I'd probably fly right into the trunk. Instead, instinctively, I flattened myself against the door, closing my eyes and hunching my head into my shoulder as the branches tore across my face, stinging my cheek and ear.

When I looked up again, the tree was in the distance, but the train was going even faster. Possibly fatally fast.

With the feeling that I was doing something incredibly stupid, I jumped.

landed with a crash that knocked all the breath out of me. I was too winded at first to do anything apart from lie there, curled in the fetal position, gasping and holding my ribs. The puncture wound felt like someone had shoved a red-hot poker into it and was jabbing it deeper with every thud of my heart. I had been half expecting that someone would notice my actions and pull the emergency cord, and as far as I could think of anything over the screaming pain in my side, I was listening for the screech of brakes and the noise of the train coming to a stop. But when the pain subsided enough for me to raise my head, I saw that the train had rounded the bend and was disappearing into the distance. Either no one had seen me, or nobody cared.

I let my head fall back and considered my options.

All things taken into account, that hadn't gone as badly as it could have done. I had landed in a pile of bracken—it could easily have been nettles or brambles, or even rocks—and I didn't think I had broken anything. My knees and ankles ached with the jarring shock of the fall, but I wasn't concussed, and when I pulled myself to my feet, nothing hurt too badly—apart from the hole in my side, which throbbed with every movement. When I put my hand under my top to check, I groaned. The dressing was still in place, but I could feel it was already pulpy with blood.

My rucksack was a surprisingly long way up the track, and as I picked my way back along the line, trying to avoid tripping over the sleepers—the last thing I needed was to fall and electrocute myself on the live rail—I tried to think what to do next. I very badly wanted to talk to Hel, but I wasn't sure if I could do so without bursting into tears. More to the point, could I risk calling her? Her phone was probably tapped, but if I used Signal at least the police shouldn't be able to triangulate my location . . .

When I finally reached the rucksack, I picked it up and began climbing the steep embankment. I needed to get away from the main line before another train came along. Maybe none of the passengers had noticed me, but a conductor would definitely spot me picking my way along beside the rails, and the last thing I needed was another train screeching to a halt and a "passenger on the tracks" security alert going out across the network.

It wasn't easy pulling myself up the steep bank, and when I got to the top, the sight of a barbed wire fence almost made me break down, but I threw my bag over and with a huge effort managed to clamber after it, ignoring the barbs that dug into my thighs and ripped a chunk out of my jeans as I pulled myself free.

It didn't matter. None of it mattered. I was over. That was the main thing. I was over and—where was I? Some kind of farmer's field, it looked like, plowed into deep ridges and sown with something that looked like turnips or beets. All of a sudden I felt weak and trembling, and I knew that if I didn't sit down—or, even better, lie down—I was going to collapse where I stood.

In the corner of the field was a huge beech, and, wearily, I forced my tired legs to carry me just a few meters further beneath its sparse canopy, and then collapsed against the trunk, the rucksack clutched to my chest. I knew I should eat something, drink something, but I was suddenly so tired, nauseous with it, that even just opening the bag seemed like an effort beyond what I could manage.

Come on, babe. It was Gabe's voice, gentle in my ear. *You've got to eat something.* It was what he had said to me so often when I got home after a night chasing around the corridors of some remote office, too exhausted to do anything but collapse into bed. I thought of our last conversation, of me bossing him around, demanding fries, bitching at him about his fucking bacon. God, what I wouldn't give for just one more kiss, one more crack, one more dad joke about one-hundred-percent vegan nuggets being made out of real vegans . . .

Gabe as a dad. The thought was too bittersweet to bear. I swallowed. Then I opened the bag and peered inside.

The first thing I checked was not how much food I had left, but the phone. It was there, and thankfully unbroken, in spite of being thrown out of a train window and dropping fifteen feet onto rocks. The next thing I did was unscrew the lid from the plastic bottle of water in the side pocket and drink about a gallon. I was, I realized, extremely thirsty—I just hadn't noticed.

So much water on an empty stomach made me feel even sicker, but I knew I had to eat something. I'd had nothing since the teacake in the cafe in Hastings, and that felt like several lifetimes ago. There were a few energy bars left at the bottom of the bag, and some instant noodles I had bought from the hostel. I didn't have any way of heating the noodles, but I opened one and crunched the powdery shards dry, and then ate an energy bar.

Then, giving way to the urge that had been growing ever since my conversation with Cole, I pulled out the phone, opened up Signal, and called Hel on her mobile.

It rang. And rang.

And then Hel picked up.

"Hello?"

"It's me," I said without preamble. Hel let out an audible gasp, and I could hear her brain racing, trying to figure out what she could say.

"Should I call you back?" she said at last.

"Sure. Use Signal and this number."

"Signal?"

"It's an app. Encrypted."

"Okay." Two syllables, but I could hear the urgency vibrating in her voice. She was as desperate to talk to me as I was to her. She hung up, and I waited. And waited. It was getting cold, and dark, and I took the sleeping bag out from the rucksack, spread it in the shelter of a hedge, and climbed into it. I was just struggling with the zip when my phone buzzed, almost making me drop it. It was a Signal call from a number I didn't recognize—a mobile number—and for a second my stomach flipped, thinking of Cole and the way he had duped me—but this was a voice call. It had to be Hel, surely?

I picked up.

"Is this secure?" was the first thing Hel said. "I used Signal and I'm on a phone I bought yesterday from that phone shop on the high street, is that enough? I'm pretty sure the police are monitoring my other phone, but I don't think they've bugged the house. Would they do that?"

"I don't know. Maybe." I tried to think, did it matter? As long as I didn't say where I was, maybe not. "Fuck, Hel, it's so good to talk to you."

"Oh Jesus, Jack. Where are you? Are you okay? Are you really okay?" She sounded like she was on the verge of tears. "I was so worried when I didn't hear anything from you. I knew the police couldn't have found you, because they're still tearing your house apart, and they've an unmarked car outside ours twenty-four/seven, but I had no idea if you were dead in a ditch. And your picture is all over the papers—did you know that? They made you sound like some kind of—"

"I know, I'm so sorry," I said, breaking in gently. "I'm okay—but Hel, listen, has Cole been in touch with you?"

"Cole? As in, Gabe's friend? No, not a word. How come?"

"If he makes contact, do *not* trust him, okay?" I felt a lump rise in my throat at the impossibility of spelling out the depths of Cole's betrayal—everything he had done over the last few days and weeks. "He's behind this, Hel—maybe not all of it, I don't honestly know, but he's been lying to me the whole time, and he set up the insurance policy."

"Insurance policy?" Hel said blankly, and I realized—I hadn't even told her about that when we met back in the shopping mall. Literally all I'd done was grab the bag and run. It was in the text messages that I'd spelled out the situation—texts I'd actually been sending to Cole. Hel hadn't heard a word from me since I disappeared into the shopping center on Monday afternoon. No wonder she'd been going out of her mind. Briefly, I explained the sequence of events: the interview with the police, the email about the insurance policy, the realization that I was being framed and my decision to flee—and then my meeting with Cole, the fake messages, the trip to Sunsmile, and my subsequent furious call with Cole—all of it. I could practically hear Hel's brain ticking as I related the whole thing.

"And he all but admitted it," I finished. "Not Gabe's murder, but the policy—he even had the nerve to claim he'd been trying to protect me. I just *wish* I'd been able to record that call. Because as it stands, it's his word against mine, and if he says it's not him on the Sunsmile call, I don't know how to prove it is. Or what if they believe it's him on the recording, but think we were in it together?"

"Quite," Hel said. She sounded incredibly troubled, as if she'd spent my breathless outpouring putting two and two together . . . and making an answer she didn't like. "Because there's holes in his story you could drive a truck through, aren't there?"

"How do you mean?" I felt desperately tired, my brain not working properly. I wasn't sure what time it was, but the sun was going down, and lying in the warmth of the sleeping bag . . . it was all I could do not to fall asleep to the comforting sound of Hel's voice in my ear, the illusion that I wasn't alone in this nightmare. "The first bit, the bit about Gabe stumbling over a vulnerability and going to him for advice . . . I think that's probably true. Gabe might well have wanted Cole's take, especially if it was something to do with phones. Gabe never did much with phones, but that's Cole's area—his whole deal is phone security and antivirus apps. And if the problem was serious enough—you know, something that affected lots of users, and compromised the security of the whole phone—then I could buy Cole's fear, and the idea that someone would kill to acquire the vulnerability.

The people who deal in those kinds of hacks aren't playing—we're talking organized crime, rogue states, that kind of thing. I mean, say it's some kind of hack that lets you see the phone's location twenty-four/seven; if you're using that as a way to track down and assassinate your enemies, you're not going to be above the idea of murdering the coder who discovered it to cover your tracks."

"But do you think Gabe would have dabbled in that market?" Hel asked a little skeptically, and I shook my head.

"No. Absolutely not. And not just out of self-protection—I just can't imagine Gabe flogging off a hack to the highest bidder. It's not . . . it's not *Gabe*, you know?"

Now I said the words aloud, I realized that that part of Cole's story had troubled me from the start. Gabe had absolute contempt for hackers who sold exploits. The idea that he'd auction off a vulnerability to any cybercriminal or oppressive government with enough money . . . well, it was laughable. The issue was, I had no idea how to convince anyone else of that fact. I knew from talking to Gabe that really big hacks could go for hundreds of thousands of dollars on the black market—maybe millions. With enough money on the table, Malik would argue, principles became cheap.

"I agree with you as far as that goes, but actually I was thinking of a different problem," Hel said. She sounded as if she was frowning on the other end of the phone. I could hear cartoons playing in the background, and if I closed my eyes and tried hard enough, I could almost imagine myself lying on the sofa in Hel's kitchen, the girls watching TV in the next room, the comforting smell of cooking filling the air. "My issue is, even if you buy Cole's argument that he was trying to save you from the same fate as Gabe, how did *he* know what was going to happen to Gabe?"

I rubbed my eyes, trying to understand what she was saying, and then shook my head.

"Sorry, I'm shattered, Hel. You'll have to give me the *Conspiracy for Dummies* version."

"I mean," Hel said, and her voice was gentle, but there was an urgency underneath that made me uneasy, "even if you accept all the rest—Gabe going to Cole, then putting the exploit on the market, and then being set up by the people he's dealing with—how does *Cole* get wind of Gabe's life being in danger? From what Cole says, even Gabe didn't know. So how did Cole see it coming?"

"Huh." I raised myself up on my elbow, ignoring the twinge of pain in my side. Now I was frowning too. "You're right. That's . . . weird."

"Wind back to the beginning for a moment," Hel said. I could tell she was getting into her own idea, pitching it to me the same way she'd pitch a particularly knotty story to her editor. "Let's buy Cole's argument and suppose that someone—whether that's the NSA, NSO, MI6, or just your regular run-of-the-mill organized crime cartel without any fancy letters to their name—let's suppose they did make contact, and Gabe listened. Let's suppose that poor Gabe ended up falling in with someone so unscrupulous, so desperate that they were prepared to *kill* to secure that exploit, and let's suppose as well, by the way, that he was stupid enough to do all that without protecting his identity or covering his tracks—which I also have difficulty buying. How on earth, in that scenario, does *Cole* get warning of what's about to happen? Let alone enough warning to steal Gabe's credit card and ID and set up a whole insurance policy in your name? No. The whole thing is absolute BS and the police won't buy it for a second. The only question is what they'll think really happened."

"Fuck. You're right." I was sitting up now, hugging myself to try to keep in the sleeping bag's warmth, annoyed with my own stupidity for not noticing this before Hel had pointed it out. "I can't believe I didn't notice that. If Gabe didn't see this coming—and I'm certain he didn't—how did Cole? And why was he so frightened when I spoke to him? Because he *was* frightened, Hel. I'm sure of that. He sounded honestly terrified, like he thought they were coming for him too."

"Exactly," Hel said. "Cole is in on this, Jack. Whether he killed

Gabe or not, he's knee-deep in this shit, and he knows more than he's letting on."

"But wait . . ." I put my free hand to my head, trying to quell the ache that was building there, but then regretted taking the pressure off the pain in my side. It was the only thing that made the wound hurt less. I switched hands with the phone and pressed again on the dressing, feeling the heat underneath it. "Hang on. The only way that he could have had forewarning of what was about to happen to Gabe—"

"Was if someone told him," Hel finished for me. Her voice was grim.

"But why?" My voice, even to my own ears, sounded like that of a plaintive child on the verge of tears. The thought that Cole, *Cole* might have had warning of what was about to happen to Gabe, but hadn't lifted a hand to save him . . . "Why would some Mafia kingpin or whoever the fuck it was bother to tell Cole their plans? The only reason I can think of—"

I stopped. Hel didn't reply, but she didn't have to, because the answer had already come to me, with a sickening inevitability. The only reason someone like that would have warned Cole about their plans was because he was already in their pay.

And the only reason he would already be in their pay . . .

"If it were me," Hel said now, "if I were running some criminal gang, or some shady government hacking firm—I wouldn't be putting pressure on Apple or Google to hand me the keys to the kingdom. I mean, sure, I'd try—wasn't there a case where the NSA told Apple to build a back door so they could get into some terrorist's iPhone? But Apple told them to fuck off, if I remember right. Because they could. They're bigger than any government, and they have more to lose by forfeiting their customers' trust than they do from pissing off the US security agencies. No, if it were me, I'd be going straight to the engineers. And not the ones at Apple, but the guys at the medium-size firms, the ones in charge of the small but popular apps. I'd be encouraging them to make their apps ask for all the permissions they

could: Camera. Microphone. Files. Call list. Exact geographical location. And then I'd put on the pressure and make them build a back
door to send that information straight to me. Because *those* people—
individuals with families they care about and bills to pay—they can
be bought. Or coerced."

"People like Cole," I said with a groan. "Fuck. *Fuck.*"

"You think I'm right?"

"I mean . . . *fuck.* Hel, I honestly have no idea, but it makes a
lot more sense than that crock of bullshit he tried to give me." My
head was throbbing, along with my ribs. "And it would make sense of
Gabe's actions too. I mean, Gabe *might* have gone to Cole for advice
about a phone exploit, but he'd *definitely* have gone to him if he discovered a problem with one of the apps Cole himself was responsible
for. Cole was his best friend—he'd have felt obliged to give him a
heads-up that the shit was about to hit the fan." My head felt like it
was about to split in two. Or maybe it was my heart. I wasn't sure.

"Exactly. Which would have put Cole in a mildly tricky position
if it was just something he'd overlooked, but a completely impossible
one if it was a back door he'd been bribed to introduce," Hel said. Her
voice was dry.

"Oh my God." I wanted to be sick. I wanted Hel to be wrong—
but it was too horribly plausible. It made sense of everything—of
Gabe's actions, of Cole's. It even explained how Cole was able to
afford such an extravagant flat. If Cole *had* been taking money from
someone—whoever it was—to leave a back door to one of his apps
open, and Gabe had stumbled over that door in the course of one of
his pen tests, of course he would have warned Cole, and of course
Cole would have gone to his handlers. He would have had to. Not
because he wanted to betray Gabe, but because he would have had
no choice but to fess up that the door was about to be closed. Only
the group didn't want it to be closed. They wanted it to stay open.
At all costs.

"Jack?" Hel said now, her voice a little worried. "Are you okay?"

"Yes. No. I don't know. *Fuck*." My mind was racing. What *was* the exploit? Was it something Cole had had access to, all this time? How much access did it give him? Had I ever put one of his apps on my phone? The thought made me feel sick—the idea that he might have been spying on me and Gabe for weeks, maybe even months. "I think you're right—you must be. But how can I prove this, Hel? They took Gabe's hard drive out of his computer."

"Didn't he back up anywhere?"

"I don't know. Not regularly. Oh Jesus." I felt like I was going to throw up. As I sat there, trying to figure out what to do, how to get out of this unholy mess, my phone gave a quiet beep, and when I looked down at the screen, a fifteen-percent battery warning was showing. With a sinking heart I remembered the battery pack Cole had lent me—still sitting where I had left it on the table in the cottage. "Shit, I've got to go, Hel. My phone's nearly out of battery, and I don't have anywhere to charge it."

"You don't have a plug?" Hel's voice at the other end of the line had sharpened with concern. "Jack, where *are* you? Are you okay?"

"I'm fine," I said, though I felt anything but. I had the strange sensation of being both hot and cold at the same time, the same feeling I remembered from being a little kid with the flu, and I felt like I wanted to be sick, though I was fairly sure that was more to do with Cole than anything else. "I should go. I'll call you tomorrow, on this number, okay?"

"Okay. I love you."

"I love you too." My throat hurt as I hung up the phone, and for a long time I did nothing except stare at the blank screen, trying to figure out what the hell I was going to do next. I should turn off the phone, save the battery, but there was one other person I wanted to talk to. Badly. I just wasn't sure if I could yet.

In the end, I switched off the phone and simply lay there, staring up at the stars through the fluttering vestigial beech leaves. I don't know when I fell asleep.

FRIDAY, FEBRUARY 10

MINUS TWO DAYS

When I woke up, my first thought was that I might be dying. I was unbearably, unbelievably cold—cold enough that the chill I'd felt in Cole's cottage by the sea seemed like a childish version of this sensation. This was cold harsh enough to physically hurt—there was frost on the plowed field, and on my sleeping bag, and my breath around the edge of the bag had frozen into a glazed sheen that cracked and flaked when I tried to move.

My second thought was that I was going to be sick. I'd felt queasy all night. But now I felt really, properly ill, to the point where I knew that as cold as I was, I had to get up or I was going to throw up in the sleeping bag.

Shakily, moving as fast as my frozen limbs would let me, I struggled onto my hands and knees and began to try to crawl out of the bag, but it was too late. Halfway out, I felt my guts clench and seize, and I threw up—a surprisingly extravagant amount, given how little I'd had to eat the day before.

For a long moment I simply crouched there, the sleeping bag down to my waist and trailing back across the plowed field like a caterpillar halfway through shedding its cocoon. I was shivering with a mix of cold and nausea, waiting to see if the vomiting had stopped. I thought it had—and then another wave hit me, but this time there was nothing to throw up, and I simply dry heaved over and over onto the frozen ground, until finally my stomach reluctantly accepted that was it, there was no point in continuing, and I sat back, trembling, onto my heels.

Well, on the plus side, I *hadn't* thrown up on my clothes. On the minus side, I felt very, very ill, and when I put my hand under my top, exploring the dressing across my side, I could tell why. My fingers came away sticky and crusted, and I could feel my pulse throbbing in the wound. I was sweating and shivering at the same time, and I knew if I didn't get to hospital there was a very strong chance I wouldn't be Cole's problem anymore, or Malik's. Words like *septicemia* and *sepsis* were floating through my head. Things that left you needing not just antibiotics but an organ transplant. Maybe even a coffin.

For the first time, the reality of what I was doing began to hit home. I had told Cole that in some ways, it would be a relief if I died, if someone cut my throat. But I had said that imagining some kind of cosmic exchange—my life in return for the truth about what had happened to Gabe. This—this was very different. Did I really want to die, pointlessly, of sepsis in some lonely field, leaving the truth about Gabe undiscovered and my body for some farmer to find when he replowed the field?

No. I wanted to follow this trail to the end and stop anyone else from suffering the same fate as Gabe. What happened after that— well, after that I didn't really care. But that meant I had only limited time left. In a day or two, I might not be able to walk, let alone dodge cops, Cole, and everyone else who wanted to see me either dead or locked away for life.

Because one thing had crystallized for me overnight. It wasn't just Gabe that Cole and his friends in high places had feared. It was also me. I didn't buy Cole's story for a second—sending me to prison to protect me from the reach of some shadowy gang? Bullshit. Whoever was behind this, they were pros. Either serious organized crime, or worse—perhaps even a government agency. If a group like that wanted me dead, they would have staked out the house and picked a time when we were both home—and I would be dead right now. As for prison as some kind of protective custody beyond the reach of the bad guys—it was laughable. People were always dying in prison— in fights, of suicide, from improper restraint. If an outside agency wanted a prisoner to die in mysterious circumstances, it would be child's play to make it happen.

No, Cole's story made zero sense—which meant that he must have framed me for some other reason, either off his own bat or at the suggestion of his bosses. The only question was why. The first possibility was that they had wanted a distraction from the killing. After all, if the police were busy scrutinizing me and my motives, they'd be far less likely to go probing about in Gabe's history for other enemies with a grudge big enough to kill for.

But they could have created a distraction without implicating me—they could have made Gabe's death look more like a burglary gone wrong, or a heart attack. They could have run him over outside our house and disguised it as a hit-and-run. There were a hundred ways of killing people that didn't look like a straight-up contract killing. So why had they gone for a method that was so obviously murder?

The answer to that question surely had to be the second reason—they'd done it this way because implicating me was part of the point. They had to get me out of the way too, locked up far beyond reach of my home and Gabe's possessions. Not dead—because with me dead they would be back to square one, with the police looking for a motive for both our killings. No, alive but incarcerated, and safely out of the way.

All of which brought me to the conclusion that even though they had taken his hard drive, they must have a strong suspicion that Gabe had made a record of the exploit—a record which his wife might stumble across.

If that was true, I had to find that record.

The problem was that their plan had worked. Okay, I wasn't actually in custody. But the police had seized all Gabe's devices and most of mine, putting his backups far beyond where I could reach them.

Given that my chances of successfully breaking into a Metropolitan Police evidence locker were basically nil—I was good, but not that good—my only realistic hope was the cloud. Gabe did occasionally back up online—not full backups, he tended to use a physical drive for those, but important documents or things he wanted to be able to access from multiple locations, those he *did* save to his online drive. But I couldn't log into Gabe's cloud backups without one of his devices. I was fairly sure I knew what the password was, but his accounts were almost all locked with two-step verification. Logging in from an unfamiliar device would trigger a text message to his phone with a code, and without that code, I wouldn't be able to get any further. And Gabe's phone was currently in the possession of the police.

Fuck. *Fuck.*

I had to get that phone. The only question was how.

t was eight a.m., and I'd forced down a nauseating breakfast of energy bars and water before I finally dug my mobile out of my pocket and turned it on. I had only a few percent of battery left. I just had to hope it was enough for what I needed.

I had come to the conclusion that I *had* to get Gabe's phone—or at least the code from it. And there was only one person I could think of who might help me to do it. The problem was, the idea made me feel even sicker than when I woke up.

I had deleted the number I was about to dial off my contact list years ago, but I knew it by heart, much as I'd tried to forget it, and now I opened Signal and stared at the screen. Every nerve ending in my body was screaming at me not to do this, reminding me of what was at stake. My pride, for sure. My self-respect. Maybe even my freedom, if Cole had led me astray about the security of the app— and he'd lied to me about everything else.

But at the end of the day, the words I had said to Cole kept echoing in my ears: nothing mattered, apart from finding out who had done this to Gabe. Nothing. Not my past. Not my wounded feelings. Not even my life. If this call got me closer to finding out the truth, I had to make it. I had to swallow my pride. For Gabe.

Fucking make the call, I told myself savagely. *Gabe would do it for you, and you know it.*

The battery ticked down one more percent.

I twisted the ring on my finger, thinking of Gabe. He wouldn't have wanted me to do this. If he were here, he would have taken that phone and stamped on it before he let me. But he wasn't here. And I had no other choice. I took a deep breath, forcing down the sickness, and dialed.

He picked up on the first ring, his voice far too cocky and drawling for so early in the morning.

"Yello?"

Even just saying his name made me want to throw up, but I swallowed back the saliva pooling behind my teeth and spoke.

"Jeff. It's me."

There was a long silence, and then he began to laugh, long and slow.

"Jack Cross. Well, well, well. You've got some fucking balls, girl, I'll give you that. You know I can see your number?"

"This isn't my number," I said tersely. "Listen, Jeff, I don't have much time—but I need—" Oh God, this was hard. *For Gabe. Do it for Gabe.* I forced the words out. "I need to ask you a favor."

"Ask away," he said. It sounded like he was grinning at the other end of the phone. "Can't say I'll necessarily grant it, mind, but it's free to ask."

"I need a code off Gabe's phone. Just a code—that's it."

"The phone that's currently in the evidence locker down the nick?"

"That phone, yes."

"You don't ask much, do you? How the flip am I supposed to get in there?"

"Can you do it?"

"Maybe." He sounded intensely amused. "You know me, I'm a man of many resources. But what's in it for me?"

"Jeff." I knew what he wanted, and I didn't try to keep the desperation out of my voice. He wanted me to beg. He wanted me to plead. It was what he got off on, he always had. Even in the early days, before it all went south, he'd enjoyed hearing me beg. He'd played it like a game then, of course, tickling me until I choked with laughter and begged him to stop, jumping out at me as I walked home on dark nights and laughing at my momentary terror and subsequent relief when I realized it was him. Now I saw those "jokes" for what they were—mind games, played by someone who enjoyed watching women squirm. Well, if I wanted that code I had no choice now but to squirm for him. "Jeff, listen to me, you *know* me. You *know* I didn't kill Gabe. And I think I can prove it. I just need that code off his phone."

"What do you need it for? To wipe one of his accounts? You know it's pointless, right? The digital forensics boys have been all over that shit, it's backed up from here to kingdom come."

"Jeff." I forced the words out. "Jeff, *please*. I'm begging you. *Please*."

There was a long, long silence. Then Jeff let out a martyred sigh.

"Fuck me, Cross. You always did know how to play me."

"You'll do it?"

"I'll do it."

"Oh my God." I didn't try to keep the relief out of my voice. "Jeff, I—" I knew I had to say it, much as it made me want to puke. "Thank you. Listen, if I call you—"

"No," he broke in with finality. "I'm not giving this stuff out over the phone. If you want that code, I'll give it to you in person."

Now the silence was at my end of the line.

"You want it or not?" Jeff said, and I could tell he knew exactly how horrifyingly torn I was, and was enjoying the moment of power.

"I can't meet you," I said at last. "I can't, Jeff. You know that."

"Then I guess you'll have to do without the code," Jeff said. His voice was smug.

Fuck.

"How can I trust you?" I said at last. I could almost hear his shrug from the other end of the line.

"I dunno. How can I trust you aren't going to do something dodgy with that code? I guess we'll just have to trust each other."

He had a point. The problem was, I didn't trust him. Not for one second. I didn't trust Jeff Leadbetter as far as I could throw him.

"Okay, I'll meet you," I said at last, reluctantly, my mind whirling and trying to figure out options. "But *I'll* choose the place."

"All right," Jeff said, surprising me. "But it's gotta be London. I'm not schlepping out to some pisspot town in Wales just to give you a piece of paper."

"Okay," I said again. I was thinking hard. Where? Where should I pick? Somewhere central, with lots of exits and clear lines of sight so I could check that Jeff had come alone. Not somewhere a person could get trapped. My mind went to places that were likely to be sparsely populated—London Fields in Hackney, Finsbury Park after dusk . . . but then it occurred to me . . . maybe there was safety in numbers? If Jeff *did* try anything, perhaps it would be harder to do it surrounded by people?

Trafalgar Square? But no. There was usually at least a handful of police patrolling there, and sometimes a lot more if there was a pro-test going on. If Jeff brought a buddy, I would never be able to spot them.

Leicester Square? No, too few exits, and too many of the lanes that did lead out of it were narrow pedestrian thoroughfares, easy to block.

A park? But I needed somewhere I could get a good overview, somewhere with a building where I could see Jeff without being seen myself.

"I haven't got all day, Cross," Jeff said, just as my phone buzzed with a five-percent battery warning.

"Piccadilly Circus," I said at last. "Next to the Eros statue." I wasn't sure it was perfect—but it was the best I could do on the spur of the moment. It had the benefit of being at the junction of half a dozen different roads, most of them major traffic routes that would be impossible to block without causing serious disruption, plus it had at least four or five Tube exits. And it was lined with cafes and fast-food restaurants, so I had plenty of options for getting a good look at the area before doing anything stupid.

"Fuck me," Jeff said with a laugh. "When did you get so suspicious? You weren't always like this, Cross. But at least it's on my Tube line. All right. Piccadilly it is. Can you make seven p.m. tonight? I get off duty at six."

Seven? I felt my pulse spike with a flicker of adrenaline. Seven was less than twelve hours away—not long to get myself back down to London and into position. Could I get everything sorted by then?

I didn't have a choice. I *needed* that number.

"Seven tonight," I agreed. "Don't let me down, Jeff." And then, my phone flashing a red battery warning at me, I hung up and vomited into the ditch.

The rest of the day was a sick haze of nerves and waiting, punctuated by anxious flashbacks at the thought of meeting Jeff.

You weren't always like this, Cross. Jeff's words kept playing over and over inside my head, like an accusation. I could have retorted with the obvious—that up until now I hadn't been on the run from the police, suspected of murdering my own husband. And that would be true—but it wouldn't be the whole truth, and I knew it wasn't what Jeff had meant. Because he was right, he and I *hadn't* always been like this. There had been a time when it had been good, although it made me nauseous to think of it.

I had been barely twenty when I'd met Jeff—not long into my fledgling pen testing career, working for a company that specialized in security tests for public sector organizations. Jeff had arrested me one night as I'd strolled out of the back door of a local government headquarters in North London—and once he'd established that I was who I said I was, he'd been fascinated to hear about what I did for a living. He'd ended up giving me a lift home, because I'd missed the last Tube, and in the car we'd talked for the whole journey about the legalities of my job, the challenges it posed, the stories I had from my encounters and near misses. He'd been funny, charming, full of a kind of teasing, provocative banter that I'd found disarming at the time, before I'd realized there was a darker side to his goading.

He'd asked me out for a drink—to pick my brain about security at the station, or so I had thought—and only halfway through I'd realized it was a date as far as he was concerned. When he kissed me that night, I'd found it funny. Me, a reformed shoplifter, snogging a cop. There had been a kind of weird symmetry to it. The red flags had come later.

The first flags had been disguised as protectiveness—a need to know where I was, who I was seeing, when I'd be home. When I pushed back, he'd dressed it up as a concern born out of the dark side of his job, an *if you'd seen what I'd seen, you'd be worried too* kind of thing.

Later, as his behavior became more unmistakably controlling, I was in too deep, and I had no one to tell me how to get out. My parents were dead. My friends had mostly left for university, and the ones who stayed had somehow fallen away in the face of Jeff's suffocating presence, made increasingly unwelcome by him on the rare occasions we did meet up. Only Hel remained—and she was mired in her finals, studying every hour she could. By the time I realized what was happening, I was trapped.

Two things saved me. The first was that in spite of Jeff's pressing the issue, we had never officially moved in together. Yes, I was sleeping almost every night at his house, worn down by the constant nagging when I spent time elsewhere. Yes, my clothes—vetted by him—were in his closet, and my bank statements—checked by him—were coming to his address. But my name was still on the flat I shared with Hel. When I did finally wrench myself out from under his thumb, I had somewhere to go back to.

The second thing was my job. Because when Jeff started to suggest it was getting in the way of our time together, that maybe I should consider quitting, taking up something a bit safer, a bit more sensible, something with a pension and career prospects, I knew that if I was forced to choose between Jeff and my work, I would choose pen testing every single time.

I had left him when I was twenty-two, almost six years ago. It felt like a lifetime—and yet on the phone to him, it had felt like yesterday.

The walk to the train station in Northampton was four miles along a dual carriageway, trudging slowly with the cars whistling past just feet from my elbow. About halfway I passed a small tarmaced stopping area for truckers, with a burger van parked up. The smell of the frying onions and hot chips was almost unbearably good, and I hovered for a long time, mentally counting the rest of my money and weighing the prospect of a hot meal against the energy bars I had left in my pack, before giving way to my watering mouth and rumbling stomach.

The owner was a cheerful older woman in a grease-spattered apron, and when I tried to pay for my veggie deluxe, she waved away my cash and muttered something about helping the homeless. I felt a rush of blood to my cheeks: a mix of gratitude and something sharper—something a lot like shame. For a moment I wanted to protest. *Oh, no! You've got it all wrong!* But . . . had she really? I had spent last night sleeping under a hedge. I had nowhere I could go home to. I was, quite literally, homeless. And I was also down to the very last of my cash—unless you counted the Bitcoin in Gabe's account, but it was becoming increasingly apparent how utterly useless that was to me. I still had to buy my ticket back to London, and since the National Rail website didn't take cryptocurrency, I couldn't pay directly in Bitcoin. And I couldn't turn the Bitcoin into notes without going to an exchange and producing ID—and I was pretty sure that as soon as I did that, the database would light up, some kind of wanted-criminal klaxon would sound, and I would find myself in cuffs.

No, the Bitcoin was as worthless to me right now as my frozen bank accounts. And I wasn't sure how much the train ticket was going to cost, but I could tell it was going to take me right down to the wire.

In the end I simply nodded, took the veggie deluxe, and said thank you.

The ticket, when I finally got to the station, did indeed use up almost all of my remaining cash, but at least, I reflected as I sank into a vacant seat, smiling apologetically at the older woman sitting opposite, it gave me access to hot water and a plug, two things I sorely needed. I washed my face in the toilet and combed some of the leaves and twigs out of my hair, trying to look a little less like someone who had slept in a field. And then I plugged my phone gratefully into the outlet beneath the seat and watched as the battery ticked up with painful slowness. The rocking of the train was making me feel almost unbearably sleepy, but I couldn't afford to nap. Still, I kept finding my head lolling and my eyes drooping as we traveled south.

"Are you okay, love?" the woman opposite me said as we approached King's Cross. She was looking at me with concern, and I realized there was a trail of drool coming out of the side of my mouth. I must have dropped off for a moment. I wiped it as surreptitiously as I could, and she added, "I hope you don't mind me saying, but you don't look at all well."

"I'm fine," I muttered. But suddenly the sleepiness had gone, replaced with the prickling watchful nerves of earlier. There was something in her expression, something in the way she was staring at my face, with a kind of worried curiosity. I didn't think she'd recognized me—her expression didn't look like someone who'd spotted a wanted fugitive—but it wasn't impossible that she would watch the news later and remember the woman slumped opposite her, with the cap pulled down over her face.

"Are you sure? You're terribly pale. And you're shivering."

"I'm *fine*," I said with more emphasis, though it was true that I was far colder than the overheated winter carriage really justified. I forced a smile I hoped was convincing. "Thanks."

I stood up and began packing away the phone, then I prepared to swing my bag up onto my shoulder, wincing preemptively at the wrench of pain that I knew the sharp movement would cause. When it came, it was worse than I had even imagined, and for a minute I couldn't do anything except stand, breathless with the pain, holding on to my side and the strap of my bag and trying not to vomit. There was a ringing in my ears and I could hear the woman opposite me chattering with concern, but I couldn't make out what she was saying. *Sit down*, I heard, and . . . *call someone for you?*

"I'm *fine*, will you please just leave me alone," I gritted out, ignoring her shocked, hurt expression, and then as the train began to slow, I moved away down the carriage, feeling my face flame with the aftermath of the shocking pain and the shame at the person I had turned into—a person who spat into the face of concerned strangers, who couldn't trust the smallest kindness. Who was I becoming? I was no longer sure.

By five to seven I was in position—on the upper floor of one of the stores overlooking Piccadilly Circus. From there I could see down to the fountain in the center, topped with the familiar cherub with his bow and arrow.

It's not actually Eros, you know, I heard Gabe's voice in my head, as clear and punchingly unexpected as if he'd just whispered the words in my ear. *It's his twin.*

The memory made my throat close with unshed tears. I had forgotten, when I chose this spot, that it had been where Gabe and I had met on one of our earliest dates. *Eros,* I had said, nodding up at the statue that Gabe had picked for our meeting point. *God of love, huh. Are you trying to tell me something?* And that was when he had explained. Not Eros, but Anteros—the god of requited love.

From someone else it would have come over as a dick move—a mansplaining *I think you'll find* of the worst order. But from Gabe . . . maybe it was his smile, or the fact that I already fancied the arse off him. Or maybe it was just that he so transparently *didn't* mean it that way, that he was just someone who liked sharing cool snippets of knowledge.

Whatever the reason, it was a mark of how comfortable I'd felt with him, right from our first meeting at a security conference, that I'd felt able to joke about something that for a while I had thought I would never trust again: love. What I'd felt for Jeff . . . well, I had called it love, once. And I was still reeling from how unbelievably wrong I had been. It had taken me a long time to trust again, longer still to use the L-word to anyone but Hel. But Gabe . . . somehow within a few weeks of knowing him, I had found myself thinking that word in the secret moments when I was alone, and my thoughts were filled with him and his body and the touch of his hands. I had found myself daring to hope. *Love*. It could happen. And this time it could be real.

Eros was lonely, that was the legend, or so Gabe had recounted it to me. And so the gods created him a twin—Anteros, counterlove. Because what does love need, except someone to love back?

It had seemed almost too perfect, that day. A meeting under the god of requited love. Was there any sweeter omen? And now I was here alone. Waiting for Jeff.

That's when I saw him—almost exactly as the clock struck seven—walking nonchalantly across the traffic in front of a speeding taxi with a swagger that still made my jaw clench involuntarily. The taxi beeped angrily; Jeff grinned at the driver and put up two fingers, and then made his way over to the fountain, where he lounged, for all the world like he was waiting for a date, the way Gabe had once waited for me. I glanced around the circus. There were no police officers—or none that I could see. There were people, of course, dozens of them, leaning against the Tube railings, waiting for friends, standing at the pedestrian crossing. I had no way of knowing if any of them were plainclothes officers. But Jeff himself looked to be alone.

"I guess it's go time," I said, very quietly, and I began to move, hurrying down the stairs of the shop, my heart thumping in my chest.

As I walked, I tried to imagine the scene as he would see it—the small figure crossing the stream of traffic, hood up, face in shadow. I saw his head go up, that shit-eating grin I hated so much spreading across his face.

"All right, Jack," I heard, and then a slow, almost amused, "Well, well, well, what do we have here."

I saw the cuffs too late—but there was nothing I could have done anyway, nothing I could have shouted, no movement I could have made to stop it happening. Jeff was a professional, with a professional's training, even though he was unnecessarily rough as he went through the steps. He'd done this a hundred times before; sub-

duing and cuffing a woman half his size was child's play. The cuffs
were on almost before I had realized what was happening—and far
before I had the wit to cry out or try to prevent it. In any case, to do
so would have been pointless—*more* than pointless—and I knew it,
but I still couldn't stop myself wailing internally at what was unfolding. I *knew* I shouldn't have trusted him. And yet I'd still hoped
against hope.

"I am arresting you on suspicion of aiding and abetting . . ." I
heard above the ringing in my ears, which was back, and louder than
ever. People were turning and staring now, looking at the woman
facedown on the grubby Piccadilly pavement and the man kneeling
on her spine, but, typical Londoners, they weren't interfering, just
backing away from the scene unfolding in front of them.

". . . have the right to remain silent," Jeff was saying, "but it may
harm your defense if you do not mention, when questioned—"

The words were hazing in and out, drowned beneath the sound
of angry panting breaths.

"Fuck you, Jeff!" I heard, as though from very far away, the words
muffled by the pavement. It's hard to speak with someone's knee in
your back and your face shoved into the ground. And I heard Jeff's
laugh, goading and irritable.

"You want me to add using obscene and profane language in a
public place to your rap sheet, Cross? Because I will."

"Oh seriously screw you," I heard, and a part of me wanted to
cheer. "And by the way, please do split my bottom lip as well as the
top, because I'll be adding that to my official complaint. I want you to
call my solicitor."

Jeff laughed again.

"You can call whoever you like. It's going to be a long night for
you, Hel."

And I stood and watched as Jeff hauled my sister ignominiously
to her feet and led her away in handcuffs, the rubber earpiece still
dangling from her ear.

*   *   *

I HAD KNOWN I COULDN'T trust Jeff. But I had also known that I had no choice. If there was even a chance that he was going to give me what I so desperately needed, I had to try. But to turn up myself, in person, was too stupid even for me.

And so I had called Hel, and asked her something I couldn't ask anyone else.

"You do know he's probably going to just arrest me?" she'd said resignedly, when we'd met up just before six, and I'd nodded.

"I know. But I don't know what other option I have. I *have* to get this number. Are you okay with that?"

"Yeah, I'm fine. I've booked the girls into afterschool club in case I end up with a night in the cells, but Rols doesn't think they'll charge me with anything much. I mean what, you sent me a message to go and meet your police officer ex in Piccadilly Circus, it's not exactly the Great Train Robbery, is it? For all I knew, you were planning to turn yourself in. That'll be my story anyway."

We had agreed, I would scope out the scene, and if Jeff looked to be alone, I would give Hel the green light via a Bluetooth headset she had bought from a phone shop en route. Hel, meanwhile, would come out of the Tube wearing a black hoodie similar to mine, so as not to spook Jeff too soon. I would be just inside the store, watching, a safe distance away, ready for Hel to read the code aloud if Jeff handed it over. We couldn't afford to meet up again afterwards. There was a very strong chance that Jeff would give Hel the code and then see if she led him straight back to me.

As soon as I had the code, I would drop the Bluetooth earpiece into a display and walk out through the store's other exit, the opposite direction from Hel. No contact and, hopefully, zero risk to me if Jeff had someone tailing Hel.

Of course, in the event, Jeff hadn't bothered with anything as elaborate as that—he'd simply arrested Hel before she'd even said hello. Given a competent solicitor, which Roland's colleagues certainly were, I didn't think she'd be in custody for more than a few hours, let alone charged with anything. But that was pretty cold comfort. In terms of accessing Gabe's backups, I was back to square one—and the thought made me want to cry.

I had only one option left, an option which had been playing at the edge of my mind ever since I'd thought ruefully of the Bitcoin sitting inaccessible in Gabe's private wallet. Because that wasn't quite true. It wasn't *quite* inaccessible. I couldn't get it out. But I *could* transfer it. And twenty thousand pounds . . . well, that was enough of a bribe to buy me my one remaining option. The only problem was, it was even more risky than trusting Jeff. And I had no idea how to go about it.

I knew the basics. Tor. Dark marketplaces. I even knew the names of some of them—Versus was one, AlphaBay another. The problem was I couldn't for the life of me remember half of what Gabe had told me. He had done his fair share of noodling around on the darker corners of the internet, not to buy, at least not after his teenage conviction for hacking, but just to keep an eye on what was being sold—admin passwords, data dumps, software hacks. Anything that might affect our clients. And sometimes he had talked about it—which markets sold what, which seemed trustworthy, and which had been infiltrated by the feds or taken over by scammers who might put your Bitcoin in escrow and then run off with the cash. Truth be told, I had never found it very interesting—it had felt like a shittier, druggier version of Craigslist, filled with an even worse combination of chancers and dickheads. Now I wished beyond anything that I had listened more carefully. Because there was no friendly *Rough Guide to Tor* that I could buy on Amazon. No *Which?* guide to dark markets.

I was about to go somewhere I knew nothing about and offer a lot of money to a complete stranger. And I had no idea if it would work or end up with me dead in a roadside ditch.

SATURDAY, FEBRUARY 11

MINUS ONE DAY

This is it, I think," I said to the lorry driver as we neared the service station on the M1 where I'd agreed to meet M4dR0XXX600—or Madrox, as I was calling him in my head, which was a lot easier to say. "Seriously, I can't thank you enough."

"Ah, it's no problem," the guy said. He shifted down a gear and moved into the left lane, shooting me an appraising look as he did. His expression was . . . well, if I had to pick an adjective, I'd say *concerned*, and I tried to sit up straighter and make the low-level shaking a little less obvious. I had been shivering fairly consistently since I'd woken up that morning, and at first I'd thought it was just the cold— I'd slept near an air-conditioning outlet in the city, but unlike the other rough sleepers in the same alcove, I'd had no wad of cardboard to protect me from the chill concrete pavement, and any warmth from the exhaust had seemed to leach straight out of me and into the hard ground. But since then I'd been hanging around shops and libraries, all places that were usually pretty overheated, and somehow I still couldn't get any warmth back into my bones. Now I was sweating as well as shivering, and I was forced to admit that maybe I was becoming seriously ill.

Most ominously of all, I could no longer really feel the wound in my side—but it wasn't because it was healing. It was because my whole torso hurt now—a grinding, wrenching pain that made it impossible to eat without throwing up and kept me hunched half over in the driver's cab of the lorry that had stopped at my outstuck thumb and makeshift sign reading *M1, north*.

"Look, love," the driver said now, "I don't want—I mean, it's none of my business, but are you sure you're okay?"

I closed my eyes. I knew what I should say—that I was fine, that it *was* none of his business. But somehow his awkward kindness, maybe combined with his age—he was probably in his sixties, about the age my dad would have been, if he'd lived—made lying feel impossible.

"I don't feel great," I admitted at last. "But I'll be okay once I've met—" I stumbled, trying to remember what I'd told him at the start of the journey. My mind felt fogged and my head hurt. "Met my friend," I finished at last, awkwardly.

"A friend, eh?" the driver said. We rumbled north for another mile or so, and then he clicked the indicator and said, as if making up his mind, "Look, love, I didn't know whether to say anything but . . . I know who you are."

My stomach seemed to lurch through the floor, and all of a sudden the fog was gone, replaced by a terrified spike of adrenaline. Everything seemed to slow down as I turned to stare at him.

"*What* did you say?"

"I said . . . I know who you are. Jacky or summat, isn't it? I didn't want to say nothing earlier in case I scared you off, but your face is all over the news. I'd show you"—he waved a hand at the phone mounted on the dashboard—"but there's cameras everywhere, I'd probably get a ticket for texting and driving."

My heart was pounding so hard against my ribs I thought I might pass out, and far from being cold and clammy, as it had been a moment ago, my face suddenly felt scarlet with a flaming heat. A drop of sweat trickled down my spine. Fuck. *Fuck.* How could I have been so stupid?

The driver was still speaking.

"I'm not going to turn you in or nothing."

"You—you're not?" I found I was trembling again—shakes from the infection, fear, shock, I couldn't have said. But I could hardly believe my ears. "Why not?"

"Agh." He waved a hand in the air, a gesture of disgust it looked like. "I can see you didn't do whatever it was. You're not the type. And

I don't trust them police neither. Never had any time for them since I got fitted up for a job I didn't do when I was twenty-one. Spent six months inside and that's how I came to be driving Black Beauty here." He patted the steering wheel. "Wasn't a whole lot of other places wanted a bloke with a criminal record. But it taught me one thing— they're more interested in putting someone behind bars than making sure it's the right bloke. So don't worry, I won't be saying anything. But you look . . . well, pardon my French, love, but you look like shit. I know going to hospital would be a risk, but . . ."

He trailed off, but I knew what he hadn't wanted to say. *Not* going to hospital might be a bigger one.

"I will go," I said at last. "I promise. In fact . . . I'm probably going to have to turn myself in, in a day or two. But I have one thing I need to try first—that's why I'm here."

The lorry had ground to a halt now, in the Heavy Goods parking lot, and the driver yanked on the parking brake and turned to look at me, his face serious in the light from the dash.

"You're not doing anything stupid now, are you?"

"No," I said, hoping it was true.

"And how are you going to get back home?"

"I . . ." I stopped. I honestly hadn't thought as far as my next move. Where even was home? "I don't know."

"Hmm." He folded his arms, looking at me as if sizing me up. I tried to smile, but my face felt clammy and numb, as if made from Play-Doh. "Well, if you need a ride, you go to the HGV caff and ask around the drivers if they know Bill Watts. If anyone gives you any crap, tell 'em you're my niece, Ella. They'll see you right."

"Okay," I said. I felt a rush of gratitude so intense it made my eyes prickle and my throat hurt. I thought of Lucius at the hostel, of the burger van owner, of the woman on the train, of all the people who had helped someone they didn't know, with no prospect of anything back but thanks. Gabe's death had brought me close to the worst of humankind—but there were still good people out there, people like

Bill, making it hard to despair completely. "Bill—I don't know how I can thank you—"

"No thanks necessary," he said, waving his hand again as if swatting away a fly. "Just you keep yourself safe. Now, you got your bag?"

I nodded, pulling it up from the footwell, and said, "Thank you again, Bill, seriously. And . . . goodbye."

"Bye, Jacky," Bill said a little sadly. He watched as I climbed carefully down from the rig, trying not to make any sudden moves that would wake the roaring pain in my side, and then I walked off across the car park, into the dark.

IT HAD BEGUN TO RAIN as I made my way to the spot I had arranged with Madrox, away from the main entrance. "By the fire exit, next to the KFC concession" the message had said. As I crossed the car park I could smell the familiar nauseating tang of frying chicken and see someone huddling under the canopy of the service station, looking down at their phone. At this range I couldn't see if it was a man or a woman—let alone if whoever it was looked suspicious.

I swallowed, hard.

What I was about to do was insanely risky—the equivalent of walking up to a complete stranger with twenty thousand pounds in untraceable banknotes. Madrox could be a cop. He could be someone who just fancied twenty grand without earning it. If he pulled a gun on me—or let's be honest, just punched me anywhere in the vicinity of the weeping wound under my clothes—that would be it. I would have to hand over the private key, and with it any chance of getting into Gabe's backup drive.

My heart was pounding as I crossed the tarmac, and I was concentrating so hard on the figure in front of me that I didn't see the speeding sports car until it was nearly on me. I skipped out of the way just in time, the blare of its horn drowning out the splash of puddle water that drenched me, and resisted the urge to stick two fingers up at the driver.

Then I drew a deep breath, trying to calm my suddenly racing pulse, and stepped off the road and onto the grass verge by the KFC.

The figure looked up as I did so, and I saw it was a man—a kid, really, probably not more than twenty. He was slight, and looked almost as nervy as I felt, and that was saying something. He was wearing a gray hoodie, not waterproof at all, and the rain was dripping off his fringe.

"Are you ReddyBrek?" he said in a voice that started off deep but broke on the last syllable, and I nodded.

"Yes." I was pleased that my voice at least sounded steady, and that my shivering could be passed off as down to the chilly rain. I didn't want to come across as intimidating—edgy people made bad decisions—but I couldn't afford to look weak. "Are you Madrox?"

"Yeah." He had relaxed a little as I came closer, presumably relieved by the fact that I wasn't a six-foot bloke with fists like hams, but now he seemed to remember the situation we were in and said, with a slight shake in his voice, "Put down the bag, yeah?"

"I mean . . . I will." I lowered the pack gingerly to the wet pavement. "But, like, are you going to frisk me as well? Should we both strip to our pants? It's a bit wet for that kind of thing." *Create a rapport. Make them laugh.*

He chuckled at that, a proper South London cackle, his face breaking into a grin that made him look about fourteen.

"Look, luv, you're fit and all, but I'm here for the cash, not the dogging."

I didn't feel like laughing back, but I forced out a weak *ha ha.*

"Relieved to hear it. Have you got the phone?"

He nodded, serious again, and held up a cheap burner mobile, the screen dark and speckled with rain.

"Yeah. My contact'll do the swap when I tell him I've got the money."

"Phone first," I said firmly, clenching my fists to try to hide their trembling, but he shook his head.

"Sorry, love. No money, no phone. Money, or I walk."

I felt sick. I had no idea how to go about this. I could see why he wouldn't want to hand over the phone without an assurance that I did at least have the cash. It wasn't like I could show him a suitcase full of notes—a private key meant nothing unless you actually knew what was in the wallet. But on the other hand, I had no idea if he was just a bullshitter with a Tesco mobile. Most of all, though, I *couldn't* afford to let him walk away. This was my absolute last chance.

"Okay, I'll transfer the money first," I said at last, "but I need to see that the mobile works. I need to know you've swapped it."

"Mate, I've done thousands of these," he said, a little nettled, and then seemed to realize that was a bit far-fetched, and amended, "Well, hundreds anyway. I'm good for it."

"Look, I believe you—but I have no idea whether—" I stopped. What I had been going to say was that I had no idea whether the police might have put some kind of lock on the SIM. But I didn't want to tell him the police were already involved in this. I had a strong suspicion the price might go up if I did—or that he might just cut and run, leaving me in a freezing car park with a useless string of numbers in a paperback book. "I'm worried the SIM might be locked. I need you to make sure the swap has gone through before I hand over the cash. You don't have to give me the phone, I just want to make sure it's worked before I press send on the transfer."

There was a long pause.

"Come *on*," I said, as persuasively as I knew how. I put every ounce of friendliness into my voice, everything I'd learned over ten years of social engineering, sweet-talking complete strangers, charming them into helping me for no reason other than that they wanted to. I made myself smile, though my face felt numb and cold. "It's twenty grand. I think I get a preview for twenty grand, no?"

The guy looked at me as if appraising my strength and size, and I felt a sick tremor of fever, or it could have been fear, run through me. I tried to hold myself steady. *Don't show them you're afraid.*

And then he rolled his eyes.

"Jeez, I must be some kind of sucker, but go on, then." He reached into his jacket and pulled out a different phone, a much fancier one. "What's the number you want swapped?"

I recited it off; he wrote it down, and then pressed a button on his phone and spoke into it, his voice low.

"Jay? Yeah, it's Mo—" he started, and then seemed to think better of the name he'd presumably been going to give and stumblingly changed it to "m-me. I'm here with the customer. I need you to do the swap now."

There was a brief pause while the person on the other end spoke. I couldn't hear what he was saying, but I had a strong suspicion he was asking Madrox whether he'd got the cash yet.

"I'm not gonna hand it over," Madrox said, a little indignantly. He had turned his back and walked a few steps away from me, as if in an attempt to keep the conversation private, but I could still hear what he was saying. "She just wants to—" There was an interruption from the speaker at the other end, and Madrox said, sounding annoyed, "She's like five foot nothing. She ain't gonna jump me, man."

More talking, more nodding and indignant reassurances from Madrox, whose hunched back was starting to look highly embarrassed. He had the air of a teen who'd been trying to be a player in front of his friends and had just been shown up by his mum. I was getting a bad feeling, a hollow dread in the center of my chest—though it was no longer about Madrox, but about whoever was on the other end of the phone. What if they didn't follow through? What if he told Madrox to take the cash and run? My work had taught me that angry, humiliated marks were dangerous ones. You wanted people to like you. You wanted them to trust you. You didn't want them to feel like they had something to prove. A friendly, cooperative Madrox I could deal with. One trying to look like a hard man for his boss, that I wasn't so sure of.

In the end, Madrox hung up and turned around, and I raised my head, trying to look like I hadn't heard every word.

"My contact's making the swap," he said, rather grandly, and I almost closed my eyes with relief. "You can test it by calling the phone. But after that, you transfer the Bitcoin, yeah?"

I nodded. There was a long wait, and then Madrox's phone pinged and he looked down at the message.

"Should be good to go. You wanna try it now?"

I nodded again and pulled out my own phone. This was it. There was no way now to avoid putting a giant target on my own back. It didn't matter if I used the fanciest encryption software in the world; the second I phoned Gabe's number, I would put the location of his new phone—and myself—firmly on the police radar. More importantly, I might have only minutes before the police noticed that Gabe's phone had been swapped and reversed the process.

I held my breath. I dialed Gabe's number. I waited, holding my breath, not sure if I was more scared that it might have failed, or that it might have worked.

There was a short pause—not more than two or three seconds. And then the phone in Madrox's hand rang.

I let out a shuddering exhalation of relief, almost a laugh, but the action was too sharp, too fast—the sudden movement of my ribs made the pain in my side flare, bright and hot, so intense that for a moment I saw stars and thought that I might pass out.

" . . . you okay?" I heard, dimly, as though through water. There was a hissing in my ears.

"Yeah . . ." I managed, grinding the words out, trying not to give way to the huge wave of trembling sickness that was threatening to overwhelm me. "Stomach . . . ache." It was kind of true—and at least that would give me an alibi if I puked. Madrox was looking at me with a mixture of concern, alarm, and suspicion, and I couldn't blame him. In his shoes I would probably have suspected some kind of ruse too. I had to get this show back on the road.

"I'm okay," I said, though I wasn't, not in the least. I swallowed hard against the saliva pooling in my mouth and the bile threatening to force its way up my throat. None of that mattered now. I needed to get that phone off Madrox and get the code before anyone realized what had happened. "Honestly, I'm fine. Let's do the transfer. What's your Bitcoin wallet address?"

He reeled it off, and I pulled out the paperback from my bag, the paperback with the number of the private key written in it. My fingers shook as I typed in the digits, and I had to concentrate, making sure I didn't mess up the long, complicated number—and then there it was, Gabe's Bitcoin wallet—a wallet which represented every remaining penny I had in the world.

For a moment, I wasn't sure if I could press the button to confirm the transfer, my hands were trembling so hard—and it wasn't only the aftermath of that shocking wave of pain that was making me shake. It was the realization that this was it. This was my last roll of the dice—every penny I had, my last remaining bargaining chip. But I knew that in reality, I had played my last card the moment Gabe's number was swapped to the phone in Madrox's hand. That phone was now a homing beacon, leading the police straight to whoever held it. Nothing else mattered now—not the Bitcoin, not Madrox. Nothing but that phone.

I gritted my teeth. I forced every muscle in my hand to *stop trembling*. I pressed send.

Madrox looked down at his own phone, tapping his foot. Then an alert sounded and he opened up the burner phone, frowning at the screen. I had been expecting him to hand it straight over, but he didn't. Instead he seemed to have changed tabs and to be typing something into another window.

When he looked up his expression was annoyed.

"You've not transferred enough."

My stomach seemed to drop, followed by a furious jolt of adrenaline. Was he stitching me up?

"What the fuck do you mean?" The words came out shriller and more angrily than I'd intended, and as soon as I'd said them I wanted to bite them back. I heard, as clear as if he were whispering into the Bluetooth earpiece, Gabe's voice in my ear. *Don't piss him off, babe.*

Too late. He looked pissed off. Very pissed off.

"Twenty grand," he said, and in spite of my own panicked alarm, part of me—the professional, social engineer part—could see he was as tense and upset as I was, as ready to believe he'd been conned. "That was the agreement. You've only transferred me eighteen."

"What do you mean?" I was baffled. "I agreed to twenty because I *had* twenty. I checked the exchange rate when we spoke."

"We spoke yesterday," he said, irritable now, as if talking to someone fairly thick. The words *you dumb bint* hovered unspoken. "Yeah, this probably was worth twenty *then*, but the exchange rate's gone down since then."

"Gone down?" I looked at him blankly. "By—what—ten percent? How can that be?"

"It's Bitcoin, innit," he said, even more tetchily. "It changes every day. If you wanted to fix a price in Bitcoin you should have said—but we agreed pounds."

"But—how is that my fault if the rate has changed?"

"Well, it's not fucking mine, is it?" he said, and even through my fury, a small part of me was whispering that he had a point. "If it had gone the other way—ten percent up—you'd be in profit. Not my fault it's gone south. You need to transfer the other two grand."

"But I can't." I spoke blankly. "I told you—I agreed to pay twenty grand because I *had* twenty grand. But that's it. I've got . . ." I looked down at the screen, calculating the tiny fraction of a Bitcoin left in the account. "I don't know, like fifty pounds in my wallet? No more."

"Well shit," Madrox said, plainly annoyed. "What are you gonna do, then? Got a credit card? There's an ATM in the service station."

I ran my fingers through my hair, feeling desperate. *Yes* was the answer to his question, and at this point I had very little to lose by using it, but I was absolutely certain that my accounts would have been frozen by now, as Jeff had pointed out. All I would be doing would be giving the police a nice clear ATM picture of the state I was currently in.

"No," I said at last. "No, I have absolutely no other money. I can give you . . ." I rummaged in the rucksack and pulled out the last few coins, counting them. "Four . . . five quid. That's literally my last pennies. And I can transfer you the rest of the Bitcoin, but there's absolutely no way I can get you two grand. Please." I put everything I'd ever learned into the words, my voice shaking with a desperation I was no longer trying to hide. I had no options left now apart from appealing to his sympathy. "Madrox, *please*, please, I honored what I thought was our agreement. I did my best. I swear it. If I had anything else—a watch—anything—I'd give it to you." I held up my wrists, showing him their bareness, and as I did, our eyes both fell on something—and the hollow at the center of my chest seemed to expand to engulf my entire body.

It was my ring. The ring Gabe had given to me when he proposed.

"How much is that worth?" Madrox said matter-of-factly, at the same time that I said, "*No.*"

"What is it, diamond?"

"Yes. But I can't. Please. I *can't.*"

"Your choice," Madrox said with a shrug. "You wanna call it off, I'll transfer you back the Bitcoin and we'll dump the phone."

Fuck. The unshed tears had swollen in my throat into a hard lump, so painful I could barely breathe, let alone speak. *Fuck.*

"How much is it worth?" Madrox said again.

"Please," I whispered. My voice was so hoarse and cracked I wasn't sure he could understand the words. I swallowed hard. "Please, I'll send you the money. I *swear.*"

"Oh, fuck this," Madrox said now, irritably. "My contact's already gonna be pissed off I came back with some piece-of-shit engagement ring. I'm not dicking about here while you make up your mind. You want this deal, or you don't?"

2 RUTH WARE

I shut my eyes. Pictures flitted through my mind. Gabe, kneeling on the sand on a beach in Norfolk, holding out the ring. *It's an antique,* he'd told me. *Seventeenth century. The diamond, it's not very big. And you can see how hard they tried to shape it, no proper cutting tools. But I thought . . . I thought you'd prefer it. It's a bit wonky, a bit unique.*

And I had picked it up and cradled it, and then slid it onto my finger, where it had rested like it had always belonged.

"No," I whispered, shaking my head, but even as I did so, I was twisting the ring, testing whether I could get it off. Twisting. Twisting it up my finger, hard against the bone. "Please, *no.*"

It came out like a sob, but the ring was already scraping against the edges of my knuckle.

I put my finger in my mouth, ring and all, feeling its hardness against my tongue, remembering Gabe's lips against mine, his body, his touch, the feel of him in my mouth.

I shut my eyes. I tasted blood. It *hurt.* Oh God, how could such a small thing hurt so much?

And then I was holding out the ring, my knuckle bruised and bloodied, one more loss, one more wound to add to everything that I had taken already.

"It's worth three grand," I said, my voice husky. I couldn't cry now. I *couldn't.* "Keep the fucking change."

Madrox gave a broad grin as the ring fell into his palm, a grin that might have been triumph but which I thought, more likely, was relief.

"Received. Thanks for the custom, ReddyBrek. Here's your phone." He held it out.

My fingers closed around it, and for a second I thought my knees might give way. I had done it. I had *done it.* But at what cost? The blood was singing in my ears, my legs felt like wet bread, and everything hurt.

"You need any more swapped, just let us know, yeah?" Madrox was saying, though his voice sounded as though it was coming from very far away. "My contact's good for most networks."

"Thanks," I said, but the truth was, one way or another I was never coming back here, and we both knew it.

I watched Madrox as he disappeared across the rainy car park and then, finally, I let my legs give way, and I sank to my knees in the muddy grass, the rain pouring down my face like tears.

I knew in my heart that it was probably stupid to go inside the service station. It was full of cameras and CCTV, and if Bill the lorry driver had recognized me, there was a strong chance he wouldn't be the only member of the public to do so.

But I was soaking wet, chilled to the bone, and a growing part of me no longer cared. I needed a bathroom, and a plate of hot food, and, more importantly, I was now holding a phone linked to Gabe's number, which meant that CCTV was the least of my worries. Every time that phone pinged a cell tower, it was leading the police right to me.

Inside the service station I went first to the bathroom. It was empty, and I locked myself into a stall, peed, and then sat in the cubicle, pressing my hand to my side and wondering if I should check what was beneath the dressing. In spite of my shivery-cold flesh, the wound itself felt hot, even through my clothes, the dressing swollen and mushy with what could have been seeping blood or something worse.

In the end I stood, stripped off my anorak, pulled up my T-shirt, and peeled back the dressing.

It looked very, very bad. But what made me most worried was not the wound itself, but the dark red streaks spreading out like tendrils across my skin. For what felt like a long time, I simply sat there, looking down at my side, and trying to control my rising panic. I knew that this had gone beyond first aid—that I was risking septicemia, organ failure . . . even death. But what could I do? Turn myself in? Not now. Not when I was so close to solving all this.

In the end I did the only thing I could—I threw away the soiled dressing, and then dug in my rucksack for a fresh one.

As I drew it out, I realized that the box was almost empty. I was down to the very last one, and I had no money to buy more. But there was no point in thinking about that. If it came to that, I had no money for anything—food, water, a place to sleep. My side was only one of a list of problems that were about to become very pressing indeed, problems that shoplifting wouldn't solve, if indeed I could pass under the radar of any security guard now, which I doubted. Pushing the thoughts out of my head, I peeled back the plastic and pressed the clean white square to the wound, holding my breath as the pain surged and then subsided again.

Then I shouldered the pack and made my way shakily to the sinks.

I looked . . . well, I looked like absolute shit, that was my first thought as I stared at my reflection in the mirror above the faucet. The second was amazement that Bill the lorry driver had recognized me, because I barely recognized myself.

I had always been fairly slight, but now my skin looked stretched tight over my skull, flushed with fever over my cheekbones but greenish white everywhere else. There were blue-black shadows under my eye sockets, and my bleached hair looked like a dirty mop head. I hadn't showered since the hostel, and as for when I had last eaten . . . was it today? Or was it the veggie deluxe I'd had yesterday outside Northampton? I couldn't remember anymore. Well, the only thing Madrox hadn't taken from me was the five quid in cash, so at least I could buy myself some fries.

First, though, I needed to wash the blood off my hands. The hot water was too hot, but in a way that felt strangely good, stinging the cuts and scrapes with a sensation that was almost cathartic. I splashed some on my face, wincing at the heat, and then moved across to the dryer.

As I rubbed my hands gently underneath the hot air, I looked down at my bruised, empty ring finger and felt that treacherous lump rise again in my throat, making it impossible to swallow.

I'm sorry, I thought. *I'm so sorry, Gabe.*

I knew what he would have said if he were here. *Don't give it a second thought. Who cares about a stupid fucking ring, babe?* But I did care. It was the last tangible piece of him I'd had with me. And now that too had been ripped away, and all I had left to show for it was the bruise. Maybe this was how it was supposed to go, though. Not with the bang of a prison door but whimpering gasps, everything stripped away until I had nothing left to lose.

You got this, I heard in my ear, and the sob rose up inside me, choking me. *I do not fucking have this, Gabe.* I wanted to scream it, sob it, wail it—*I can't do this anymore, do you understand?*

But I had to. I had to do this. Because there was no one else.

The dryer cut out, and I swallowed down the pain in my throat, shouldered the rucksack, and pulled up my hood. Then I made my way out of the bathroom and into the bright lights of the food court.

At McDonald's, I ordered the cheapest, warmest combination I could think of—a large tea, fries, and ketchup—and then took my tray over to a booth in the far corner, where I sat, picking at the fries and trying not to drip rainwater onto my MacBook.

I had warmed up now, or should have, with the heat inside the building, the hot water, and the dryer, but I was still shivering, and my fingers felt stiff and stupid as I tried to input the password. After two botched tries I had to force myself to slow down, breathe, and make sure of every letter. A third failure would mean I was locked out until the counter reset, and I couldn't afford that.

But the final attempt, I got it right, and the laptop fired up.

The service station Wi-Fi was, surprisingly, not too bad—and this time, as I navigated to Gabe's backup cloud, I didn't bother with the VPN. I had already blown my cover. Now, if something happened to me, I wanted the trail to be clear and visible—bread crumbs large enough for Malik to follow and figure out what I had been doing.

I typed in Gabe's email and password, taking immense care over each letter, and the screen hung for a moment while the site considered—making me hold my breath with agony.

Then, *Send verification code?* asked the log-in screen.

I let out another shuddering breath, more carefully this time, not wanting a repeat of the screeching agony in the car park.

I clicked *OK*.

And then I waited.

And waited.

And . . . waited.

My remaining fries were going cold, but I suddenly felt too sick to eat them. Why wasn't the code coming through? Had the police already noticed the loss of service on the phone sitting in their evidence locker and managed to block the swap? Or had Madrox and his "contact" double-crossed me after he left the car park and changed the number back? It was possible—though I couldn't imagine what they would have got out of it.

I glanced up at the top right of the phone screen. I still had service—three bars of it, plus 4G. The SIM card was working fine.

And then a horrible thought occurred to me. The phone in Madrox's hand *had* rung when I called Gabe. But I had never seen the screen. I had no way of knowing if it was my call that was making it vibrate, or if Madrox had sent a secret message to his contact to call him, in order to make me think the phone was now linked to Gabe's number. Maybe his contact didn't work in a phone store at all. Maybe he was just your garden-variety con artist. Fuck. *Fuck.* I had thought I was being so clever, calling the phone to check the swap had gone through. Why hadn't I waited and made Madrox answer it, to check it really was Gabe's number?

I was still staring in cold horror at the phone in my hand, trying to work out how I could figure out whether I'd been double-crossed, when I heard footsteps behind me and looked up to see a member of staff walking towards the quiet corner of the forecourt where I was sitting.

I looked down at the phone again, more to hide my face than because I really expected the code to have come through, but I could still hear the footsteps, clicking and purposeful, coming closer and closer, and to my shock, when I glanced furtively up for a second time, I saw that the staff member wasn't walking past or heading to another area. She was coming straight to my table. To *me*.

Oh God. Oh God.

Had I been spotted? Was it worth making a run for it?

I looked down at the table, at the open laptop, at my bag, and then at the security guard standing by the big glass doors, boredom in every line of his stance. He looked tired, and not exactly athletic. On a good day, I might have risked it. But like this, with a pack that felt increasingly like a leaden weight, sweating and shaking with the wound in my side, I would never make it. Not even if I abandoned all my stuff—and I couldn't do that, not now. Not the laptop, anyway. Not when I was so close.

My heart felt like it had stopped dead inside my chest. The woman was almost at my table.

I swallowed and pasted what I hoped was my friendliest smile on my face, though it felt like a grotesque, clammy attempt at the real thing. Then I looked up. "Everything okay?"

"You forgot your tea!" the woman said. She was smiling. In her outstretched hand she held a paper cup with a plastic lid.

Blankly I looked down at my tray. No tea.

"Sugar?" the woman asked.

"Oh. Oh God, I'm so sorry. I'm such an idiot." *You can say that again.* "You shouldn't have come over." My heart had restarted, shallow with relief. I felt a stupid, giddy grin, a real one this time, spread over my face. "Honestly, you didn't have to." Then, realizing she was still waiting for an answer, "N-no, no sugar. Thank you. I mean, no thanks."

"No probs!" the woman trilled. She set the tea down on the table, and then turned on her heel and left.

I tried not to slump too obviously.

And when I looked down at my phone—the code was there.

I typed it in. There was a brief pause as the screen hung blank for a moment, thinking about its response, and then Gabe's backup drive opened up in front of me.

My first feeling was triumph. The second, following very closely, was despair.

Not because the drive had been wiped, as I'd half feared, but the opposite. It was utterly stuffed. Folder after folder, file after file. How on earth was I supposed to find a needle in this programming haystack?

A bunch of the folders seemed to be personal—pictures, scans, useful documents relating to the house. Another set related to our company. There were files of VAT returns, invoices, bank statements and spreadsheets. For the love of Mike, had Gabe ever just saved something, without backing it up?

However, by far the largest section of files seemed to relate to ongoing projects. Glancing down the *A*s, I saw *Arden Alliance*, but it was just one of many, starting with *Aardvark Inc*—a company we'd never worked for, as far as I knew, but when I clicked through there were notes on some responsible disclosure reports Gabe had made, flagging up a vulnerability in their online email portal. Below Aardvark were folders labeled *Abel Inc, Ace Electric, Adelaide Systems, Adelphi-Core, Ajax & Cline, Anoraxis, Apex Finance, Arcturus Publishing* . . . and that was just the *A*s. The list went on and on, through the whole alphabet, and I had no idea where to start.

I scrolled down to *C*. A file named *Cole* seemed like too much to hope for—but Cerberus Security was the name of Cole's company, and it didn't seem impossible that Gabe would have labeled the folder that way. But there was nothing. I felt like crying.

My side was hurting, along with my head and my joints, which ached like I had the flu, and now I shifted in my chair, feeling the clamminess on my back sticking my T-shirt to my spine and then peeling away as I moved. Under my clothes the new dressing felt stiff, the adhesive pulling at my skin in a way that somehow seemed to aggravate the wound. I had probably been bending when I put it on, and now it was too tight, but I knew I couldn't start repositioning it now. If I unpeeled it, there was a good chance it wouldn't stick down again, and it was the last one.

Instead I popped a couple of ibuprofen and scrolled further down the list, trying to ignore the pain. Past *C* to *D, E, F,* and then further through the *L*s, *M*s, *N*s and on. There was nothing, or nothing that meant anything to me, at any rate. There were names of companies, names of programs, some unfamiliar, some recognizable from projects we'd worked on together—but nothing I saw seemed to relate to Cole. Had I got this all wrong?

And then I saw it. Right at the bottom, below *Unrivalled Software* and above *Upside Down Design*. A folder labeled *Unsubmitted.*

That was it. Not Unsubmitted Inc., or Unsubmitted Software. It could have been a company name—but something about it, and the size of the folder, made me pause and click through.

Inside were a bunch more folders, these much less tidy, mostly labeled with names relating to website URLs, apps, or programs. And right at the bottom of the list was a name I knew well. *Really* well. Watchdog. It was the name of Cerberus's flagship security app.

I clicked on the folder.

I don't know what I expected. A ticking bomb, a bunch of warnings to flash up. Instead, what I got was a load of files I didn't recognize, some text, some in what appeared to be computer code. I had no idea what half of them were.

Mentally crossing my fingers that I wasn't going to make anything explode, I opened one of the files. It was a long string of code—and I had no idea what any of it did. But at the top were a series of what I assumed were Gabe's notes to himself. I had seen them often enough, a kind of to-do list for that specific project, filled with reminders of

loose ends and tasks left unfinished. This one was no exception—
there were half a dozen items listed at the top, most of which seemed
to be programming related and made little sense to me. But the last
few . . . they made my heart stutter.

THIS HAS NOT BEEN PATCHED YET
TODO: Notify Cerberus next week
TODO: Check Puppydog concerns w Cole

There it was. Cole's name—in a document Gabe had been working on right before his death—alongside a clear implication that he
was about to go over Cole's head, direct to Cerberus. The "last modi-
fied" date on the file was Friday—the day before we'd done the Arden
Alliance pen test. The day, according to Cole's own account, that the
two of them had spoken by phone.

What Cole had presented as a routine catch-up must, in reality, have been something quite different—Gabe, following up the
warning he'd given Cole with a polite heads-up that he'd be filing an
official report with Cerberus on Monday. It was the kind of routine
disclosure he'd done many times before as an ethical hacker—one
following a tried and tested process. But that friendly warning, *I'm
sorry, mate, but there's a problem with your code*, had cost Gabe his
life—and here was the evidence.

Maybe it wasn't quite a smoking gun—but it was a whole lot more
plausible than the Sunsmile theory Malik and Miles were working on
right now.

But it was the reference to Puppydog that really made me shiver.
Because Watchdog was bad enough. Watchdog was the home security app that Cerberus made most of their money from—a 360-degree
monitoring system that hooked up everything from your home hub
to your doorbell to a single app. But Puppydog—Puppydog was the
parental monitoring app that was fast coming up the charts to beat it
in popularity. Puppydog gave parents complete access to everything

on their child's phone—their contact list, their browsing history, and most importantly of all, it tracked the physical location of both parent and children, so they could always find each other.

If someone could hack Puppydog, they could monitor not just you—but your kids. What kind of money would someone give for that? Access to a celebrity's child? A political dissident's family? A chill ran down my spine that was nothing to do with the fever burning through me. And as it did, as I stared at the screen trying to process this and wondering exactly what Cole had got himself involved in, Gabe's phone began to ring.

For a long moment I just stared at the screen wondering, stupidly, what was happening. The number was a landline, a London one, and I had no idea who it could be. Although Gabe's number had been SIM-swapped to this phone, nothing else had been transferred, which meant his contact list was blank. It could be anyone from Gabe's gym, to his parents, to . . . well, anyone. The question was, should I pick up?

The phone was still ringing, vibrating across the table, and I was still trying to make up my mind when a woman strolled past, pushing a sleeping baby in a buggy, and remarked, "Well it ain't gonna answer itself, is it?" with a kind of weary pissed-offness that put my back up.

You have no idea what I'm dealing with, I wanted to snap at her. But the truth was, that went both ways. Maybe she had lost someone too. Maybe she was afraid. Maybe she was mired in postnatal depression.

Okay, she almost certainly wasn't on the run from the police, a suspect in her dead husband's murder. But either way, she was right. The phone wasn't going to answer itself, and I wasn't gaining a great deal by letting it ring. It had already connected to the cell towers, beaming out its location to anyone who knew the number. Picking up wouldn't change much. And the truth was, the ringing was starting to drive me crazy, boring into my aching head like a drill.

I took a deep breath. I picked up the phone. I pressed answer.

"Who is this?" the caller immediately demanded.

I blinked. The voice at the other end was immediately familiar—but I couldn't place it. The speaker was a woman, and it sounded like she was somewhere busy; I could hear the sound of computer keyboards clicking in the background, people talking. For a crazy minute I wondered if it was Keeley calling from the Sunsmile call center—if she had tracked me down to demand what the fuck I had been playing at. But no—that was insane, of course it was. She didn't have my number, let alone Gabe's. And glancing at my watch I saw that it was too late for Sunsmile to be open. But I *did* know that voice. Was it one of Gabe's friends?

And then, as the caller spoke again, repeating her question with a sharper intonation, "Who *is* this?" I knew.

t's me," I said very quietly.

There was a long silence. When the caller spoke again, she didn't sound abrupt anymore. In fact, there was a warmth in her voice, a smile like someone whose Christmases just came all at once.

"Hello, Jack," she said. "It's really, *really* good to hear your voice."

I shut my eyes.

Malik.

DS Habiba Malik. The woman I had last heard calling me through the sea mist, threatening to hunt me down with dogs. And now her voice was in my ear, with an intimacy that made me shiver. Because it was that voice, *her* voice, that had grilled me hour after hour on the night of Gabe's death, and then again the next day, pulling apart my story and putting it back together in the most damning way. It was Malik who had urged me through my account again and again, winkling out details I barely remembered, picking up on inconsistencies I hadn't even noticed myself—and it was her voice that had made me run, when I'd heard her out in the corridor, urging my arrest.

And although she'd been wrong about my guilt, she'd been right about practically everything else—more often than I wanted to admit. This case *had* stunk, from beginning to end. It *was* all wrong, just as she'd told Miles that night. And she'd had me pegged too. Where Miles had looked at me and seen nothing but a harmless, grieving widow, Malik had seen me for what I was—someone steely, someone determined—a flight risk. And she'd been right.

Fuck. In one sense answering the phone hadn't done much—Malik must have known, as soon as Gabe's phone lost service, that I was behind it. But I had given her certainty where before there had been doubt. Now the police knew exactly where to look.

"Jack, look, I understand," Malik was saying in my ear. Her voice was kind, sympathetic—the tone she'd used on that first night, when she had helped me pick out clothes to take to the police station and wash Gabe's blood off my hands. But I knew that kindness was a means to an end. I had done enough calls like this myself—calls where you just wanted to keep your mark on the line long enough to get the information you needed. I was Malik's mark. And she was good. "Your sister told us what's been going on," Malik was saying now, her tone warm. "She told us you didn't do this. But you can't help yourself by running. We *want* to believe you. We *want* to find out who did this, but we can't do that without your help. Will you help us, Jack?"

"I know who did it," I said. My voice shook. "At least, I know who led them to Gabe. His name is Cole Garrick. He works for Cerberus Security. And he is—" My voice cracked. "He *was* Gabe's best friend. And you need to arrest him *right now*."

"We're looking into all—" Malik began, but I interrupted.

"Listen to me—this was a contract killing, by the people who employ Cole. He's probably got an alibi up to the hilt because he wasn't the one who actually cut Gabe' s throat, but he *was* the person who started all this, and *he* was the person who put Gabe into their crosshairs, and if you wait to act, they will kill Cole too. If you want him alive to stand trial, you need to take him into custody *right now*."

"Let's talk about all this at the station," Malik said persuasively. "You must be exhausted, Jack. Let me send a car to pick you up."

I put my hand to my head, feeling something very close to a hysterical laugh bubble up inside me. Exhausted? Exhausted didn't even begin to cover it. I felt . . . I felt like I had nothing left to give, nowhere else to go. My side hurt. My joints hurt. Everything hurt, and I felt constantly on the verge of throwing up. Was it really time to stop running? Maybe it was.

But then I heard something. My head went up, listening. It was a police siren. And when I put my head down and looked out of the food court window, I could see blue lights slicing through the darkness of the car park.

If I gave myself up now, I would have to trust Malik to believe my story, read Gabe's garbled notes, understand the significance of what I had found, and, more importantly, act on it, before Cole's handlers got to it.

Because whatever Cole had done, whatever he deserved, I didn't want him to die. I wanted him to end up in prison for what he had done to Gabe, but I didn't want him killed.

Most crucially of all, I wanted that zero-day exploit—the exploit that had cost Gabe his life—patched so that no one else could ever benefit from it. Whatever those people were doing, whatever information they were gaining, it was worth killing for. And Gabe had taught me there was only one sure way of making certain that patch happened.

Publicity.

"Goodbye, Malik," I said, and I stood up, packing away the laptop.

"Jack," she said, and her voice was sharp now. "Jack. Don't—"

I hung up. I turned off the phone with Gabe's SIM in it, and my own, and shoved both into my rucksack.

Then I began to walk. Not particularly fast. Just the brisk walk of a woman with somewhere to go and something to do. And not towards the door, where I could see another pair of blue lights pulling into the forecourt. With my head down and my hood pulled up, I was walking the other way. Deeper into the service station. Towards the stairs, and the overpass that lead to the southbound service station.

Pulling myself up the steps was more of an effort than I wanted to admit, and as I rounded the halfway landing I had to hang on to the banister and hold myself up for a moment before I continued up the next flight. When I reached the top there was cold sweat running down the hollow of my spine, and it was all I could do to stop my knees from giving way. The pack on my back felt like a dead weight, and now I dug inside it, pulling out everything I didn't need—the wash bag, the sling, the water bottle—every bit of weight except the things I would need to see this job through to the end. I let the items fall to the floor, then pulled the half-empty bag back onto my shoulders, straightened up, and began to walk again. Mercifully, the corridor was quiet, no one around, and I was able to hold on to the wall as I half walked, half jogged through the tunnel, over the six lanes of traffic below.

As I passed, I could see the lines of cars beneath, see another police car speeding north, from London, towards the service station, and a part of me almost wanted to laugh. Three cop cars. Who on earth did they think they were dealing with, Osama bin Laden?

I was halfway across now, but looking back over my shoulder I could see the blue lights clustered around the entrance to the food court, and could imagine the police fanning out inside, searching the booths, the loos, the back exits.

How long before they noticed the overpass? Another patrol car was speeding north on blue lights, siren wailing, but this one passed underneath and I knew probably heading for the next junction, intending to double back and search the southbound service area. I had to get across before they made it.

I quickened my step, feeling the perspiration prickling at the back of my neck and across my upper lip. My whole right side was throbbing now, from my breast to my pelvis, pulsing with every beat of my heart, but I pushed myself on, stumbling once, and just catching myself by grabbing hold of the windowsill of the tunnel. I groaned, not trying to hide the sound, for there was no one up here, and held myself up while the tunnel stopped lurching and swinging, then carried on, trying to breathe with short, shallow pants, as it hurt to fill my lungs completely.

I was at the stairs now, and I skittered down them, trying not to look like someone on the run from what was now quite an obvious collection of blue lights on the other side of the motorway. Another car screamed north underneath the pedestrian tunnel, heading for the flyover at the next junction. What was that, five now? Six?

As I came down the stairs into the eerily identical southbound foyer, I was half expecting to be greeted by a matching collection of uniformed police, but there was no one there apart from a second, equally bored security guard, who did not look up as I walked quickly across the beige tiles and out into the night.

Outside I looked left and right, trying to figure out where the fuck the HGV area might be. Did they have a separate terminus? I couldn't see one—but on the far side of the parking lot was a collection of rigs, and peering through the spattering rain I could see at least two had lights on inside the cabs.

As I stood, trying to decide what to do, blue lights appeared on the slip road leading from the southbound motorway, and my heart gave an involuntary leap in my chest. The sight made up my mind, and I took a deep breath and began to walk as quickly as I could through the rainy night, towards the lighted cabs.

"DO YOU KNOW BILL WATTS?" I asked, for the fourth, or maybe fifth, time, and for the fourth, or maybe fifth, time, the driver shook his head.

"Sorry, darlin'. Is he a driver? Have you tried inside?"

He nodded back towards the service station, and I looked over my shoulder to see a second police car sliding to a halt in front of the steps. I turned back, hoping my face wasn't too obviously ashen.

"I've already been—"

"Bill Watts?" A voice came from behind me, and I turned again to see a rig, not too far away, with the window cracked open and a cloud of vape smoke coming from the slit. Now the driver rolled it down further and peered out. "I know him. Chatted to him on the radio earlier. I think he's heading north, though. Darlington or summat? Doubt he'll be here."

I felt a rush of relief.

"I'm actually not looking for him. I'm his—" I swallowed. I was someone who lied professionally, for God's sake, so why was it so hard doing it now, when it mattered most? "I'm his n-niece, Ella. I'm stuck and he said maybe if I asked around, someone would give me a lift south?"

"Where are you looking to get to?" The guy had opened the door and now he slid easily to the ground. He was a lot younger than Bill, nearer my age, and powerfully built. He looked like when he wasn't driving he probably spent every hour in the gym.

"London, ideally."

"No bother. I'm doing a drop in Greenwich. I can't get you much closer cos of the Low Emission Zone, but if I left you round there, would that help?"

"Are you kidding?" Greenwich was only a few miles from Cole's flat. I could walk the rest if I had to. "That would be amazing. Is there any chance . . ." I glanced over my shoulder, trying not to look too obviously at the police cars idling by the main entrance, radios crackling over the still night air. "I mean, I'd be incredibly grateful either way, but I don't suppose you're leaving soonish, are you?"

He glanced at his watch, then nodded.

"Yeah, just about done my break time." He tapped something into a log on his phone, then said, "Hop in, Ella."

For a moment I had no clue who he was talking to, then I realized and a smile spread across my face. Ella Watts. For the next couple of hours, that was me.

"Thanks. And you are . . . ?"

"Mike. Michael Rake to the DVLA. Or Micky Take to my mates." He held open the door for me, and I climbed up into the cab.

AS WE SPED SOUTH ON the motorway, the flashing blue lights receding behind us, Mike kept up a steady stream of chat, asking me questions about myself, my work, my supposed uncle Bill . . . I answered at random, trying to keep up the pretense of being related to Bill while mixing in "facts" I could plausibly pull off without research. I told him I lived in London, worked in a call center, wasn't married. Saying those last words gave me a stab of pain that was nothing to do with the wound in my side, and I couldn't stop myself glancing down at my bruised and empty finger. I remembered Gabe's face as he had held the ring out to me, the light in his clear brown eyes. He must have known I would say yes—but even still, he'd looked nervous, had stammered over the words, "Jack, will you m-marry me?"

I saw again the slanting light, smelled the ocean, felt the sand between my toes as I'd crouched in the dunes, saying *Yes, yes, yes* . . .

Oh God, I thought, *I love him.* And for once, I didn't have to painfully correct myself over the tense, because it didn't matter that Gabe was dead. I still loved him. I would always love him. What was I going to do when all this was over, when I had no reason to keep putting one foot in front of the other?

"Ella?" I heard, dimly, over the roar of my thoughts, and I looked up to find Mike watching me curiously.

"Sorry . . . sorry, I was . . ." I swallowed. He could clearly see something was wrong. He was looking at me with a mix of concern and that alarm men show when they think a woman is about to cry. "Actually, to be completely honest, your—your question hit a nerve. I lost someone. M-my partner. He—well, he died. Not long ago. Saying it aloud just made me feel—"

I stopped. The words were stuck in my throat. I took a long, shuddering breath, and for the first time I was grateful for the pain in my side, distracting me from everything I was trying hard not to feel.

"Ah, right," Mike said. There was something else in his face, though, not just sympathy but a kind of relief. "To be honest that's a bit of a— Nah, sorry. Ignore me. Me and my big mouth."

"No, go on," I said, a little curious now. He was looking both relieved and profoundly uncomfortable, and anything was better than trying to keep up with my own lies and fibs about Bill. "You can say it."

"Well, to be honest, I could see I'd put my foot in it and I was a bit worried . . . I thought maybe he was beating you up. I can see—" He waved a hand at me, taking it all in: my hunched stance, my bruised knuckles, my good arm curled over my bad side, unsuccessfully masking the fact that I was clearly in pain. "You look like you been in the wars. I thought maybe it was him did it."

His words hit me like a slap. The fact that I looked ill, I could admit that. I wasn't delusional. Even the fact that I was more and more often being mistaken for someone homeless, I was getting used to it, though not to the guilt of accepting sympathy under false pretenses. But the thought that I looked like a battered wife . . . the idea brought the lump back to my throat, as though I'd betrayed Gabe in some way, though I knew that wasn't true.

"No," I said, huskily now. "No, he was . . . he was amazing. None of this was his fault. I was in—" I swallowed hard, trying to think of a story that would explain the state of me without prompting Mike to drive me to hospital. "We were in an accident. He died. I'm still . . . I'm still recovering."

It was a lie, of course it was. Nothing about Gabe's death had been an accident. And I knew in my heart I would never recover from this. Maybe I didn't want to. Because the more I thought about what lay ahead when all this was over, the less I wanted to face it. I just wanted to lie down, close my eyes, and wait for Gabe.

"I'm really sorry, pet," Mike said, his voice a touch gruff. He cleared his throat, staring fixedly ahead at the road as though he didn't want to look at me and set himself off. "Really sorry. That's—that's rough. Really unfair."

"Yeah," I said. My throat hurt so much I could hardly get the words out. "Yeah. It is. It's really unfair."

We drove in silence after that, the lights of the motorway lulling me, until at last the lorry swung around a mini roundabout, jolting my head against the windowpane, and I felt Mike touch my shoulder.

"Ella. Ella, wake up, love."

I blinked, my tired brain taking longer than it should have to figure out who he was talking to. Ella. Ella was me. Fuck. Had I been asleep?

"Are we there?" My voice was croaky, and my mouth felt dry, with a strange taste. My head was throbbing. I wiped the thread of drool coming from the side of my lips and blinked again. The streetlights swam in and out of focus.

"We're just coming up to Canary Wharf," Mike was saying, "but I wasn't sure which side of the river you wanted."

I rubbed my eyes, trying to put the pieces together. The lorry was idling in a layby just off the North Circular and I could see the O2 behind us and the Blackwall Tunnel signs not far ahead. We must be pretty close to the Thames. I could get the DLR from Greenwich . . . but what time did that close?

"What time—" I croaked out inaudibly, and then cleared my throat and tried again. "Sorry, what time is it?"

"Coming up to midnight. You gonna be all right?"

"Yeah. Yeah, I'm fine. I—my friend lives in Wapping." Another lie. Cole wasn't my friend. And if I managed to do this, he wouldn't be living in Wapping much longer. Wormwood Scrubs Prison, hopefully.

"I reckon you'll be better off here, then. I'll drop you in Canary Wharf," Mike said, and in spite of my protestations, he swung the wheel and pulled off the North Circular towards the cluster of towers.

Ten minutes later I was climbing out of the cab into the cold night air, thanking Mike profusely and trying to ignore the concern in his expression as he watched me navigate the steps down from the cab with a lot more care than someone my age should have needed.

"Are you *sure* you're all right?" he said again, and I nodded, trying to put as much conviction as I possibly could into my face.

"I'm completely sure. Honestly, thank you so much, Mike, you—" But I didn't know how to put it into words, what he'd done for me, what he'd saved me from. "You're a lifesaver." Maybe literally, if that exploit was being used for the kinds of things I suspected.

He watched me go, doubt still written all over his face, and I tried to keep my body as straight as possible, not give way to the pulsing pain that the climb down from the cab had jolted awake. I could feel his eyes on me as I walked across the deserted street and ducked between two buildings, and then at last I heard the big HGV engine rev and his rig pull away into the night.

Slowly, when I was certain he had gone, I let myself collapse in a doorway, panting with the effort that looking normal had cost. I couldn't be more than a couple of miles from Cole's flat, but I was no longer sure I'd make it there.

As I knelt, shivering, on the cold pavement, I heard a church bell tolling the hour. One, two, three . . . all the way up to midnight.

The final chime faded away, and I straightened and forced myself to my feet. Only one more hurdle to go. And then I could rest.

SUNDAY, FEBRUARY 12

ZERO DAYS

I was weak and trembling with pain by the time I got to Cole's flat, my teeth chattering in spite of the fever I knew I must be running. At one point I tripped on a curb, jolting the pack against my ribs in a way that sent pain radiating through my whole torso, and I couldn't stop an involuntary cry escaping my lips, a sound that echoed eerily around the deserted wharves and narrow passages, making me freeze like a small animal spotted by a hawk, waiting for windows to open, footsteps to come running to see what the sound was.

I shouldn't have worried. This was London. If anyone in the flats and offices round about heard a woman sobbing in the night, they didn't come out to ask what was wrong. But then again, these were expensive places, with triple glazing, soundproofed against the London nightlife and the foghorns of passing boats. Maybe they just didn't hear at all.

There wasn't much I could do against the pain, apart from pop two more painkillers from the fast-emptying packet in my bag, and I wasn't sure that anything over the counter would do much against the throbbing that was starting to engulf my chest. Still, it was better than nothing. I crunched them dry, and the taste of the ibuprofen was sour on my lips as I steeled myself to straighten and walk the final few yards to Cole's flat.

As I drew closer to the beautiful old warehouse, I found myself marveling afresh at the difference between this place and my modest little two-up, two-down in South London, and wondering how Gabe and I had never questioned it before. On one level it was a mark of how much Cole's and Gabe's lives had diverged since their childhood, afternoons coding and gaming together in Gabe's bedroom. Cole had chosen the tried and tested route of an Oxbridge university, then the corporate ladder, with everything that meant in terms of share options, corner offices, and bonus rewards. Gabe, by contrast, had made his own path, following his principles and the anarchic curiosity that had been his hallmark all his life.

For the most part, it hadn't seemed to matter. Gabe had made cracks about Cole selling out to the man; Cole had responded with jibes about how principles didn't pay the bills. But it was all good-natured, two friends whose shared love of code had taken them on different paths to the same goal—making the world better through technology.

Still, I knew the kind of offers Gabe had turned down from software companies bigger than Cerberus—and somehow the sums had never quite added up. *Now*, of course, it made perfect sense. How long had Cole been taking money to build back doors into Cerberus products? Five years? More?

As I reached the front door of Cole's building, I realized that I hadn't actually planned this far, hadn't thought about what I would do if he refused to let me in. What would happen if I pressed the buzzer and he told me to piss off, or called the police? Would he risk that? Or would he do something even more drastic? He had let his best friend get killed to protect this exploit. I didn't flatter myself that he valued my life any higher than Gabe's.

I needed an insurance policy for if this all went south.

Pausing in the shadow of the porch, I pulled the laptop out of my bag, fired up a hotspot on my burner phone, and began logging into Gabe's Twitter, Discord, and Instagram accounts. They all wanted two-factor authentication, and I felt a tremor as I dug the SIM-swapped phone out of the rucksack. My finger hovered over the power button. This was it. As soon as I turned on this phone, Malik would know. How long had it taken them to find me in the service station? Thirty minutes? Maybe forty at a stretch. And this time—in central London, surrounded by police stations—they would be faster, I was sure of it.

But I needed Gabe's accounts, not mine. His were connected to the people who would understand what all this meant—for whom the code would be not a screed of gobbledegook but a map of what Cole had done, and why.

I had no choice.

I pressed the power button, and waited.

Then I logged into Gabe's accounts and began to upload the files from his drive, one after another.

"Attention all hackers, OPSEC, infosec, cybersecurity experts," I wrote. "I'm Gabe's wife, Jack. I need you to see something that Gabe was working on before he died—something connected with his death. I believe it's a serious unpatched vulnerability that affects one—maybe several—of the most popular security apps on the market. Please check out these files, and for your own safety, forward them to everyone you know. Demand that Cerberus fix this exploit. You are not safe. Your phones are not safe. I believe that my husband was killed to keep him quiet, so please—be as loud as you can."

I pressed post. My hands were shaking.

Then I picked up the phone, shouldered my bag, and walked over to Cole's door. I had done all I could. I had maybe fifteen minutes of freedom left. Now all I had to do was face Cole.

ello?" The woman's voice was croaky, and more than a little alarmed. "Who is this?"

"Yeah, hi." I put my face close to the camera, so the person watching the screen couldn't see what I was holding, and made my voice sound tired and bored, like someone at the end of a long shift. "I've got your pizza."

"Are you joking?" The alarm was gone, replaced by a flash of irritation. "It's midnight! I didn't *order* a pizza."

"I've got the ticket right here, pizza for a . . . Cole Garrick, flat four."

"He's in flat *fourteen*, for Christ's sake. I was *asleep*. Can't you lot take an order right? Ugh, look—" There was a buzzing noise and my heart jumped in my chest, full of hope. "Just—go on up. And tell him from me, *e-nun-ciate*."

She slammed the phone down and I leapt forward, pushing at the heavy metal front door with an alacrity that made the wound in my side shriek and then grumble with pain as the door closed behind me.

For the first time in hours, I didn't care. My exhaustion was gone, the pain dulled beneath the buzz of a dopamine high. My nerves felt like they were singing, and for the first time in a long time I knew that I was back in my rightful place—*predator, not prey.*

The foyer was full of touches that looked like they might be industrial leftovers from the building's past but might equally have been expensive commissioned props to make the prospective purchasers feel like they were in touch with history. Either way, the lift was a giant metal box with a sliding grille, and now I stepped inside and pulled the door across, my heart thumping with a mix of fear and excitement.

It clanked and groaned as it rose up through the floors, until at last it stopped right at the top, and I pulled back the grille and stepped out.

Now, I had to get inside Cole's flat—and this would be the hard part. But I was a pen tester, even sick and wounded. Getting into places I wasn't supposed to be was what I did.

I considered my choices.

Option one was simply ringing the bell and hoping—but even if he was stupid enough to answer the door without peering through the peephole, I didn't think I could force my way inside. Maybe I could have done before all this. I wasn't a match for Cole in size and strength, but I was wiry and quick and trained in self-defense in a way that he almost certainly wasn't. But now, shaking with a mix of nerves and fever, and with a weeping hole in my side—not a chance. If it wasn't for the huge adrenaline high I was coasting on, I probably wouldn't have been able to stand. And at some point that high was going to run out.

Option two was breaking in—and that felt like a better bet. I had my picks in my bag. The problem was, the door facing me was solid metal and expertly fitted, not so much as a crack anywhere. And the lock was a Bramah, notoriously difficult to pick. Given enough time, I might be able to manage it—but I didn't fancy sitting out here waiting for someone to hear the telltale clicking of my picks.

As I looked around the hallway, searching for inspiration, my eyes fell on another door—the only other one on the landing. It was marked *Fire Exit*, and, more out of curiosity than anything, I pushed it open and peered through.

It took a moment for the security lights inside to pick up my presence and flicker on, but when they did I saw a staircase—two flights, one leading up to an unmarked door, the other down into darkness. Cole's flat was the penthouse, which meant that the door almost certainly led to the roof.

Holding the banister with one hand and pressing the other to my ribs, I began to climb. It was only one flight, twenty, maybe thirty steps, but it felt like three times that, even harder than the stairs I had climbed at the service station, and I was panting and shivering when I got to the top. Every breath hurt, and I found I was breathing in little shallow gasps, trying not to wake the slumbering monster of pain below my ribs. The realization that I was worse even than just a few hours ago sent a flicker of panic through me. I was sick—really properly sick, there was no skating around that anymore. But I wasn't sure that I cared. Nothing mattered now, apart from exposing Cole.

When I got to the top I saw that the unmarked door did in fact have a small sign by it that read *Roof Access—Authorised Personnel Only*. No alarms were visible, so with a silent prayer I turned the security handle and pushed. The door swung outwards, and I stepped out onto a graveled parapet.

The area I found myself on was much smaller than I'd imagined, just a neat access area cut into the warehouse's sloping roof. But when I walked to the side and peered down, I could see what I had been hoping for—Cole's balcony, directly below. The problem was, it was very, very far below. The penthouse had high ceilings, and the drop had to be at least ten feet, maybe twelve. Even a week ago, I would have winced at the prospect. Now, in the condition I was in, I thought I'd probably pass out if I tried to lower myself off.

There *was* a balustrade around the balcony—but it was a fancy slim one, with very little to stand on. My best hope was lowering myself down as carefully as I could and trying to balance on the edge. But if I fell to the wrong side, I would be killed—there was no way around that. The roof was five or six stories up, with concrete below.

I pulled off my rucksack and took out Gabe's phone, shoving it into the pocket of my jeans. Then I took off my raincoat and folded it into a thick, wide band. Pinning one sleeve under my armpit on my good side, I wrapped the band around my body as tight as I could, groaning as I pulled the fabric taut, and then tied the arms together to form a makeshift brace. It hurt like hell, but at least if I fell, the jolt might not be as shockingly painful.

Then I took out my lockpicks, shims, and housebreaking tools, rolled them in a T-shirt, and dropped them as quietly as I could onto the balcony. I waited for a moment to see if the balcony doors swung back and Cole's outraged head came poking out, but nothing happened.

Lastly I took out every other piece of clothing I had left in the rucksack. My spare tops. My fleece. Even the sleeping bag, which I unrolled and spread out on the roof, thanking my lucky stars that I hadn't abandoned it in the service station with my heavier belongings. I tied the fleece to the top of the sleeping bag, looping it through the drawstrings to give as much purchase as possible on the slippery material, and then the two tops to the fleece, interlocking their arms. Then I tied the arms of the topmost shirt to the metal balustrade that ran around the roof and flung the whole lot over.

I peered down. It looked . . . well, it looked better than a straight drop, but not a lot. It was also hanging considerably short, although I couldn't tell exactly *how* short. Whether it would hold my weight was another question—and one I didn't have time to worry about.

I thought about what Gabe would have said if he were in my ear right now. *Step away from the ledge, you stupid woman*, most likely. *No pen test is worth risking your life.*

But I could no longer pretend this was just a routine job. And it *was* worth risking my life for. If my actions could bring Cole to justice, if I could bring home to him what he'd done to Gabe, what he'd cost me . . . then yes. It was worth all of this. And more.

I love you, I thought, and I remembered looking up at the security camera at Arden Alliance, blowing Gabe that flirty little kiss, knowing that he was watching me, feeling like I could do anything with him at my back.

I shut my eyes, and I heard his voice in my ear, as clear as any headset. *I love you too, babe. You got this. Now, tick tock.*

Tick tock indeed. I took a deep breath. Then, I put first one leg over the balustrade, then the other, and I began to slide down the makeshift rope.

The first part was . . . well, not easy. I was ridiculously weak and the muscles in my arms were shaking like I'd just completed a long workout. I could also hear the fabric in the seams creaking and snapping in a frankly worrying way. But all that was easier than what came when I reached the sleeping bag. The material of that was too slippery to get any kind of grip on, and I found I was slithering, first faster than I wanted, and then totally out of control. The material ripped through my fingers, the zipper scoring my palms and spattering blood—and then it disappeared completely, and I was falling.

I hit Cole's balcony wall hard with one hip, a thump that jarred every bone in my body, and ricocheted off to land in a crumpled heap on the decking. I should have been thankful that I fell the right way, and not to the concrete apron five stories below—but I was past thanking anyone, past even thinking. I simply lay, curled up on my side, hugging myself against the surging pain and trying not to scream. It was unbelievably painful—a kind of roaring fury that ebbed momentarily only to come flooding back every time I tried to draw breath. The only saving grace was that I was too winded to cry out properly, even involuntarily. I could hear little gasping whimpers of agony which I knew were coming from my throat, but which I had no way of controlling, and a far-off part of me knew that there was a strong chance Cole had heard the crash and was about to find me lying on his balcony, incoherent with pain—but it was buried too deep for me to care.

Nothing happened, though. No one came. And at last I pulled myself back onto my hands and knees, eyes watering with a mix of shock and pain. My hip hurt where it had hit the balcony wall. I had bitten my tongue. My ankles and knees ached like I'd suffered a beating. But most of all, my side was throbbing worse than I had ever experienced, the pain so intense I thought I might pass out. The makeshift raincoat brace had come undone, and now I sat back on my heels and let it drop. A familiar hot trickle ran down my side where the dressing had come loose, but there was nothing I could do—I had used up my last dressing. More to the point, at this stage I simply didn't care. I had nothing more to lose.

Come on, Gabe's voice whispered in my head, so real it felt almost like a hallucination. *Jack, love, you can do this.*

I wished, more than anything I had ever wished for before, that he were really here, urging me on.

But the voice in my head was nothing more than memory. Memory of the thousand nights we had spent together, doing just this. Now I was alone. And this was endgame.

Slowly, my lacerated hands leaving bloody streaks on the tiles, I groped around for the bundle of lockpicks I had thrown down. Then I used the balcony doors to pull myself upright. I took a deep breath, trying to calm myself—there's nothing harder than picking a lock with trembling hands.

But as I let it out, I saw something I hadn't been expecting.

There was no lock on the outside of the sliding doors—just a handle, and a blank metal frame.

My heart sank. It made sense in a way. You might want to lock the doors from the inside, but I couldn't imagine a scenario where you'd need to lock yourself onto your own balcony. But it left me in a very nasty position, trapped here with no way of getting into the apartment or back down to the street. I tugged on the handle, just in case, but it was locked. I considered knocking—but the first thing Cole would do would be to pull back the curtains—and then he'd see me, and either call the police to come and fetch me from my self-imposed prison, or else . . . well, I didn't want to think about that. But the image of the concrete five stories below was still strong in my mind, and Cole would have a ready-made explanation for any "accident."

There was only one thing left to try. Forcing it.

In the bundle of tools I'd thrown down ahead of my climb was a slim jimmy a bit like a small crowbar. Carefully, holding my breath, I inserted it between the doors. They were well made and I had to force the tip into the narrow crack, bending and scratching the powder-coated aluminum in a way that gave me a mean satisfaction. This was not something I would ever have done on a job. *Leave no trace* was my motto, accidents aside, and barring the odd broken ceiling tile, it was something I usually managed. But Cole's fixtures and fittings were the least of my worries—I would have kicked in the fucking glass if it hadn't been reinforced.

As I pulled on the jimmy, sweating with the effort, the doors groaned, as if in sympathy with my throbbing side. The gap between them was growing larger, millimeter by millimeter, and now I could see the metal bar of the lock shining in the moonlight. When the gap was about a centimeter wide, I reached in with the tip of the crowbar and pulled the latch sharply upwards. There was a click—and the doors slid back.

I let out a shuddering breath—and stepped into the darkness of Cole's flat.

nside, it was absolutely quiet apart from the sound of a man snoring. Carefully, I reached into my jeans pocket and switched on Gabe's phone, then dimmed the screen and slipped it back into my hip pocket, with the top inch poking out.

I had been in Cole's flat several times before, and I knew the layout, roughly, but in the darkness everything was strange, and I groped my way towards the snoring, edging round ottomans and coffee tables and almost stumbling over a book that had been left splayed on the floor. My whole side throbbed, hot to the touch, and I was light-headed, almost dizzy—but not in a completely bad way. My heart was hammering, but it didn't feel like the sick, shallow flutters I'd experienced in the service station. It felt almost like . . . excitement.

I was right outside Cole's bedroom door now, and I pressed it open gently, praying that he would be alone, that Noemie would still be abroad. He was. He was naked, sprawled facedown across the sheets, and he looked like he had been drinking. There was an empty wine bottle on the nightstand, and a glass tipped sideways on the floor beside the bed.

I walked across to the nightstand where his phone was charging, faceup, glowing gently in the dim light, and switched on the bedside lamp.

"Wake up, Cole."

"Jus' sec," he slurred, and turned over, hiding his face from the light.

"Wake *up*, Cole," I said more insistently. "You're going to want to see this."

I don't know what was different about my voice that time, but something got through to him, and his eyes shot open. For a second he simply stared at me, completely nonplussed, and then he jerked onto his back and scrambled backwards up the bed, clutching the sheets to his crotch.

"What the *fuck*?" he gasped. "How did you get in here?"

"Check your phone, Cole." I nodded at the phone lying on the polished wood.

"I'm not checking anything, what the *fuck* are you doing in my apartment?"

He was staring at me, but I saw that he had inched across the bed, and that one hand was reaching for something in the drawer of the far nightstand. Before I could react, his fingers found what he was searching for, and he sat up sharply. I was staring down the barrel of a small pistol. There was a click as he removed the safety.

"Get the fuck out," he said, with a kind of snarl of satisfaction. There was a *you messed with the wrong person* edge to his voice. "I don't know what you've come here for, Jack, but get the fuck out."

"Check your phone."

"How hard is this to understand? Get out or *I will shoot you.*" He said the last words very slowly, like I might be too stupid to understand them. I couldn't tell if he meant it. The pistol was still pointing at me, trembling very slightly, but he was close enough to kill me no matter how shaky his aim.

Either way, it didn't really matter.

"Shoot me. I don't give a fuck, Cole. Don't you understand? You've taken everything from me and I genuinely don't give a shit if I live or die. Shoot me and explain that to the police."

"I don't have to explain anything," he snapped back. "Someone burgled my apartment in the middle of the night. I don't think it's unreasonable for me to take—"

"One," I broke in, ticking the objections off on my fingers, "I highly doubt that gun is registered; it doesn't look very legal to me. Two, check your phone. It puts a pretty big hole in your story."

"I'm not checking my fucking phone," Cole ground out, but in spite of himself, his gaze flicked to the phone sitting on his bedside table, and I saw his eyes widen involuntarily at the sight of the notifications blinking on his lock screen. Twitter mention. Twitter mention. Discord call. Instagram tag. Twitter mention. They had already maxed out the counter and were showing as 99+ which, as anyone on social media knows, could mean only one of two things: either something very good had just happened . . . or something very bad.

Cole didn't need to open the screen to know which it was. He had already begun shaking his head, his face ashen.

"No. No, no, no, no, fuck . . . Jack, what have you *done*."

"Check your phone," I said, quietly now, for the fourth time. And this time Cole put down the gun and picked up the phone.

His gasp sounded like a man who had been smacked around the face, and when he looked up at me, his skin had gone the color of skimmed milk—ghostly blue-white in the light from the screen.

"What the fuck have you done, you stupid bitch?" His voice cracked. "Don't you know we'll both be killed?"

"Don't *you* know—" I put both hands on the bed, leaning in as though to confide a secret—though the truth was, my legs were shaking and I needed the support. "I. Don't. Care?"

"What do you want from me?" He pushed past me, frantic now, searching around for his clothes, not caring that he was naked and I was standing right there watching as he dug in the drawer for his jeans and pulled them on. "What do you *want*? Do you want me to die?"

"I don't care what you do. Everything I want is in the past. You can't undo what you did. You can't bring Gabe back. I just want you to admit to my face what happened. I want you to tell me you're sorry."

"Okay, I'm *sorry*," he said, but the words sounded forced out, each one spat like something that tasted rank. He picked up the gun from where he'd left it on the pillow and stuck it into the waistband of his jeans. "Okay? I'm sorry Gabe died." He yanked a T-shirt down over his head, so hard the material ripped at the neck. "I'm sorry he went poking around in files no one asked him to check, finding exploits no one wanted him to know about. I'm sorry he didn't listen to me when I said I'd deal with it. I'm sorry he was a fucking puritanical shit who'd never have done the sensible thing and taken a payoff to shut the fuck up. I had no choice—whatever I did, whether I patched the app or not, if he lived, he was going to tell Cerberus, and then we'd both be dead. I couldn't save us both, so yes, I picked *me*. And I know what kind of a friend that makes me. But *I* didn't kill him, okay? I didn't, Jack. So stop trying to make this my fault."

"So, tell me," I said, making my voice as persuasive as I knew how. "Tell me, Cole. If you didn't kill him, who did? Who are you working for?"

"I don't know!" He was crying now as he searched through his drawers, pulling out a laptop and a bundle of cash. "They came to me—I'd only just started at Cerberus, I was working on some crappy app that never even launched, and they said they were government agents, they had this whole spiel about doing my bit for my country and getting paid for my service. It was small stuff at first. Not much more than what we tell advertisers. But then later . . ."

"Later they came to you about Watchdog, and Puppydog, and you were in too deep," I said, feigning a sympathy I didn't feel. I just needed him to keep talking. "Were they really government, Cole?"

"I don't *know*," he repeated. His voice throbbed with a desperation that wasn't faked. "Maybe some government—not ours, though. I realized that fairly fast. These people are very well funded, very organized, and they're killers, Jack. We're both utterly fucked."

He was stuffing things into a holdall—clothes, money, three passports in an elastic band. He was barely paying me a second glance. I could have leaned over and pulled the gun out of his waistband and held it to his head, but I didn't need to.

"Give yourself up, Cole," I said softly. "Come on. This is over and you know it. You won't even make it to the port."

"Stay. Away," he ground out, and brandished the gun at me one-handed, the other reaching for his bag. Tears were running down his face, but I didn't think they were for Gabe. He was crying for himself. "Stay *away.*"

"Where are you going?" I followed him to the door. "Cambodia? Belarus? It's not just the police you have to worry about, you know that, right? These people may be government, but I doubt they care about extradition treaties—they'll hunt you down wherever you run to."

"Shut *up.*" He was out in the hallway now, jabbing at the lift, and when it didn't come, he opened the door to the stairs. "Stay back or I *will* shoot you, Jack."

"Give yourself up," I said again, but now the pain in my side had come back, more intense than ever, the rush of adrenaline that had got me through my encounter in the bedroom beginning to ebb. I could feel trickling wetness against my skin.

But Cole said nothing, he just shook his head, swiping away the tears with one arm, and headed for the stairs. I followed, pressing my hand against my ribs to try to quell the throbbing.

"Cole, don't do this."

"Who the fuck's going to stop me?" he said, and beneath the sob in his voice there was something close to a choking laugh. "You? You're practically crawling, Jack. Look at yourself—you should be in hospital, not destroying yourself for a man who's already dead."

"Don't do this," I said again, but he was halfway down the first flight, and I could only follow much more slowly, holding on to the banister.

"Leave me alone," he shouted back up over his shoulder. "Leave me *alone.*"

"What are you going to tell Noemie?" I called, but I was panting now, my breaths coming sharp and shallow, and I wasn't sure if he'd heard me. He was two flights down. I suppressed a groan and made my legs move faster. "Are you just going to abandon her?"

"Fuck you," he sobbed back.

Three flights down now, and I had barely made it round the fourth-floor landing. Was he really getting away? That wad of notes wouldn't last him very long, but the three passports spoke of someone with a plan in place—a plan that probably involved a fat crypto wallet and a bolthole somewhere without extradition to the UK—and much as I'd talked the talk about his bosses hunting him down, in truth, if he kept below the radar and didn't shoot his mouth off, I wasn't certain they'd waste their energy.

Malik, I found myself thinking, *Malik, dear God, please be the cop I think you are . . .*

And then, as I rounded the corner of the next flight, I heard them: sirens.

Cole was at the ground floor; I heard the screech of the fire door into the lobby, and then the clang as it slammed shut.

Every breath felt like a knife in my side, and when I looked back, I saw I was leaving a trail of blood up the stairs, little drops the size of pennies on every step, more where I had paused to try to gather my strength for the next flight.

What if I didn't make it?

"Cole," I croaked, but I was sure now that he couldn't hear me. "Cole, give yourself up."

No answer, just the wailing sirens. I forced my feet to go faster, but they were numb and stupid, and now I tripped, stumbling down the last half flight and only saving myself from falling completely by grabbing hold of the rail with a jerk that made me cry aloud.

"Cole!" I shouted again, as strongly as I could, but my voice was drowned beneath the rising scream of the sirens, and there was no answer.

I was at the door to the lobby now, but it was heavy, so incredibly heavy. I put my shoulder to it and leaned with all my might, sobbing with the effort. It creaked open. I pushed, and pushed, feeling the muscles in my side ache with the effort. How had Cole barged through so effortlessly?

And then the door opened enough for me to slip through, and I stumbled into the lobby, blinking at the blinding blue lights that were suddenly flooding the little room.

Outside I could see police spilling out of patrol cars, and they were coming for me, I knew it. I just had to pray that Malik had been listening, watching, taking note. Because Malik, of all people, had been the one who had known something was wrong. She just had no idea how wrong.

The police were opening the lobby door now, moving in formation, like hunters taking down a wounded animal. They were holding out weapons—guns, Tasers, I wasn't sure. I put my hands up. My legs were trembling so hard, I wasn't sure I could stand for much longer.

"Did you arrest him?" I tried to say, but the words seemed to stick in my mouth, hard to get out.

"On the ground!" shouted one of the cops. "Get on the ground! You are under arrest!"

I obeyed, shakily kneeling, though the phone sticking out of my hip pocket jabbed into my stomach and made the movement awkward.

"Did you arrest him? Cole Garrick? Did you arrest him?"

"On the ground!" the officer shouted furiously. I nodded and put my hand to the phone to take it out. And I knew as I did so, as I saw the officer reach for his baton, that I'd made a huge mistake.

"Hands on the floor!" he roared, and I heard, dimly, from far away, Malik's voice saying, "Jake, it's just a—"

But before she could finish, his baton came down on my hand, the hand reaching for the phone. My wrist, and the baton behind it, slammed into my bad side, whacking against the wound with a force that made me drop like a stone—no longer caring about the phone in my pocket, no longer caring about anything except the red-hot eruption of agony radiating from my side.

"The phone!" I tried to say, but I don't think the words made it out of my mouth. Perhaps I screamed. I don't know. I don't remember. All I know is that I saw an explosion of dark stars and a pain so intense I can't even describe it shot through every part of my body. And then I passed out.

MONDAY, FEBRUARY 13

DAY ONE

B abe." It was Gabe's deep, soft voice in my ear that woke me, and I blinked and then turned my head to see him lying next to me in the rumpled sheets, the sun bringing out peat-colored lights in his black hair. He was smiling lazily, with that grin that pulled at the edge of his mouth like he couldn't help it, and my heart clenched with love and longing.

"Hey, honey." I rolled over to look at him, drinking him in, running my hand over his smooth shoulders, down the ridges of his ribs to his hip, feeling the heat of his skin and the hardness of his muscle and bone beneath my fingers.

"I love you," he said, and I didn't know why, but it was as if something inside me was hurting, cracking. Something was wrong. Why did those familiar words hurt me like a knife in the side, like a physical pain in the flesh beneath my ribs?

"Gabe?" I asked. "What's wrong?" But he only shook his head.

"You gotta wake up, Jack."

"I *am* awake," I said, but even as the words left my mouth, I knew it wasn't true, and Gabe was still shaking his head, moving away from me. I reached out for him, but he was already slipping away. "Gabe," I said, and it came out like a sob, "Gabe, no, please wait, *wait for me.*"

"Wake up, Jack," he whispered, and I tried to scream: *No, no, no, I don't want to go back.*

But it was too late. I *was* awake now, properly awake, and I could feel sun—actual sun this time—on my closed lids. I was back in the real world. The world in which Gabe was gone, and the pain in my side was sickeningly literal. My heart ached. The dream had felt so real, so unbearably real—and I hadn't wanted to wake up.

Something felt different, though. For the first time in . . . I couldn't remember how many days, the surface beneath my shoulder wasn't hard and cold ground, but the spongy softness of a bed. There was a strange distance to the pain, which yesterday had been sharp and immediate enough to take my breath away. And I was warm—almost too warm.

I opened my eyes. The room was bright—blindingly so—and for a moment I just blinked, trying to figure out where I was. I seemed to be in some sort of . . . tent? The walls were made of a kind of curtain material. Only, no, not a tent—because there was a ceiling, and a double-glazed window behind the bed.

Before my aching head could figure it out, I realized something else—I wasn't alone. In a chair beside the bed was Hel, scrolling through something on her phone.

I tried to speak, but only a croak came out. It was enough. Her head came sharply up, and an unmistakable expression of enormous relief flooded her face.

"Jack! Oh, thank God. Don't try to talk, sweetie. You're in hospital. You've been—well, you gave us a pretty good scare, to be honest."

I swallowed. My throat was dry as a bone, and I felt more than a little sick. I tried to pull myself up the bed, but I seemed to be tethered by something attached to my hand, and the movement made my side ache and twinge in a decidedly strange way. After a moment's struggle I gave up and let myself sink shakily back into the pillows.

"Am I under arrest?" I managed, or at least, that was what I tried to say. It came out more like a slurred, croaky *ama underess?*

Hel understood, though, and shook her head.

"I don't think so. I'm not sure, but nobody's said you are, and there aren't any police here. That Malik woman came past, while you were asleep. She wanted to talk to you, but the doctors sent her away."

I coughed, and she jumped up and poured some water into a flimsy plastic cup, then held it to my lips. I took it, swallowing the flat, warm water like it was vintage champagne, and then coughed again, trying to clear my throat.

"Where's Cole?" My voice was oddly hoarse, my nose and throat raw in a way I couldn't explain. Was I coming down with something?

"I don't know," Hel said regretfully. "Malik didn't really tell me anything."

I let that sink in, trying to process. Was Cole in custody? Had he escaped? If he had, how long had he been on the run?

"What time is it?"

"It's . . ." Hel looked at her phone. "Ten thirty a.m. Just gone."

I put my hand to my temple, trying to do the mental maths, though the simple sum made my head hurt. The movement gave me a painful twinge in the back of my hand and when I looked down at it, I saw that the thing I had taken for a tether was a cannula taped just below my wrist, its snaking tube attached to a drip bag.

My last memory was of chasing Cole down the stairs, then being tackled by that police officer. It had been just gone midnight.

"So I've been asleep for . . . ten hours?"

Hel's face changed. She shook her head and said gently, "Ten thirty on *Monday*. You've been unconscious for over twenty-four hours, hon. I was really worried. We all were. You did come round a bit in recovery, but I'm not sure if you knew who I was."

"Recovery?" I tried to compute what she was saying. "What do you mean, recovery?"

"Surgical recovery—they had to operate."

"*What?*"

"On your side. You've got a ton of stitches. The doctor said . . . Christ, what was it? Septicemia and a delayed ruptured spleen, or something like that? What on earth did you do to yourself? Did you get shot?"

I suppressed a groan. Suddenly the drip bag and the strange pulling sensation in my side made sense. Stitches. Of course. And I was probably still doped up to the eyeballs, which explained the oddly distant quality of the pain and my muddled thoughts.

"No, this was completely self-inflicted. I stabbed myself on some kind of spike. Climbing a wall."

"Of course you did," Hel said. She was smiling, but there were tears in her eyes. "Of course. What else. Christ on a bike, Jack, I was so worried. I was so, so worried. I can't—I couldn't lose you too. Not after Mum and Dad. You're all I've got!"

It was the same thing she had told me . . . how long ago? It felt like a lifetime, back in the kitchen of her house, before all this started. Now she leaned in, hugging me gently, and I shut my eyes, feeling her arms around me, hugging her back and wanting to cry—but not for the reasons she meant. Because it still wasn't true—not for Hel. She had Roland, and Kitty and Millie, a whole new family of her own.

But it *was* true for me.

I had done what I'd set out to do. But nothing could bring Gabe back. He was gone. And now I would have to face my future alone.

I swallowed hard, and Hel gave a shuddering breath and wiped her eyes, laughing at herself. As she straightened up, groping for a tissue, a noise came from outside the cubicle curtains.

"Knock, knock. May I come in?"

"Sure," I said shakily. And then the curtain drew back, and DS Malik's face came through the gap.

My body reacted before my brain made the connection—a huge jolt of adrenaline pulsing through me and setting my heart racing at a speed more suited to escaping predators than sitting in a hospital bed. It felt like I'd been on the run from this woman forever—it was hard to make myself remember that I'd stopped running.

"How are you feeling?" she asked, a little tentatively. I pulled a face, trying not to show how her appearance had jolted me.

"Pretty crap. But did you—did you arrest him? Cole?"

Her face changed at that, cleared.

"Yes. He was somewhere up the road when we caught up with him, but thanks to your recording—"

"Recording?" Hel broke in. "What do you mean?"

"I take it you haven't been on Twitter recently?" Malik said, a little dryly. Hel shook her head, puzzled, and Malik gave a short laugh—

halfway between amusement and exasperation. "Your sister's gone more than a little viral the last twenty-four hours. As if uploading an exact guide to hacking one of the most popular security apps on the market wasn't enough, she then decided to livestream breaking into the culprit's house. It's going to make the whole court case fairly interesting. Christ knows how they'll find a jury who hasn't seen the livestream. But I don't think we'd have a case against him without the recording, so . . ." She shrugged.

"*What?*" Hel said. She looked from me to Malik, bewildered.

I shut my eyes, too tired to explain, but remembering that split-second decision when I'd pulled Gabe's phone out of the rucksack, turned it on, pressed record, and then slipped it into my hip pocket, with the camera facing into the darkness. I'd had no idea if it would capture Cole's face, let alone his voice, or whether the whole thing might turn out to be a messy, inaudible dark blur. But it was that phone I had hung all my hopes on—that phone, and the homing beacon it was sending out to Malik, telling her exactly where to find me . . . and Cole.

And Malik had heard it.

I had been reaching for that phone when the arresting officer hit me, the bastard. Not that I could blame him, exactly. I should have known better—my work had taught me that if there was one rule about an interaction with edgy police officers, it was that you didn't reach into your clothing without warning them what you were going to do. And then, on the run from the police, wanted for murder, what had I done? Reached into my pocket without asking him first. He couldn't have known about my side. But he didn't need to hit me so fucking *hard*. Presumably it was that blow from the baton that had ruptured my already damaged spleen.

"So . . . my sister's cleared?" Hel was saying now, frowning. Malik nodded.

"Yes, I'm authorized to tell you that you're no longer a suspect in your husband's murder," she said. She was answering Hel's question, but she was speaking to me, her dark eyes shining with compassion. "I'm so sorry for your loss, Jacintha."

"It's okay," I tried to say, but the words would barely come. My throat was suddenly choked with tears, and in any case we both knew that it wasn't true. It wasn't okay; nothing about Gabe's death was okay, and I would never be the same person again.

"And are you charging Cole as an accessory to Gabe's murder?" Hel was asking. Malik shrugged, not quite a *don't know* but a *maybe*.

"Not my decision. My gut says that even with the taped confession, that one might be hard to make stick. But there's plenty under the Computer Misuse Act. He'd compromised Watchdog and Puppydog to the point where they were effectively running twenty-four-hour surveillance on everyone who used the apps—camera, microphone, location, you name it. And he could be facing counterterrorism and espionage charges too, when we find out where the information was going."

"So you're closing in on whoever was behind this?" Hel asked.

Malik nodded. "Not my department, but between us, I think MI6 have a pretty good idea of who they're dealing with, it's just a matter of tracing back the digital bread crumbs. They'll get what they can out of Cole, of course, and I'm sure there'll be some horse trading regarding sentencing in exchange for testimony, but he'll be going away for a long time, regardless of what he coughs up."

I swallowed, feeling the tears brimming at the edges of my eyes, trying not to let them spill over.

"Thanks," I whispered. "Thank you."

Malik nodded, just once, rather brusquely, as if she too did not quite have the words for the moment.

"Well, look, we'll have a few more questions, but they can wait until you're feeling a bit stronger. For the moment, take care of yourself, Jack. And if you need anything . . ." She put a business card down on the bedside locker and tapped it. "Just call."

"Thanks," Hel said. She glanced at me, then stood up. "I'll walk you out. I think Jack needs a rest. Is that okay, Jack?"

I nodded, not trusting myself to speak, and watched as the two women slipped through the gap in the curtains. I heard their footsteps fading as they walked up the ward, then a swing door opening and closing, and then silence.

I shut my eyes, feeling the hot tears I had been holding back for so long, ever since Gabe's death, spill over, running down my cheeks. And a great sob seemed to rise up, a huge choking gout of grief that felt like it was ripping me apart from the inside.

It was over. It was really over. And I had no idea what to do next, what was left for me now. There was nothing else I could do for Gabe. There was no reason to keep going anymore, keep putting one foot in front of the other as I had forced myself to do, day after day after day, in the hopes of finding his killer.

I had found him—if not the person who'd held the knife, at least I'd found the person responsible for leading them to Gabe.

And now what? What did I have left?

I had wished I could cry so many times since Gabe's death, and now the tears were here. They were coming thick and fast, and I didn't seem to be able to stop them. They were running down my cheeks, soaking into the clean white sheets, and my chest hurt with it—not the decorous weeping I'd imagined, but great hacking sobs that seemed to be wrenched uncontrollably up from somewhere deep inside of me, tearing my heart and my throat as they came. It was a real, physical pain, one that pulled at the stitches at my side, tore at my heart.

"Hey," a voice came from outside the curtains, and then the fabric twitched back. "*Hey.*"

A man was standing there in a nurse's uniform, hands on hips, looking concerned. Behind him was a lunch trolley loaded with covered plates.

"What is all this?"

I couldn't speak. I only shook my head, trying to get control over myself enough to say *Please, I'm not hungry, leave me alone.* But the words wouldn't come, and the nurse moved across the cubicle to take my hand comfortingly in his.

"Come on now, there's no need for all this!" His name badge said *Harrison Carter.* He had a Jamaican accent that reminded me of my elderly next-door neighbor in Salisbury Lane, the one whose wall I'd vaulted, and the memory of home made me sob harder. "We can't have this. Are you in pain?"

I was, and the sobs were making it worse, but I shook my head. That wasn't why I was crying, and no amount of morphine was going to stop this tsunami of grief for Gabe.

"Here," Harrison said. He turned away, rummaging on his trolley, and then stood up, holding a plastic tray with a covered plate. "Have some lunch. There's nothing like a bit of food to make everything feel better. I've got a lovely veggie shepherd's pie."

He held the tray out towards me, and a school-dinner waft of hot Quorn filled the cubicle. A wave of nausea rose up inside me so strong that I thought I might actually be sick, and I turned my face away, trying to get ahold of myself.

"Come on now," Harrison said cajolingly to my back. "Can you not manage a bite for the sake of the baby?"

For a moment I thought I hadn't heard right.

"I— What?" The tears had stopped, as abruptly as if I'd been slapped, and now I turned my head back to face the nurse, but he hadn't noticed my shocked expression. He was talking as if I hadn't spoken, smiling reassuringly.

"I can get a doctor if you're worried, but it's all looking good on the scan."

I had to dig my nails into my palm, concentrating on that small pain so that I didn't scream in his face about the knife in the side his words were twisting. This was too fucking cruel, a brutal reminder of all the possibilities that had died with Gabe. My throat, when I spoke, felt tight and raw with the unfairness of his mistake.

"I'm not pregnant." The words were forced out through clenched teeth, each one hurting. "You have me mixed up with someone else."

Harrison looked puzzled. He picked up the chart from the bottom of my bed and glanced down at it and then up at me.

"You *are* Jacintha Cross?"

I nodded. His expression changed to one of deep, compassionate concern, and he said, very gently, "No mistake. Oh, child, did you not know?"

I felt everything go cold. My heart seemed to stop and then restart again at an uneven pace, and I could feel a strange prickling in my fingertips, a physical manifestation of the shock.

The nurse was talking again, but his voice sounded strange and faraway.

" . . . picked up on the routine presurgical tests. I'm sorry, they thought you knew. Is it good news?"

I didn't reply. I was too busy trying to remember back, remember what day we were on, what *month*. How long was it since I'd had a period? Four weeks? No, more. It had been . . . God, it must have been sometime between Christmas and New Year. And I remembered, vaguely, putting my Mooncup into the bag I'd packed to go to Arden Alliance, in case my period came that night. Only everything that had happened after had driven it completely out of my head. At the time, I hadn't given it two seconds' thought—my cycle wasn't that regular, so a few days here or there was nothing.

But we must be in the middle of February now. Which meant . . . I swallowed hard, doing the maths. That meant I was six, maybe even seven weeks pregnant.

With Gabe's baby.

And suddenly so many things made sense. So many things I should have noticed but hadn't. The fact that I hadn't had a period for more than six weeks. The constant nervy exhaustion. Even the nausea—which I'd put down to the festering wound in my side, but which suddenly seemed a lot like morning sickness. In fact, the only thing that *didn't* make sense was that the baby had survived everything I'd been through: exhaustion, infection, and now this—a ruptured spleen on top of everything else. Was it really possible?

"How do you feel?" Harrison was asking, his expression worried now. "Do you want me to get the doctor?"

There was a lump in my throat, but I forced the words out.

"You said it—the baby—it's okay?" I knew I hadn't answered his question, but he nodded.

"Yes, completely fine. They did a scan. And the antibiotics you're on are all safe for pregnancy. You don't need to worry about any of that. *Is* this good news?" he asked again, and now his face was really concerned.

And for the first time in . . . I didn't even know how long. For the first time since Gabe's death, I realized, something actually was.

"Yes," I managed. "Yes, it is good news."

His face broke into a smile.

"Phew! I have to admit, you had me worried there, my darling. But I'm pleased you're pleased. Now, shall we talk about that shepherd's pie?"

And suddenly I was very hungry indeed.

MONDAY, FEBRUARY 12

DAY THREE HUNDRED
AND SIXTY-FIVE

The police station was hot and stuffy and my spine was sweating as I walked quickly down the corridor, glancing right and left and attempting not to look too obviously like I was not supposed to be here. The first thing to do was get some kind of disguise. I was known at this station now, and consequently I stuck out like a sore thumb.

Trying doors at random along the corridor, I found two that were locked, one that opened into an empty interview room, and then I hit the jackpot—a changing room, lined with lockers, each fitted with a padlock.

About half the padlocks were the kind operated by a key. I was pretty sure that I could pick any of them within a few minutes, and if I couldn't, the small bolt snapper inside my rucksack would have made short work of the flimsy hasps, but more out of a sense of curiosity than anything else I tried the combination locks first. Picking the closest, I put in my old favorite, 1234. Nothing happened, and I spun the numbers back to a random configuration and moved on. The second lock, however, gave a satisfying little *click* and the hasp swung open. Grinning, I laid the padlock on top of the cabinet and opened the locker door.

Bingo. I had found the mother lode first try. Inside was a freshly pressed uniform complete with hat and ID badge and, even better, it was a woman's. Okay, I was forced to concede as I tried on the trousers, a woman who was considerably taller and a fair bit broader than me, but it was nothing a couple of turns to the waistband wouldn't solve, and fortunately the jacket hung down far enough to cover the rather unofficial-looking fix.

I was already wearing a white shirt, which was good because the shirt seemed to be the one piece of attire that was missing. Otherwise the uniform was complete—there were even shoes, neatly paired and shining at the bottom of the locker, but they looked to be at least two sizes too big, and besides, my faithful black Converse were more comfortable and quieter. If someone got as far as examining my footwear I was probably sunk anyway.

I folded up my jeans and jacket and put them in my backpack and then considered the next question—what to do with the pack. Police officers didn't typically carry bags, and striding along the corridor with one would attract attention I didn't want. In the end I took out my picks, compressed air, and radio, and shoved them in the capacious uniform pockets. Then I bundled everything else back into the pack and shoved it into the little alcove behind the bin, fervently hoping no one mistook it for rubbish and threw it away. *That* would be an expensive outcome—one I really couldn't afford in every possible way.

With the uniform on, I felt a rush of confidence, and I strode out of the locker room with my head held considerably higher. When I rounded the corner and bumped into another officer, I didn't even hesitate.

"Oh, hi, sorry to bother you, I'm Kate Lederer, from—" Shit, what had Jeff's station been called? "Eltham Green. I've been sent over to interview a suspect in your custody suite, but I've got a bit lost. Can you point me in the right direction?"

"Sure." The officer's eyes swept over me but didn't seem to notice anything amiss. "I don't think we've met before, have we?"

"No," I agreed. "I'm new. Well, new to the Met. I just transferred from Thames Valley. Nice to meet you . . . ?"

I trailed off inquiringly.

"David Moran. Nice to meet you too." We shook, and a smile quirked at the corner of David's mouth. Was it my imagination, or was that a hint of flirtation? He was tall, and very good-looking, with an Irish accent. Glancing automatically at his hand, I saw there was no wedding ring there, though that didn't necessarily mean anything. Lots of officers took rings off when they were on duty. Still, married or not, I didn't think I was imagining the flash of interest in David's expression, and maybe I could turn that to my advantage.

"The officer on reception told me which way to go," I said, putting a touch of chagrin into my expression and smiling back at David. "And then of course I immediately forgot what they said. It's quite the place you've got here, and I've never been able to keep a chain of directions in my head."

"Yeah, it is a bit of a labyrinth." David glanced down at his watch, and then seemed to make up his mind. "Look, d'you want me to show you to the custody suite?"

"Are you sure? That would be amazing."

"No bother. I'm supposed to be in a meeting in ten but I've got time to take you there first. So, what's Eltham Green like? I hear old Patterson's a bit of a . . ." He trailed off, grinning, with one eyebrow raised, and I laughed and let my arm brush his elbow as we rounded the corner.

"Yeah, 'bit of a . . .' is right. I'm not gonna lie, I prefer working for women. My old boss was a woman."

"Yeah? Me too," David said. "I think they bring a better energy to the team."

We continued talking as David led me along a corridor I recognized, and then one I didn't, landing us up at a reinforced door with a bell push and a swipe card reader. He touched his pass briefly to the reader, pulled open the door, and ushered me inside.

"Hi, Jake," he said to the officer on duty at the desk. "This is Kate Lederer from Eltham. Here to conduct an interview. Well, Kate, I'll leave you in Jake's capable hands, but nice to meet you."

"Nice to meet you too," I said, smiling at him. I watched as the door closed behind me, and then turned back to the officer he'd called Jake, mentally preparing myself for what I was about to say. I didn't have time to do more than open my mouth, though, before my earpiece crackled and an apologetic voice came over my headset.

"Jack? I'm so sorry to ring you at work, darling, but she's just thrown up everywhere."

Fuck.

"Sorry," I mouthed at the officer behind the desk. "One second."

I turned my back to him and touched my finger to the headset, hoping Jake would think I was taking a work call.

"Verity, I'm so sorry, this is a *really* bad time. Can I call you back? We're talking ten minutes, tops."

"Of course, darling. I did think about not bothering you, but you did ask me to call . . ."

"I know. And I'm glad you did. Has she got a temperature?"

In the background I could hear a high, throbbing wail that made my breasts suddenly swell agonizingly with milk. *Shit.* I hitched at the borrowed trousers, conscious that they were starting to sag. They must have come unrolled on the walk to the custody suite.

"Who did you say you were here to see?" said Jake's voice from behind me, a touch of suspicion in his tone now, and I cursed under my breath and tried to press one arm to the trousers, which were inching perceptibly further down my hips.

"One sec, Jake."

"I don't *think* she's got a fever," Verity was saying, a little doubtfully. "John and I had a go with the ear thermometer, but she had a bit of a paddy about having something in her ear, and we couldn't keep her still long enough to get a reading. She doesn't *feel* hot."

"Okay. Thank you, Verity, and please don't worry. I'll head home now. See you shortly."

I touched the headset and then turned back to Jake.

"Right, change of plan. I'm not here to see a suspect, I'm not actually a cop, this was a pen test organized by Detective Inspector Habiba Malik."

"It's a what?" Jake said, looking a mixture of outraged and annoyed. "Wait, did you say you're not an officer?"

"Jack!" I heard from behind me, and I turned to see Malik walking through the doors of the custody suite, a big smile on her face. "How on earth did you get in here? And—" Her expression changed to one of puzzlement, and then to an outright frown. "Wait, is that one of *our* uniforms?"

"Yes," I said. "You *really* need to tell your staff not to use 1234 for their locker combinations. Also, there's a bag stowed behind the bin in the locker room which could have been full of explosives but definitely isn't, so if you could tell your staff not to call the bomb squad, that would be great. I need it to get home."

"You're leaving?"

"Yes." I was shrugging off the jacket. "I'm sorry, Gabby's not well. I thought about canceling but I didn't want to let you down. I've got enough for the report."

"If you got in here in full uniform, then I bet you have." Malik looked considerably put out. "Oh bloody hell. I *really* thought you wouldn't get past the front desk."

I smiled, sympathetic but not trying to hide my triumph.

"I know. I'm sorry. I'm afraid you owe me that drink."

"Ugh. Anything else?"

"Just the usual. Don't let your staff buzz people through. Don't let secured doors swing shut behind you without checking they're actually closed. *Definitely* don't reuse passwords."

"Reuse . . . ? Oh God, Jack, do I want to know?"

"Don't worry, I didn't look at anything sensitive." I gave her a one-armed hug and hitched again at the borrowed trousers. "Right, sorry, I have to get going. I need to return this uniform and retrieve my bag before one of your staff blows it up in a controlled explosion."

"I wish," Malik said with a groan. "It sounds like it could have had a ticking clock pasted to the top and they wouldn't have noticed, judging by everything else. Go on then, get out of here. Give Gabby a squeeze from me. No . . . hang on." She seemed to remember something. "I'll walk you to your car."

"Do you not trust me to get off the property?" I said, laughing, and she shook her head.

"No, it's not that. There's something . . . something I've been meaning to tell you. Look, give me five minutes and I'll meet you in the locker room. Okay?"

"Okay," I said, a little puzzled, and then Malik buzzed me out of the custody suite.

MALIK CAUGHT UP TO ME in the locker room a few minutes later, but we were all the way out to my car when I finally said, "Well, you said you had something to say. So spit it out, whatever it is. I have to get going."

"I know," Malik said. She looked grave. "It's—well, it's actually two things. I'm not sure . . ." She stopped, and I felt a flicker of alarm pass through me. Habiba Malik and I were something close to friends now, but after what had happened last year, I wasn't sure if I would ever be *completely* comfortable in the company of the police.

"Look, what *is* it? You're worrying me."

"It's Cole Garrick," she said, turning to me. Her face in the sharp February light looked older than it had when we first met, fine lines around the corners of her eyes. "He—well, he's died, in jail. Awaiting trial."

"Fuck." I had been trying not to swear so much, for Gabby, but now the word slipped out of its own volition, and honestly there wasn't anything else I could think of saying, so I repeated it. "*Fuck.* So he'll never stand trial?"

"No. I'm so sorry. They had him in protective custody, as you know, but evidently he found a way . . ."

"*He* found a way? Are you saying he did this to himself?"
Malik shrugged.

"He was found hanging. How you interpret that . . ."

"Fuck," I said again. I pressed my fingers to my eyes. Images flickered through my head—Cole on the beach at Brighton, laughing and diving through the waves. Cole on the balcony of his apartment, drinking dirty martinis and grilling giant prawns on the barbecue. Cole's face in the candlelight of the cottage, his lips on mine. His expression that last time I had seen him, in the darkness of the penthouse, his features twisted with anger and despair. His voice: *Stay back or I will shoot you, Jack.*

Would he have done it? I still didn't know.

"I'm sorry." I heard Malik's voice as though from very far away. "I know this isn't what you wanted. It isn't what *we* wanted. We wanted to see justice done."

Justice. The word had a sour taste in my mouth. Some might argue it was a kind of justice, what had happened to Cole. A life for a life. All I knew was it didn't feel like it to me.

"What about the people behind him?" I said now. "Do they think . . . did they do this?"

"It's being looked into very carefully," Malik said. She was watching me, her face grave and patient, and full of sympathy. "And you know, Cole had given a huge amount of testimony before he died. Believe me, *every* thread is being followed up at the highest level."

I nodded. I believed her. I didn't flatter myself that MI6 were particularly bothered about the death of a lowly hacker. But who knew how many journalists and dissidents had had their phones compromised by Watchdog, their whereabouts tracked by Cole's software. Who knew how many people had been quietly assassinated at a time they had believed they would be safe, how many diplomats' children now had their photographs in biometric databases in some far-off country, thanks to Puppydog.

What had happened to Gabe—that was on Cole, and now he had paid the ultimate price. And the men who had cut Gabe's throat, well, I would never know for sure, but last summer two corpses had been found floating in the Thames, with DNA that matched microscopic traces recovered from the bathroom window. When Malik had told me the news, I knew what she'd wanted me to feel—that it was over, that the people who had killed Gabe had been, if not caught, at least run to ground, and in a way it was true, but though it was strange to admit, I had never been that interested in the men who'd wielded the knife that night. To me they'd always felt like bullets in a loaded gun—killers, yes, but in a strange way, not the ones ultimately responsible for Gabe's death. To me that had always been Cole . . . and his handlers. And now Cole was dead. But the group behind him was a more shadowy, amorphous thing, and in spite of what Malik was saying, I didn't know in my heart whether a group like that could ever be pinned down, let alone brought to justice.

Whoever the individuals were behind the Puppydog hack, they were just one part of a vast dark web of unseen players, a network that encompassed everyone from national security agencies to organizations like the Lazarus Group, right through to some kid in his bedroom in Canada or Poland or Bangladesh, pressing buttons and causing havoc because he could, just like Gabe had once done. And yes, they could be fought, maybe some individuals might even be arrested, but you might as well try to prosecute cancer. They would always exist. Slippery, shadowy, forcing their way through the cracks in our online security and the doors we left open for them in our digital lives.

All I could do was tell myself that I had closed one door—the door Cole had carved out for them—and thousands, maybe millions of people were safer for it. And now I had to let it go.

"What was the other thing?" I tried to force my voice into a semblance of normality, but it came out strained and false, and I knew that Malik knew, and was sympathetic, but was trying to be business-like for both our sakes. "Any better?"

"Maybe. I hope so, anyway. I'm not completely sure if this is public yet, but I wanted you to be the first to know."

"Yes?"

"I just heard from Eltham Green. The investigation's been concluded. They found Jeff guilty of gross misconduct."

"You're kidding?" My face felt strange and stiff, as if it wasn't sure what expression to make, or whether to laugh or cry. "What does that mean?"

"It means . . . well, he's been sacked, basically. He can't work as a police officer again. And two of his colleagues have had formal reprimands over their behavior towards you after the breakup. I know it's probably too little and it's definitely far too late, but, well, I hope it's something."

"Oh my God." I felt like I'd had a punch to the stomach. I put my hand there, feeling the twisted knot of scar tissue beneath my T-shirt, where the hospital had cut into the ragged, suppurating wound in my side to take out my spleen, and not completely succeeded in repairing the damage. For some reason, the feeling of it—the raised, tender edges, the still-perceptible traces where the sutures and surgical staples had been removed—anchored me. I had survived that. I had survived Gabby's birth, accumulating more stitches, more scars. I had survived Gabe's death, and I was still here, not whole exactly, but still standing.

"Thank you," I said at last to Malik, and she gave a nod, a little formal, as if she too wasn't sure what the two of us should be doing with this information—whoops and high-fives didn't feel that appropriate, and Malik knew it.

"Okay. Well, that was it. I'm sorry to spring it on you now, and a double whammy, I know that. But . . . I wanted to tell you face-to-face."

"I know," I said. I touched her arm and forced a smile. "Thank you. I mean it."

And then I got in the car and drove away, Malik watching me as she grew smaller and smaller in the rearview mirror.

I was almost at Salisbury Lane, lost in my thoughts, lost in memories, when a song came on the radio, one that I couldn't place at first. I only knew that the intro, an insistent little repetitive refrain that ticked along with the indicator as I waited to turn into our road, gave me a strange feeling—a mix of panic and wistfulness and yearning.

And then I realized. "This Must Be the Place." The song that Gabe and I had played at our wedding, the song we had danced to on a warm summer's night, surrounded by our friends and family, holding each other, and then laughing as we beckoned Cole and Noemie to join us on the dance floor, Hel and Roland, Gabe's parents, all the other friends and family who had come to wish us well in our life together.

But the panic was because beneath that was the other memory, of Cole, whistling the refrain as he came through the sea mist towards me, as I huddled in the dunes, in fear for my life, not knowing if he was friend or foe.

Cole. Cole, who had betrayed his best friend, who had driven me to the very edge. Who was now dead in a prison cell.

I stopped the car at the curb and sat there, listening, as David Byrne sang of love and dreams and the hopes of being human—and the meaning of home.

I found there were tears on my face—I seemed to cry a lot these days, though not always from sadness—but it was Gabe in my head as the song wound to its end, not Cole. Gabe's hand in mine as we danced together under a hundred glimmering lamps, his arm around my waist, turning me, leading me, holding me in the warmth of his love and the promise of our future together.

And then the song ended, and I wiped my eyes, switched off the engine, and got out of the car. I turned to face our little house, the house where Gabe had lived and loved me and died, and the house where our daughter had come wailing into the world—a wailing I could hear now, even from outside the front door.

My heart filled with a joy that was so close to pain, I wasn't sure if I could have told the difference, except that this time I was smiling through the tears. Because behind that door, our daughter—mine and Gabe's—was waiting for me, and she was gorgeous and red-faced and furious, and everything I needed her to be.

I opened the front door. I was home. And that was where I wanted to be.

ACKNOWLEDGMENTS

I have a litany of thank-yous for this book, which is always the case when tackling a subject you knew little about before you started writing.

This book was born in large part out of the many, many podcasts I listened to in lockdown, podcasts that I first became intrigued by when writing *The Turn of the Key* and *One by One*, which explored the world of technology and apps from very different angles. There are many shades of cybercrime and just as many intriguing podcasts on the subject, but the one that had the greatest influence on *Zero Days* was undoubtedly *Darknet Diaries*, hosted by Jack Rhysider, where I first heard professional pen testers and social engineers speaking directly about their experiences, in sometimes hair-raising detail. So first thanks to Jack, for making a complex subject so very accessible and entertaining, and second thanks to all the hackers and security experts who shared their wealth of knowledge, and who help to make the world a little safer.

Thank you also to the multitude of experts and friends whose brains I picked on the subject of law, policing, crime scene processing, surveillance, and hacking. Neil Lancaster, Clare Mackintosh, Katie Robinson, Graham Bartlett, Sam Gordon, and HD Moore, I am more grateful than I can say to you for reading sections, giving advice on plausible (and implausible) scenarios, and generally allowing me to ask stupid questions without making me feel stupid. Needless to say, any mistakes and stretches of the imagination (plausible or otherwise) are my own. Thank you also to Derek for your invaluable help on the inner workings of insurance call centers, and I hope you enjoyed the shout-out to your namesake in the book. And as for Gytha, who told me, "I'm as swift as a fox. An old one. With osteoporosis. Run over by a 4x4. Ten days ago." You know what this means and you owe me a drink next Bloody Scotland!

Thanks always to my brilliant agent, Eve, to Ludo, Steven, Rebecca, and everyone working on behalf of the EWLA to get my books out into the world. And heartfelt gratitude to the teams of people working tirelessly behind the scenes at Simon & Schuster in the UK, US, Australia, and Canada, and at my publishers in other languages and abroad. To Alison, Jen, Suzanne, and Nita, thank you for your joint editorial brilliance and your belief in me as a writer. To Ian, Jonathan, Jessica, Sydney, Sabah, Katherine, Taylor, Adria, Natasha, Felicia, Kevin, Mackenzie, Gill, Dom, Nicholas, Hayley, Sarah, Harriett, Matt, Francesca, Jennifer, Aimee, Sally, Abby, Anabel, Caroline, Jaime, John Paul, Brigid, and Lisa—your care and brilliance never cease to amaze me, and I'm forever grateful for all the hard work you put into getting my books into the hands of readers.

To Paul James Hillman, thank you so much for your generous bid to help Young Lives vs Cancer. Your donation is supporting young people through some of the toughest times, and I am so grateful.

Thank you to my family for giving me reasons to emerge from my imaginary worlds, and making the real one so much fun.

Finally, to my readers—what else to say, apart from the fact that you make it all possible. Thank you from the bottom of my heart for reading this far.

—Ruth

ABOUT THE AUTHOR

Ruth Ware worked as a waitress, a bookseller, a teacher of English as a foreign language, and a press officer before settling down as a full-time writer. She now lives with her family in Sussex, on the south coast of England. She is the #1 *New York Times* and *Globe and Mail* (Toronto) bestselling author of *In a Dark, Dark Wood*; *The Woman in Cabin 10*; *The Lying Game*; *The Death of Mrs. Westaway*; *The Turn of the Key*; *One by One*; *The It Girl*; and *Zero Days*. Visit her at RuthWare.com or follow her on Twitter @RuthWareWriter.